MISSING FAY

FICTION

Ulverton
Still
Pieces of Light
Shifts
Nineteen Twenty-One
No Telling
The Rules of Perspective
Is This The Way You Said?
Between Each Breath
The Standing Pool
Hodd
Flight

POETRY

Mornings in the Baltic
Meeting Montaigne
From the Neanderthal
Nine Lessons from the Dark
Birds with a Broken Wing
Voluntary

TRANSLATION

Madame Bovary
Thérèse Raquin

NON-FICTION

On Silbury Hill

MISSING FAY

Adam Thorpe

JONATHAN CAPE
LONDON

1 3 5 7 9 10 8 6 4 2

Jonathan Cape, an imprint of Vintage Publishing,
20 Vauxhall Bridge Road,
London SW1V 2SA

Jonathan Cape is part of the Penguin Random House group of companies whose
addresses can be found at global.penguinrandomhouse.com

 Penguin
Random House
UK

First published in the United Kingdom by Jonathan Cape in 2017

penguin.co.uk/vintage

A CIP catalogue record for this book is available from the British Library

ISBN 9780224098007

Typeset in India by Thomson Digital Pvt Ltd, Noida, Delhi

Printed and bound in Great Britain by Clays Ltd, St Ives PLC

Penguin Random House is committed to a sustainable future for
our business, our readers and our planet. This book is made from
Forest Stewardship Council® certified paper.

In memory of Ernest Wistrich

Every angel is terrifying.

Rainer Maria Rilke,
The Second Duino Elegy

1
DAVID

15–16 August 2012

There might be bigger crabs when the tide's right out, he suggests to the kids. Worms, anemones, brittlestars and the countless small crabs have not grabbed them. Stephie has just done a project on giant crabs at school, and is further up the beach, stooped over with a red bucket and a net. Noah is stabbing at bubbling air holes with a stick.

'Don't do that, Noah,' says his father. 'You might kill whatever's breathing down there. Those holes are like their nostrils, OK? Little critters that thrive in salty environments. Pretty special.'

A brief pause, and then his son stabs at them with even more enthusiasm, now they are nostrils. Nostrils of concealed salt-loving monsters.

'I said, Noah. Don't do that. An intertidal mudflat is an amazingly rich habitat but it's also . . . what? Noah. What is it? Remember? Begins with *F*.'

Noah mumbles a word that sounds very like *fucking*.

David is momentarily speechless. Surely not? Not at six years old? Noah glances up at him with a secret little smile. 'Fracking,' he repeats, loud enough to be heard over the sea's restless wash.

The father chuckles in relief, to Noah's delight. 'OK, OK, I get it. The word is actually *fragile*. Remember? *Fragile*. A very important word, Noah.'

The boy is now pretending to be a burly hard-hatted fracking operative, from the look of it, adding drilling noises. His father turns away, defeated. He was woken at dawn, shivering in the tent, by a cacophony of rooks massing directly overhead, and he feels shit. The damp sand is silky-hard under his feet and surprisingly cool. He presses his toes into it, kneading the grains, not making much headway and releasing a sulphurous odour: the natural decay of organic matter, on which all life depends. His toes' impressions are black. He is not an imaginative man, but he tries to picture himself as a hominid walking here a million years back, with a very simple life pattern, with straightforward thoughts and feelings and finely tuned sense receptors. Wetness, light, the healthy stench of mud, the cries of his blood progeny, the tribe's future. It is difficult picturing this, what with a huge bright-blue shipping container in his sight line, dumped for no discernible purpose in front of the concrete seawall, its patched ugliness topped by a metal fence.

Noah has left off fracking and has picked up one half of a sword razor shell: creamy white, almost opalescent. David begins to relate the amazing story of bivalves, tapping the shell in Noah's small palm. A helicopter, the bright-yellow rescue type, thumps into view some half a mile inland. The chopper's slapping rotors are loud, considering its distance. Noah points the long shell at the heli and makes a surprisingly effective space-gun noise, followed by an explosion.

'Noah! You're really pissing me off! What is that heli doing?'

'Blowing up.'

'It is not blowing up, stupid. It is flying off to rescue someone, someone badly injured or drowning or critically ill!'

Lisa is meditating out of sight in the dunes, with a view down to their van parked in a lay-by on the very straight and very depressing coastal road. Luke is in the van, dreaming whatever toddlers dream. Lisa doesn't like her husband to swear in front of the kids, breaking into one of his hissy fits, as she calls them. Maybe it's his red hair, she says. True, he can't help it. Not that it happens very often, these days. He has better self-control.

'I'm not stupid,' says Noah in a voice that mixes defiance with deep hurt.

Steph skips up to join them, to the father's relief, the bottom of her bucket seething with whelks, hermit crabs and various wrigglings yet to be identified. 'Wow, well done,' says David. He'd forgotten to check on her. You never know with beaches. Noah crouches down and examines the bucket's interior without touching, Steph standing over it with crossed arms.

At least there aren't that many people on the beaches of Lincolnshire, if you stay clear of places like Skegness or Mablethorpe. The North Sea is off-puttingly cold, even in August. They've seen a few folks in the water, still only up to their waists about half a mile out, it looks like. The weather's supposed to be getting a lot drier and hotter (or less cool) in a couple of days' time. It is just unfortunate that most of the coastline has a rampart of static caravans and bungalows, which somehow they did not expect, while the coastal towns are basically run-down housing estates with amusements. Looking on the map, he just assumed that the miles and miles of broad sand would be lined by fields and trees beyond the dune grass, as they would be back home, where there are thousands of miles of wild beaches. There are nature reserves here, but they are pretty small and you can't camp overnight. The one open stretch of grassy shoreline they drove past lifted his hopes until he saw the first bunker. He didn't want his kids brained by golf balls travelling at 70 mph, especially as the few people on the fairways looked well into the doddery stage.

A retired couple from Birmingham with what looked like salt-blistered skin told them this morning, while they were rolling up their tents at the inland campsite, that it's amazing north of Mablethorpe in the Saltfleetby-Theddlethorpe Dunes, but you can't camp there, it is another nature reserve.

'Could we camp sort of on the edge of it?'

'Well,' the man said, 'there's always Pleasure Island Family Theme Park at Cleethorpes. Or is it Fantasy Island? There's that lovely site near Skeggy, lots to do for kids, plenty of toilets. Pool tables and whatnot. What's its name?' he added, turning to his wife.

'Fantasy Island's just down by Ingoldmells,' said his wife sternly. 'Ten-minute drive from here. You can't have missed it. Britain's first-ever theme park.'

The Milligan parents have so far managed to conceal the big resorts' attractions from the kids, on the basis that unappeased desire is crueller than ignorance. They thanked the couple anyway, although the man persisted in going on about the campsite near Skegness. 'Fifteen minutes' walk and you're on the esplanade with all the amusements,' he said. 'What the heck's it called? We used it three years running, didn't we, pet?'

His wife's sagging jowls shook. 'Haven't a notion which one you mean.'

'Superb pitch sizes,' he continued as the Milligans bundled their gear into the van, agreeing to spend the day in the dune area with the unpronounceable name. 'Superb!'

*   *   *

David is sitting back on his heels apologising to Noah for calling him stupid. They give each other a cuddle, which topples David backwards into the yielding sand, both of them laughing. Noah has the most extraordinary squeal of a laugh, reminiscent of a juvenile kea. David first heard keas on South Island in Kahurangi, and made their mating patterns the subject of his thesis. 'They're probably the most intelligent bird species in the world,' he told Lisa at the time, when she questioned his choice. Really, it was so he could live in the mountains for a while, but he found it lonely: Lisa did not join him for long enough. The kea squeals got on his nerves, were sending him crazy, and now they're haunting his son. Memory transference maybe. There's a lot we don't know.

The nature discovery exercise is turned into a game in which they get points for spotting something new on the soggy flats, from worms to waders to rusty cans which they can't touch. The bigger crabs have made a collective decision to stay under, it seems. Size isn't everything, he tells the kids, not in the natural world. Intelligence counts for a lot. Finding your niche and sticking to it. They don't seem convinced. They have a little rucksack rattling with shells, including some pretty whelks, but there's nothing here to equal the beautiful specimens back home, especially the huge patterned volutes. Yesterday he told them about his favourite, the famous black-foot paua, iridescent with blue, green, purple and silver once you'd spent a long time scraping and scrubbing it, but that just made them more fed up. He took out a couple of slipper limpets and pretended they were his ears. Noah, despite David telling him that they are a product of the plastics industry and choke birds and fish and could even choke Luke because they look like sweets, has started a collection of blue nurdles.

When the rain starts in earnest, gusting into their faces, the three of them slope back to the van. Lisa is inside, her meditation already relocated to the van itself and disrupted by Luke filling his nappy and wailing. The cramped interior stinks. 'This is supposed to be my holiday too,' Lisa groans.

They find a spot in the simple campsite a mile away, a little close for comfort to a casino and a games arcade, but pleasant enough and only ten minutes' stroll from the beach proper. There's a café and a dilapidated mini-golf nearby. They sit in the site's wooden clubhouse and play cards, before venturing out to Swan Foods, the local store, for supplies. The row of shops includes one selling mobility scooters, which Noah thinks are for kids and the best gadget he's ever seen. There is a bright flyer for the Cleethorpes theme park pinned to the corkboard near the till. The kids are investigating the vast lolly display, thankfully.

David joins the queue, bored already. A small handwritten plea to find a home for Fluffy, an eponymous angora rabbit, red-eyed from the flash. A MISSING poster next to it. *Did you see Fay?* Thin, toothy, pale. Looking straight at him.

Lisa is nominally in charge of the confectionery department. The kids' expressions are agonised, unable to choose within the strict parameters allowed by their parents. Sour Ears, Strawberry Clouds and Cobbers do not exist here, but the Brit substitutes are almost as foul and just as enticing, tempting you at every corner, every counter. It's a kind of comestible porn.

David's glance wanders back to the girl called Fay. Hair not as red as his and Stephie's, not a proper auburn, but the poster looks faded. He doesn't think the hair's dyed, although henna red has become fashionable. Fourteen is a bit young to dye your hair, and she looks a very young fourteen. Old beams in the background, real old English cottage beams. Nice middle-class English girl. She'd still be called Ginger or Carrot Top. Copperknob in his case. Trousers pulled down by the

Matthews gang when he was fifteen to check his pubes. Howls of laughter.

Her eyes of course do not look away in embarrassment but are still bolted to his, straight into the camera. They are a clear emerald green and her mouth has a child's large teeth, her bone structure yet to mature around them. One front tooth is growing crookedly so it looks pointed. She will need a brace. She is amazingly alive, he thinks. Fay Sheenan. Irish roots, probably. He has nothing much else to read, so he scans the words over and over. Last seen in *distinctive leopard-patterned trainers with pink laces, orange tights, a fur-lined hooded coat.* And with *a small mongrel dog.* Some maniac with uncontrollable urges. Or maybe she has just run away. Home situation. With an ugly little bitser. Her only friend.

'David?'

Lisa is gawking at him. Infuriatingly he blushes. The kids show him their lollies in their paper bags as if they are jewels. How can anyone harm anyone else, let alone a child of fourteen? Steph will be eleven in the autumn. What if his own red-haired daughter was to go missing, her pink laces carefully tied? Fragile, that's the word. The lollies look sticky and alien to him. That's how you know you're abroad: by the unfamiliar confectionery. Among other things. His EcoForce colleagues, for instance, so passive-aggressive, so British. He loves his kids to bits, nurdles and pink laces and all.

The adjoining shop sells beach and pool toys, including a dolphin ride-on eerily like EcoForce's logo, blown up and on display. A mere eight pounds. The kids want it. Even Luke points at the window and burbles in the same acquisitive manner as his siblings. David tries to explain that it's made out of cheap plastic, no doubt in China, and will last about a week, if that, before creating yet more toxic waste for the planet. Also, the sea is really cold. 'We can use it in the pool,

Daddy,' Steph points out. Lisa is further up the street, looking at a clothes shop. He walks towards her with Luke, who is in the pushchair; the other two cross their arms and stand firm. It is rare for them to show mutual solidarity. This will all lead with horrible inevitability to the need to find a swimming pool, to being squeezed by overweight campers with armpit and nasal issues: a living hell. Lisa points out that he's left the other two behind.

David shrugs. 'Oh, they just want to buy, buy, buy. Ignore it.'

'Your problem to sort out,' she says. 'I'm on vacation.'

Steph runs up, Noah following her a few yards behind. She says in a mournful tone, 'Daddy, we really love dolphins, just like you do.'

They wake up to a cold, clinging fog that soaks the outside of the tents. It is forecast to clear by mid-morning. It's that time of year, the campsite manager tells them. 'Yeah, we get these sea fogs in Wellington,' David comments. Lisa grunts, 'And how's that supposed to help?' They are tired after a bad night so decide to stop this upping-sticks lark and stay the morning in the immediate area, trying to be mindful instead of hopeful. Lisa's been edgy ever since they hit Lincolnshire, for which she had great hopes. Or maybe it's just PMT. Or the weather. Someone she respects at the toddlers' group – a woman called Penny who has published a novel and lives in Muswell Hill – called Lincolnshire 'authentically mysterious and eerily unknown. Tennyson!' she added, which Lisa at first thought referred to sports facilities. England is so tiny, how could anything be mysterious and unknown? 'The land that time forgot,' Penny added with a giggle, her overactive son banging the bongo drums like a maniac. David had stayed in Lincoln in January, representing EcoForce at a conference on *Engaging with the Televisual: New Ways of Visualising the Environment.* A complete waste of time full of unpleasant media types, but he could confirm the (relatively) wild emptiness of the area, although he'd only glimpsed it from the conference bus on a wetlands tour. A quick meander through the Wolds on Google Street View sufficed. It was beautiful. And relatively inexpensive to camp in. And a lot nearer than the Outer Hebrides, which was his first choice.

David would have quite fancied a walk through the Saltfleetby-Theddlethorpe Dunes themselves, spotting birds, but the kids screamed in the negative; yesterday, when they first saw the trees and open meadows full of swirly rye grass from a winding lane, they pronounced the reserve 'boring' and Noah claimed car-sickness. They stopped the van and Lisa had to hold him from behind as he imitated violent retching, disturbing the peace of this miraculous parcel of unspoilt countryside. So the attractive walk plan has been delayed until further negotiations come the afternoon.

David has hardly used his binos. The birdlife is supposed to be fantastic, but so far all they've seen, apart from rooks, sparrows and so forth inland, is gulls and a couple of shelducks and the odd wader on toothpick legs in annoying silhouette against the dazzle-wet sands. Today is a no-no for anything outside, but then it clears in around ten minutes and the future looks bright.

The kids keep interrupting an adult argument about migratory patterns with demands for a go at the mini-golf. If they can't have that dolphin ride-on, then . . .

Its puddled dilapidation attracts David, and probably explains why it's free. You get the clubs and balls from the café next to it, an old-fashioned place called Nelly's Teas where jellied eels are served up in a polystyrene cup. Lisa says she'll sit with Luke at one of the outside tables and asks David to

9

order her a cuppa. The others go inside and wait at the counter for the waitress, who is clearing tables very slowly, as if underwater. Another *Did you see Fay?* She's becoming almost familiar, surveying them in their family bliss. Dimples, toothy smile, that long red hair. Mutant gene 40,000 years ago. How did the first coppernob survive? Regarded as a freak, a god, a curse, a blessing? Very pale skin, freckles scattered over her nose. Born to keep to the shade, skulk in the shadows. The lightless back of the cave, among the stalactites. Her coat was *reddish-brown*. He missed that last time. Why not red-brown? Or brownish-red? Maori. Apache.

The kids are desperate for him to have a taste of jellied eel, but he explains to them that eel numbers have fallen by 98 per cent in the last five years thanks to pollution and overfishing. What he doesn't say is that he ate eel back in NZ years ago, and the slippery cold flesh made him feel sick. It was almost as bad as those grilled caterpillars in the Congo during his fairly disastrous post-doctorate research stint on African greys. He mentions the caterpillars to divert their attention, and it works.

She's probably fine. Most runaways are. Alternatively she could be naked and strangled at the foot of some hedge or other, like a skinned rabbit.

The busty young waitress hands over the clubs and balls. She's called Colette, according to her name tag.

The three of them survey the course. He tells the kids how, as a boy, visiting his grandparents in Manawatu, he would play mini-golf every day, clearing pine-needle clumps out of the holes just as he is doing right now.

The first hole is simple, just a chicane. Before they start David explains that it is not as easy as it looks, that they mustn't shout or have a hissy fit if the ball doesn't go in the hole like they want it to. Winning is not what's important, he tells them.

'We're here to have a fun time together, OK? I played a lot of mini-golf when I was a kid, so don't expect to be as good as me and go mental when you aren't.'

Steph insists on going first. She has Lisa's strong character. She hits the ball.

'Remember, Steph,' says David, 'there's a lot of luck involved. But well done. Wow. Oh, wow. Beaut, Steph. A hole in one. Look at that.'

Noah hits his sideways. He gets the ball into the hole after twelve hits, and is already in tears. David's ball clips the chicane and leaps up out of the run like a comet and straight into the weeds and pine needles and probably dog mess.

'You're in the lead, Steph,' says David, knowing this won't last.

Steph's ball has a magnetic attraction for the hole. Noah, four years younger than his sister, gets angrier as he gets worse, and vice versa. As for David, he finds that the club is not right for him, or maybe it is Noah's anger: his ball keeps going haywire. He clocks up nine strokes trying to get over a double humpback bridge with a chipped sidewall and a brown puddle of rain in the middle. He was pretty good at mini-golf as a boy. His ten-year-old daughter, having never played it before, is beating him by five strokes.

To take the heat off, he tells them about the fun course he would play all those years back in Manawatu. The ball had to pass between these two big round cheeks, he says. It looked just like a bum. The kids screech with delight when he says this word. *Bum.* The upper half of the construction, which was a clown's eyes and nose, had been smashed by vandals. It wasn't supposed to be a bum, it was supposed to be the cheeks on the face of a huge clown. He clips the ball with smooth confidence.

11

'Beaut,' says Noah with an unpleasant grasp of the snarky.

'Why can't you play now, Dad?'

'I *am* playing, Stephie.'

'But you're no good.'

'I'm just giving you and Noah a chance,' he fibs.

'Oh yeah,' jeers Noah. 'Just because you're losing, Dad.'

'It's not a question of winning or losing, Noah. I told you. Don't take that attitude, please. It's so *competitive.*'

There is a loop-the-loop now, with dribbly swirls of graffiti on the side. Noah throws the ball, and Steph shouts at him not to be a piker. Their mother is dimly visible through the chicken-wire fence, still seated with Luke at one of the café tables.

An electric shock passes through him. Shit, he never ordered her cuppa!

His dismay is distracted by some noise. Another group has come onto the course. Oh no. They are probably from that bigger campsite a mile or so up the road: a sprawling place with 'entertainment' and a heated swimming pool teeming with microbes. The Milligans studiously avoided it after a preliminary spec. The group has already caught up, and is waiting at a tactful distance for David to get his ball into the loop-the-loop. Steph's ball has shot through far too fast but somehow bounces back off the low side wall to end up inside the hole, sitting like an egg in its cup. Now his daughter is leaning on her club like Tiger Woods, watching her dad. The campsite group is also watching.

David thinks he hears laughter and begins to feel sweaty and faint. They are bikies, from the look of it – huge with leathers and big boots. David is wearing minimal esparto sandals modelled on an archaeological find, according to the owner of the green shoe shop in Lincoln. It was surprisingly full of people. Crazy name. What was it? Itchy Feet. Served by this old hippy in a wheelchair, whose own feet were bare and brown as though carved out of kauri. Would they itch, in fact? Noah kept staring at him like he'd never seen a ponytail before, let alone a wheelchair. The sandals are uncomfortable and keep falling off; maybe that's why he is losing. (Lisa bought a pair of reiki flip-flops, which are fantastic, she claims; she can feel the energy in her ankles.) Noah is sulking under the pines, face in his hands, partly because his sister has called him a piker. At last David's ball makes it up into the loop-the-loop. There is a rattling noise and a pause and it trickles out again from his side, bashfully. David covers his face with his hands in half-meant despair and the bikies laugh in a weirdly raucous way, as if he is entertaining them deliberately.

This time the ball makes it to the other side. He taps it into the hole.

'Eleven,' says Noah. 'They're German. Yuk.'

'What do you mean?'

'You took eleven for that one, Dad. I counted.'

'OK, great,' says David, his voice rising. 'I'm sure you're pretty pleased.'

He waves the bikies through. They are tall and bulky, grinning and nodding at him in their leather bib pants, their cut-offs festooned with sewn-on badges. Are they mocking him, or is there a cultural misreading here? Noah was right: on some of their backs is a big circular patch showing the German eagle popping its biceps with PROUD GERMAN BIKER around the edge, with the eagle echoed in tattoos on square-shaped bared shoulders. They are very good at mini-golf, despite not knowing shit from clay. He just wishes they would keep their voices down as they rasp, growl and gargle their way from hole to hole at blitzkrieg speed.

13

'They're typically German,' says Steph, having looked impressed and a little scared. It was as if she was dutifully echoing someone adult.

'That's cultural stereotyping. They're human beings.'

'No, they're not,' Noah says. 'They're stupid coconuts.'

'Noah,' David shouts, making him jump. 'Never *ever* use that word!'

'Not even if I'm eating one?'

'I mean in the context of an insult. And you know why, don't you?'

Noah leans on his mini-club and nods slowly and theatrically. 'But they're not *real* coconuts,' he points out. 'They're all white.'

'It's a racist term, and I don't *ever* wish to hear it from your or Stephanie's mouth.'

He really feels upset.

'And from my bum?' jokes Noah.

Steph explodes into snorts. 'Coconut from your bum!' she wails deliriously, a kea's mating screech. 'That's so yuk!'

David leaves them to it. The long tunnel looms.

'*That's* not a bum.' Stephie giggles. 'It's something else.'

Noah gives a snort, as low and guttural as a dirty old man's.

'Give it a break, thanks,' says David, adjusting his bum bag around his waist as if by association. He doesn't quite know how to respond to Stephie's comment, but his body is responding with a hot-flannel feel on his forehead. It's a kind of appalled panic. Maybe it's the bag interfering with his swing, but if he puts it down he'll forget it and they'd be sunk, stranded here for weeks or maybe for ever, like illegal immigrants. He can't believe he forgot to order Lisa's tea. He glances over through the chicken wire. Still with Luke at the table. He should nip back and correct this. Oh, she'll realise eventually. She's a grown woman. He'll abase himself, drop to his knees and beg forgiveness. All will be well.

Steph wins by a number of strokes that only their author has kept track of. 'Sweet as!' she cries, punching her fist. Noah is permitted to place the ball in the hole manually. His juvenile maleness is undergoing a terrible trial. David's ball has done nothing right. Maybe he was not actually very good at mini-golf in his youth down the far side of the planet. It is hard to say because he only ever played by himself.

'All good,' he declares as they head for the gate and the tables. Lisa is animatedly reading to Luke. Before he can open his mouth, she says, 'Looks like you were having a lotta fun.'

'Steph won by yards,' he tells her. 'Hey, look, I completely forgot to—'

'Don't sound so surprised. Girls can be excellent at sport too.'

'She cheated,' Noah declares without any conviction, already flinching in his sister's proximity.

Steph snorts and shakes her head. 'So sad.'

It is, David reflects. It really is. She is so *dominant*. She'll end up an exec director for sure, breaking other people's crayons. Jesus, how can he think this of his own *daughter*? 'Really sorry about forgetting your tea, Lisa.'

'I'm fine. Aren't we, Lukey-Lukes? Hey, why did you lot keep slapping your own bottoms and shrieking? Kinda weird.'

He tells her about the broken clown face back in Manawatu.

'I don't think that's very sensible,' she says.

'*What's* not sensible?'

'Lavatory humour.'

'You cannot be serious.'

He married a scamp of an Aussie and her mischievous sense of fun. The scamp became a responsible mother and the fun has all but dried up, although she laughs on the phone or on

15

Skype with her friends. The children want a second turn, and Noah slips off the bench and shows his bottom – pulling his shorts down, taking the undies with them. People at the other tables are looking.

'Just stop that,' snaps David, blushing furiously because he knows what the people are thinking. He would blush as a kid when a teacher asked who had stolen this or that, even though he'd done nothing wrong. It was uncontrollable, a freckled white to crimson, blushing under his red hair *because* he was blushing and so subsequently blushing an even deeper crimson. But now he was an adult! For Chrissake! 'If you don't want it whacked, Noah, pull them up. Right now!'

Lisa shakes her head. 'Whacking a kid in public is illegal.'

'Yeah, but I don't ever get to whack a kid in private.'

'Your threat was all bluster.'

'Well, bluster works. Ask my colleagues.'

Their voices were technically quiet, as if they were talking through headphones, and they weren't looking at each other. 'What worked was your fairly aggressive tone of voice. Empty threats are not a great approach to firm parenting.'

'OK, I'm a shit dad. Say it.'

'You're a good dad. But not a perfect one. You have to admit now and again to making mistakes. Telling that story about bums was probably a mistake, if you think about it. *Bum* is a trigger word, like *arse* or *tit*. Nobody's going to beat you for it.'

His face is melting in the self-stoked fire. 'I didn't make any mistake, Lisa. I was just telling them a funny story from my childhood. They thought it was funny too. Please try to be less *judgemental*, it's pretty tiring.'

'You have a problem about being judged?'

'You never used to be so judgemental.'

16

'You'd rather I just shut up while you yack on? Play the obedient Sheila?'

'Dolphins are our favourite animals because they're threatened from stinction,' Noah says with an infinite sadness in his eyes.

'I hope I don't yack, Lisa.'

'You do talk quite a lot, actually. Ever since we started.'

He turns to look at her. 'That's maybe because I'm relaxing. I'm actually enjoying myself for once.'

'Dolphins are even more intelligent than me,' Steph announces with an arch look.

Lisa scoffs. 'I mean started started. From the beginning. *Ab ovo.*'

They started at uni some fifteen – no, seventeen years ago. He has always thought of himself as quiet and considerate. Never in seventeen years has Lisa accused him of being an earbasher.

And his wife, in certain company, talks a great deal. She can stay on the phone or on Skype for *hours*. He hesitates before saying it. He could just retire from the scrap right now, like sensible animals do. But he is a non-sensible human.

'And, of course, *you* never open your own mouth, Lisa.'

Lisa shrugs. 'I think you just assume that the man has more right to talk than the woman, unless it's about domestic issues.'

'You're *nearly* as telligent, though,' Noah concedes as if after careful thought or out of solidarity.

Luke is slapping his mother gently on the face, then not so gently, as if testing her resilience. Already the male brute. David's mouth is tense, a tense coil of rope. Out of this mouth might come words with which he could hang himself. The pasty, bored-looking and mostly fat folk seated outside the café are watching him, as Brits do. Not minding their own business. Stickybeaking into private matters. Neighbourhood

17

fucking watchfulness. He glares back and they turn their heads away.

'Let's go sit in the dunes,' he says. 'With an ice block. What d'you reckon?'

They all go inside Nelly's Teas to return the golf gear and buy their ice blocks. The young waitress called Colette takes the gear and says, 'Dead good is mini-golf, but it's not a thing any more. Like yo-yos.' David smiles in fake agreement. Her thin white kitchen coat exaggerates her bust. One button is missing. No sign of Nelly herself, presumably long dead, but it's a nice café apart from the filthy tables: very English and shabbily authentic down to the name. There are truffles for sale, made in a local monastery. A leaflet claims its gift shop sells stuff like pottery, fudge and honey, apart from books. Our Lady of Grace Abbey. They can visit it, David thinks. Despite believing that monotheistic religion is a historical and environmental disaster, he is attracted to monasteries. The contemplative life.

In the end they collectively succumb to ice creams in the form of Magnums, and Colette digs through the freezer with loud rustles as if their choices are annoyingly unusual. Monasteries and murderers, what a world of extremes. The *small mongrel dog* gives him hope it might not be murder, in fact. The girl went missing in late January. Almost six months ago. *She was last seen at 16.22, Friday 27 January 2012.* So precise! No doubt by a CCTV camera. Through a chill winter drizzle. *Pink laces.* Steph has a pair of pink laces, as far as he recalls. It's not looking good. January cold, and now it's summer, or what passes for summer in England. Maybe she's begging somewhere on a busy pavement, with the dog next to her. Vulnerable. He'll look out for her when he's back at work. A daggy bundle in a furry parka by the mouth of a Tube station, mournful eyes the same as the dog's. *Take me to London.*

'Sorry, Steph?'

'I didn't say anything.'

'No,' he insists, 'you just whispered something.'

'Er, no. I did not. Daddy, are your ears going mad?'

Maybe it was Noah, who now asks, 'What is that girl missing?'

'Herself.' He has unaccountably blushed to the roots of his equally red hair, a steaming hot flannel pressed against his skin. Except that he knows it's all in the head; no one else can see it. 'She's gone missing.'

'Whoa, go easy on the detail,' Lisa murmurs.

Noah frowns, looking up at his father. 'You mean she's lost in a wood? Why have you gone really really red, Daddy? Like Postman Pat's van?'

'Crikey,' his wife chuckles quietly, 'so you have.'

'It's pretty hot in here.'

Steph snorts. 'She's chopped up in a basket, more likely.'

'Yuk,' says Noah, his little hand twitching inside David's.

Lisa sighs. 'Where on earth do you learn that kind of silly nonsense, Steph?'

'I want to go find her,' Noah pronounces. 'I have to go find her,' his son continues, crossing his arms and stamping his foot. 'I have to. Not if she's chopped up,' he adds cautiously. The waitress returns from the freezer with the five Magnums, and Noah's determination unravels into an outstretched hand and the huge eyes of a starvation victim. If his son and his wife have noticed, David thinks with alarm, then everyone must notice.

There's an awed silence as the Magnums are distributed. 'Guys, I've an idea. This great idea.' David's blush is retreating, it helps to speak, to be proactive. There again, it has no logic. 'You go start on your ice creams outside. Leave this to me.'

Lisa ushers the gang out. As he sorts through his change, he asks the waitress if she's got any more copies of the missing poster. The waitress stares at him under her mop of curly hair, then draws her little white coat closer over her breasts as if he's been peeping into their deep gully. She can't be eastern European, David thinks, as she's not smiling.

'I'm just standing in,' she says, her voice hoarse and knowing nevertheless. 'Seriously, like, I haven't the foggiest about anything,' she adds with a cheery cackle.

'The point is, we live in London so I could put a few up there. Posters. Unless she's been found?'

She turns round slowly and studies the poster as if she's unfamiliar with it, pulling her coat over her buttocks. 'I imagine not,' she says. 'The campsite up the road can do you a photocopy, like? They've got a colour one.' She turns back to him, her full upper lip winking with gloss. 'Are you from Australia or South Africa or summat?'

'I'm a Kiwi.'

'Don't mind me asking, but why the heck have you come here then? It's just a mudflat the whole way along. Water's full of sewage. They don't even bother replacing the light bulbs in them Las Vegas illuminations in Skeggy.'

'We're not staying long,' David admits, startled by the sewage info. 'Just passing through, really. My wife's family came from here about a century ago.'

'Changed a bit since then. To be honest. Do you really want it?'

He nods. She turns back to unpin the poster, struggling with her sharp bright-green nails, then hands it over a touch slyly.

He rolls it up. 'I'll bring it back today. What time do you shut?'

'No urgency,' she says, leaning her elbows on the sticky counter. 'But I'll probably get a right bollocking. Have you tried the seal sanctuary?'

'Temporarily closed.'

'That's what people round here have got tattooed on their brains.'

Which earns a chuckle from him. She smiles back, looking straight into his eyes. Christ, it feels good.

The others are well through their ices outside by the time he joins them, somewhat perky. His own Magnum has started melting – he has a struggle to unwrap it cleanly, asking Lisa to hold the poster.

'We'll photocopy it and take a few to London.'

Lisa looks at him as if he's doing something slightly perverse. The kids are too busy with their lollies to be interested.

'Let's shift back to the beach,' he suggests.

'Are you OK, David?'

'Yeah, why?'

'Dunno. You never stand like that.'

'Like what?'

'I dunno. Legs wide. Like my brothers. Like you're used to straddling horses. Weird. It doesn't really work. The jackaroo look,' she adds with a kind of giggle that reminds him of the old days.

They sit on the sand between two big tufts of grey-green marram grass, safely hidden from stares, shivering a little, within sight of the wetter grey that is the sea. It's attractive here if you don't look to the right too far, where the concrete re-appears a few hundred yards up. Why couldn't the whole coastline have been preserved? Who is in charge of Lincolnshire?

21

Gulls flock screamingly overhead and then find someone else to harass. He knows what he has to do, apart from being careful about the way he *stands*, for Chrissake. He'll carry out a personal word survey, quantify his vocal output, establish indices of nattering density and then establish long-term, year-on-year monitoring of the spew coming out of his mouth. He'll ring certain home-grown words and record their re-appearance, like *reckon* or *heaps* or *keen*. Won't he just?

'What's up now?' Lisa asks, frowning at him.

He blinks innocently and mentions the monastery. Organic allotments, herb garden, beehives. This could be a good contact.

'Your parents would be *delighted*,' Lisa says in a tone made more caustic by her Aussie twang.

'I think we should visit. They're completely organic. Reach out, build the network.'

'Try selling it to the kids. The monastic peace would be shattered. Forget work for a day, yeah?'

Lisa was a social worker back in Auckland, and is currently struggling with her doctoral thesis on the use of *manaakitanga* in mental health risk management – *manaakitanga* being the Maori concept of hospitality. It seemed a great idea at the time. She's yet to find a suitable supervisor in the UK, but Skype comes in useful. David reckons she misses her job and is resentful of his. She's already chomped her Magnum all but down to its stick. Despite her veganish ways, she has a sweet tooth.

Sex on a stick. You'd be so lucky.

If he catches her burying it in the sand, with the idea that it's organic . . .

He looks out at the sea, narrowing his eyes like a sailor. There's a silvery line of hope out there, right on the horizon. He hunkers into his silence.

Lisa is now teaching the kids a tongue-twister: *She sells seashells on the seashore.* She's really relishing her latest minor victory, kicking him when he's down, not letting him limp away to nurse his wounds. No, she's a tough woman, brought up on a farm in the Outback with five huge and deeply unattractive brothers; she knows how to weld, for Chrissake. Steph's inherited all that. Lisa once told him, in the early days, that she appreciated his feminine side. Her brothers reckoned 'your Bluey' was as camp as a row of tents, she said, simply because he was slight and couldn't lift a tractor with one hand. They both laughed. He told her about the time he'd met a black tiger snake when out birdwatching on Bruny Island and stayed to watch it swallowing a lizard head first. 'The fourth deadliest snake in the world,' he added as if she didn't know! 'Yeah,' she smiled, 'but it had its mouth pretty full already.' True too. Most of what she says is a reality check. Rows and rows of little boxes to tick. A blob of Magnum gunk hits his T-shirt like a seagull dropping. The chemicals will no doubt eat into the organic dye.

He gets up and goes over to the trash can behind the grass clumps and drops in the unfinished bulk of his ice cream. The two older children run up to ask him why he has done this. He explains to the kids that commercial ice creams are full of synthetic chemicals and that actually they have never seen a drop of cream or even fresh milk and that their reputation is the result of careful globalised marketing or, in other words, lying, and that many of them use palm oil, which is responsible for terrible deforestation. A great flock of words, he realises. Too many to count, screeching overhead, on and on.

'Does this one use palm oil?'

'No, Steph, as it happens, but most of them do.' The kids are frowning, absorbed in sending all those colourings and flavourings and emulsifiers down into their innocent and miraculously constructed stomachs at massive profit to Unilever. The corporate cynicism lingers on his tongue, oily and synthetic. Serves him right. If they'd bought a chilly bin they could have stocked up on healthier snacks, but he didn't want to look too equipped and disconnected from the natural world, humping it all about.

He eventually collects the sticks – Lisa's is bitten raw – and they clatter in the trash can. He holds his youngest child's hand and walks a little way on the long slatted path towards the beach proper, with Steph and Noah already there. Luke is bandy-legged but steady, a small precious weight pulling on his own enormous hand. Bits of shredded plastic and gunge-food wrappers blow past them in the sudden gusts as their toes hit the harder, cooler sand. A dog and its walker break away from what looks suspiciously like a canine crap in the middle of the beach. Wow, folk are selfish. He's seen dog poop all over the place in Lincolnshire, actually. Wild animals do it discreetly, terrified of being tracked. Perhaps Lisa was right about him being an earbasher. And so what? It isn't exactly the greatest of reprimands. He feels good, rationalising his rage into self-judgement and self-awareness like this. His father would've given Mum a black eye in the name of the Lord.

He looses the two older kids onto the beach like live balls, swinging them away to where they can hurtle about, trying not to think about sand-speckled sausages of dog poop. Soya sausages of poop. *And a small mongrel dog.* Owning a large dog is equivalent in sustainability terms to owning an SUV: he's seen the figures. Luke toddles behind them now on his chubby little legs, freed of his nappy, naked except for his top. The sky has patches of blue and the sun shines way out in a definitely broadening strip of silver that David stares at again, appreciating the delicate beauty of the light and colours, its diminished northernness. The offshore wind farm is now far more visible, its elements rimming the horizon like tiny skeletal trees. It is the beginning of the future. Clean and sensible. He finds it both ugly and beautiful. A hopeless gesture, really, against the infinite kilowattage of nature herself, soon to come pounding in on gigantic breakers, sorting out all this trash. Not even revenge. Just physics. There are other people scattered on the beach; those sitting down are looking at their mobiles, not the sea. That's what we'll all be doing the moment the climate apocalypse happens. We won't even lift our heads from those tiny screens.

Lincolnshire spreads out behind him, as flat and featureless as the Outback. He'd go insane if he had to live here. Bungalow roofs, patches of foliage and the usual in-your-face glint of antennae and pylons. That's about it. The kids hate walking so the Wolds were hopeless. Nothing he has ever seen in the world outside New Zealand is anything like as spectacular as New Zealand, but this is ridiculous. The waitress asked a valid question. Why have they come? Why did he leave New Zealand in the first place? To be more connected, less out in the planetary wop-wops? Connected with what? The great liberal-capitalist highway lined with fuckin Macca's and KFCs?

He wanted foreignness too, and this is a foreign coastline. Because this is a foreign country. Where when he says stuff like, 'I'm just gonna have a kip,' his UK colleagues say something like, 'Make me a cup too, there's a good chep.' Because of crazy London property prices, they are condemned to living in a small semi-detached in Borehamwood.

A bloke with a camera behind the railing on the raised concrete strip, telephoto lens, half-naked Luke in his field of view. Against the law, probably. Repeat shutter clicks. To be reproduced on the web without permission. Should he go over? Or maybe it's just zoom shots of the sea. The man is elderly, in a raincoat, with a check scarf and matching cheese-cutter cap on his big round head. Could be harmless, could be evil. Turning away and walking on now; got what he came for. The kids' souls in his bag maybe.

How come so much of life is tainted?

Lisa stands nearby, packing a sad yet again – staring out to sea like she's waiting for her lost man to return from his epic voyage. Her figure is running to stout, says a little voice. It is a political move. She once dressed to kill and now she dresses to evade any kind of sexual overtones. Her hair in a practical but unattractive bob.

She is unattractive to him now.

When he first met her she looked very young, like someone's little sister, mid-teens. She was so thin her clavicles showed through her cotton tops. Her skin was amber; she was lithe and laughing, with freckles over her nose, and he fancied her like crazy. She had an Aussie frankness about her. She'd spent her childhood sunbaking (as she put it) on the farm that her father and her brothers ran with their leather whips and their massive horses. She was a wild girl, or that's what he believed. She wasn't, not really. She was in her first year of sociology, had wanted out of Australia. No one is truly wild. But that's what he projected onto her, the suburban boy from Auckland. Now his terrible secret is that he no longer feels physically drawn to her. He doesn't know what to do. The feeling is mutual, he reckons. She has only grown tired of his voice because she no longer desires him.

He goes over to her and puts an arm around her shoulders. Her back slopes. Her mouth has a pout to it that he knows well. He's seen photos of her as a kid, with exactly the same pout. Then, she looked sultry and pretty as a flower, a skinny nut-brown scamp on the farm. Now, somewhere inside her beyond the tired eyes is that same amazing kid. He feels a great nostalgic love for her, welling up in him like springwater in a dry place.

Stephie and Noah are running around with Luke in a large circle, kicking up the sand and chanting, 'We're the clever dolphins! We're the clever dolphins!' He likes to see them happy and free. It makes him feel he is doing his job, that he and Lisa have brought their ankle-biters up to relish the natural world. It costs nothing to run about on a beach kicking up sand. Not even eight pounds. And it costs the planet nothing either. He feels good about this, that he resisted the ride-on. A tiny victory for Mother Earth.

Luke stoops over, screaming like a swift. David feels his life mate flinch and stiffen under his arm.

'He's got sand in his eyes,' she says flatly, as if she has known this would happen all along.

She runs over to Luke, but David walks. There isn't any point in panicking.

'Don't rub,' he calls out. 'Luke, don't rub your eyes or they'll scratch.'

Lisa looks as if she is clawing at Luke's face, trying to brush away the sand, which is covering the little boy's features like breadcrumbs on a fish. She must know all about grit in the eyes. Maybe this is a tried and tested technique. His little snout of a willy is also coated. David hopes that girl was inventing the stuff about sewage.

'Was that you, Stephie?' he shouts.

Steph explodes into angry wails, perhaps out of fear that Luke is really in trouble.

'There's no point in telling her off,' says Lisa. 'That doesn't help.'

David swallows a newly furnaced slag of rage and says, 'Let's go find some water. You want to splash him. You don't want the lenses scratched.'

27

'He's not a camera!' yells Stephie, then, after a pause that feels like surprise at her own brilliance, resumes wailing, but half-heartedly.

Lisa takes no notice and is now flapping a tissue over the screaming child's face, blowing at the eyes.

'Go get some water, then, David,' says Lisa. 'Stephie, stop wailing. I can't concentrate with you hollering as well.'

David lopes off to a tap outside a concrete structure that houses a pair of loos. The smell of effluent stubbornly holds out against the sea wind. He has nothing to put the water in. A discarded Coca-Cola can has been placed carefully on the sill of the dunny window. He fills the can up, wondering if it would still have about it a tang of Coke. Appallingly overt graffiti sends toxic darts into his unpolluted consciousness.

'What's that?' yells Lisa as he runs back.

Luke instantly stops screaming and sticks his hand out, hiccupping mournfully.

'Me,' he says. '*Hic.*'

'No, it's water for your eyes, Luke,' says David.

'Me! Me! Coke! Me Coke me!'

The sea crashes on the sand, neither good nor bad but ruthlessly neutral.

''Sup, Luke? You said you wanted water, it's water.'

BRONWEN IS A FAT CUNT. PEADOS GO BAK TO POLAND.

Stephie and Noah are watching the proceedings with their arms folded. They hope to catch a Coke out of this. He can tell that's what they are up to.

What they ought to be up to is scouring the beach for interesting animal specimens. For signs of natural life, bivalves and crabs and worms and waders. For all the living wonders of this remarkable world.

'Me Coke!' screams Luke, his face impossibly distorted.

'Us too!'

Coca-Cola is an evil ogre of a corporation, and the drink little better than paint stripper disguised by sugar, but the agreement, the deal, is that one or two Cokes per vacation are permitted so as to avoid the kids feeling like weirdos, since David always felt such a weirdo as a kid – not being allowed television, not being allowed comics, not being allowed toys, not being allowed Christmas.

'Just let me photocopy the poster,' David says. 'I have to give it back to the café. Two birds, one stone. Won't take two minutes,' he adds, already turning up the path.

The campsite's main hut is thirty yards away. But that trip is enough to make him a free man for a moment. He feels different, on his own, as if breaking into a clearer space. Not watching his back, not permanently checking the kids out in his peripheral vision. He makes ten copies: the face of the girl called Fay looks washed-out in the copies, the machine suffering (according to the overweight teenage campsite operative in his tracksuit, DARREN on his name badge) from some unidentified ink-flow problem. Darren looks at him warily.

'You know her, then? Family?'

'Not at all,' David assures him, securing the rolled-up posters with a free lacky band. 'But it says spread the word, and we live in London.'

'Gotta car? Put it in your back windscreen then.'

The café seems crowded now: the German bikies are responsible. The waitress is too busy to acknowledge him at first, leaving a vapour trail behind her of sweat and cheap scent. He rests his elbows on the counter. The seated bikies glance at him but don't seem to care any more – too busy slurping, too intent on laughing like hyenas. Eventually, the waitress called Colette comes over only to tell him she is out of Cokes because of the bikers but they are sold on the bigger campsite nearby. He feels vaguely upset that she is treating him as if she has never seen him in her life before. The English blow hot and cold, he reflects. He returns the poster, and she takes it without comment. He leaves without saying *Au revoir, Colette*.

They drove through the bigger campsite yesterday. There were one or two tents like army staff headquarters; otherwise it was the usual oxymoronic spread of immobilised mobile homes populated by ageing bogans. There was a man shovelling white gravel from the boot of his Mitsubishi Shogun SUV (David had done the pollution report on this very model) onto the area in front of his massive white touring caravan in order to make a terrace. There were clipped bushes in tubs, and televisions, and huge tasselled parasols. It was a vision from consumerist hell, David remarked, not helped by the dismal weather and the flood defence ramparts hiding the sea.

Lisa laughed. 'You'll be saying it's all Satan's fault soon.'

There's a village a few miles away called Hogsthorpe – everything is either Thorpe-something or Marsh-something round here – but they aren't going to burn fuel into the atmosphere just to go get some fizzy drinks. If they are that keen to drink Coke, they'll have to tramp it.

The kids are impeccable on the pleasant half-mile walk through the dunes to the bigger campsite, as if holding their breath in anticipation. Steph and Luke hold hands, David holds Noah's. Three mobility scooters pass them, one with coloured balloons tied to it, but Noah takes one look at their drivers and keeps quiet. The place looks even worse up close. The main paths between the caravans and camping cars and the odd tent are actually metalled, with judder bars every ten yards; it's all zoned by letters and there are further signs indicating beach volley, karaoke, massage, mountain bike, two bars, disc golf, boule, zorbing and trampbilar. The last is a Swedish import, and the campsite is so like the same sort of place in Sweden, if not as cool, not as full of young, handsome types (understatement of the year), that David reads the signs unconsciously with a kind of Swedish accent.

'What's trampbilar, Daddy?'

'It's really hard to do, Steph. It's ice skating but uphill.'

Lisa darts him a look. 'Is it?'

Noah is agog. 'Can we have a go? I bet I'd be really ace.'

David has no idea what trampbilar is, in fact. He pulls a stupid-dickhead face. Stephie slaps him on the bum and Lisa *actually smiles*. Another spring of contentment unexpectedly rises inside him. He is so lucky. So spoilt. Such a lovely family and it is all his. Well, ours.

Reception, with 'Since 1925' above its door, has proper tiles on the roof and flowers in hanging baskets outside and nice wooden window frames and an A3-size Fay in the glassed noticeboard, staring out at them with that much more force in her big green eyes. Dead but won't lie down, he thinks irreverently. Again he sees Stephie in place of this kid he doesn't know, precious Steph grinning out at the world and MISSING, and the pools left by the flood of contentment are instantly sucked away to a barren dejection.

'We should've bought them the truffles,' he says. He is so weak. 'From the monastery.'

'Truffles are basically whipped cream and chocolate,' says Lisa.

'Exactly.'

'What's that supposed to mean?'

The sun is breaking through the great white fleets of cloud: the blueness beyond gives hope. The fitful glare feels almost as strong as the southern hemisphere's, and Lisa wonders whether the kids should slop on some of the gloopy 100 per cent natural suncream factor 60 that lies on the skin like a cross between paper glue and clotted cream. David claims they need their vitamin D – leave it, the sun's in most of the time. His mouth is bone-dry. He wishes he'd not forgotten his hat. Condemned to UV-challenged skin, he's already had five benign carcinomas in his life; his mole-map is checked out every other year. Life is a minefield, bro.

Bulky dads stripped down to stomach-lapped togs and jandals are already using the barbies, set out in rows in a small field beyond a low wooden fence. In the distance, pulsating with screams and shrieks, is a huge swimming pool with slides. The kids don't seem to notice. They are evolving well, he thinks. Or maybe Coke is their priority, and their brains are too small as yet to multiply intention simultaneously: the gunk has flooded their neurophysiological substrates, he muses, smiling to himself. As they approach the campsite's fizzy-drinks source, housed in a fetching red clapboard hut, a teenage girl comes up with pamphlets.

'German?'

Do they look German?

'English,' says Lisa, although they aren't English. Or maybe she means the language.

'Are you coming from far away in England?'

The girl could be anything: Serb, Latvian, Polish, Estonian, Romanian, whatever. Although aren't Romanians dark-haired? 'No, just from London, though to complicate matters we're not English, in fact,' Lisa tells her. 'I'm Australian, my husband's from New Zealand. You can tell.'

Why is Lisa getting so happily involved?

'Cheers but no,' says David firmly. He goes unheard as the girl is now leaning down and saying, 'Are you wild kids? Would you like to learn about being out in the nature?' She gives each of them a glossy pamphlet on which is written, WILD KIDS: LEARN ABOUT BEING OUT IN NATURE!

Lisa takes one and says, 'Oh, this looks great, ta.' The girl, a titanium blonde with caramel skin, is in a fetching yellow T-shirt tied with a knot under her breasts to reveal a sun-soaked belly that David clocks as not being firm and flat but slightly bulbous and probably spongy, although her waist is willowy enough. McJunk, high-fat diet, but she is somehow bizarrely attractive, despite his predilection for thinness in women. Her white shorts reveal thighs covered in a peach-fuzz down visible only because the sunlight makes it gleam like silk. She is probably on a zero-hours contract or even unpaid, an intern learning nothing except how to wheedle money out of innocent passers-by.

'You kids will love this like *crazy*,' she is saying. 'It is an adventure that is so good. I know because I did it for three years ago when I was a kid myself in my home country? We learn you about birds and trees and sports in the nature like—'

'Not really our thing,' David interrupts, alarmed by how hot he is for her, suddenly, without warning. He starts to walk away but finds himself on his own. The girl – a child three years ago – is sitting back on her heels in front of Noah, Steph and Luke; Lisa now holds Luke's hand. The pamphlet is headed with a logo for an outfit called WildNature. It must be an international franchise preying on campsites and so on, a kind of vulgar troll version of EcoForce's moral warrior status. McNature, more like. MaccaNature with chips.

'When are you all born?' asks the girl, her bright voice making it over to him despite the electronic dance music thumping from someone's caravan, or maybe it's ambient campsite stuff to keep everyone happy. David can see the girl's coccyx at the bottom of her long curve of spine.

SUK MY HARD COKK DRY.

Noah puts his finger on his chin, squirming in thought. This foreign girl must reckon his son pretty slow – not remembering

33

his own birthdate. Lisa is encouraging him, looking slightly anxious. Noah has learning difficulties, but they are sure it's shyness, oversensitivity, his mind too creative for the rigours of school. He is 100 per cent going to end up an artist, they reckon. This teenager would have no idea. In her world everything is perfect, her arse is perfect and her brown legs are slender and her teeth and her hair shine in the sun. Her labial hair, David thinks behind a protective white noise of irritation and alarm, would be spun silk, all but invisible.

'Would you like a really funny swell time,' the girl is saying, 'in the nature?'

'Yessir,' says Steph, nodding fiercely, still flushed with her success at mini-golf. *Yessir* must be something she's heard on the telly. She is losing her native speech.

'What kind of stuff do you do?' asks Lisa.

'We have real fun scouting antics like doing a big fire, cooking marshmallows, seeing animals, grilling green frogs, finding treasures in the forest and leaves that are eating by people,' says the girl.

What forest? Those spindly clutches of trees? Birch, aspen, pine, the usual?

'We're not part of the campsite, sorry,' says David, walking back to his hijacked family with a firm tread. 'We're going to the dairy. I mean, the shop.'

The girl looks up at him. She has large grey eyes that seem to envelop him like mist. 'You're doing wild camping?'

David nods. 'We're just here to buy drinks, that's all.'

'A shame. It sounds like heaps of fun for the kids.' Lisa smiles.

'I really really want to do it,' Noah says. 'I want to grill some green frogs. Twenty-one November,' he adds.

The girl is already glancing away, noting a family of five – three big-shouldered boys – strolling past in fluorescent jandals and striped shorts to just above their knees. They are rolling an enormous transparent beachball. They remind him of Lisa's brothers all those years ago, who said things like 'Jeez, it's as dry as a dead dingo's donger.' These kids are a few years older than the Milligan brood, which makes the parents seem like veterans.

'Come on,' David says. 'Let's go get some Coke.'

'And some crisps?'

'Maybe, Steph.'

He can smell the girl, a butter-biscuity muskiness of sweat and sun oil and maybe raspberry shampoo like something dripped onto a cake. Imagine a world where anything was allowed, where there were no moral rules: apes lived in it. Hominids, once. Chattering monkeys. Chimps kill and eat a rival group's young, no questions asked. Most animals live in that kind of world. Birds, especially. Any rules in their world are survival-bred. Surveying the tree canopies for days and weeks in Kahurangi taught him that. And a kea may well have the intelligence of a four-year-old human somewhere behind its beady eyes, according to the studies. The sun-oil touch makes him realise how he misses the southern brightness and sharpness: they've had three grey days out of five. He's been so busy finding his sea legs at work that he's barely noticed, and London is London: you don't scan the skies. Today's showing has expired already behind a sudden thrust of gunmetal cloud moving faster than the high white galleons.

'Coke!' cries Luke.

'Can't we do the wild thing?' asks Stephie.

'I suppose,' says Lisa, glancing at David.

'Keen as, keen as, keen as!' shouts Noah.

The girl has straightened up in one sinous movement, is turning towards the beachball family, her pamphlets at the ready. She has old rock-festival bracelets on her slender wrists.

She is a schoolgirl. She is now laying a hand on the huge ball, almost the height of her.

'Lisa,' David murmurs close to her ear, 'this isn't our thing. They'll charge us a fortune.'

'I want to grill a green frog,' Noah whines.

'I don't suppose they do that for real,' says Lisa. 'It was just her English.'

The girl is now talking animatedly to the family hunks, shaking her impossibly tumbling locks next to the shaven-haired dad, whose broad and naked chest is golden-furred, his eyes a laser-like blue in a face that is so regulation Aryan that David feels ugly and freckled and useless. The man has fiery tattoos all down one muscular arm, as meaningless and as ugly as graffiti. The guy can't be English, but what is a Swedish or an Icelandic (or whatever) family doing near Skegness? They'd have the girl for breakfast, probably in turn or all at once. All at once, in and out, slippery and warm.

For Chrissake!

Noah adds, addressing Stephie with appropriate movements, 'I really want to see it bubble and really swerm in agony.'

'I think you mean *squirm*,' says Stephie.

'Noah,' David snaps, somehow invaded by the girl so badly that his dick is pressing up against his thin hemp-fibre shorts. He lets the tube of photocopied posters rest idly on his groin in case. 'You know you don't mean that. Frogs are in danger of extinction. We don't cook them; we don't kill them in the first place.'

'No,' says Noah, miming even more vigorously, 'we can cook them living. That's why they *swerm*.'

He glares quite evilly, showing his canines, as if the extremely unattractive and even terrifying element in the human race, in the branch of it called *Homo sapiens*, which has effectively

36

committed genocide on all the other hapless branches up to and including the quieter, more modest Neanderthals, and is right now trashing the planet to bits, has welled up in him and is claiming this small boy's soul for its own. David taps his son's shoulder with the back of the knuckles quite hard and Noah acts as if he's had an injection.

Lisa frowns. 'Did I see you do that?'

'Well, did you hear? What our son said?' The girl and the blond athletic family are looking at him. His dick has obediently retreated, but it was touch and go. He is not blushing. 'Let's split. This place gives me the creeps.'

'That was a *slap*,' says Lisa as they walk away. 'Now you'll be arrested.'

Noah is acting not as if he's been injected but as if he's been hit in a shoot-out with some PlayStation alien, gripping his shoulder and wincing and staggering along behind his father. The athletic family and the fragrant teenage girl are looking concerned. David is boiling inside, the dance music now switched to heavy metal, completely antisocial and drowning any vestige of whatever dim ideal this campsite originally stood for back in 1925, when it was probably all tepees and Woodcraft Folk.

The beachball was a zorb, according to Lisa, a hollow sphere with straps for your hands inside. You crawl into it and roll off down a slope. Sounds a bit like life, starting in the womb and ending over a cliff. There is a gentle zorb run for children on the far side of the campsite. Lisa could not believe that, as a Kiwi, he hadn't known about zorbs. 'Of course I do. I know about them, I just didn't recognise it. I've had other priorities in my life.'

There are these gaps. No telly, no radio. Satan made the world. Jehovah would save it. Or a few thousand of us. The Brethren.

So unbelievably right wing. Fascistic. Everyone not of the Brethren was evil. Dad and Mum – crazed fanatics.

The heavy-metal beat comes from the woods, where a fun run involving rope bridges, mud pools and slippery mats is being undertaken by a variety of ages, some of them advanced. The Milligans watch in the grass from behind a rope, sucking up their agonisingly expensive Cokes through plastic straws and sharing one bag of crisps, beef-flavoured at Noah's insistence but at least these have never seen a cow. Steph has left most of her share after they gave her hiccups and has resorted to the banana-flavour chewie she inexplicably succeeded in buying with her *own* money against fierce parental disapproval. Noah consumes his Coke with the concentrated fervour of a deprived addict, then blows through the straw to make wet-fart noises amplified by the can. Luke holds his own enormous-seeming can like a Titan, legs straddled, upper lip stained, and swills his new teeth in a mouthwash of gunk sufficiently acid to clean a car's engine. Lisa is reading to the kids from the volume of fairy tales she picked up second hand in a chaotic bookshop in Lincoln. 'Crikey,' she says at the end, looking up at David. 'I didn't know it ended like that. Where's the woodcutter who saves her with his axe?'

'I think there are different versions,' David suggests. 'It's like evolution. In some it's a hunter, right? With his gun?'

'Why didn't she just chop up the wolf herself with a big old knife?' asks Steph.

Lisa chuckles. 'You mean Red Riding Hood or her granny? These days it'd be the granny. Grey power.'

'Wolves are yukkie yuk,' says Noah. He has a handful of blue nurdles secreted in his pocket and is now counting them in his palm like beads, like treasure.

Lisa suddenly beams at the kids one by one like they aren't her own. 'Hey, the story tells us she took cake to her granny. What kind of cake was it, do you think?'

'Chocolate poo cake' is Noah's creative contribution, with an evil cackle. Lisa tells him not to block, which to David's mind is itself a block.

He doesn't remember even reading any fairy tales when he was a kid because he was home-tutored by those creeping-Jesus nutcases. Even poetry was banned, unless you count the Bible as poetry. He only ever did one year at a primary in Witherlea when his mother was ill and he had to do actions for 'Some One' by Walter de la Mare and won a consolation prize. He still knows it by heart.

> Some one came knocking
> At my wee, small door;
> Someone came knocking;
> I'm sure-sure-sure . . .

Downhill ever since, bro.

'Wolves shouldn't be killed at all,' he suggests. 'They were here long before we were.'

'But they're really wicked, wolves are,' says Steph. 'Not like dolphins. Daddy, can we go to the pool? It's really ace here.'

She's got an English accent, David realises. She's sloughing off her Kiwi skin. He won't know her soon. He won't understand her vocabulary.

'Are they fragile, wolves?' ventures Noah.

'Faced with us, with the human race, any creature is fragile,' David explains, his heart swelling with love for his son, to whom knowledge and understanding has been miraculously transferred, making it past his Coke moustache. The nurdles have vanished, he hopes not thrown into the grass.

39

'Do you mind,' says Lisa in the harsh voice that always exaggerated her Aussie accent. 'We're reading fairy stories, not attending an endangered species conference.'

Steph pretends to stifle her laugh with a hand over her mouth.

'I'm just defending the wolf from the usual pastoralist propaganda,' David insists, genially playing along rather than taking a cricket bat to his spouse's head.

Lisa just pushes him around the whole time. He is a typical Kiwi, too passive and accommodating. Some New Zealanders do beat their wives to pulp, admittedly, but they are a minuscule minority and unfortunately a fair proportion are Maori. Poverty. Domestic issues. A conquered race. Massacre and disease. He'd craved to be Maori in his youth. Anything but a filthy all-conquering white man. With fucking red hair.

The smell of Stephie's bubble gum wafts around him in faint gusts, weirdly reminding him of his weed-smoking days. So long ago. Free to be an idiot. Let loose and roving. The discovery of girls. Way over the top, he went. Way over. Like a lacky band stretched taut all those years and then released.

He wishes he had his tinnie on him right now. Opening the foil package to pungent shredded home-grown leaves, rolling and licking and drawing on it deep. But he hasn't smoked in years. He has temporarily ditched the prehistoric sandals and his feet are now bare, toes curling, liberated. He could just walk off and keep going, keep going, until, I dunno, Alaska.

'Ready to quit?' he asks, turning to his family. 'We can put one of those MISSING posters up in our rear window,' he adds, waving the tube about.

'Noah wants to go zorbing,' Lisa announces, lasering out his suggestion.

'What?'

40

'It's a Kiwi invention,' Lisa adds. 'A part of his ancestral culture.'

'If I can't cook green frogs,' says Noah, quietly taunting. 'Or go to the ace pool.'

'Daddy, this morning Noah said my poo's like chocolate toothpaste.'

'Did he? I'm sure it isn't, Steph.'

'You're not *listening*.'

David is certain that if Noah goes zorbing, something terrible will happen. Everything is just a matter of threads and choices, second by second. Sometimes a crack opens and you see what the outcome might be, and instinct kicks in. It is evolution's little hint, the helpful whisper. The hominid smelling the unseen beast on the wind. A telephoto lens clicking. The teenage girl not taking that path, not right then.

'Sorry, Noah. That's definitely a no-no. Noah's no-no. And the Lord said to Noah, no.'

'Daddy,' enquires Steph, screwing up her face, 'are you going mad or something?'

'Lemme see the poster,' says Noah.

David unrolls one of the photocopies on the cropped grass. Fay looks up at them, as suddenly distant as a bird call over chasms and waterfalls, over the forest's endless upper canopy, trees and more trees to the horizon.

'She's *miss-ing*,' says Noah, his finger hovering over the black capitals at the top.

'For the moment,' says David. 'We're going to help find her, by putting this up in the van. It's our mission.'

'I'm Miss Milligan; she's Miss Ing,' says Stephie brightly.

'Miss Ing-land!' shouts Noah. He looks about him, surprised at his own wit. 'Miss Ing-land! Miss Ing-land!' Like a football fan.

'I don't think this is very appropriate,' says Lisa, scowling at David as if it is all his fault.

Steph scowls at Noah in turn. 'England's spelt different, stupid.'

David rolls the poster up. He mustn't let the rage overwhelm him. 'No worries. And let's not forget her little dog, guys. We have to go find that bitser too. Her only friend.'

'That *what*?' shrieks Steph.

2
FAY

'That's not a Staffie,' says her friend Janice, chewing and chewing with her mouth wide open so the banana smell makes Fay want some. 'It's a mixture. What's its name? Stinky Gingernob? Stinky Gingernob Two?'

When Fay tells her the name, the slag collapses like she is having a heart attack. Then she puts her head on one side and puts her hands on her hips like Mrs Pratt over your desk when you've not done your coursework and she says, after cracking a bubble, 'Whyyyyyyyyy?'

Fay doesn't really like Janice. Apart from the stupid slag calling her Gingernob all the time just because she's jealous (Ken says you're not ginger, you're ruby-red and beautiful), there is something about her. Hands on hips, mascara, bright-green coat, not even fourteen. She's in the year below. Fay is fourteen and three months, with freckles on her nose that she would like to scrape off. She feels even older since she did her Year 4 work experience fortnight in the toddlers' clothes shop on Totter Hill back in the autumn. Now Sheena, the owner, gives her odd jobs to do on a Saturday because she did good with them snotty little kids and Sheena is the best person in the world. Old enough to be her gran, probably,

43

but still as beautiful as a film star when the light isn't too bright, when she isn't stood under one of them spotlights in the shop. Fay hasn't got a proper nan. Her mum Rochelle had a mum who copped it when Rochelle was born, and there was no dad because he was in prison, so her mum had to be adopted and the family were cruel twats, according to Rochelle – they didn't like the Irish!

Sheena said on the third day of work experience, 'Fay, with your green eyes and red hair you're a second Maureen O'Hara.' 'Eh? Come again?' Sheena laughed, although sometimes she could be in a right mard. 'Maureen O'Hara was a gorgeous actress in Hollywood, she looked fantastic in Technicolor.'

Fay says to Janice, 'Pooch is a he, not an it. And Ken says as he's more than half Staffie.'

'What's the other half?' Janice says, wiping her eyes. 'Your mum's ex? And I don't mean yer dad, neither.'

'Jack Russell, moron.'

Janice grips Fay's wrist and tries to give her a slap but Pooch bounces up and down barking his head off until Janice backs away. She's stopped chewing.

'I've swallowed me chuddy, I'm gonna suffocate to death,' she says, gripping her own throat as Fay laughs.

Rochelle says not to go on her own to this place and that place, on account of the dealers and the pervs, which means Fay pretty well can't walk further than their own crescent, so she pretends she is going with Janice or Evie. Mum sees dealers and pervs everywhere. She says everywhere round here is a shit hole.

Pooch is worth ten friends, any road. A few weeks back, walking up Riseholme Road, he snarled and showed his yellow fangs at a couple of nobheads who'd normally mell your head in. They were jumping up and down in their trackie bottoms behind the underpass railings.

'Weapon dog, is it? Luvvit. So ugly it kills with a single stare, like.'

'Oh, Raging Bull, so scary,' said the other, whose voice cracked in the middle. She told them to bog off but they didn't come any nearer. Trouble being, when she headed down to the leisure centre, where there were some good grassy bits and where some dead-fit blokes with loads of muscle were smoking outside, Pooch snarled at them too, and they whooped and laughed and made her feel a right div.

She walks Pooch up to the Nene Road playground, where her stepbrother Craig has gone with his mates, passing the weird church with a roof that looks like a giant has thought the godshop were a horse and sat on it. She went to a comedy show there, year before last, with the school: *Little Red Riding Hood*, loads of singing that hurt her ears and a bloke with a stupid wolf face what wouldn't stay on. Her friends kept laughing. Baking hot and the seats were frickin uncomfortable, but she was stuck in the middle of the row. Torture, it were. There's a big patch of grass behind the church for Pooch and her to run around in, but then someone'll only come out and give her a Bible or a bollocking.

Pooch interrupts the boys' football, dreaming he's Mario Balotelli, and Craig gets really annoyed, and it's him who gives her a right bollocking because it's him what's a goal-scoring machine and not a fuckin ugly dog, OK? So Fay ties Pooch to a bench and has a go on the swings until some fat-arse from St Francis calls her a baby. 'Ginger, gingertwat baby.' She gives him a mouthful of abuse after untying Pooch and runs off towards Burton Road and the bypass, face hidden inside her furry hood.

The gate into the fields and woods coming up to the over-pass has barbed wire along the top. So does the stone wall. She could climb over except she doesn't want to tear her

45

leggings and add to the holes that are already there but are invisible because she's splotched orange lipstick in the right places on her thighs. She is out of the estate now, and she feels free and a bit frit, being here on her own. But she isn't on her own. Craig should not have tried to stamp on Pooch's head. It was wrong. Her stepbrother doesn't have the same feelings as she does for animals. He's only eleven and yet already the spit of his dad. Craig's mum passed away a long time ago. Fay's mum has to be his mum too after Ken (and the dog and the bass guitar) moved in, along with Craig. Ken is Craig's dad and they come from London, and Craig thinks he and his dad are number one and that everyone round here is mentally disabled.

In the first week, when Fay was eight, Ken walked in with red eyes and put his hand on her head and said, 'Your stairway lies on the whispering wind, me little sparrer.' He's never ever tried it on, though. She'd have bitten him on the face and screamed if he had.

Why couldn't they all have moved in with Ken and Craig in mega-cool London, instead of staying on in the Ermine?

'You don't want to be going to Sin City, duck.'

'But there's never nothing to do here, Mum, except from sitting in town.'

'You don't know as how lucky you are, Fay. You could be in Louth.'

Rochelle took a long, deep drag from her cigarette. She'd been told to stop by the health visitor because of her weight.

'I were raised there,' she added as if her daughter didn't know. 'Fuck knows how I survived.'

Pooch came free with Ken and his tickly goatee beard, as Rochelle would joke. A tiny puppy. Rochelle doesn't like dogs, but puts up with Pooch just like she puts up with all sorts. Maybe she hasn't noticed the fresh holes in the carpet, which is dead manky and already had holes in it. Ken doesn't bring a lotta dosh in, as he calls it, except when he was delivering out of a van for a while, but he's stopped Rochelle from ending up in the clinic. Fay isn't sure what that means exactly. Janice told her a clinic was a loony bin, but Sheena said it was where you went for a bit of mental calm. It's because Rochelle has problems remembering names and getting her tongue round words sometimes. She has trembly hands and shaky legs that can only just carry her big body up the stairs. But that in't going insane, is it?

'I'm not feeling over-well today,' her mum keeps saying, as if it's summat new, as if she hasn't said the same thing the day before. 'But I'll save me tears for the pillow.'

Fay walks along Burton Road's grass verge and onto the concrete bridge with the bypass underneath it like a raging river, four lanes wide. She stops to do up the hot-pink lace on her right trainer but it isn't easy with Pooch pulling. She yells at him to stay put. She can feel the bridge tremble when a big lorry goes underneath. There's a splotch of mud on the trainer that is pretending to be part of the leopard pattern. She wipes it away with her tissue then throws the tissue as high as she can but the wire fence is higher and the breeze here is too strong.

She's never come this far before, not on foot. The fence is there to stop people throwing worse things than tissues at the cars and lorries thundering along far below. But you can still chuck a can or a brick high enough to get over the top wire, because stuff like that doesn't care about the wind. Maybe it's to stop people throwing themselves over, people who've had enough of Lincoln. The sign advertising the Samaritans is still there stuck to the fence, but it is all faded. NEED TO TALK? PHONE . . . Someone has crossed out the number and put their own number with *FOR A MEGGAAA COCK* after it. Nobhead. That could kill someone, if they are almost decided to top themselves but not quite and Hull had beat Scunny or whatever and there en't more to life for them than football.

The sign made Ken laugh when they were in the bus together once, when his car was off the road; he had a solo gig in the White Heather halfway up that dead-straight road to Scawby near the roundabout. She was supposed to watch his gear when Ken's new mate Damien with the red eyes never turned up. It was a big posh bungalow with a carvery and there were loads of tossers only there to get kegged who'd never heard of T-Rex or The Who or even Creedence Clearwater Revival, and Ken said never again – I'm back to the pavement and a fucking hat – so they went home early and watched *Shrek II* with Rochelle through a cloud of dope. Fay was allowed one puff. It burnt her throat. That was the idea, laughed Ken. 'Dunno bout them tossers,' she'd said to him in the late bus going back, 'but I reckoned you was tops.'

He'd been looking out of the window, so the big cross with wings tatted on his neck was all she could see, and the scabby zits under the hairline, and the copper earring. And then his face appears and he slops this drooly wet kiss on her nose which probably the others are thinking is a bit paedo and says, 'Oh, and there's me looking forward to phoning that number on the bridge.'

It's true, his goatee beard does tickle.

She presses her hands against the cold wet wire and then her lips, squashing them against it. Gimme a kiss, Mason Greyback! She's Selena Gomez today, not Maureen O'Hara. Wizard of the Year. It's so high up here, it's what flying in a plane would be like. Magical powers, turning all them lorries to jelly. Gerroff, Mason, I'm concentrating on a spell! You don't ever reckon it's a high bridge from the road because of the trees before it and the road just carrying on as normal, then you get onto it and you are flying. She can see miles and miles over fields and woods, right out to Scunny probably, although she isn't sure she is facing north. She knows Scunthorpe is in the north of the county because they've just had a fieldwork test in geography and some perv had crossed out the *S* and *horpe* on the land-use map she had to use. There is something on the horizon, she doesn't know what, a bit like a castle, but it is probably a massive power station she can hide with her little finger. There is steam or smoke above it. The sun comes out and everything is lit up and she is happy and all she needs now to be perfect is a cherry Coke.

Pooch keeps tugging on the lead, not looking at the view, scrabbling to get off the bridge on the far side where the road carries on. There are no buildings on the far side, only fields of mud and bare trees; she can see that from here. You must be joking, Pooch. That's like the wilderness in Ken's video games: enter at your peril. Scorched earth, he calls it. A big motor is coming from town. It is slowing down. A big SUV with tinted glass so you can't see in. Not red, or she'd scarper. Ken says if you see a flash red Land Rover and the old geezer offers you a lift, saying he's a mate of the family, never take it. Never. Promise?

Who the frick do you think I am, Ken?

This one's green. But only pervs slow down, even in smart cars like this one. Her heart's hammering suddenly.

Passing her, the window slides down and there's a sad bloke's face, but not old. Staring at her. Then stopping a few yards further on, near the Samaritans sign. Fuck! There en't no one around. She runs back off the bridge towards the estate and home and safety.

Only halfway back does she think he was stopping to top himself, maybe.

3
HOWARD

27 January 2012

He wonders if he has the right to call it a day. They've played
five games and are halfway through the sixth and nothing
good can happen to him now, too skint to recover. They are
all steaming in Don's new tacked-on heated conservatory with
its hibiscus, balsams and a gaudy one called a Congo cockatoo.
A few months back for the summer match last year they were
out in the garden, where a pleasant breeze played havoc with
the lolly, and even the Chance cards ended up in the gardenia
bed. Now the garden is nuclear bare. New year, fresh start.
Mizzle, though. It'll start getting dark soon.

He's a wheelbarrow man, has been trundling round the
board with an uncanny ability to miss desirable properties –
and as usual he's bought into stations and utilities, a strategy
which he's kept to over the years, despite its minimal returns.
A feller of habit, he is. They all are, although their annual
Monopoly pub crawl is a shadow of its former self. Last
year, starting from the browns – the Lord Nelson in the Old
Kent Road – they fizzled out in Northumberland Avenue,
bloody Ian Glossop a virtual stretcher case. That was age.
And the bar-girls never knowing what ale was, now they are
all foreign.

He tilts his chair back and regards the other players with fake bonhomie. Lunch was the usual microwaved nosh, followed by the deluxe box of holy chocolate truffles from Our Lady of Grace Abbey that he'd found in Waitrose, believe it or not, on the way here. In memory of Diane, who regularly insisted they drive to the monastery, out beyond Tealby towards Kirmond le Mire, for the truffles and their holy cucumber body cream. Just as well he brought it along, because Trevor's donated some home-made toffee that breaks your face. As for drink, the various six-packs of Stella are history, furled cardboard, empty cans stopping the kitchen bin lid from closing properly and making that ear-splitting din, particularly painful now he's on hearing aids. He has an awful thirst, he's played badly, his best properties keep flopping over, white bellies up. He's about fifteen quid down. He picks up his Chance card:

Go to Bucket. Do not pass Scapa. In so many words.

Win some, lose some.

He needs a breath of fresh air. In the old days he'd have stood in the garden and smoked, but he's long given up. Chain-smoker too. The hotels line the board like the Monte Carlo waterfront, if line the waterfront they do in Monte Carlo, and not one of them is his.

'Gangster land,' he murmurs.

'Eh? Whassat, Howard?'

'Who'll put me up for the night?'

'You mean,' says Don, sliding his yappy little Scots terrier past his luxury strips, 'in real life, or on the board?'

'I can't risk the drive back,' Howard admits. 'All them Friday patrols between here and Swinderby. I want to enjoy myself.'

'Order a sherbert,' suggests Don.

The bastard didn't want him using the spare bed. That'll be his Sandra fussing. As if he might be incontinent or something.

He keeps schtum, just declares himself a bankrupt. Don's eyes light up. 'You throw the towel in too easily, Howie. Persist is my motto.'

Remember who you're talking to, schmuck. 'I'll bet none of you bastards know what day it is today,' he growls.

Gary checks his watch. 'January 27th.'

'And?'

General shrug. They're all still in the game and calculating, cogitating.

'National Holocaust Memorial Day.'

'Something about it on the news this morning,' says Eamon.

The others say nothing. The game continues.

'I might take a butcher's at the, er, the park,' Howard announces.

They all turn to look at him. He's giving his specs a wipe, breathing on them and rubbing the lenses with a relatively clean hankie. Helps to keep busy.

'Is that prudent?' says Trevor.

'Take care, now,' says Ian as if it's a trip to Somalia.

'Don't forget your hi-vis jacket,' Gary jokes. He hasn't understood.

'Now that's another bloody ridiculous thing,' moans Eamon as is his wont. 'Fluorescent yellow everywhere. Bicyclists, police, jumped-up traffic wardens. Have you seen them school kids in them? Just to walk to school. European mollycoddling, I call it.'

'Don't be a lemon, Eamon,' says Don.

Howard hears the laughter as he's closing the front door, its St George's flag streaked here and there with bird muck from the nest on the porch. Has Don noticed?

Good mates, still. He adjusts his tartan cap and matching scarf – prezz from Diane for his sixty-fifth – and watches his step on the crazy paving. Don's massive Land Rover, cherry red, means he has to squeeze past. The garage is reserved for Sandra's new Dodge Challenger.

Just don't ask. That way trouble lies.

The park is either ten minutes further from the street than it used to be when he was living in this part of town, in the days when he and Donald were next-door neighbours – Sandra and his Diane nattering over the wall – or he walks a lot slower. What's more, he'd be pushing Andrew's pushchair or going at the speed of Lily's four-year-old legs. No excuses. It's a seventy-four-year-old's puff, this one. The grey mizzle has cleared with the blustery wind, it is cold but bright, blue-sky stuff, everything sharper. It reminds him of their weekends away in Skeggy and Mablethorpe. A quick motor out to the edge. Hood up, get blown about. Fish and chips. A few snaps with his trusty Ilford Sportsman: the waves, Diane in her swimsuit, kids frolicking, reckoning he's Lord Snowdon. Best of British, Ilford. All the Fun of the Pier. Now it's a digital Canon with a zoom. Jap. Fake click.

He pauses at the iron gate. He hasn't been back here since. Wally, he calls himself. He loved this place once. It was always intimate. He liked its sloping nature, an open sweep all the way down and running with the kids through the rough grass in Hobbler's Hole. You could cross from here into West Common of course, which is probably still full of horses and more for dog-walkers and such like so you'd have plenty to slip on.

Birdwatching, courting, then the kids. Before they moved to Dunholme. 'I want to live in a village,' Diane said. 'In a quiet close for the kids. I'm a farming girl.' The piner after London! A twenty-minute commute: he should have used a pedal bike all those years. The extra quiet meant they could hear the training aircraft droning over, mostly from Wickenby.

The Red Arrows at Scampton were the closest, but for some reason their racket didn't nark her so much: sharp and quick it was. All them smoke trails playing noughts and crosses in the sky. Helicopters are the worst, but there weren't so many back then. Blade slap, you call it. Thump thump thump. Even Lincoln's got it bad with them these days: police, surveillance, private. London even worse. All them rich A-rabs and Russkies and whatnot. He put in double glazing but she could still hear the droning. It didn't bother him, his ears were already buggered for that sort of pitch, but he wondered why it bothered her when she'd been brought up on it. Out in the fens, on the farm, right under Coningsby's flight path they were. The in-laws.

The iron gate needs grease in the hinges, squeals like an alley cat. 'Know when to stay in Jail,' he mutters as he enters the park between the same old brick pillars, taking his mind off. The rest of the gang have stayed put, even though most of them are Londoners like him. Bow bells bong bong. Or from the south-east, anyway. He's lost about fifteen quid, he reckons, totting it all up. Three crisp Godivas less. *Monopoly money*, as someone always observes.

Like them video games are not real war. Four years older than him, yet she was still a little brat when she'd seen the first-ever lot to bomb Germany heading off – Handley Page Hampdens, cramped as a suitcase, sharp taper to the wings. Long thin tail like a dragonfly's. That's how he knew what she'd seen passing overhead. And the noise. 'What a fearful din they made, Howie.' Out of Scampton, that must have been. 'Might have done for me mum and dad,' he said. 'Oh no,' she replied, 'they were trying to save your mum and dad.'

When a crippled Lancaster had come down short on the return trip, the hedgerows were ablaze. Running up to help with slopping milk-pails, she was, her father scorching his hands. And the gippos making a line, handing on the pails. Loads of gippos in them days, helping with the harvest, she said. Always had been at harvest time. Their nice wooden caravans, all painted. Their hard brown hands. And then a Wellington's crew falling like stones one by one onto the family acreage one winter, their parachutes more flame than silk. Never talked about what she found. It was them Phantoms in peacetime, eventually. By then Diane was living with him in town. Nice change of a Sunday, to tread the muck on the farm, lift a few hundred beetroot or cut some broccoli just to give a hand, tuck into a roast after.

'I wouldn't mind them nuclear rockets,' her mother remarked one day, looking up at the sky as a jet ripped over, loosening their fillings. 'They don't make so much as a whisper.'

It was the first sign, of Diane's sensitivity to noise. Half of it in the mind. And her sight going. Still, he couldn't see why, with all that water to the east, they couldn't use that to fly over, like them Typhoons do now from Coningsby. Quick Reaction Alert. Saving the nation from intruders.

Look, sweetheart, we are under the trees. There are red apples on bare branches, unbitten by frost. Crocuses and snowdrops. In January! All that global warming nonsense. They'll always be dreaming up something to scare you out of your wits. Floods of immigrants. The demise of the indigenous. Bye bye, England.

Well, he quite likes smoked sausage and pickled herring out of the Baltic.

Mild for the time of year, but still a chill in the old bones. Damp and misty. His cap catches on a low thorn, unpicking the tartan. Look on the positive but remember to duck. He's got about an hour before it gets dark. There are days in January when it never gets light.

He strolls around the pond, remembering. This is going all right. Coming back, walking through them gates, no big deal. Therapy, even. You can avoid too much in life, makes a man weak. Andrew in the pushchair still and Lily scampering about. It hasn't changed, not much, in four decades. The swans look like the same ones. How long do swans live? Should have brought the Canon, a few artistic black-and-whites.

He enjoyed living in town, he thinks. This end of Lincoln. First job, first love, first kid. First proper job, anyway. British Steel from bloody zero hour. Crankshafts for heavy goods vehicles.

'How romantic,' Diane said humorously, first time he met her on that bench in '58. 'Jet engines,' he added. 'We do them too. I've applied for a transfer.'

That was probably what bagged her in the end, him getting an in-house transfer to the jets. 'He forges stuff for Rolls-Royce,' she'd say to her many relatives in their muddy gumboots. Adding, 'Avro Vulcan bombers,' in case they'd got the wrong idea. Farmyard stink. Lincolnshire innocent, she was. Still is, mate! Eyes wider than the Wolds.

Truth is, it was all in decline. Loss-making by the time Andrew was born. Thatcher sorted them out. Spirit of bloody Grantham.

Not Lincoln, though. It was the aerospace angle. Up-to-the-minute. Thermonuclear capabilities. They still cattle-prodded him out on early retirement: too expensive, mate. As was the oil-fired boiler in Dunholme. So it was a solid brick bungalow from the 1950s, all to gas, in pretty Swinderby. A pond in the garden. Decent neighbours: snuffling old Tom Parks on one side, out in the garden rain or shine; Maureen Henderson on the other, quiet widow doting on her even quieter boy, Gavin. Would hardly have known he existed, except for the occasional blast of teenager's music. Dreadful acne, poor sod. The occasional row audible over the fence. But who doesn't shout at his mother now and again at that age?

And when the kitten was adopted off the farm, scrambling over her knees or swinging off the curtains by its miniature claws, Diane would say, 'You know what, Howard? My life's complete. Could you turn the heating down? It's like a sauna in here. Look at what she's up to now. Smudge! Little rascal! You, c'mere, now!'

'You've never been in a sauna, poppet.'

'No, there's a lot I en't done, Howie.'

Lincoln, Dunholme, Swinderby.

Bloody yo-yos, Don called them.

The ducks flap and quack and the swans glide about but there's no one with him to squeal and point. He'd bring them here every Sunday while Diane did her bit for the Baptists. Life went so quick, and now the kids are into their second marriages and he's one of them oldies he never thought he'd become, all woolly coats and tender skin, and Diane is in the rest home for good, over in Bassingham, nice spot by the river. Doesn't matter where she is now – Timbuctoo, for all she knows. He tries to go over every day. Dress rehearsal, he jokes to the staff. His clothes smell of the place, that's the trouble. Pretty nurse or two, gladdening his heart. The raven-haired Romanian one is the best, in terms of efficacy and general all-round charm and the type of bristols you can't help privately admiring. His mates don't want to know. There are always exceptions, they say. Stolen someone's job, she has. Someone native. *Yeah*, he always thinks, *with warpaint and bloody feathers, whooping*. Better to keep your head down, though.

For the big summer match he came in shorts – a whopping mistake: gnarled calves, varicose veins, sandpapered knees.

They should be put away, he remarked at one point, looking down at his legs which ended in red socks and sandals. Don had asked, 'Why the socks, Howard?' Because without them he felt vulnerable. No, because it has always been like that, sandals or no sandals. Auntie Eva's orders all those years back. Sturdy, thick-strapped sandals for the bomb sites.

'You're not a street urchin,' she'd snap. 'Or an African.'

Didn't tell them that, though. He can't remember what he told them. Some bloody self-effacing jest. Another season, another life.

Terrible, being this age. You look ahead and see your life in slices. Wafer-thin slices. Work it out. Can't be much left. Almost the whole of 2012 still to go and sounding brand new, like science fiction, but come December he'll wonder where the year bloody well went to.

And then what?

He takes a circuit up to the bowling green on the edge of the park, walking briskly, pushing the ticker a little. Doctor's orders. He remembers telling weeny Lily, when she asked what lay beyond the first row of houses, 'More houses, sweetheart.' Now there are even more: Lincoln has spread like margarine. Big smart new houses too, but probably cowboy-built just the same. Not necessarily by Polacks or Lithuanians. Good old British lazy arses. Badly finished joints, fungus on the skirting boards. Leaks. Wiring all over the place. His children are thousands of miles away now. Miami. Bloody Auckland! It might've been nice to have had their company more often. But they weren't interested. No grandkids, unless they'd had them and hadn't let on. The odd Skype, when he gets it to work. No little kiddies secreted in the background, no poster-paint masterpieces, no toys. No continuation of the blood line, so far. To think what Auntie Eva would say. 'Oy-oy-oy,

I hope your mummy and daddy aren't looking down on us.'
Something like that.

Diane is dead to the world mentally, so she won't be hurt
if they turn out not to have let on. The newbuild in Swinderby
found the cracks in her mind after a year or two. Freezing
cold air under the floors, she said. Ice burns on her ankles.
True, there were draughts, place thrown up in a fortnight
probably, wonky handles, Persimmon just pocketing the
money, but only she could feel the freezing cold nature of it.
Bitter, it was. He'd started with masking tape over the draughts,
then tacked bubble wrap, carpets, foam rubber up the walls.
Electric blanket at night. Heating on full. Furry boots. It was
coming from inside her, that was the trouble. The power of
the mind, feebleness of the body.

'You'd not feel the chill at Skeggy,' he'd joke. 'Blimey, we
could hardly stand upright.'

Like living in a sauna, it was.

'I'm in thermal shock, Howard. Look at my feet. Blue!'

Mind you, it was all good at first. She liked Swinderby: the
bungalow, the church, the shop, an occasional Sunday roast
in the Angel. Driving out between them soggy fields. He can
still see her sitting by the pub's log fire when he goes over for
a pint or three.

It was the shock of finding Smudge dumped on the doorstep,
that's what did it. Claws pulled out (a pair of pliers, must have
been). Eyes gone. Blood in its nose. That would've been enough
to have turned anyone's mind for the worse. She loved that
cat. Whoever was capable of doing that to a helpless little
creature deserved the same treatment, was Howard's own view.
It wasn't the first time, they said in the pub. Oh no. Don't
think it's aimed at you two personally. There's a torturer of pets
in the vicinity somewhere. Maybe a gang. Louts from Lincoln.
One of them Polacks or Lithuanians. It was in the *Echo*, and

the vicar touched on it in the parish magazine. All creatures great and small. At least Smudge was buried proper. The lad next door, quiet Gavin, volunteered, probably encouraged by his mum. 'You've got a bad back, Mr Bucksbaum,' he said, 'and you're in deep mourning.' The most Howard had ever heard him say in one go. Dug the hole with great alacrity. Probably the first physical effort the youth had made in months. Not short, but thin as your little finger. Spots, greasy black hair like a helmet. Diane in the house, still shaking like a leaf. At least some young lads have morals.

That's what turned her. Pure evil. Never mind what the vicar said about forgiveness in the parish rag. *Show us ways to turn darkness into light.*

Switch the bloomin light on, Rev.

The park's air is fresh rather than cold, full of all those pancake-flat fields between here and the sea. Half of them put to rapeseed eventually, the horrible hi-vis crop that Diane's brother Kevin got into before his breakdown. Diane hated it. Kevin said rape was a good break crop between the wheat and the barley, and the CAP subsidies were 'summat to take home'. And *he* was the farmer now, he said, 'and not you, nat'raly'. Truculent type. Or fratchy, as Diane called him. You'd need a bloody dictionary, sometimes. And now it's Kevin's cousin Nathan managing it for whatever insurance company bought the place for its shareholders, screwing the life out of it. Typical Dobson too, all cast from the same mould – except for Diane.

He burps, feeling gassy. Too many Nelsons in his belly. Give me bitter any day, but Don's a lager man. Not a bad schmuck, when it comes to it.

You get a good view of it all from the park's slope, he remembers, and no rapeseed in January. He walks slowly over to the right spot, but the trees have grown higher. Still, there are gaps between the bare branches. Makes him think of Diane back in their courting days. He's glad he's come. Why be prudent? Being prudent didn't get him very far, did it? Fifteen quid down. It's Don who takes the gambles, buying up everything he lands on, going for broke, piling up the properties, while Howard sticks to stations and utility companies. I'm backing Britain, as he jokes. It means he never loses much, makes modest gains. Prudent! It applies to life too. Don and his conservatory, his top-of-the-range Land Rover, his South American holidays. Just don't ask. There are rumours. Play the wise monkey. Women too, probably. Sandra was always a looker. Knew it. Smuggling a pair of peanuts under her blouse, warm days. Good days. You could see her Alans on the clothes line from their bedroom, all lacy and black. Diane laughing.

There used to be a bench here, for the view. Or was it over there? That was how he met Diane. On a bench in Bexhill-on-Sea, end of the pier. Both far away from their respective domiciles in Lincolnshire. What were the chances of that occurring? One in a million. Could have been anyone. They might not even have got talking, but that her ice-lolly wrapper blew from out of her fingers onto his lap. The winds of fate. What was it? A Cornish Mivvi.

'Oh, my favourite,' he quipped, although it'd landed sticky side down on his new trousers. 'Can I keep this to lick?'

'I thought you were ever so saucy,' Diane was to tell him years later.

But he hadn't intended sauce.

Here's the bench, a new one with a brass plaque on it. IN MEMORY OF BOB SPRINGFIELD, WHO LOVED THIS SPOT. WE MISS YOU. THE KIDS. He parks himself on it. Someone has to. Like sitting in Bob's lap. Ghosts. Springfield as in Dusty. Diane's favourite. Now there was a voice.

A few trees lopped for the view. Sacrificed. Which came first, the bench or the view? The mist's not on his lenses either, though it feels like it.

Howard sighs, feeling very much on his tod, aware that no one would dedicate a bench to him. His offspring are too far away to be bothered, and Auntie Eva long gone. Slipped on a cabbage leaf in Borough Market. Nearly thirty years back! There's no one else, is there? He's never looked into it. Unless the British Steel Old Codgers Club, Jet Engine Division, Lincoln, would cough up for one. Alias the Miserable Gits Society. Always at Don's. A good all-gent schmooze, the one time in the year that Don's trouble has to make herself scarce. Fewer of us these days. Like war veterans. Natural attrition. Before they split tonight (although he still plans to bed down in Don's spare, once the git's too bladdered to care what Sandra thinks), they are going to watch Liverpool versus Man City – supping on their Vera Lynns, digging into their takeaway curries, playing the experts. He is looking forward to that, and a warm glow of anticipation floods his chest.

The damp's made it parkier, and the mist's gathering thicker. Well, it is nearly February. Already! Time marching on, takes no hostages, faster and faster. Always too hot, the home. But not for her. Never for her. She misses him if he doesn't go for a day or two. Those bleary blue eyes. Pulled the short straw, she did. It was all hidden. Eating away for years. They've not a notion what causes it. Like his glaucoma: makes him drive too near the middle of the road, apparently. One day he'll be entirely reliant on cabs to get there. Or anywhere. Buses being hopeless. Splash out. Lean back and be driven. British Steel pension, ho ho.

He's gone inert. What he needs is a good massage. Under the mitts of some beauty called Ludmila, he thinks, smiling to himself. No smoke without fire, but he can't raise a spark these days. Don's had his prostate out but still ruts like a ruddy rabbit, or so he claims. Doctor's orders! Private too, with that robot thingie. All on Bupa. That was never part of the British Steel pension plan.

63

Keep your hooter out of it, Howie. Asking for trouble.

He hears kids' squeals, like an echo. There'll always be kids to keep things going. He heaves himself up, knees complaining, and heads for the sound, the bare trees dissolving to swings, a slide, a climbing frame in a little paddock, mums and dads and their safe, fenced-in toddlers. Big bright scarves. Faces all colours. And then Jimmy Savile turns up, waving, and they usher him in among them, laughing and bedazzled. You could hardly warrant it. Always found him creepy, but Diane considered him a bloody saint. 'Don't be an old grump; you know he does so much good in the world.'

No, I didn't know. A perv in a shell suit. Should've had his nuts cracked in public. To the cheering millions who'd thought him the Barry McGuigan.

What about the swings?

The old pair, not this spanking-new lot. All bright-yellow and postbox red, with rubber safety mats – heavy-duty rubber compound, those are. A kid would bounce off. No bloodied knees and hands. So would a dead cat. You've got to learn your own parameters from bitter experience though. Life isn't all padded walls and floors, mate. It's a jungle, with thorns and claws. Wolf country.

Maybe the old lot of swings are still there. Or maybe not. Maybe they took them away, afterwards. Out of respect. They'd been there donkey's years before he came along, probably. He'll take a peep. Just a peep.

He goes off to the left, between the laurel hedges, his ticker speeding up from anticipation. A little out of the way the old swings are, which is why he always liked the spot. A spread of turf, the trees just behind, deep in bracken in the summer months. He's puffed. That's the nerves, heart reminding him of its miraculous fidelity to the job in hand. Day in, day out. Banging on. Pistons.

He clears the laurel and sees them: just the metal frame now in brown shags of winter-dead grass. Six rusty legs and a horizontal bar. Walking to nowhere. The chains and wooden seats have gone; just the frame has survived, with its four hefty eyebolts rusted in. You can understand it, the dismantling. A little dip where the shoes scuffed, now grassed over. A healed scar, that.

He positions himself right where he'd stand in front of Lily on the swing. He'd always make ugly monster faces as she came squealing towards him, and then he'd give her a little shove to set her swinging back again, tick tock, tick tock, the chains creaking and squeaking against the eyebolts, time passing, the frame a touch loose, ground anchors needing adjustment probably. Andrew gurgling in the pushchair.

Lily loved that. So did he for some reason. He has the right to look again, remember the happy times.

He crouches stiffly and sticks his tongue out and growls. The gobble monster! Yaaaah! Raaaah! Oi, Lily! Look this way, pet! Raaaaaach!

A girl, twelve or thirteen, hard to tell at that age, right in his line of sight beyond the uprights, a bit dark against the mist. Gawping at him. Close enough to talk to. Christ alive. It could have been . . . He thought for a second, just a second, that it was . . . Nearly bust his old ticker, thinking that. That's all it takes to be carried off. A bolt loose, the shock. So where did *she* pop up from? With an ugly little dog, on the path, appearing out of the shadows. She's staring at him. Petrified. She was camouflaged by her muddy-red coat and big fur hood – blimey, more effective than a combat pattern, if you discount the orange leggings visible over the verge. His monster face dissolves and he straightens up with difficulty. He tries to smile reassuringly but she hurries off, the dog following.

Thin, white, toothy face. Pink laces on her trainers, like Lily once had as an infant, but they're all the rage for all ages now.

Pretty with it, however. Big eyes. Must have thought he was barking mad. A girl like that can't be too careful. Big eyes like a calf's. Her slim body budding all over like the trees. And so it goes on, life. Natural. Slim body budding all over. Little buds.

A shock, though. Even though she was too old to be . . .

There's a creaking, a squeaking and a creaking. Faint.

Eh?

He stays standing exactly where he stood long ago when pushing the swing seat, his own little angel on it squealing with delight. Now there's no little angel and no bloody swing. He cocks an ear. Tinnitus from the factory floor, the forge, the engine-testing. That's what it is. Don said once that he ought to get a hearing aid. 'Not on your nelly, mate. I prefer catching only half of what you say.' And then he had to, anyway. Now he reaches behind one ear and presses the button: up to the stronger level on two beeps. Space flooding in, like walking into a cathedral. Funny that.

Squeak, louder. Then a creak. Then a squeak. Tick tock. Trees can creak like that, and he glances over his shoulder at the clump of bare trees, feeling the age in his neck. Still a dark place. Bracken dead like skinny white fingers.

He turns back and something bumps his shins.

'Ouch,' he says.

He takes a step backwards, sways a little. Internal spirit level's pretty well shot these days.

Then something hits his chest. He shouts out what you'd never shout in front of the kids, all but coming a cropper as he backs off, stumbling. He knows what it is, what hit his chest: a tiddly pair of shoes.

The creaking is longer in duration now, with a little skip in it at the apex of the arc. The arc, pausing in the eyebolts to descend again. What the swing is making. Change of the pendulum. Sweeping past.

Squeak. Pause. Squeak.

Except that there isn't a swing; just the empty frame, not even shuddering a bit, as it used to do if Lily swung high enough up.

He wants to scarper, but he can't. Paralysed. He takes hold of the frame's nearest upright and stands there, to one side, out of range, mouth wide open, sucking in air as best he can. The ticker barking and barking.

Broad daylight, but his head is moving from side to side, following the squeak, the creak, the squeak with his eyes, as if the swing seat and the chains are still there solid as steel and not vanished.

He doesn't dare walk in front to see if he gets hit again. He wants to, but he doesn't dare. It'd be like walking in front of a plane. So what he does is, he leans close, hand on the rusty upright, still short of breath so he has to take pauses, 'I'm sorry, little girl. I'm so sorry.'

What was her name, now? June? Julia? Gina? Then he remembers it in a flash.

The creaking stops.

He doesn't know where to look, that's the worst. He is waiting for it: the little cold hand in his. It is waving about, looking for his own sweaty hand to tug. But he's now got both of his hands clamped under his armpits.

Taters, it has suddenly turned proper taters in a nasty way. Beginning to get dark too. Or is that his eyes? He looks up. The sky bright enough, the mist swirling a bit darker in between, but yellowish. No, they'll be closing the park soon. Dusk. A rustle in the dead bracken under the trees. He looks there. Butterflies flickering about in the spots of sunlight, a cloud of midges, a thrush. Summer has come all of a sudden, bang into the latter part of January.

It is a very good thing indeed, saying sorry. He's always believed that. One of the great virtues, the ability to apologise. His chest feels bruised.

'Sorry, Judy,' he shouts towards the dark clump of trees knee-deep now in green bracken. There is no response. Everything going on as before. Butterflies. Midges. Wobbly spots of sunlight . . .

You'll be lucky.

They are now in the sitting room, the cricket highlights on Sky Sports: Pakistan versus England. All frying under the Dubai heat, the pitch a dust-grey rectangle from crease to crease. Nice for some. They all look up as if they've been worried.

'Have a nice stroll, Howard? Out in the chill?'

They are finished with the game and are embarked on the Veras, clinking nicely under wodges of lemon. The Miserable Gits Society has only three rules, apart from having sweated away the best years of your life for British Steel Special Steels Division and not arsing about with your mobile during get-togethers even in emergencies: no cheating, no dirty talk during the game, no gin until six o'clock. It is just past five of the clock.

He slumps into an easy chair and says, 'I saw her. I bloody did.'

'Eh?'

'I saw Judy Beeswick.'

Gary, who only joined three or four years ago, says, 'Who's she?'

'Little girl what was done away with,' says Don, picking up the remote and cutting the volume on the adverts. 'In the park, at teatime, July 1971. We advised you not to go, Howard. Ice, lemon?'

Howard nods. Don knows you can't drink the stuff without the clinking, the bobbing about, the burn of it on the upper lip. Why ask?

'You look very pale,' says Ian.

'As if he's seen a ghost,' Trevor remarks.

Howard says as he didn't really *see* her, visually speaking. He explains. The others nod sympathetically. Silent white puppies are knocking over pyramids of white toilet rolls, silently. The heating is on too high. He undoes his coat. Tickles of sweat from his armpits.

'The missus likes that one,' says Trevor, indicating the screen with his arthritic ring finger.

'Andrex,' says Eamon pointlessly.

'I'd have used ermine,' Ian says. 'The royal touch. Puppies running over ermine.'

To rhyme with vermin. Not like the fine, benign, draw-the-line Er*mine* council estate. Now there's a mystery.

'Animal rights,' Don points out. 'Charlie isn't going to wear ermine robes at the coronation.'

'Told you, has he?'

'Trevor, I have ears in high places.'

They all chortle except for Howard. There is a little, strained silence.

'So what exactly were *you* doing that afternoon, Mr Howard sir?' asks Gary.

Quite the joker is Gary, but that one falls flat as a pancake. He is too young at sixty. Howard cradles his double Vera. No one has commented on the breaking of their own rules (senile indulgence, probably), and he explains to the new boy what happened. The others stay respectfully schtum, even though they've heard it a dozen times over the years.

'The thing is, I loved taking the kids up there, on the swings,' says Howard, gazing into his drink. 'Making me monster faces. Lily loved it. Loved being frit, as they say round here.'

'Do they?' Trevor chuckled.

'But I couldn't stand the creaking and the squeaking. It was the council's job, but that's just it. It's too simple, isn't it?'

'Chronically incompetent, that lot,' says Don, who has nevertheless greased a few of their palms in his time. 'Where does one begin?'

'As the Somalian taxi driver said,' jokes Ian, although no one gets it. Always a deep one, Ian Glossop.

The cricket tutting again, the Abduls hitting to the boundary. Bloody horrible neon-yellow stumps. Look at them. In case the bowler is myopic. Eamon's right: hi-vis everywhere like a disease. Eurobollocks.

'Overspenders,' Howard presses on, 'unless it's on something useful. They'd have replaced the swings with a brand-new set, using our money. Paper money to them. So I took it upon myself. Grease. Wheel-bearing grease, state-of-the-art, safe from high thermal exposure and wet. Took me half an hour. Hey presto, silent as a lamb.'

'You can tell he was in the Jet Engine Division,' jokes Trevor.

'The next day,' continues Howard, 'Judy Beeswick vanishes.' He gulps without meaning to. It makes him cough for a few seconds, like something's caught. 'Sorry.'

Ian stirs. 'Take your time, Howie.'

'Right. Found twenty-four hours later.'

'Strangled,' adds Don with a squirt of relish.

'On the swings one minute, slipping off into the trees the next. Naughty, that was. Because even at five years old she knew it was wrong, slipping off like that into the bracken while her mum was deep in a book.'

'She'd be deep in her bloody mobile these days,' murmurs Don into his tipped-up glass, the ice sliding into his mouth, where he audibly crunches it. As if he never uses one.

Howard leans forward on the sofa with some difficulty and fixes Gary's eye. 'She – the mum – says to the papers how she never heard the swing stop. She never heard it stop. She would never have heard it bloody start. Because someone'd greased it.'

After a polite pause Gary says, because he is younger, 'That's confusing cause and effect, mate.'

The others chuckle. The gin's viscosity is as high as ever, oiling his thoughts already, all those little molecules creeping in. Maximum cold cranking. His bladder tells him he needs a gypsy's, urgent, but his mind is thick-skinned. Outside is now night. Or that's the impression from in here. The floor-to-ceiling curtains need closing. He can see himself, reflected. Old and haggard. No surprises there. You think you're Paul Newman in his twenties until you catch your reflection or someone takes an instant on their mobile. Then it's a rude awakening. Diane withered down to her dentures, if they bother to put them in. Such a beauty once. Spilling his birdlime. That flowery swimsuit, all clinging polyester. Always up for it. His hand under them hard wet cups. Right there on the pebbles, under the seawall. And leave the rest (chuckle) to me. Play the Frankie Vaughan at her funeral, why not? Not a dry eye in the house.

'Christ, another four for the Pakis,' says Don, making him jump.

'Too many Pakis, too many runs,' says Ian.

Gary crosses his stretched legs at the ankles. 'There aren't too many of them over our way, over here, though. Are there? Mostly doctors or teachers or summat.'

'We don't want 'em,' says Don. 'Not on top of the Polacks and whatnot. Romanians. Any minute now.'

'Roma,' says Ian. 'Watch your throats.'

They're not the same thing, you berk, thinks Howard. The drop-dead gorgeous nurse at the home told him. But remonstration just makes enemies, as he learnt long ago. 'She's still on them swings,' Howard continues almost to himself. 'And they need more grease. Forty years of use. Silent and deadly.'

Trevor clears his throat and says, 'They never did find the bloke, did they?'

Eamon, the quiet one until a chance to moan offers itself, pops up again from his turtleneck. 'Too many nutters about. And the worst ones are even more ordinary than you or me,' he adds, surprising them.

Ian has another go: 'We lost fair and square this time, eh, Howie? But it's only a game.'

'I'll drink to that,' says Don, who has cleaned them out by sixty-five quid, so he is happy. But his glass is drained.

Howard says, quietly, staring into his own half-supped mother's ruin, where the melting ice is making flow patterns like a wind tunnel's, 'Win some, lose some. Win some, lose some.'

Don licks his lips. 'That's the spirit,' he says. 'Drink up. You're two behind us lot, if we're talking *lez aperiteefs*. If we're talking women, I have no idea.'

'To Graeme Swann, still the best off-spinner in the world,' says Ian, raising his glass at the screen. The others don't budge.

Irreparable damage, Howard thinks. He needs to move.

'I tell you what,' he announces, staring at the screen. 'I'd like a memorial bench when I'm burnt bread. Seriously. When I fall off me bike. In the park somewhere where you get that view eastwards towards the sea. IN MEMORY OF HOWARD BUCKS-BAUM, WHO SAT HERE WITH HIS DIANE. You can add whatever you like after that. Something biographically relevant.'

SURVIVOR OF THE KINDERTRANSPORT, he was assuming. Obviously.

After a little confused silence, Don says, shaping the plaque in the air with his finger and thumb and enunciating each word with care, 'A GOOD LOSER.'

4
COSMINA

12–23 May 2012

When she finds herself sitting under the hedge, it is an effort to recall what happened, how she arrived in such a position. The car struck the bicycle in some way – clipped it more like, and she was thrown bodily. She remembers nothing more. Her arm is painful and her thumb hurts and her bottom is sore; she has blood on her face, bright red blood. She feels her face all over, then checks her teeth with her tongue. The lane's verge is soft enough and the hedge is not thorny, it is something like laurel – evergreen anyway. On the other side of the hedge are the grounds of some exclusive club or hotel – she passed the sign and then the large gate of wrought iron. The big red SUV did not even stop: maybe the driver had not felt her, had not noticed when he roared past.

She examines her bicycle, which is lying like a wounded horse after a battle: half on the verge, half on the road. She is breathless and wonders if her chest has been damaged in some way, or whether a blood clot might have formed in her brain from her head hitting the ground and in a few minutes she will drop dead, having thought herself free, let off to live another day or another lifetime in this strange and wonderful country.

The bicycle seems fine but on wheeling it a little way she sees that it has been subtly twisted and the chain makes juddering noises. The front wheel is stroking the support bar (if that's what you call it) and she feels upset. Her day has gone cabbage: she was planning to visit the monastery near Tealby, having the afternoon off before the night shift. Buy a jar of honey, send up a little prayer. The monastery is in the Wolds, which she has never seen and which seem to her special and mysterious. The weather has been sunny and cold for days, but now on her day off it has turned grey and cold, even though it is May. She wants to find out where the blood is coming from on her face because she has several tender spots but no actual breakage of the skin.

Then she feels her ear, leaning the bicycle against her thigh, and twitches with pain. The blood is trickling from her ear down her jaw and her neck, and when she feels her ear it is like touching half-melted sugar in a pan. In the shell of her ear there is a creature, a sand-covered lump of gristle. On the tip of her finger is a smear as black as plum jam. Does blood go black that quickly? She realises she has landed on her ear and cut it up.

She reaches for her phone. It isn't in the pocket of her cycling jacket. She looks in all the pockets. Then she sees something glinting on the road. The phone has been crushed, the screen starred with fractures. It still lights up, but she can't press the screen without slicing her thumb. She cries a little and swears through her tears and works out how many long hours she has worked to pay for this brand-new iPhone, but then thinks how lucky she is not to have lost her life. It is a bargain in Heaven: five hundred pounds against her life. No one else passed her on the lane, which she chose because it was too narrow for lorries and in the right direction for the monastery.

She sets off towards the next village, wheeling her bicycle. She passes either a squashed rabbit or hare, it's hard to tell from the mess. Her grandfather, bringing in a hare from the lower fields: the sinewy meat. *You must not run after two hares at the same time.* The neat hedge becomes a scruffy hedge that runs all the way along this part of the lane, with a tangle of trees and saplings behind it. She desperately needs to pee. It must be the shock. She waits for an opening in the hedge – there are quite a few gaps; it is more like undergrowth than a hedge – and slips through, tugging her bicycle after her. She steps a little deeper into the grey and dingy wood and crouches down. There are tiny woodland flowers and beetles and ants. Beech trees. The leaves are still fresh and green; then the sun comes out and they turn translucent, like the emerald tiara of Princess Elisabeta. Visiting the Natural History Museum on Şoseaua Kiseleff with her father and seeing it behind glass, and *tată* saying, 'At least that lot had class. But if you think they'll be coming back any day, you're fighting the windmills with a broom.'

As she buttons herself up, she is brought up short by what in the first horrible flash she believes is a sheep torn apart by a wolf. Shreds and bunches of grey wool scattered next to a fallen and mouldering trunk: the brown skin, the crumpled flesh. It is a memory flash, instantaneous, from when their flock was attacked years ago and she was taken to see the result. 'They bunched together and the dog growled,' her father said, 'and I knew there were wolves but you never see the evil bastards. They are there, watching you, but you never see them. That's why I hate them.' They tore at the stragglers from behind, and one poor animal was killed, along with her lamb. The lamb survived for an hour or so, in fact, but was dead by the time Cosmina went up to look with her mother, its tongue lolling out and blood in its nose, insides spilt like stew. She was five. 'Why did God make wolves?' she asked her mother. 'That's what we've all been asking ourselves from the oldest times,' her mother replied. 'But one day the lamb shall lie down with the wolf, God willing.'

It is only a harmless item of clothing: a brown coat, maybe once red, its arms spread wide. Her heart is still pounding as she stares down. It must be delayed shock from the accident. She distinctly pictured a sheep or a lamb. Just to make sure, she picks the coat up, holding it between her thumb and finger like something poisonous and giving it a shake to release the soggy leaves stuck to it. It is quite small, maybe a child's coat, with a big furry hood that something has ripped into clumps with its claws. A dog or a badger. No wolves here! Not in gentle England.

As she lets it drop back onto the mush of dead leaves and nutlets, she feels an unaccountable depression come over her, as if she is standing in a very dark room without a candle. Maybe she feels as worthless in her soul as this discarded coat. It is litter, like the crisp packets and sweet wrappers scattered here and there along the verge. Condoms even. A child's rusty pushchair. But it is worse than them: it looks as if it might rise up and point at her, with its empty hood pulled forward. What a horrible thought!

She hurries back through the gap in the hedge and quickens her step along the bright lane, keeping the nearest pedal away from her leg, feeling suddenly vulnerable.

In fact, she feels a little sick and faint.

She reaches the outlying houses. The odd person she passes, walking their dog, turns round and stares at her, frowning. A woman emerges from a semi-detached house with a box of plasters, some antiseptic and a sausage of cotton wool in plastic. The woman's chubby middle-aged face beams.

'It's dangerous, bicycling is. All this traffic. You should wear a helmet, pet. Look at that ear.' The woman points to the low brick building over the road. 'That's the surgery,' she goes on. 'You'd best go and use it. I've only got these small plasters. Where are you from?'

Cosmina wipes her neck with a big tuft of cotton wool. 'Romania.' The tuft turns bright red.

The woman's face falls a little. 'Oh. Don't see many of them. Not yet. Well you'd best go and use it, any road.'

She waits an hour for the doctor between screaming infants. He tells her that her ear has saved her life. The upper ear was pierced right through by a sharp stone but took most of the force of the collision, like a rubber guard. Just behind that part of the ear is a spot that all assassins know about, which leads directly to the brain with no bone in the way. A thin stiletto blade can fit into it perfectly. The ear is an elaborate protection and a shock absorber. The village doctor, who seems to be Indian – Asian, at least – is knowledgeable and chatty behind his large pockmarked face, his moustache and his busy hands. People in England are always chatty and smiling when they aren't drunk or in their cars – when something turns them into scowling monsters. He sprays a sort of medical glue over the perforation and cleans her up with wet wads of cotton wool that sting. 'You should never use dry cotton wool on a wound,' the doctor says, probably because, when she arrived, she was still clutching the reddened tuft. 'We have to pick out all the threads with tweezers.'

'Thank goodness I never did that,' Cosmina says.

She asks to wash her hands and does so in the little sink in the back room off the surgery. There is a poster in there in English and what looks like Polish, showing a sad child with bags under its eyes. The Polish ends in an exclamation mark, but the English doesn't. TVS, PHONES AND SCREENS SPOIL KIDS'

SLEEP. The TV in the little flat in Lincoln that she shares with Anca from Timişoara keeps having fleas, as her father would say: static interference. *Spoil* is a funny word to use in this context; she thought it could only be used with an object or the word *life*. Spoiling my tablecloth. Spoiling my life. Not to be muddled up with *soil*. Soiling the bed linen. She would always stupidly confuse *spoil* with *spill* in the early days.

She tries not to feel unlucky. It is too easy. On the way here she stood on the station platform where she had to change trains, somewhere dull between the mountains and Bucharesti, somewhere grassy and full of dust off the road, four hours still to go on the slow journey, and there was a big Roma family on the platform, filthy kids running about, the baby without a nappy, two dark men and two dark women, and she somehow knew they would be in her carriage, filling it up, shouting and laughing and eyeing her luggage and her necklace and maybe her throat, the baby shitting from its bare arse. She felt so nervous she began to sweat, feel giddy. Then the train came and the Roma family stayed on the platform, sitting on the concrete, teeth tearing at sausages. Perhaps they were squatting there; Gypsies squat anywhere. She felt stupid with her fatalism, her pessimism. The only other person in her carriage was a university teacher, retired: a little lady with a thick book and spectacles who told her all about Constantin Brâncoveanu – things about the great man and holy saint that she was never taught at school. It was a wonderful journey.

She suddenly feels homesick for her village, for the glowing light from the dewy meadow grass beyond their wooden fence, for the cow bells clinking afar and for the blue haze of the mountains and the long shadows of the trees sprawled up the steep slope running down to the farm. For the spruce trees stabbing up from the mountain crests. For the sweet incense of the air. For the orchard and the chickens and the pigs in their mudbaths, for the rattle and sway of the hay waggons and that sweet hot smell, for the neat ricks, for the only spot in the garden that picks up a mobile signal, so close to her mother's big red roses that you get scratched. But Mother won't dig up her roses for anybody! For Mircea the shepherd passing and waving to her from the track, his big boots splashed with mud and at their heels his vicious, drooling dog – vicious to anyone it doesn't recognise, which is a rare occurrence in her village. And in the winter the deep snow, the ice, the frozen ways. Even the harsh winter she misses. But her nostalgia is mostly for harvest time, the ripeness of the hay piled onto the waggons, so high you can hardly believe it will not fall off.

She might have been killed on her bike and all her plans to make the world a better place would have been wiped out in a second.

At least her English is improving fast. Soon she'll have enough money to go to journalism classes, to make contacts, to push upwards. No one here could care less that she is already a graduate, except that it has allowed her into the country in the first place. She is useful, that's all. A spare pair of hands in the care home. Night shifts very often. They give her a lot of work, a lot of responsibility, but she is treated as if she is slow and stupid. Clear, loud instructions. As if she is an inmate! Yet her professor reckoned she was doctorate material. She could have had Doctor before her name, like this real doctor. Not in medicine but in political science. Sometimes she does the job of a nurse, even. She knows how to take blood and give an injection. She learnt this on the farm, staying twice a year as she would, and when her grandpa was very ill and the snow would often cut the village off, she was taught emergency treatments by the doctor. But she is only paid as an assistant.

81

She dries her hands on a large paper towel, one of a pile that lies next to the sink, and throws it into the pedal bin, in which she glimpses bloodied plasters and a syringe. COUGHS AND DISEASES SPREAD DISEASES. An old, faded poster. Full of microbes itself, probably.

'Feeling better? I wondered what had happened to you. Lucky it's quiet today.'

'Thank you, yes. I am sad because my phone was really squashed,' she says, producing the evidence, careful not to cut her finger on the shattered screen.

'Dearie me. Buy another one. Apple's profit. Dreadful company.'

The doctor is from New Delhi. It is a group surgery. He is very chatty, although she has trouble understanding every sentence. He asks her about Romania and whether she is ever confronted here in England by racist types. There are problems in the area from these racist types, who complain that they never see the doctor they want, which always happens to be the two others, who are white women. He is scathing about these racist types. It was probably one of these types who hit you and then sped off, he says.

Cosmina shakes her head. She says a woman was very kind and came out of her house with plasters, antiseptic and cotton wool. She hasn't used the cotton wool on the wound, she adds quickly. She is feeling woozy and wants to find a place to lie down. The doctor seems a bit fed up that she is disagreeing with him about the villagers. His room is clean and white, with lace curtains over a frosted window and various items of steel equipment. A Mac sits on his desk. The desk is an antique type, heavy and dark with carvings of dogs and boars under the lip. It looks out of place in here. A colour photograph of a child with its mother sits in a gilt plastic clip-frame on the desk, positioned so that both patient and doctor can see it.

The mother is white, the child is half-and-half, a bit like a Roma kid but cleaner.

The doctor sits down and wipes his face with his hand, distorting it, and makes out a prescription. He's applied iodine to the wound, and she must continue with it. The medical glue will dissolve in time. The ear will recover its shape. Cosmina has still not seen it – there was no mirror above the sink – but it is clearly a bit of a cabbage. If the ear doesn't recover, then she'll drape her thick dark hair over the mess to hide it.

As the doctor is making out the prescription, tapping it out on the computer, Cosmina feels a wave of euphoria. She feels as a soldier must who has been lightly wounded, visibly wounded, in a battle. She likes to think of herself as a warrior sometimes, fighting evil and injustice. An Amazon! She asks if there is anybody in the village who might straighten out her bicycle and the doctor makes a humming noise without taking his eyes off the screen. Cosmina wonders whether he heard her. She doesn't want to push her luck. The doctor's eyes rest on hers for a moment.

The weather turns a little warmer and the sun comes back from its hole. Everyone says how at last May is behaving properly, although the air is still cool. On Wednesday, working the early shift, Cosmina goes outside into the garden in her coat for her main break; the sun on her face is definitely pleasant. She is having her usual snack lunch of *zacuscă* spread and smoked yellow cheese, brushing the flakes of crust off her knees and thinking how lovely the fat red roses are, almost as good as Mother's. They were only buds last week. She is breathing in their fragrance, even stronger than usual in the sun, when she hears a voice inside her head. It is intent on keeping something secret and is speaking in some kind of whispered code. The voice is not all that different from the noise of the little river sliding past in its lazy way beyond the lawn, but when she looks about her she sees that there is no one else nearby: the care home through the bushes looks as big and dead as it always does, its brick giving nothing away, just waiting, always waiting, as Catholics always are. Redemption. Salvation.

She squeezes her eyes shut and opens them again, feeling an obscure sensation of fear and dread. Her ear is healing remarkably quickly – the black blobs like plum jam have almost disappeared – but she can't help thinking of the perforation and the blade of a stiletto entering the vulnerable point of the skull. She suffered a light headache for two days but that in turn has faded. Her phone is unmendable, they said, and it wasn't insured. She has bought a bottom-range mobile, pay-as-you-go, chunky and with giant letters, until she has worked enough hours. Or maybe she won't bother to buy another iPhone. The doctor was right. Apple computers and exploitation. Child miners! She wants to live right. At least the bike has been straightened out. That wasn't cheap either. Eighty-five quid! She can't send any money home this month without starving. Sometimes when on nights after meals in the home she brings back untouched leftovers to the kitchen for her own consumption, but there are limits. Everyone here throws everything away, even before it's finished. And this is the country, not the city. Yet it is worse than Bucharest.

She wonders if she was overconfident about her injury and is now being punished. She is only twenty-two and a part of her wishes her mother was right here, sitting next to her on this bench. There would still be snow in the mountains. She lays down her bread roll and stands up, brushing caraway seeds off her blue tunic. The little voice is coming in and out of the other sounds. She walks about a bit on the grass and bends down at a place where the water laps vigorously at a sandy spit formed by the seasonal action of the water on the crumbling bank. She dips her fingers into the very cold water, resting her chin on her knee. She feels fit, mentally and physically. She cycles a lot, though she was never into sports very much back home; going back each summer with her parents to help with the harvest on her grandparents' farm was exercise enough. Picking raspberries without crushing the fruit! She would like to build her own log house in the meadow next to the farm and look after her grandparents in their extreme old age and then her parents when they retire and come back from the city and grow very old in turn. One day she will do that, when she has the money and has lost her ambition, but right now she has other dreams. When she first came up here she had no choice but to work under a gangmaster cutting broccoli and cabbage that stretched to the horizon, feeding them onto a conveyor belt. Imagine how much money is tied up in these huge fields!

She isn't sure she likes all these agricultural advances, this economic efficiency. The food here tastes of nothing. The fields are monotonous. The locals don't work in them; there are no horses pulling ploughs or waggons. Maybe she is just her great-grandmother reborn, grumbling about the new ways. An ignorant rustic under her university degree. Or maybe she is ahead of her time. The German couple who have bought the farmhouse next door to her grandparents claim to be the future, the only possible future. They are politically green, let rooms out to tourists, grow organic vegetables and fruit, have a composting toilet. They said to her grandmother, 'We are learning from *you*!' Cosmina translated, laughing with her grandmother. Up until then everyone had said to her grandmother, 'Your peasant ways are finished. Thank God we're in Europe now. We can advance.' But her grandmother's house has a proper flush toilet, installed just a few years ago almost before anyone else's in the village. A proper shower, thanks to her father, working so hard as a plumber in Bucharest. They are saving up for a dishwasher, even. This did not impress the Germans. What had impressed them was the dung heap in the yard, the hens coming into the kitchen, the filthy, mud-bespattered pigs at the bottom by the fence. 'They're fighting with the windmills,' her grandmother said when they'd gone. And laughed, showing all her missing teeth.

Cosmina kneads the water as she imagines the rest of her life, picturing an empty place like a chair and no one coming to occupy it. A slight pressure is creeping around her head, like a migraine. She's had two attacks of migraine in her life and they both laid her low for three days, lying in bed unable even to read, the curtains drawn and every shaft of light an agony.

The May sun dapples the river through the small over-hanging trees that line the banks. It will be lovely here in the high summer. The water is too shallow to swim, or she might strip off when it gets hot and wade in. She laughs inwardly. No, not really! Never! Because opposite is a footpath, and then gardens, and then a group of modern houses before the fields begin. They also look as if they are waiting, with the dark eyes of their windows.

Blind windows that can see.

It is like the view from their apartment in Bucharest: yet more blind windows in the tower block opposite. Her parents remember when the heating was kept to ten degrees even through the harshest winter, the pipes frozen solid: government orders. 'You were born the day after Christmas Day,' she keeps being told, 'but not any old Christmas Day. The day the devils were executed. You were our angel of hope, Cosmina.' That is a big burden. A great weight, being an angel of hope. Her wings should be bigger. Not sparrow size but swan size. A heron's wings.

She is back again in her grandmother's cottage, its yard and its chickens and its wooden swing; the family's vegetables and their orchard are on a slope beyond the last of the hamlet's houses, before the forest starts. The tiny whitewashed church has a bell with a crack in it, and after three peals it turns dull, as if (as her father jokes) someone has put their sock in it. She closes her eyes; she can smell the waxed wooden benches and now she is hearing the creaks of the floorboards in the aisle. She misses the mountains but she also likes the flatness of everything here, the huge skies. You don't see those in Bucharest either. Here it is like the first time she went on a boat on the proper sea. She can breathe and spread her wings to the horizon.

She keeps her eyes closed and searches through the sensation of pressure, looking for clues. The doctor looked at her eyes and said there was no sign of concussion. But sometimes bleeding can build up on the brain afterwards. She is trained to be aware of this in the rest home. Floors and walls and the edges of furniture don't like old folk, they spend their time battering them black and blue.

Cosmina stands up and snorts in self-derision. *Varsa!* A weed to be plucked! That's all she is!

She can't hear what the voice is saying. Whether it is speaking in Romanian or English or some invented language. People pick up radio signals with their metal fillings. Maybe it is just that.

She stretches and thinks of the dream she had last night, in which a huge wolf out of the dark forests munched through her bicycle while she was up in a tree, looking down at the scene. The wolf was demonic, with glowing eyes. Her mother would tell her at bedtime about the wolf who persuaded three young goats to let him into their house. The mother returns to find blood splashed on the walls and the heads of the two eldest children lying on the window sill.

'What happened to the little one, *mămică*?'

'She was tucked up in bed, all safe and warm, *bibic*!'

Through the thin wall they could hear her father shouting, 'Go get fucked by kangaroos!' He was shouting at the radio. At the politicians. They'd got rid of the two big devils but not the system. They *were* the system. The same crowd, the same minor devils. *Oportuniști!*

'You know what, my sweetie,' he would say later on, when she was a young teenager. 'Romania has almost no memory in its brain. It's like a goldfish. A memory of five seconds. I have a memory almost as long as my life. I remember everything. Everything.' He'd strike his head to show how it was all still full of his terrible memories. 'But fighting people with no memory? It's to kick a wooden leg.'

Dear *tată*, I miss not being with you, even though you still shout *Go get fucked by kangaroos!* at the TV (in colour these days).

England is stretching all about her, with its English trees and birds and grasses in which English insects crawl and spin and hum and jump. The English river swirls past and English fish rest as if dazed by the sunlight in its current. She feels young and vigorous but at the same time blighted by concern, by worry. She wishes she had found a nice English boyfriend, yet the thought of trailing after someone else is anathema to her; she appreciates the solitude of the life she is tasting, the choices it leaves her free to make.

Madalina wants her to come to Grimsby, where there is skilled work available in the fish-processing factories or the chilled-food plants. Madalina is already assistant team leader in 2 Sisters Food Group after only a year. Better, she claims, than being a healthcare assistant. You could join 2 Sisters Food Group and rise to manager status, buy a house with a garden after a few years, with Romania properly in the EU so no permanent-residence problems. 'You don't want to look a gift horse in the teeth, *drăguţo*.' But Cosmina doesn't fancy working for 2 Sisters Food Group or anyone else in some massive cold warehouse or factory smelling of fish or soup or rubbish food, whatever the money, the opportunities. Madalina always treats her like a little girl, telling her what to do, what is right. It's a kind of joke, but it's not funny.

She likes working here in the care home. The beauty of this riverside garden is settling into her like fine sand, laying down a sediment of memory uncluttered by conversation or relationships, the kind of annoying feelings that even a good friend like Madalina provokes.

Cosmina pictures her brain (a brain picturing itself) impacted by the darting spots of light, the sprinkles of birdsong and the smells of the green river and the garden flowers, of the cells filling up with this liquid honey, of her own inarticulacy in the face of such profound moments, for she has never written so much as a poem outside those exercises ordered by school.

She yawns and feels a sharp thorn-prick in the temple. Her mother has described how her uncle died in the war, when the proud Romanian army was fleeing before the German onslaught: his skull had got dented by a piece of shell which infected the brain in some way. Cosmina rubs her temple with her finger. She has bought a helmet since the accident, and the ridged plastic can be felt through the foam when she is riding along. It is uncomfortable, it has probably created the headache out of nothing. Why do doctors always want to worry you? It is a question of power. They want to control you.

A swirl of lather emerges from behind a rock and makes its way spiralling slowly like a galaxy past the sandy spit, spiralling out of itself yet remaining intact until a dip in the current takes it, and it disappears like she will one day disappear. And then? Black. Not an ever-changing black like her thick hair but completely lightless. She no longer believes in Heaven. She gave her rosary to a street child in Gare du Nord, where the orphans sleep and beg and sell themselves: the kid might earn a few *leu* from it. She believes in *this* life, in making the most of this life and not spoiling it instead of waiting for the next one. But she would never tell her mother or her sisters that she believes in this life more than the next. Her father would understand, always working out where the leak is, how to run a pipe behind a wall, fixing taps.

It is time to go back to the old folk until she is off at two, to change their soiled sheets and offer them milky cups of tea that have to be just the way English people want them, like a secret recipe she hasn't yet found. The air inside is always so hot and stuffy and thirst-making, except when the boiler breaks down, but you can't open the windows because the damp currents of air find your ears and neck in this country worse than in Romania: it's like being in a train going through a tunnel where someone's yanked the window down. But Bronwen and the others like to open the windows, and when it is cold the home always loses one or two to pneumonia. No one minds, because there is a long waiting list. The owners have no need to worry.

She takes a last deep gulp of the red roses and feels fine now, smiling to herself as she makes her way over the soft, perfect lawn to the back door and its sign that says, NO VISITORS. PLEASE USE FRONT ENTRANCE. NO SMOKING PERMITTED. KEEP CLOSED.

The voice has faded, like a mobile signal. She pulls herself straighter, lengthening her neck. That usually helps. Less pressure.

She pushes at the heavy fire door, and it swings open to the faint smells of antiseptic and tomato soup and sour *pişat*, which cling to her clothes and hair all week. The smells seem stronger than usual, which is a bad sign. Migraines mean she can only endure one smell: lavender. Her grandmother's lavender scent.

Diane has soiled her bed yet again. Cosmina tries to see the point of Diane's existence, the poor woman's eyes staring blankly at the ceiling, her body shivering under the heavy blankets, her tender parts calloused with bedsores, but she can't. It would be better if Diane were dead. But Diane refuses to let go. She clings on to her pointless existence as if it is precious. Her elderly husband in his flat cap comes in almost every day and talks to her, but she never responds. He claims Diane squeezes his hand now and again. That is probably the pain, but Cosmina doesn't tell him that. Instead she says, 'That's lovely, Mr Bucksbaum.'

A few weeks ago he said, 'Cosmina, you're an angel. And I mean that. Call me Howard, by the way.'

She won't ever call him Howard. The rules are that everyone who is a relative or friend must be addressed properly, formally.

'I am not allowed to, Mr Bucksbaum,' she said.

'Rules are for breaking, princess. Angels break them all the time. They don't even obey physical laws, do they? I was called an angel, once. A real one, y'know? Angel of hope. Mind you, I was only two.'

She didn't tell him that she was also called an angel of hope. She tries to avoid him now. Some older men can go all silly when it comes to the younger staff in their uniforms. Janie Watkins' son is more sensible at least. Very polite. Shy. He

91

once tried talking to her, and of course it was about Ceaus͵escu, as if the tyrant hasn't been dead for twenty-two years. 'Yes,' she said, 'he was a very bad dictator.' And the son said, 'You mean as dictators go?' She didn't quite understand him, and she was busy, but she said yes anyway. Then she had a puncture two or three weeks back and he gave her a lift home. He offered to buy her a drink in the White Horse and she said yes because there is no question of anything silly with him: he is very introverted and probably gay, in love only with his books. His name is Mike. The only problem is that sometimes he smells. She talked too much about herself in the pub. Then he went on for a long time about shops in Sheffield, and she pretended to listen. But she told Anca that it was quite enjoyable, on the whole.

As she turns Diane and changes her with the help of the new, frightened-looking nursing assistant from Latvia whose strange name she has already forgotten, Janie is wailing like a cat on heat. Her son doesn't come enough, she complains, when in fact he always tries to come at least three times a week, but she has dementia and short-term memory loss. For her the son never comes, he has abandoned her somewhere she doesn't know.

A few days later the son tells Cosmina that if she ever needs good books to practise her English, he sells them second-hand on Totter Hill. He's already told her this before, and maybe more times, but she's usually busy and tired when he talks to her and she doesn't always take it in. Again she replies that she hardly ever goes into the centre of Lincoln; she works too much (this is an exaggeration). Again he says she can order them through the Internet, as the shop has just moved into the twenty-first century. This time, however, she replies that she doesn't have her iPhone any more, and the tiny flat she shares above the betting shop has only one computer, which is really Anca's, and Anca doesn't like anyone else using it except in an emergency.

'Was your iPhone stolen?' 'No, it was run over by a car,' she tells him, trying to concentrate on Janie's medication.

'How his face dropped!' she tells Anca afterwards, scrubbing the dishes in their tiny sink. '*Atât de surprins!* Like I was joking with him! He is very sensitive. He asked me how and when it happened. I told him. I parted my hair to show him my ear.'

'What's his name?'

'Mike.'

'Is Mike rich, Cosmi?'

'What? He runs a second-hand bookshop! I dunno, maybe even a stall on the pavement. Like that barefoot guy on the Strada Doamnei, back issues of *Click!* spread out on the ground next to nice old books. Maybe I shouldn't have accepted that drink in the pub. I felt sorry for him. And I was thirsty after my shift.'

'What a mistake.' Anca laughed. 'Feeling pity for an old bookseller! Cosmi, you are just too good for this world.'

She doesn't tell Anca that he offered to show the phone to a friend who can mend anything. Or that she fetched it from her bag in the nurses' room and handed it over. Neither did she tell Mike that if ever she needed a book, she'd go to the library (where she could also use the computer). Or Oxfam or Age UK. They even have some tatty Romanian novels in Help the Aged. She pretended that she'd come to look at his books, 'the next time I will be in the centre'.

He seemed pleased. Even if he smells of alcohol and body odour, he has kind eyes, he listens. This was only yesterday, but his mother would already have forgotten. Like running uphill on ice. The TV in Janie's room was working badly; there was static interference. Mike fiddled with it. He said things about the universe, but she wasn't concentrating; the extra night shift at the weekend had exhausted her. 'In Romanian we say the TV has fleas,' she told him. Mike laughed. His face completely changed again. Maybe he should laugh more. She seems able to make him laugh quite easily, although mostly he looks depressed and so reminds her a little of her daddy. About the same age. At least now you can see his face. When she first met him he had a huge beard like the priest in their village back home, Father Daniel. Then one day a strange man came into Janie's room and it was Mike, with much less *barbă*.

As she takes the stuff she needs – swabs, ear cleaners and so on – out of the drawers in the dispensary, she thinks about him and his reduced beard. He is obviously very intelligent, like her *tată*. She feels sorry for him. Another idealist. Not an opportunist. She feels sorry for idealists. Their ideals are always betrayed by the thugs and then the opportunists.

'Nu-urse!' the sing-song wail breaks in, chasing away her deeper thoughts. 'Nu-urse! Where the fuck are you?'

Just after six on Monday morning, as her own parents are tucking into their *mămăligă* and eggs and pickles because it is eight in the morning at home, Cosmina enters Janie's room, and the poor thing is sitting in her chair, dressed and shouting the same words. It is business as usual. Those on night duty are always being told to wake and wash and dress the inmates early, to make things less busy for the day staff and to make it fairer, but Cosmina thinks this is cruel: who wants to be woken up at 4 a.m.? Yet the fact that she can come back to something that hasn't gone away, been taken away from her, feels like a miracle. She must focus on that. Not give in to that little voice she heard last week or to any other voice. The flashing lights.

'Hello again, Janie. How is it going?'

'What do you expect me to say, pet? Bloody marvellous? Who are you, anyway?'

'Hey, is it your birthday, sweetie?' There is a present on the tray next to the bed, good-quality gift wrap: fancily penned words on the paper instead of pictures. She reads the repeated sentence where it isn't hidden by the folding.

The valiant never taste of death but once. William Shakespeare. The valiant never taste of death but once. William Shakespeare. The valiant never taste of death but once. William Sha . . .

The label isn't addressed to Janie Watkins, but to herself. 'Is this for me? I'm thinking it is, Janie sweetie!'

'Eh? Where's me tea? No sugar.'

'You always have sugar. Why you have this idea you don't like sugar, sweetie?'

'Open it, then.'

The old woman's eyes are excited. Cosmina has never seen this in her eyes before.

'Why you don't open it for me, Janie my darling? You're so good at these kind of thing. If you do it carefully, we can keep the paper. It is so nice.'

The knobbled fingers work away feebly at the ribbon. Cosmina sits on the bed and helps her. A bell rings, meaning another inmate needs something. Nurse Bronwen can see to it for once. She is fat and lazy and sweats a lot; she especially likes to open windows as if she is the only one who can't feel the cold currents of air. Shuffling about with a carrot permanently up her arse. She'll kill all the inmates soon. One by one. Then Cosmina remembers that Bronwen is on the following shift. It's so complicated! Every week it changes!

The glossy wrapping paper rips apart suddenly – Janie is stronger than she looks – and reveals an iPhone box, white as snow. On the box, written in black felt pen, are four words: *Take care of me.*

95

'But who's this come from, Janie?'

Cosmina knows of course. All Janie says is, 'Daft bugger. He stole that, you know.'

'I don't think he would steal a thing, your son.'

'The ugly fucker always stole. He had a whole room full of books he stole.'

'Janie sweetie, your son is so kind. He'd never do an ugly thing. Would you like to see the flowers in the garden? How about we go out together into the nature after your tea?'

'Oh, I'd like that. I would, you know. I've always liked roses. And delphiniums. And them others, what are they called? I do lose names. Can't remember me own, sometimes.' She's better today.

'Daffodils?'

Cosmina only knows the names of about three flower species in English, and a few trees: laurel, beech, oak. She'll have to learn some more – each night, looking in her dictionary. She used an app before the accident. What is she going to do with this phone? She can't accept it, can she? She'll have to return it to him, quietly but firmly. His mother is scowling at her.

'What are daffodils when they're at home?'

'Yellow, sweetie. Early in the spring.'

'Oh, them. He stole that, you know. Or maybe you did. That used to be mine, that thing. My stuff's always going missing. I'll have to tell Bronwen about it. You're light-fingered, Cosmina, like all them fucking foreigners. I know all about daffodils.'

Cosmina looks surprised. 'Sweetie, you are so better at remembering names.'

'Am I?'

'So better because you even remember my name.'

'Oh.'

Janie Watkins smiles a lovely smile.

The sun stays out as Cosmina wheels the chair slowly through the thick gravel. How stupid to lay gravel in front of a rest home! The poor old treasure loves the roses, their fragrance, the silky petals, and learns their colour in Romanian: *conabiu.* You have to keep challenging the brain, not let it soften, poisoned by the pollution of dementia. '*Conabiu*, Janie. You learn my language, now. *Conabiu.*' A whisper comes out. Another. 'Sweetie, you are brilliant.'

'I was. I was.' Janie pulls at her false teeth so they protrude, then sucks them back in with a click. 'Now I've got this, what's it called? Demonwhatnot.'

'Dementia.'

'The Devil crawled into my ear, that's what he did. And where was Jesus? Down at the betting shop, that's where.'

Cosmina would like very much to keep the new iPhone, but she doesn't want to be in this man's debt. He said he would find someone to mend the old one, that's all, although it was unmendable. After the excursion in the garden there is very little time left. She opens the box to check the contents just in case it's a joke, and finds an envelope containing handwritten instructions on how to activate the phone, the address of the shop and some more instructions. The phone is indeed brand new. Her old SIM card is also inside because it was not damaged. She can keep her old number, say Mike's instructions, but she will have lost anything she didn't back up onto the SIM. She is annoyed at the way he has taken over this little aspect of her life.

Cosmina writes something very quickly. A scribble. No correcting.

Dear Mr Watkins, I don't know what is your motive for this gift except kindness, but I am sure to not accept it, sorry. It is TOO kind! I will look your web library and buy a book. Your mother is actually doing great. Take pity please for my

English. With best regards, and so much thanks to you, Cosmina Dalca.
Sa aveti o zi buna! (Have a nice day!)

She folds the paper neatly and places it in the box, sealing it again in the wrapping paper after removing the old SIM card. She has to hunt about for Sellotape. She tries the Christmas-and-birthdays drawer, but someone – probably Bronwen – hasn't put it back. They have just celebrated a hundredth birthday: Amy, born 20 May . . . in 1912. She isn't missing a single stave – the full barrel! Poor Janie kept thinking it was all for her and choked on the *Amandine prājiturā* that Cosmina had made.

'Totally unsuitable for the residents,' says Bronwen, chocolate smeared around her mouth, cutting another slice out of the sponge. You can always tell a bird by its feathers.

She finds the Sellotape in one of the kitchen drawers, among graters and serving spoons. Bronwen is so lazy, moving the minimum she can get away with. The iPhone is now in Janie's cupboard, properly wrapped in the Shakespeare paper. She lets the matron know, the one called Esperança, who always looks as if you are talking Russian and yet her own accent is quite strong. She is about to retire, thank God.

'What am I supposed to do with it?' Esperança says.

'Just tell the son that it is lying in his mum's cupboard for him to take. I have put a message on it.'

'What?'

'A message. Writed on it.' When Cosmina is nervous, her English starts to disintegrate.

'*Written* on it. You mean a text message? Look, tell him yourself. I'm busy actually.'

'OK,' Cosmina agrees. It is always worth agreeing with Esperança. In fact, there is no other choice. 'When he comes, if you can tell him, please. I don't know when he comes here this week, and I don't have his contacts.' Esperança is taking wipes and pads out of the storage-room cupboard, tutting. Cosmina is not going to get any further without being snapped at by the old crocodile. People very often don't listen in life. 'I am off to home now, Matron. Bye.'

No answer. No answer is like a slap on the face. Like the slaps Esperança gives the old folk, saying *Shut up your mouth*. When Diane whines like a dog, like one of those big shepherd dogs back home when you wave a stick at them to keep them off, Esperança slaps her on the shoulder or the head.

But the memory of Janie's smile softens the impact.

She sleeps badly that night, partly because Anca told her she was mad refusing the present, but also because it is suddenly much warmer. 'Did you think he'd go asking to stick his dick in you, or what?' Anca probably *would* have accepted. She is a simple, hardbitten girl from Buzău. Give her an inch – or five inches! – and she'd turn into a hooker tomorrow. Two thousand pounds a week. Although she isn't that good-looking, really. Teeth, scarred chin. The thought makes Cosmina shudder. Her headache has not evolved into a migraine, at any rate. She feels she has been interfered with in some way, although she did give him the phone to mend in the first place. She wakes up with sweat on her face, the blanket thrown off.

When she comes to start her night shift the following evening, arriving as usual fifteen minutes early so that she can discuss any problems (or issues, as the staff call them) with the previous shift, she is surprised to see Janie's door wide open; it lets in a draught from the front door whenever it's open. Even though it has suddenly turned really warm today, to old folk a draught is a draught and will swirl around Janie's ears like a lot of little devils, and she will catch cold and maybe pneumonia. But Janie isn't there to catch cold. The drawers are empty, the cupboards bare, the bed stripped not only of its linen, but also of its mattress. There is just the bare base and its springs. Nurse Bronwen, who is finishing her afternoon shift, confirms that Janie 'passed away' around supper time – at least Bronwen came in with the trolley and found her staring up with her mouth open. It was obviously very quick – she looked 'astonished'. The son has been and gone, taking what he wanted, which amounted to the dented and faded biscuit tin that was a part of his childhood, along with a few photos and some necessary papers.

The clothes could go to charity, he said. 'Be incinerated, more like,' Bronwen snorts, pulling a face, 'although I didn't tell him that. I'm back at six tomorrow morning and I'm not even finished. Barely enough for a decent kip, by the time I'm home. Ellen's sick; I'm standing in. Well, someone has to save the day, don't they?' Bronwen always stirs from her sleepy fatness when one of the inmates passes away. This energy usually gives out after a few days, as if the last breaths have entered her slow-moving body to be gradually used up.

Cosmina checks the drawer for the phone in its reused wrapping. Of course, it isn't there. He has read her note and taken it back.

She is glad she chose to wheel Janie out into the garden to experience the flowers during the poor old sweetie's last week on this earth. Janie smelt the red roses with closed eyes and a big smile. What could be more special, while life was still yours to enjoy? A vivid yellow-and-black butterfly she knew from home settled for a moment on a blue *zambilă*, folding its wings. Each wing had a white and a black spot that Cosmina pointed out. Then it flew off. Janie was delighted. 'That's my private angel,' she joked. 'Look at it go, the bugger.'

'What's these flowers, sweetie?'

'Bluebell, dumbo.'

The dead must grieve for such simple pleasures; she was sure they never miss the expensive pleasures.

She is alone in the nurses' room; the others are still chatting in the corridor, where the two shifts have exchanged information. Now they are just gossiping, even though it is ten o'clock at night. She understands only half of what they say when it's gossip or jokes. She tidies her hair in the mirror, smooths her blue nurse's top and tightens the drawstring of her comfortable trousers, removing from her many pockets any debris from her last shift – balled-up tissues, a folded bunion plaster. The soft hum that the care home always generates (perhaps the giant industrial boiler, or the giant industrial dishwasher, or the giant industrial washing machine down in the basement, now dealing bravely with Janie's wardrobe) reminds her how life always carries on, skirting past death and actually unstoppable, except that as individuals we fall away from this ineluctable process. She doesn't know why she's feeling so philosophical so late in the evening, with her bed wondering where she is.

Her thoughts are interrupted by a faint, angry sound. It is a kind of whispering anger. Sss-sss-sss-sss.

It's not that little voice again, she realises, because it's coming from the floor-to-ceiling metal cupboard where they deposit their civilian clothes and shoes and bags. Heart thumping, she opens the cupboard door. It's her cheap new pay-as-you-go mobile calling for her attention from the depths of her yellow shoulder bag, whose leather still faintly smells of Bucharest, of sharp cigarettes and of the slimy green water of the Dâmboviţa. A silent call. She's been getting quite a few recently. She's relieved that it is not bad news from home, where it is now nearly midnight. The ringtone is 'We're Not Gonna Take It'. She got it for free, following some complicated steps on the Internet. She hates heavy metal, it sounds like a lot of dustbins crashing together with someone screaming as if they are having their arm cut off, but this tune means a lot to her father, who heard it on a smuggled cassette one day in 1986 and thought, That's the anger we need to change things. It makes her think of her father and warms her heart. It is better than the default ringtone on her iPhone, Marimba. Whenever she hears it, it reminds her of her first days here, when she started in the fields cutting cabbages and broccoli all day with the Poles and Latvians under Ted the gangmaster (who wasn't so bad, when he wasn't eyeing her bottom), because Marimba was her alarm. Hearing it even now makes her sweat, heart racing. If she'd slept through it, she would have been sacked, got a bad reputation among the other gangmasters.

Her eyes stray towards Bronwen's horrible leopard-print handbag, completely plastic. It is bulging, and the zip is not quite closed. She has to close it or something terrible will happen. She gets these thoughts several times a day: that door must be closed, that jam-jar lid screwed on properly, that knife and fork straightened, or else a call will come from home with dreadful news . . . The zip is sticking, the bag is just so cheap, and as she struggles with it she notices a bulky whiteness inside the bag. Without hesitating, she tugs the zip open the other way and sees what she knew she would see. The box no longer in its gift wrap. *Take care of me.*

'Y'all right there then, Cosmina?'

She whips round, startled. Nurse Bronwen's small eyes in her piggy face, complete with white piggy lashes, are glaring at her. It is past ten o'clock, but she is still in her nurse's top and trousers, maxi-size, bags under her eyes.

'Get your dirty bloody foreign mitts out of my bag this moment, if you please.'

Then she yells for Matron down the corridor, as if Cosmina is an inmate herself, who doesn't let go of the box in a guilty fashion but opens it. She wonders whether Janie's son gave Bronwen the phone simply because the nurse was present and he was upset at his mother's sudden death (a huge stroke over her Horlicks, they said), or whether Bronwen took it for herself before the son arrived, like a filthy thief. Cosmina believes it was the second because her letter is still inside. She just has time to check before Esperança arrives, squeezing past Bronwen hovering by the door and practically rolling up her sleeves with a triumphant gleam in her black eyes.

Bronwen claims that she was dead scared that Cosmina might stab her. That's what they do in Romania. Gypsies. Knives. Dirty thieves. Roma. 'I would've fetched her one, otherwise.'

'I am not Roma,' Cosmina snaps, really annoyed with the stupid woman. Fetched her what? A knife? 'I am Hungarian-Romanian. You should learn some history.'

Of course Esperança calls the police, even though it is ten at night and they'll have other more urgent problems to deal with; she won't listen to any explanation. Cosmina places the iPhone box on the table.

When the policeman and the policewoman arrive in their bright yellow jackets, Cosmina tries to explain but she is shaking and her English has collapsed like old Bucharest before she was born (the dust billowed over us for days, her parents would say). Bulldozers. Demolition balls. All she wants is her soft pillow, to float away into sleep.

'Where are you from, madam? Romania? Let's have a look at your ID. Righty ho.'

They look in her bag. All in order. The policeman picks up the iPhone box and turns it in his hand then puts it back on the table. Bronwen says nothing, leaves the talking to the matron.

Then something amazing happens: the police have an argument with Esperança, a sullen Bronwen contributing the odd word. Esperança wants Cosmina to be taken to the police station. 'She's Romanian.' The police say that the accused is not in possession of any stolen goods so they can't take her in; they can't even give her a caution as it is only one person's word against another's. 'Two people,' snaps Esperança. Then she is raising her voice and soon she is almost shouting like she shouts at the old folk, and the police tell her to stop getting 'irated' or they will start getting 'peeved'. What a strange country! Esperança's anger is echoed from some of the rooms, and a nurse also on night shift pops her head round the door, curious.

The police ask to speak to Cosmina in private, outside. The main door swings shut behind them with a clunk. The moonlight is streaming through the trees like a painting in a church.

'I'm not saying you were stealing anything here,' the policewoman says, 'but do think twice before adopting a modus operandi that involves petty theft. That's my advice.'

'I was not stealing. I have never stolen anything except once, a stale loaf of bread. It was a hard time. My father couldn't work for six month after he fall down a . . . a . . .'

'Staircase?'

'Liftshaft?' suggests her colleague, chuckling.

Cosmina shakes her head. It is coming. Let it come.

'Ladder!' she cries. 'He fall down a ladder!'

'Or slid down a snake?' says the policeman, smiling. In the eerie grey of the moonlight something strange has happened to his bright ginger hair and blue-green eyes. According to her grandfather, such hair and such eyes mean that he will return after death as a vampire.

The policewoman turns to her. 'Know that game, do you? Snakes and Ladders? Very English.'

'Ah yes. I think it come from India, really.'

'Climb a ladder, slide down a snake. More snakes than ladders, in real life . . .'

Supposing someone kicks the ladder away? Someone powerful, who doesn't even know you. But say nothing.

When Cosmina goes back into the home to start her shift the matron is still furious at the way the police reacted. 'Completely ridiculous,' she spits over her cup of coffee, eyeing Cosmina with real venom. 'Now get a move on. You've wasted half an hour. It'll be docked off your pay. That is clear, yes? Docked off!' Bronwen is nowhere in sight. Scuttled off back home, the iPhone safe in her ugly, cheap bag.

'No problems,' Cosmina couldn't help saying. 'No problems at all.'

At around dawn, towards the end of the shift, as Cosmina is wheeling the trolley full of dry pads and wipes, the plastic bag for the wet ones dangling like a bulging bladder, the Spanish monster comes up to her in the corridor. 'We have taken our decision. I have talked to the manager. She won't give you any more shifts. Thanks God! You'll never get another post like this anywhere in England, understand? No letter of recommendation. The opposite, in fact.'

Cosmina looks at her, straight into those two eyes, black as night is at home. 'You see, I am so upset, tears are down all my face. You know what? I don't care. One day they will catch you hitting the old people, and it's yourself they will arrest and they will send you back to Spain.'

Esperança goes white. 'Get out of here,' she hisses, 'you stupid whore of a Roma bitch! And I am from Portugal!'

The woman smells. It is peculiarly like Bucharest in the heat of summer: old fish and cinnamon, a urine stench from the craters in the pavements, each one filled with litter. Or maybe this is just Cosmina's own homesick projection.

* * *

105

The sun is shining. It is still hot. Cosmina, after a fitful sleep in her room, is settled on a bench on the cathedral's lawn, facing the statue of Tennyson. She likes this statue because Tennyson was a poet and his dog is gazing up at him and he's holding a ragged flower in his hand, looking at it as if he's checking his messages. She sits a while, thinking, and then phones Madalina in Grimsby. Is there a job for her in the 2 Sisters Food Group? Snowdrops – the care home – owe her a month's work but they will never pay it. A month's hard work for nothing. She doesn't tell Madalina why she has been sacked; she just says that she's had enough of incontinent old folk. She hopes that 2 Sisters Food Group won't need a letter of recommendation.

Madalina is delighted. There are vacancies going in Five Star Fish in the coldstore, or for fish-packing operatives. There always are. 'Not in 2 Sisters Food Group?'

'Five Star Fish are part of 2 Sisters Food Group,' says Madalina as if everyone ought to know this. 'Like almost everything to do with processing food in this country. It's run by Mr Ranjit Singh Boparan. The coldstore is at minus twenty degrees Celsius, but they provide you with thermal clothing.'

'*Aoleu*, I don't think it sounds all that tempting,' Cosmina sighs, although it is very warm outside on this peaceful bench.

'What do you expect? That's how *I* started. Mr Ranjit Singh Boparan himself started out by cutting up chickens in a butcher's at the age of sixteen with no qualifications. Now he's a multi-millionaire with a heap of chicken-cutting sites in the UK and Europe, apart from all the other divisions. Pizzas, biscuits, fish, chilled meals, sandwiches, red meat. You could be part of a really great enterprise.'

'Madalina, you make it sound like a religion. Mr Singh as the pope. The grand imam.' She laughs at her own joke.

There is silence at the other end of the phone. It was the cathedral's great stone walls that made her think of religion.

'Madalina, I'm sorry, it was a joke.'

There is a click, then silence. Cosmina tries ringing again, but gets cut off twice. She can't even leave a voice message. Two ambulances wail past on the road the other side of the low brick wall: she has to block her ears.

Madalina sounded different. She sounded as if brainwashed by some cult. Ready to drop her friend for insulting her beliefs.

The policewoman explained, afterwards, what she'd meant about there being more snakes than ladders in life. Cosmina had not agreed.

'Only if you get yourself into the wrong company,' the policewoman said.

After four thirty there is no entrance fee and so Cosmina moves into the cathedral itself, enjoying the vast cool space. An idea comes into her head. The care home refused to give her the contact details of Janie Watkins's son; it was private, and Cosmina was a thief. Luckily she has written down the address of his bookshop website in her diary. She doesn't want to phone him or to go to the bookshop itself; it is all too difficult. She can go to the library or the Internet café and use a computer to send him an email. Ask him whether he gave the iPhone to Bronwen. If not, then she would have written proof that Bronwen stole it; the manager would understand and give her a letter of recommendation.

She sits down on one of the hundreds of padded dark-blue chairs. For the first time since coming to Lincoln, she bows her head and prays. Not for herself, but for Janie's soul. Then for Diane. 'Please, Lord, take her into your arms. There is no point in her existence. Amen.' And she doesn't even believe in Heaven! She's not so sure about God. Who can be?

Then she goes to the Internet café and sends her email, spending too long on it because she doesn't want him to laugh at her English. She doesn't leave her number. Then she sees how you apply for a vacancy with 2 Sisters.

Her cheap phone rings her dad's tune. She answers quickly.

'I don't get it,' comes his voice. 'Why didn't you take the phone?'

'How did you get my number?'

'Why didn't you take what was a simple gift?'

'It's on my duty to help myself to this life.'

'To help yourself? I don't understand.'

'My English. I'm so sorry, Mr Watkins. I mean, Mike. And I am sorry about your mum,' she adds, only then remembering.

'It's OK. Cosmina, all my life I've been misunderstood. Join the club. We need to talk this over.'

'Over what?'

'A cup of coffee and a cake. Somewhere like Polly's Kettle on Bailgate, for instance. Know it? Nice and quiet. This afternoon? I'll close up early.'

It is always like this. He sounds as though he's been running. All she wants is for him to tell the police that he didn't give the phone to Bronwen but instead gave it to her as a gift, that it was her property except that she hadn't taken it so that it was still his property. Simple. But no, he wants to date her. To take advantage. Immediately. Pushing her on too fast. Like an object. His voice, distorted by the cheap mobile, hissing and quite sinister. How did he get her number? From the care home?

'Cosmina? Maybe we can talk about Janie too. Your memories of my mum. Janie. It would help my loss. I can't quite take it in.'

Maybe she does need something cold and clean, in fact. Like swimming naked in the mountain lakes. Minus twenty

108

degrees. Smoky breath. Maybe she would rise like her friend – assistant manager, decent pay, a garden. The coldstore is not like a walk-in fridge after all.

'Hello? Cosmina?'

'Sorry. It's OK in fact. Sorry. Bye bye, Mike. Bye.'

She looks it all up again on the web. The Five Star Fish coldstore covers an area of two thousand square metres. It supplies Iceland, Morrisons, 3663 – everybody. Even she knows these company names.

Later, when the mobile keeps screaming that it can't take this any more, over and over, she switches it to silent. She is embarrassed about showing this nasty thing in public, and hides it in her bag as she walks through the centre among the Saturday shoppers. Until she turns it off, people frown at her every time it rings, because the ringtone is so aggressive, but that's because they have never suffered as her nation has suffered. They have no idea what fear and frustration are like when mixed together into one liquid. It bubbles and spits.

Nearly twenty-five degrees, like yesterday. Everyone in summer clothes. Soon she'll be earning enough to buy a new iPhone, if she does overtime in the coldstore in Grimsby. Sharp, cold air.

A little ladder, leading to another one. Then another. Each like the very old wooden ladder her grandpa scrambles up each year to pick the apples and the cherries. The crooked ladder, made a hundred years ago by her grandpa's own grandfather out of cherry wood, and still intact. Rising into the leafy branches in the dazzling sunlight of the mountains.

'You see, sweetie? As good as new. It'll never let you down, believe me. There's one you've missed, just there. Don't stretch too far! Leave it for the birds. *Halal!* That's it, sweetie. Always leave a few for the birds, the pretty thieving bastards.'

She wipes salty moisture from her upper lip, thinking hard. She returns to the Internet café. There is one place free, next to the far wall. She searches for the Five Star Fish website to apply for a post online, but there is only an email address. This is the wrong approach. She rubs her eyes, exhausted. The noticeboard on the wall is full, and only a part of one notice is visible, but some words on it catch her attention.

She was also wearing a reddish-brown coat with a furry hood.

She has seen this poster before in Lincoln, she believes, but has never read it. It is for a missing girl called Fay. Fay Sheenan. She lifts the rock concert announcement that hides the rest, sending a drawing pin tinkling across the lino. The victim's face smiles out. *Fay is a happy, outgoing girl.* She and the family dog (*black and white, mixed breed*) went missing from her home in Ermine West, Lincoln, on Friday, 27 January this year. *She is described as a white girl, aged 14, about 5ft 2 ins and of slim build. She has long red hair, green eyes and distinctive freckles on her nose. We are keen to piece together where she went after leaving her home on Friday. Any information, no matter how insignificant you consider it, might prove crucial in helping us find Fay.*

It is a local constabulary notice. She thinks of the coat lying twisted in the woods near the road. She should tell the police. But the girl went missing four months ago and the coat looked older than that, streaked with moss and decayed and its furry hood torn. But how does she know what a piece of clothing left in a damp English wood would look like after four months? She has no idea. It was brown, not reddish-brown, but maybe that was the effect of cold and rain. Maybe there are long red hairs left on it!

She shivers at the thought. At the end of last month, she remembers, a couple of weeks or so before her accident, it poured and poured, water trickling like a stream down the streets and lanes, umbrellas not coping. Any hairs would have been washed away. She is afraid of going to the police, anyway. Of provoking them. They were nice to her, but now they might think she was wasting their time. They would only need to take her name and check on the computer. Coats with hoods are very common. *No matter how insignificant you consider it.* Surely they wouldn't be angry with her for trying to help! On the other hand, the poster is already four months old, with tears in it and marks of drawing pins poked through. That's why it was half hidden behind a notice for a rock concert this week. Perhaps Fay has been found. Or – and here she shudders again as she did in the woods – perhaps it is too late and she has been found murdered.

She types Fay's full name on the search engine, adding 'Lincoln' and 'missing'. Photos of the girl, of the posters (there are two types), a couple of local articles dated from the end of January, and nothing more. The mystery has not been solved. She looks around her. Mostly teenage boys, except for an old man who might be the source of the sour and (to her) familiar smell. The blips and hissings and stutterings of computer games.

She leaves quickly, without applying for a job as a cold-store or fish-packing operative. It would be too like death, like working in a morgue. She feels cold already, as if she is deep underwater, deep in freezing water, despite the air outside feeling so warm, everything ablaze with sunshine so that this rainy island feels like somewhere else – Lincoln is like a city in Spain or southern France. There are people standing drinking outside the pubs or sitting under parasols, laughing and talking loudly, reflective sunglasses flashing, the streets full of the sweet sickly smell of beer and sun lotion mixed together, one bare-chested man showing fiery tattoos, his plump white flesh bright red at the neck and on lower arms sprinkled with gingery hairs. He whistles at her, and there are guffaws from his mates. They have T-shirts with stupid words. No one knows how cold she feels inside. She knows that shock makes you feel cold however warm it is outside: a dip in blood pressure, that's all. Blankets, hot-water bottles. A warm hand in yours. A kiss on the forehead.

Everything she is missing. This is the best, most perfect time for the mountains. May. The summits sharp against the blue sky, the air fresh as snowmelt, meadows carpeted with flowers, so much later than here, but so much brighter and more plentiful!

And then that voice starts again as she walks down the steep hill, but it is whispering this time. Urgent, a child's voice. That pressure. She wants to go home, like a child. To come home. All she wants is to come home, safe and no longer striving for something better. For something impossible. Fighting with life. Fighting.

All she wants is to come home.

5

FAY

24 January 2012

She's running with Pooch to the massive field off Lincoln Road. Half on it is TO LET – the grassy half, up to a ditch running across the middle. Ken says it is all going to disappear under more poncy offices and restaurants and hotels and Audi fuckin car dealers. The bypass is like thunder there because that's what the field ends on. Once you're onto the field's bumpy grass, everything outside is hidden behind bushes and trees except for the edge of the estate – a long row of way-off houses with tiny windows spying on her. You'd need binoculars, though. She's really out of breath.

TO LET: DESIGN AND BUILD PREMISES. A spanking-new building stands facing the road near where the field starts, with a big car park behind. SOLICITORS. She hasn't been here since the summer, when this patch was just muddy trenches. Soon there'll be buildings all over, looking like the estate but more modern. She slows to catch her breath a bit then runs with Pooch into the field and keeps on running and shouting and thinks, This is what our garden looks like to an ant. Pooch runs like he is in the Olympics, in his own world of adventure. Ken reckons he is really intelligent. The teachers say her stepbrother Craig is intelligent enough for university, but Ken says you have to be loaded to go to that waste-of-time.

On the way back, sparkling all over but puffed, she stops to read a poster in the bus stop, saying the words under her breath: '*I always wanted to study at a university with first-class sporting facilities on campus. Thanks to DMU's new £8 million leisure centre now I can.*' So she reckons Ken must be right. He *is* right usually, more's the shame.

Now I can. But how?

Eight million!

Today is food-shop Tuesday. Tomorrow she'll bunk school and go to Sheena's after lunch. Wednesday en't Saturday, but who cares? Work's work. Sheena gid her a big hug last time and a ten-quid note.

She ties Pooch's lead to a drainpipe outside the store. She can smell burnt cheese from the pizza place next door, but they've treated themselves already this week. She's spent a quid of what she got from working at Sheena's (three packets of Fizzy Fangs) and put the rest (three pound coins) in her savings box under her bed. She is too late for the Co-op's discounts and there's only 10 per cent off the pasta shapes she doesn't even like. Rochelle has given her a fiver, but it won't stretch what with the milk and bread and margarine and stuff, so a budget packet of Edam happens not to get clocked up on the self-service till.

Pooch thinks what she did is really clever and wags his tail like a hairy windscreen wiper.

'Oh look, Pooch. There's yer brother!'

Fay is looking at the news-stand outside. A photo of a Jack Russell takes up most of the paper's front page. UGGIE: A DOGGONE STAR! Ken likes to read the paper now and again, to keep up with the news, even though his head is back in the Seventies when he was a baby, and she still has 30p. He prefers the *Mirror* but this one's the *Sun*. It's all rubbish anyway, he says. If he don't like it he can do one.

'Full Story – Pages 4 and 5'. She sits on a wall under a street lamp before they reach home, reading out loud for Pooch and starting on her Fizzy Fangs. She doesn't like reading out loud in class, especially when the others make stupid noises. Hollywood's top dog. The canine genius born to be a showman. Crazy and very smart, says his trainer. Who saved the cheeky Jack Russell from being put down and guided him to fame. Uggie, skateboarding star of the Golden Globes. In line for Oscar glory.

'The talk of Tinseltown, he is,' Fay goes on, tucking a fang under her upper lip and letting the tip of her tongue taste the fizz. 'The world at his paws.'

Pooch doesn't really look like Uggie, unless you screw your eyes up into a fog. Ken says Pooch's face is like he's been licking yellow snow off nettles all day and it's got stuck.

But looks en't everything, are they? Ken's no picture. Not when his eyes are bloodshot. Back of a tram in a crash, as Mum says of blokes on the telly. Fay scares Pooch with her Dracula teeth but he only wags his tail, thinking he's going to get nosh out of her.

By the end Pooch is panting and whining, showing his own canines, his paw on her knee like Uggie on the front page. Uggie's paw is on a golden box. His owner must be dead chuffed. The fangs are now a slippery lump and she swallows them. Sour and sweet. Dead good day, so far.

'Youch, but that's an ace start, Pooch.' She holds his paw and feels his dry pads in her palm. 'I love you,' she says, gazing into his yellow eyes. Heck, it is raining and the newspaper tears like wet Kleenex, goes all crinkly. She throws it onto the grass and they race each other home.

Ken is on the sofa. All Fay can see is the back of his head and the tat on his neck, that big cross with wings. Smoke curling up. The telly is showing posh types in suits, a village with snowy mountains behind, igloos like the North Pole. Then words.

World Economic Forum Annual Meeting 2012.

Ken swears and stabs his spliff at the screen and says without looking round, 'Bloody Davos. They're taking the Michael out of us all, Fay. Selling us crap that goes bollocks so we have to buy more crap. And we don't lift a finger. We should do, right? But we stupid knackers just let 'em.'

'It mightn't have been me. Could've been a deadly killer.'

'Pongo Dog here gave you away,' says Ken. Pooch jumps onto the sofa but Ken shoves him off. 'OK, the stink's on me hands now. Progress or what?'

The Great Transformation: Shaping New Models.

'It's the wet on his coat,' says Fay, shivering. The wet on her coat – her long shit-brown coat, Mum's hand-me-down, used to be red – has got through to the inside fur. She takes it off and hugs her thin body, rubs her damp leggings.

She asks Ken where Mum is and Ken says, 'Tantrum factory has retired to bed. Refused to take her meds. She says to me, can you take the sheets to the bag wash, I says no, I'm on the phone, speak proper English, it's called a laundrette. So she loses it. Swears at me an all. National Debtline's engaged all day, but I done me best, yeah? Not like them sick prats poncing about in the snow. Did you get a paper?'

'I only had nosh dosh,' Fay lies. Nosh dosh is what Ken calls grub money. She likes his expressions because they are London, like *EastEnders*. He talks posher on the phone, though.

'Give us a sweetie,' he says.

He can smell it on her breath. Just one, Ken. He stubs out his spliff really carefully in the ashtray on the table so he can puff on it again and shoves the fangs in under his upper lip and plays Dracula, waving his fingers like in a magic show and rolling his eyes at her. Like, so original.

She goes into the kitchen and puts the shopping away, heart sinking because she'll have to play MasterChef tonight when all she wants to do is start on the training and then tomorrow she'll have to take the dirties and wait an hour in the bag wash and half the folk'll be staring into their phones. She's going to give it all she can. That's what you have to give it, the training. Fame and money don't come out of the blue. It is passion. It is all about passion and putting in the work. That's what Katie Perry said. And that's what the dog trainer said in the *Sun* too. Passion and hard work, like magic ingredients mixed in with canine genius. She'll have to bunk off school again.

She goes back into the sitting room and now there are clips of film stars in shimmy dresses, lights flashing, golden skin. The Oscar nominations. She sits down next to Ken, waiting for the star pet to skateboard on. The commentator is excited too. She'll get herself some bronzer before hitting Hollywood, even doing her white bum, because them dresses split in the middle and you have to wear thongs.

'Yeah, we're all breathless with anticipation,' Ken growls and changes the channel again. Fay moans but he doesn't hear. Adverts.

'Give us another.'

'Finished.'

'Piglet. Bad for your teeth, right? All them fillings.'

He changes channel again. The North Pole.

'Davos Man,' he says and swears softly. 'Superhuman powers. Camping it up in the woods. Minted bastards. Buying their own sodding stairway to Heaven. They call it making history. Not for us, though, is it?'

117

He shoots off to have a piss. He's always going off to have a piss. You can hear it like a waterfall. Hardly ever a bob, though. Fay switches to the Oscars. When he comes back he tries to grab the remote from her and they end up on the floor, with him tickling her around the waist. She goes all paralytic when she's tickled. 'Fuck off,' she squeals, still laughing almost to death, unable to catch her breath. 'I really hate you, Kenneth, you slob.'

He sits back on the sofa, grinning, and plonks his ugly bare feet on the coffee table. He switches over to the cricket somewhere so hot they have white hats on and sleeves rolled up. Sky Sports. A ball rolls along and bumps over the boundary edge. Everyone waving in the stands.

She could smell the soap off him, at least. She stays sitting on the rug. His feet are like the cricket bats.

'I think you've damaged my internal organs. Like, mega-bad.'

'Fuck off,' he says in a high voice nothing like hers. He laughs and picks up his spliff again. 'Watch your language, princess.'

'What's happening, Ken?'

'Slogged straight past the slips,' he sighs, clicking on his lighter. 'Umpire gives the Hitler salute. Four for the bacon sarnies.'

Sometimes she doesn't understand a frickin word he says.

6
SHEENA

29 September 2011–25 January 2012

Whether it is the leaves turning yellow and flying off or a sudden sense of panic at her lack of fulfilment in the personal arena, Sheena senses something moving in herself one wet and windy morning, something solid that has uncoupled from its station. Her 2011 Scotland Panorama calendar in the scullery tells her that today is Michaelmas Day. Big deal. Last year she missed Australia Day in January and Tony couldn't believe it.

She looks it up on the Internet. St Michael the Archangel, fought against Satan and the evil angels. Used to be a big deal. Very big. End of the farming year. Not much mileage in it now, though, and certainly not for retailers.

'Raffety, don't touch,' drawls a loud mother with a nose like a shark's fin. Raffety goes on touching. As his fingers and mouth have been on recent and intimate terms with Nutella, Sheena goes up to him and leans over.

'No way, petal,' she says in a soft and menacing tone that would freeze boiling lava. And she presses his little fingers away from the toadstool bodysuit, all thirty-five pounds worth. She is glad she's painted her nails violet today: Raffety is clearly impressed.

When the squall of tears is safely out in the lane with another customer lost to the shop, she says to the useless part-time assistant with a bead in her nose like a bogey, 'I'm just popping out, Brittany.'

Sheena remembers her as a weeny whiny tot. Forbidden to call her Britt. Not-Britt, Sheena secretly names her. Useless Not-Britt.

She nips upstairs to her flat to check the face. Scary, but it will have to do. She taps a sprinkling of perfumed talc into each shoe. What she needs is a pair of elbow-length gloves. Her ears are still ringing from Raffety's squeals. They triggered her tinnitus, made her teeth ache. It will all be in some mumspace blog by tomorrow, but what does she care? She'll leave her cleavage as it is.

She makes straight for the lower end of Totter Hill in her smartest fur-trimmed coat. Not really liking his stuff, she's never bought anything over the years, only chatted. Itchy Feet, daft name. He looks up as the bell tinkles, a ghost of a smile. 'Sheila. Hello, stranger.'

'Sheena.'

'Of course, just talking to a Sheila on the phone.'

Liar. 'Long time no see. Happy Michaelmas.'

'Is it? Oh. Tea?'

'Shoes, would you believe it. Time to spoil myself.'

Paul Cannon doesn't turn a hair. He touches the shoes as if they have no weight, scratching the back of his neck where the greying locks bunch into that Crusoe ponytail. She likes the way he handles her feet, professionally. His big hands on her small feet with their pronounced arch. She's had boyfriends who've gone weak over her feet, who've undressed them as if they were extra women on the end of her legs. That was before her left big toe started curving in like her mum's. Age is such a sneak. She has to wear a rubbery toe stretcher. She's forgotten to remove it.

'Better than the op,' he says. 'Better still, avoid tight shoes. Or any shoes.'

Kind man, but it's hopeless. She glances at his own bare feet, their long toes: 'You're like a teetotaller in a wine merchant, Paul.'

An ado in a long coat comes in at this point, hands in his pockets, headphones on his ears, and shuffles about by the leather boots in the corner. Maybe not ado, maybe just young. Even thirty-year-olds are beginning to look ado to her these days. He's jiggling his head to whatever rubbish is giving him early hearing loss. His headphones are fur-lined, as sported by those bods who wave their arms about on a runway. He's not missing much in the shop: the music is weird, spaced out, not very suited to the clientele. Sheena is sensitive to this sort of thing. Every aspect of a boutique has to be angled towards the hearts and minds of its customers. Paul's music is more suited to a hippy craft shop, which goes with his barefoot thing, his ponytail. Yet the decor is so simple as to be neglectful: slatted pine painted white, the only relief being a poster of an eagle hovering high up over crags.

'I always wanted to be a wildlife photographer,' she says, nodding at the poster. 'Hanging off cliffs somewhere remote and windy.'

There's no reply. Maybe he has to concentrate. She refuses a pair of moccasin boots as not quite her, not *quite*. Too funky, too wild. She is subtler. But there isn't a lot of choice in here. It is all a bit peculiar. There are even trainers that look like feet, with individual toes. Creepy.

'Why sell shoes, then?' she asks. Paul looks up from the rustling box, his hand around the calf of a bootee made out of 'black microfibre, suitable for vegans'. As if she's going to eat it like Charlie Chaplin in that film.

'Why do I sell shoes?'

121

'Yup. And not, I dunno . . .'

She can still feel his hand on her foot through the tights. She wants to say 'cheeses' – she can just see him in a striped, old-fashioned pinny with pockets, selling lovely cheeses on straw mats. But he'd have to wear appropriate shoes. Or you'd think the pong was his feet.

'Go on,' he insists. 'Surprised I'm not selling what?'

She closes her mouth and puts a finger to her lips in thought. She encourages her dimples to appear. She raises her eyes to the ceiling. It needs cleaning.

'Let's see now,' she says. 'Old clocks?'

He snorts softly, fitting the lid back on the box, giving it a little pat, replacing it on the shelf from where he drew it five minutes ago. She has miscalculated. Maybe he has a touch of Asperger's. Somewhere early on the spectrum. It is more and more common.

'Books? Old books?'

'I don't read,' he says. 'Dyslexic. Can't even spell the word.'

'Blimey, neither can I. So was John Lennon,' she adds, blinking quickly.

'And Einstein. Faraday.'

She can't quite recall who Faraday was. His jeans look great on him, considering his age. Forty-eight? Forty-five even? She hovers around forty-five like the needle on a speeding car, compromising for safety's sake. They've shared the same lane for years, fifty yards apart. Incredible. Mother Hubbard towards the top, puff puff, Itchy Feet near the bottom. Since they were young enough not to find the hill a stretch. *Totter* is the operative word, although it's old Lincolnshire for a lookout apparently, which makes sense. Your early thirties is bloody young. She took too long to make the first contact. Approaching forty. Maybe he was still married back then, anyway. She remembers a woman with

122

lots of dark hair, now she thinks about it. The young man in the corner is looking at her. She wishes he wouldn't; it makes her feel older.

Jenny of the organic deli informed her last week that Paul is divorced, not gay. Into some dangerous sport or other. Rock climbing, perhaps. Can you climb in bare feet? Maybe why he has this slight crookedness to his shoulders. Came down to earth with a bump one day. She'll bring it up.

Paul proffers another pair of microfibre boots, long ones and black as liquorice. The youngster stirs and comes over. Black hair, very dark eyes, a crumpled Oxfam coat. He shifts the headphones onto his neck. If it wasn't for the zit on his nose and his experimental haircut (shaven at the sides, bunched into curls at the front), he'd be good-looking. In a pretty way.

'No,' Paul replies to his question, 'we don't do steel toecaps, sorry. Try Sports Direct.'

The lad glances at her again as he leaves. Meaningfully, his black eyes twinkling. Could she still pull men young enough to be her progeny? Paul is staring at her. She shifts herself into a straight-backed, businesslike pose on the bench, which has the unintended effect of pushing her tits out.

'At least you don't have coat hangers,' she says, picking up the thread a bit late. 'Swish and clatter. There are people with coat-hanger phobia. Kylie Minogue for one. Maybe I'm another.'

He has got down on one knee to fit her boots. Then he sits cross-legged on the little rug, all yogic, as she stands and tests them out. He is the only shoe salesman she knows who never wears shoes. Not even moccasin slippers. What about the dog shit? What about bits of glass? Soles like dark leather. Rough as sandpaper in bed, probably.

'You do yoga?' she asks.

He smiles for an instant as if the question is amusing. 'Nope.'

She walks about, feeling self-conscious. The long black boots make a clicking noise on the planks. Hollow heels? His smile was affectionate, not just amused. Something has broken through. Everyone loves a client who buys; maybe it's just that. She likes these boots, even though they're a bit pricey and not real leather, not off a cow flayed alive by the Chinese or whatever. He is looking at her walking about, a solo fashion show. She'll purchase these boots to remind her of this moment.

As she pays him, she notices the small picture in a frame propped next to the till: a bishop with a mitre stroking a swan. 'I didn't think you could stroke swans,' she says. Blimey, he is a born-again Christian.

'He's a saint. Saint Hugh of Avalon. Bishop of Lincoln way back.'

The name rings a bell, but not as loud as the real bloody bells, tolling the time *da-dee-da-da bong bong bong*, or clanging away all at once. And that's just the rehearsals. 'I like the carols,' she adds. 'It's Michaelmas Day today. End of the harvest, in the good old days when folk went to church. Archangel Michael versus Satan.'

'The patron saint for you and me.'

Her heart leaps. 'You and me?'

'Shoemakers. Well, in the old days cobblers sold shoes too, so I think we're counted in.'

'I only do a small selection of footwear. Accessories, really. Minute moccasins, hand-stitched suede bootees from Italy.'

He's waiting for the machine to do its thing. 'I was in India for two years, on a course, learning the tabla.'

That was apropos of what? 'Is that those funny drums?'

'Twenty-odd years back.' He nods. 'Cross-legged. Bare feet only. As in a Hindu temple. Got used to it.'

She laughs. 'Very ironic, you ending up in a shoe shop.'

'Married into it, so blame my ex.'

124

'Doesn't it hurt?'

'We went round barefoot for millions of years, right? Desert sand, deep snow. You develop protective calluses. And the toes were nicely spread. No bunions. Good arches. Feels good. Thousands of nerve endings in each sole.'

'Are you Buddhist?'

'Nope.'

'Show me them again.'

He has splayed toes. She hopes it isn't a fetish thing.

'I wouldn't fancy it on Lincoln pavements,' she says.

'You just have to look where you're going. And you become more sensitive to danger,' he adds with a slight smile, meeting her eyes.

Blimey. Is she danger?

'Funny, though,' she presses on, 'with you selling shoes.'

'You don't wear kiddies' clothes.'

She's not ever had kiddies either, though she doesn't tell him that. All she's had is pregnant dreams, woken up from with a sigh of relief. He tears off the receipt and she takes it, fingers touching for a microsecond.

'Do you still drum, then?'

'I was crap.'

'You're good at rock climbing.'

'Says a little bird who's got it wrong.'

She leaves it at that, ta-ta-ing him goodbye and nearly tripping over the sill. You do have to have the patience of a saint, in fact, to work in a shop.

He mentioned his ex. Must have been that one with all the hair and the good figure. Strange man in some ways. Nothing wrong with being dyslexic, though.

When she gets back to hers, Not-Britt is nattering to an equally well-pierced girlfriend on the pavement under a smoke cloud. 'Brittany, have you heard of Hugh of Avalon?'

'I'm not that thick, durr. Want to see my GCSE school project on him?'

'Mine was better.' Her friend laughs.

Always so *loud*.

She notices the dark-haired youth again, standing on the pavement opposite, in front of the bookshop but with his back to it. Because he's staring at her. Or at Brittany and Friend, maybe. Except that when she turns round, they've scuttled back inside. At least they have some notion of guilt.

'Know him, do you?'

'Who?'

'The pale young feller with jet-black hair and headphones over the road.'

They look out through the window, but he's vanished. The glass needs bloody cleaning *again*.

Drifting down once, when he was smoking a beedi. 'We're almost cellmates.'

He nodded. She could see confetti. His and hers.

'Out on parole, yeah.'

Many years ago, gesturing with her fag at his shop sign behind, she actually made him smile.

'A little like the unfortunate name I saw in sunny Provence a while back,' she said. 'Athlete's Foot.'

'Itchy feet isn't a medical complaint; it's a psychological need.'

It took four years from the outset before he offered her a cup of herbal tea inside. She liked the way she prepared it, tipping the leaves out of his palm, stirring the brass pot. He is always tanned, which is a bit dodgy in Lincolnshire, outside of the farmworkers or the foreigners. Daily sunlamp? He never really goes anywhere, apart from the India business in his youth. So they talked about tea, weather and how best to clean brass.

She doesn't speak to him for weeks at a time, though. That's the pattern. He is just too far along for her to wander over in a natural way, and the lane is steep – not the illustrious Steep Hill itself, but its neglected sister. Prettier, some say.

'I'm at the posh end,' she jokes to him. 'We talk different up there.'

Not altogether a joke, in Lincoln.

So she is stuck with Alan and Des from the sandwich bar next door, or fusspot Marco in his poncy waistcoat at the speciality coffee house (beans only) two doors up. Who wears bright-red bovver boots. Or hipster-bearded Mike Watkins with his used books, bang opposite her, as tatty as his shop. Except he's not a hipster: fashion has caught up with him and will move on again, leaving him stranded and more misery-guts than ever. Pretty, posh Hannah has On the Hob a few doors down. Kitchen knick-knacks. She's a well-meaning soul. 'Puts us all to shame,' Des commented with his usual wiggle. Last year, for Australia Day, Hannah covered the shop in green and gold and hung up stupid koala bears and kangaroos, and wondered why she wasn't besieged by Lincolnites. 'It's a long way from Lincoln,' Sheena pointed out.

Hers is called Mother Hubbard: *smart clothes for small kids.* She reckons *smart kids* would be better, but it's not her decision. It is housed in a sixteenth-century cottage with see-saw walls and floors, drawing the sort of mum who drives a silver Lexus RX and whose budget cares for itself. Sheena's prices are also hand-knitted, as she jokes to friends. She put up a notice saying PLEASE FOLD PUSHCHAIRS and someone added AND WHEELCHAIRS? so she took it down. None of her customers ever call her duck or say 'ey up' or 'bless'. At least there is that. A duck-free zone.

She's sold the business to a man called Tony Bartlett, operating out of Worksop. He owns three other similar shops in the East Midlands, all called Daisy Chain, though she's hung on to the name Mother Hubbard because of the shop's reputation. This is pending her breakout. There is only so much you can take of toddlers, woolly rompers, tandem buggies the size of her Mini Cooper. Friday and Saturday evenings you get the yobs banging on the metal shutters – overspill from the High Street area. On top of that, like a crusty layer in a Beatrix Potter bowl, are the accounts. Not being her own boss is a relief. Someone else's burden.

She's agreed to stay on as manageress for a two-year period, until both she and the shop are sorted. She does, however, own the warren of rooms overhead, living under and between the knotty beams of oak (like the proverbial rabbit) with Mungo, her plump ginger tabby. One day soon she'll downsize to somewhere wild, windy, idyllic and cheap. The Outer Hebrides, maybe, where some of her stock used to come from, smelling of sheep's grease and rough seas.

Under pressure from the terrible Tony, the shop has begun to inch downmarket. He's forced her to change most of her suppliers: to ditch the hand-knitting ladies in Iceland and the Orkneys for sweatshop machine-operators in China – the wool shipped out there soaked in pesticides, or so she read in the *Mail* over a steamed-milk espresso chez Alan and Des. Same prices, though. It gets her blood boiling. Tony told her to snip off the MADE IN CHINA labels and she told him to get stuffed, that she'd be done for selling counterfeit goods, but he just laughed.

'No one can tell the diff,' he said. 'Can you? It's product, not plastic surgery.'

Honestly, she shouldn't be caring less. She'll be gone soon. Tony isn't bad-looking, past his nasty suits. He once made a pass, hand on bum, but she would never mix work and pleasure. It's the thrill of the chase that interests her. Or absolutely forbidden fruit: the youngish dad, cute and hassled, mooning in the shop among knit shrugs and pointelle cardies and monkey slippers. Tony once said, 'Sheena, it's all about concept. You're on the front line. It's face-to-face transactions. You don't need to dress to slaughter in a kids' boutique called Mother Hubbard.'

'It's not the clothes, Tony,' she replied, 'it's what's in them. I can't change that.'

The toddlers she started out with have whizzed up into lanky teenagers with spots. Not all lanky; overweight, some of them. Squishy juvenile bellies.

'The worst's those little runny noses meeting my nice woolly jumpers,' she confides one morning to Paul. She spotted him smoking and wandered down with her fag. A deadly quiet day. 'Snail trails on the collars. I'm not wiping it for them. The mumsies don't notice, they just go on jabbering.'

Paul suddenly sticks his hand out and makes it go floppy, wrinkling his nose. 'We have it in every size except yours, sir,' he says in a girly, high-pitched voice. Then he looks down at the cobbles. 'Oh, is it Camembert or double Gloucester today?'

She's a bit shocked at first, then smiles. 'Crikey. Got a bit worried there. I mean, that you were being prejudiced about gays. Did you actually watch that, then?'

'Before I'd even started in the shop. Classic British comedy. Loved it. Only lasted two or three seasons. Living it now, except the joke's on me.'

'I used to laugh and laugh,' she admits. She wasn't about to, she was going to pretend it was beneath her. *Have You Got My Size?* was proper trash, she always thought. Very silly and very camp. She tries to think of one of its punchlines, but it was a long time ago.

They have the same taste, anyway. Good sign. He has it in him to be funny. Unless he liked it because it was full of homo in-jokes. 'You can probably find every episode on YouTube these days,' she adds. He's lightened up. A glimpse underneath the crust. Tasty.

Recently she's begun to feel low more often. Lower than usual. Sitting alone in her flat, in the quiet. Chewing through her spinach and ricotta cannelloni freshly nuked in the microwave; she can't be bothered to cook properly these days. Chips dipped in lemon and coriander hummus will do her just fine. Fancy cakes and a coffee. The mice scratching in the roof, whistly noises up the chimney. Wondering where it's all gone to, heading for fifty. The best years. And the toddlers: she could be their grandmother, easy-peasy. Granny Sheena. Dear God.

She meets Paul by chance in front of WH Smith's in Cornhill. He's listening to that busker with the tattoo on his neck who used to do deliveries *chez elle* for a bit. He has a lovely voice and plays old rock numbers on his guitar. Led Zep. The Doors. It is T. Rex right at the moment. Homeless type, but a bit of a cutie. Better than most of what you hear on the radio, she remarks. 'It's because this guy's pure, Sheena. No microphone. No electrics. I wanted to *be* Marc Bolan when I was thirteen.' His feet must pick up the chewing-gum splats, she thinks. She was still reading *Bunty* when Bolan was glam.

And subsequently spots him down the slope a few times, unlocking the shop. A wave.

She faces the full-length mirror in her fishnet teddy and it is scary: the face doesn't go with the nice young body, naturally rounded breasts and all. She has to wear glasses to see the prices these days, looking over them at the customer like an old biddy. The pastures might be new but the rest never is.

Not that her life hasn't been rich, out of hours. She's left quite a trail of proper boyfriends, aside from the no-strings hooks. Rovers, most of them. A Spanish bass guitarist called Sandro, love of her life until she realised she was sharing him with the drummer, Cliff. A mildly schizophrenic puppeteer. Several husbands over the years – but never hers. One leading to another by various local connections. The longest fling being with a London-commuting knockout called Bob, Bob Springfield, while his wife said nice things about Mother Hubbard's shop frontage on the council. Already old history – almost a decade ago! Kicked the bucket recently: coronary. Not much past fifty. Always full of fizz, but overdoing it probably. Designed robot spot-welders of all things, mostly for the Chinese. Nice hams.

Though Lincoln isn't quite as local these days. *Burgeoning* is how estate agent Damon now puts it in his flash corner window at the top of the hill where the old record shop used to be; *burgeoning* blah blah in its *sylvan setting between fen and wold.* Quite the poet. Burgeoning with foreigners, that's for sure. Damon looks about nineteen but is not her type, not one bit. Big-bearded Mike bang opposite her is tall but has very rounded shoulders and a moth-eaten cardie with dandruff down the front in sort of floury streaks. He's probably about her age but going on seventy. She's never so much as dipped a toe into Chapter Seven: too dark and off-putting behind its peeling bay window, and you can't give used books as presents. She'll smile at him across the cobbles as he fiddles with his stock, but she's lucky if he smiles back. He's had these drop-jaw gorgeous young assistants now and again, both sexes. Pays them nothing, apparently: good for their CVs. Maybe that's what she should do. She's had schoolkids doing their Year 10 work experience, more trouble than they're worth, but what she needs is some young Johnny Depp lookalike to help fold the tiny buttoned cardies. Highly unlikely, and he'd be homo.

An intriguing diversity of independent shops, fast transport links to London and excellent schools help to under pin property prices.

'Why are we *intriguing*, Damon?'

Damon shrugs, taps the cobbles and pulls on his fag.

'And I think you'll find *underpin* is one word,' she goes on because he is cocky. 'Like underpants.'

'Are we looking at something we don't like?' he says to her, meeting her eyes through the smoke.

'I'll give it a shot.'

He snorts derisively, as if she is being serious. Shallow end of the gene pool, him.

She's still tasting the barbecue she had last night at the smart new Korean place. Not much flesh for the price. This town has consumed her. Five minutes' puff from the cathedral, yet the only time she goes is for the carols at Christmas. Quite calming, that is. Every year during that hour in the pews she loves England and vows to attend services and concerts on a regular basis, but the tourists and the evangelical types put her off (lame excuse).

Yet if she were to die suddenly in a tragic accident, the *Echo's* obituary would go on about her zest for life, her many friends, her passionate love for the city and for the local countryside. With a blurred picture of her grinning out at the world. The immigrant from Hemel Hempstead, land of mini-roundabouts and Wally World. At least she can talk English proper.

Or maybe there won't be anything at all. Not one word.

On Monday morning, just before opening time at eleven o'clock, shoulder aching from working the squeegee, she notices a young girl loitering in front of the shop the other side of the sparkling glass; she's in burgundy school uniform which clashes with her hair, which is dark red. Natural colour because she has a redhead's chalk-white skin and freckles on her nose. This is all I need, Sheena thinks, cold dribbles of water in her sleeves:

Year 10 work experience. Forgot all about it. Looks twelve but must be fourteen.

She unlocks the door and greets the girl, voice turning husky and ending in a cough. Tormented by thoughts of Paul Cannon, by memories of his firm fingers on her feet, by dreams of shoes slipping from their moorings and travelling far out on the ocean's glitter, she's had one of those lonely weekends that demanded help from the vino quarter. As they say round here, she got *fairly kegged*. Now she looks at the girl through a blear of headache and an overtaxed liver, her haggard complexion disguised somewhat by the judicious use of spray tan. The return of the undead. Why does she never learn? At least she didn't find sick in her hair, this time.

'Me name's Fay Sheenan,' says the girl straight off.

A pause to catch up. 'Oh. Sheenan? Well well, I'm Sheena Fleming. We're going to get muddled!'

'I don't think so, Miss Fleming.'

It's written on the form the girl is holding out. 'Miss S. Fleming.' Along with all the guff about health 'n' safety and safeguarding. What on earth do they think could happen to a teenage girl in a kids' clothes shop?

Fay is so thin she might be anorexic, Sheena surmises as she makes them both an instant coffee in the scullery at the back. It makes her teeth more prominent and her eyes bigger. The girl lives in the Ermine, on the west side, which is the rougher half of the council estate up on the northern edge of the city, when you'd expect the rough half to be the east. As a matter of fact, *edge* isn't the right term because the estate *is* pretty much the north of Lincoln. Sheena has never more than skirted it. Parts of the city are no-go, or no-go for faint-hearted law-abiding types like herself. The local paper reports the details every week with calm nonchalance, as if splintering a stranger's jaw or tipping someone out of their mobility scooter or walking about with a broken cocktail glass in your pocket is totally normal behaviour. It was like that even before the Poles and whatnot came flooding in.

This is the first council kid she's ever had; the work-experience candidates usually come from upmarket families who are ex-customers, the teenagers nostalgic for their distant toddlerhood or pushed into it by their mothers for the same reason. 'Oh,' they always say, 'it's so much *smaller* than I remember!' This is Fay's first time. Her green eyes are like a cat's in the dark, letting in as much light as they can. She doesn't seem too demanding, doesn't smell or look grubby like one or two of her middle-class predecessors, although she has an irritating way of tapping the chair's bar with her foot.

A quiet Monday, the shop taking its time to warm up on a chilly autumn day, means there is time to explain things. Always greet the customer but don't be too intrusive. Don't display too much stock or too little. Keep an eye on those sticky toddler fingers. The worst are the even younger siblings left in their buggies beside a rack of dresses, half a soggy rusk in their hands and the other half on their face, who like to explore the texture and smell of clean cloth. Fay listens carefully. Sheena has no idea whether any of it is going in. For all she knows, the girl might have learning difficulties. Then Fay says, 'You could just get really irated and then they'll never forget.'

'Technically a good idea,' says Sheena with a sudden rush of affection for the girl, her matter-of-factness and total absence of side. 'But, practically speaking, impossible: the mother would never come back. She may even accuse you of emotional abuse. You get all sorts, but the customer is always right, Fay. Rule number one, until you feel pushed to break it. The customer is always right.'

134

Later in the week, the girl says, 'Who's that weirdo over yon side?'

Sheena loves Fay's expressions. A tall, angular mumsy suppresses a giggle. 'Not quite so loud, Fay. That's Mike Watkins – owns the bookshop. Ever been in?'

Admittedly Mike does look different, judged objectively. Somewhat like Tennyson, the local celebrity bard. What was that poem about the man with the beard? Probably not by Tennyson. *There once was a man with an enormous beard.* Something like that. Learnt it with Miss Wiles at primary. Fay shakes her head.

'Have you ever actually been in a bookshop, Fay?'

The mumsy suppresses another giggle. Why did she say that? So crass!

Fay looks at her temporary employer past a rack of Armani Junior plum-coloured coats. 'I wanted a book last year, so I looked in the library. Now they've shut the library down. It's got a big padlock on the door.'

'Try Mike's then,' says Sheena, feeling bloody awful. 'They're used books, so there are a good few bargains.' She admires this girl, who will always stand out from the crowd with her deep-red hair and snow-white skin. For good or for ill. The look becomes more attractive with maturity, in general – if she can keep from getting overweight. The thinness isn't anorexia, Sheena reckons; it's more to do with a restless energy, burning up fat. Like working-class kids a generation ago. Scrawny, ferret-like. The opposite now. She could discuss this with Paul. He probably has a funny ecological diet, would have theories about obesity. Boston, fat capital of Britain. Or certainly of England. England-and-Wales-and-Northern-Ireland. 'You can go over to the bookshop now, if you want. I'll give you half an hour off.'

'Off what? You're not paying me.'

The kid can say these startling things. For instance (an hour or so later), that her friends mostly do their fortnight in Asda or Carpet Warehouse, because Asda gives you this certificate, a City & Guilds Accreditation Certificate. *Whatever that means,* Sheena would like to add. *These bloody chains.* Instead she says, 'I can give you a certificate too.' She's folding a Ralph Lauren polo neck with faux-suede patches on the elbows. 'The Mother Hubbard Certificate for Removing Sticky Fingers,' she says, surprised at her own inventiveness.

'I'd prefer to have a special cake in your flat upstairs,' says Fay, stroking the gold embroidery on a Roberto Cavalli dress on special offer for £299. 'If you don't reckon I'm being too lippy.'

'Honey, I like your lippiness. Look after the shop for ten minutes while I go get us a cake. Can you stay on another hour? We can phone your mum.'

'I'm not allowed to be on my own. They told us. Elfnsafety.'

'I take full responsibility. And I trust you.'

The girl grins broadly, showing her long and crooked front tooth. That ought to be sorted, at least.

Fay clearly loves the old beams, the cosiness, the shaggy rugs from New Zealand, the pots from Málaga, the cat Mungo from out of the Lincoln rain one evening. Or maybe it's the Mr Kipling Viennese Whirls that Sheena's dug out from the back of the kitchen cupboard. 'My secret indulgence,' she tells the kid, which isn't true; she shoved them to the back because they're cheap and sickly. Can't recall which gentleman brought them. The girl buries her face in Mungo, who is also ginger, but Fay's hair turns darker in contrast, almost carmine. She tells Sheena about her dog, Pooch. Stepdad Ken's dog, really. She takes Pooch for walks and if some nobhead starts on her, Pooch starts on him. He's without fear. Sheena finds it depressing that Fay walks a world where louts want to bully her. It seems a far cry from pink cashmere and sailor outfits at a hundred and fifty quid a throw, or from this cosy flat with the hearth flickering (gas but very realistic).

'One day you'll meet a nice kind-hearted lad,' Sheena says, 'with that lovely hair of yours.'

Fay shakes her head. 'They're all stupid moppets and nobheads who think they're the cat's mother. Stuck up their own arse. What the heck. How bout you, miss?'

Sheena smiles. 'Oh, I've known a few Prince Charmings.'

'Why didn't you marry one, then?'

An image of Paul floats in her head, obscuring the others. Paul would like Fay, would find her original. Would he? Sheena has no idea, really. Of what he likes and dislikes beyond shoes and tea and music. She can only surmise. She's not even capable of saying what dangerous sport he's into. Could be rally driving. Or bungee jumping. All she knows is that she very much enjoys being in his somewhat depressed company. That's love.

'Miss Fleming?'

'Call me Sheena. I sound like your teacher, otherwise. Why didn't I marry one? Good question. Because Sheena is a ditherer. In other words, Fay, I am incapable of making a firm decision when it comes to love and commitment. I am about as clear and decisive as a mini-roundabout, of which there have always been loads in Hemel Hempstead. Where I hail from, as I told you. Voted one of the ugliest towns in Britain.'

Fay reflects for a moment. A serious girl. Sheena knows there's something wrong with the mother and that the step-father has had run-ins with the law. Fay may well think her employer is also a touch daffy, as they say round here. The firelight flickers on the girl's face, giving its paleness a touch of rouge. The freckles on her stubby nose look painted on. One day the duckling will become a swan, of that Sheena is certain. She's seen it before with redheads. A green-eyed swan. Sheena feels her toes curling in the deep woollen pile of the rug. In some ways she wants this moment to continue for ever.

'Sheena, like . . . have you heard of Uggie?'

'Wait there,' says Sheena, not listening. She returns with her new camera, a digital with a swish lens. She cancels the flash: the light is adequate and she can't bear red eyes, gleaming canines. Fay complains but then poses in a very artificial manner, hand under chin, a Facebook smile. Quite pert, really. 'Try to look natural,' Sheena says. Fay asks what she means by *natural.*

'Normal.' What's normal? We're all bloody freaks. The hand comes away from the sharp little chin. The camera clicks its fake, electronic shutter-click several times. They both take a look. The last one is approved by the sitter, 'cos I look less of an ugly twat'. The background is the ancient oak beams she so likes.

'I'll send it to you. Email?'

'Only our Ken's got a mobile. We've got a flatscreen, mind.'

Sheena returns to Paul's on the following Monday, having given ye olde hair dye a day to settle. Fay has phoned to say she can't come in the morning, a problem with the mother (the stepdad not being around). 'She's gorra bag on,' whatever that means. Don't tell the school! Itchy Feet opens at ten, Mother Hubbard opens at eleven. She has an hour.

She is glad she has stockings, as the veins stand out on her uppers these days. The left foot looks almost deformed. Maybe he is right. She likes narrow shoes. More flattering. Bunched-up toes. Cram them in.

'I'm off to Tenerife for a few days, bang in the middle of the pre-Christmas rush,' she says.

'Sensible.'

'Yup. I was thinking about some sandals. Or maybe even flip-flops.'

She finds her toes are curling now, like an excited little girl's. She will take him away from the shoe shop. He is meant for better things. It is time to get serious. She's not felt like this in years, not since Sandro. At least a decade. And did she ever enjoy just being in Sandro's vicinity so intensely?

He looks up after a pause, as if he is thinking about something else. Her heart begins to slide down. 'I've got some Havaianas straight from Brazil,' he says finally. 'I don't stock polyurethane, so it's all hemp. Hemp's less of a barrier against the earth's negative electrons, which are good for you. Rubber or plastic cuts them off. We'll all be wearing these when the environment finally collapses.'

'Oh dear,' she says. 'Too much choice. This one is jolly.'

She has picked up a flip-flop with a sole covered in a rainbow from a shelf where all the flip-flops are cheerily coloured.

'Oh, that. Reiki. A kind of Zen without the pain. Reiki shoes. The all-seeing eye or Buddha or rainbow sends healing vibes up through your feet.'

'Through all those thousands of nerve endings.'

He gives an amused grunt. 'Until, one presumes, your sweaty soles have rubbed the design away. I prefer the earth, if we're talking energies.'

'Some folk will buy anything,' she sighs, although she is tempted. He isn't very good at client persuasion; just the opposite. He'll be talking flying saucers next. She glances at her watch. 'I've left yet another useless nose-pierced ado in charge,' she fibs.

139

'I wouldn't choose conventional sandals,' he says with professional briskness. 'I can offer you some minimal esparto sandals made in Spain to my specification. Copies of prehistoric footwear from the sixth century BC . No heel, no arch, nothing. Very thin, tough soles. Better than flip-flops. You'll learn to touch down on the balls of your feet rather than the heel, if you're on a hard surface. And most surfaces are now hard, unfortunately. It's almost as good as going barefoot.'

He presents them. They are like squashed bits of old baskets. She frowns. 'They're not really my thing. I'll get calluses.'

'Exactly. Calluses are nature's footwear. Look at dancers' feet. Yoga teachers.'

'You're talking yourself out of business.'

She tries on some Roman-looking faux-leather sandals, with curly ties instead of buckles and well supported under the sole. 'You don't have someone breathing down your neck, like I do.'

'These days, no. It was my wife's shop, originally. It came with Rebecca. Ever know her?'

She shakes her head, unable to recall Rebecca as more than that blur with a lot of hair.

'I was floating about,' he goes on, 'after spending six years sick.'

'Six years?'

'India. I got four diseases, one on top of the other. Came back with them stuck to me like giggling schoolgirls. In bed at my mum's down the road near Boston for nine months.'

Giggling schoolgirls? thinks Sheena, smiling uncertainly from her chair. Oh dear. In bed with his mum carrying in treats on trays. Maybe she won't get him to meet Fay, who finishes her stint at the end of the week. 'Scary,' she says.

'Nah. Frustrating. I wasn't really sick as such, just harrowed. As we say in Boston. Harrowed. Exactly how I felt. I once

140

knew a chronically depressed bloke whose daughter was murdered,' he says unexpectedly.

'Oh my God.'

'He was never depressed again. It sort of jolted him out of it.'

She wanted to ask him about kids, but now backs off. All she knows about him for certain is that he lives out near Tupholme, very remote, drives a blue van. Their eyes meet and she feels a pleasant quiver, as if someone's put sherbert in her blood. The door jingles and an elderly female hobbles in.

Sheena turns back into a customer, sliding off the chair and picking up her bag. She is seeing them – her and Paul – stood among vegetables growing in neat rows out of peaty earth, with mountains in the background. Maybe it is his hands, which are large and broad and furred with dark hairs – a farmer's hands, not a shoe handler's hands. So he is a local, in the end. That is disappointing, but she can live with it.

'We ought to have a drink some time,' she breaks in, touching his elbow. 'Discuss trade and the clientele. Oh, or other things. The meaning of life, if there is one.'

'Nice idea.'

'Go for a Chinese?' she pursues. 'Pop by or give me a buzz. I'm in the book. Or I'll text you.'

He smiles, which makes her scalp go fuzzy, and says, 'Look forward to it.'

The cathedral's ringing its bells. Sometimes when the wind's right they float down here. Wedding bells! She is too old, she thinks, to be playing this sort of lark. Batting above her average. She walks towards the door and is brought up short by the shock of her bare feet against the doormat's bristles. Forty thousand nerve endings. She can believe that. 'Oops,' she says, turning to him. 'Senior moment.'

He is holding her shoes out, his fingers curling into each warm interior. She notices the heels are worn. Standing up all day. Eyes on hers, directly on hers. Holding them together.

'Go unshod,' he says. 'Pad gently like the beasts.'

He's poetic, not dull.

'You're putting yourself out of business,' interrupts the elderly bitch with a stupid laugh – who, Sheena later thinks, is probably only about fifteen years older than herself and has very striking pale-blue eyes. Much more amazing than hers. Upstaged as ever. There's always someone who upstages the bride.

'Shooting himself in the foot,' Sheena quips, slipping one of hers in.

But no more chuckling. When she glances back through the window from the lane, he's nodding and smiling at the elderly faggot as if they're hanging out together.

She is forty-eight, looks mostly younger, especially in sunglasses (not much call for those here). If they were to have a baby, there is more than an even chance it would be healthy. He is trapped. She is trapped. Together, they have this enormous potential. She would text him but doesn't know his number. He probably doesn't do mobiles. He doesn't phone, anyway. He doesn't pop by. When she goes for a Chinese, she invites Fay. 'It looks right posh, dun't it?' She drives the girl back home afterwards, somewhat nervously. She turns off Burton Road into the estate. There are a few gaunt blocks, but the brick houses are neat and rather sweet, with gardens in front. Some have upmarket cars parked outside. Well, the state's paying the rent, tenants decently salaried, or just plumbers and whatnot overcharging. Admittedly several of the gardens are rubbish sites or overgrown with weedy bushes, but it is nothing like she imagined. Fay's is a maisonette, no more than three storeys, in red brick with big concrete balconies and a thick hedge encircling a lawn. It is almost dark and the autumn breeze has a chill on it. Maybe she'll be invited in. Meet the damaged mother, the dodgy stepfather. Both on state benefits, of course. Victims or scroungers? Like the eastern Europeans. Some work hard. Some steal. Boozers too. Crunchy glass underfoot the next day.

Sheena gets out of the car when Fay does. No invitation. They give each other a little hug. The girl feels bony and slight. Sheena squeezes her a bit closer out of affection. Fay lets her. This girl needs so much love, Sheena thinks. They are hugging when a slash of bare-bulb light appears on the first-floor balcony and someone emerges. Standing there behind the handrail is the man with a tattoo on his neck, the guitar player in front of Smith's. Who *used* to be in front of Smith's. The busker. A bit of a dish. He peers out at them in an old T-shirt. He must be freezing.

'Oh, it's the wonderful busker.'

'Yeah, everyone says it. His head's a mess, though. Bye, Sheena. I've gotta go cos he won't be doin nefin or else. Guess who's the cook tonight?'

'Tell him from me that I love his music, Fay.'

'Tell him that yersen and he'll start coming on to you right warm.' She laughs.

'Better not, then.'

'Makes no difference that you're old enough to be his gran, not with our Ken.'

'Not quite that ancient, hun.' God, this is how Fay sees her: the withered granny. 'Nevertheless, feel free to come back on Saturdays. As I said, yeah? A bit of extra pocket money. No need to warn me beforehand. Just turn up.'

As she gets back into the car, she hears Fay get an earful from the balcony and pauses before starting the ignition. They're only half an hour late; should she explain? She hovers for a minute as Fay disappears round the corner. The door shuts, the shaft of light vanishes behind a curtain. A group of lads are hovering across the way, hooded and menacing. She turns the ignition and tries not to get the hell out of there too obviously. Blinking the odd tear from her vision.

Fay returns at eleven on the Saturday following, out of uniform. The coat with its fur-trimmed hood is slightly too large for her, the cuffs hiding her knuckles. She's excited. 'Tennyson had a fire.' 'Sorry, angel?' 'Tennyson block. At school. Burnt out two classrooms. What? You think I done it or what?' Sheena asks if anyone was hurt. 'Nah, it was at night. Some nobheads got kegged for defo. I dunna who. Can't say or they'd kill me. Slowly, like.'

Sheena worries that she's been too forward. Most teenagers would loaf about in bed till midday, but the girl has this restlessness. She'll go far. She is good with the toddlers, makes them laugh, talks to them in a sing-song voice that is a little loud. It is busy, and Sheena is on an adrenalin high.

She sends Fay off to do some shopping for the weekend, handing over a twenty. Fay is totally trustworthy. She comes back with the bill and the change, but Sheena doesn't bother to check it. They eat lunch together upstairs, Mungo smelling the dog on Fay's jeans. The mumsies look at Fay down their noses because, apart from her broad Lincolnshire twang, she is so obviously dressed in bottom-of-the-range clothes sparking with artificial fibres: orange leggings with a drawstring fastener, a long-sleeved T-shirt with a WEST COAST CALIFORNIA logo, leopard-patterned trainers laced in neon pink. The coat is a touch grubby and was once red.

Sheena enjoys the irony of it all. They probably think the girl's a shoplifter at first. On Saturdays the dads always come in, looking lost, clutching punnets of organic raspberries they've been forced to buy by the older sibling after her saxophone lesson or whatever, bewildered by the sight of their children, whom they never see in the week (the office, not marital separation, not yet) and having not a single ounce of control over them. Sometimes it's both mum and dad – but equally lost, in this age of gender equality, without the nanny. London commuters, escaping impossible house prices, enjoying their four-bedroom stone cottage, double garage, and huge lawn for under four hundred thou. And getting raspberry juice over bloody everything.

Fay leaves mid-afternoon, home-duties-bound. She has earned a tenner and the bus fare. That was always their agreement. She seems satisfied. She doesn't know if she can make it every Saturday. Next Saturday is frickin PJ Sports Day at her school, raising money for a frickin orphanage in frickin Romania. 'Oh, another nice English cause, I see,' comments Sheena. 'That'll be fun, running for the Roms.' 'No,' says Fay, 'I hate it.' 'Is that because it's embarrassing, being in smelly pyjamas?' Fay makes a snorting noise. Sheena wonders if the poor thing even has a pair of PJs. An acceptable pair, anyway. 'Don't fret about it, honey. The point is, you can just turn up. But I'm away for the last week of November.' 'Where you going, then?' 'Tenerife. Bag up on sunshine to see me through to March.' She didn't suggest Fay came in to help Not-Britt cope with the pre-Christmas rush, ho ho. (Retail suicide, Tony called it. 'Tony, would you rather the murder of a client on your hands? Blood all over that lovely carpet?')

Fay's eyes are full of imagined sunshine. She's been a few times to Skeggy in Ken's van, apparently, and a school trip to Boston for coastal erosion when she was sick in the coach, and that's it.

At the door, a leaving present of a jaffa cake melting in her hand, she turns into the moderately busy shop and calls out,

in a chance lull, 'You en't allowed to say that, any road, Sheena.'
Sheena bustles over to her. 'Say what? Please don't shout.'
'That Romanians are Roms, like. It were racist. You'll get Miss
Crabbe after you. Discriminising.' Sheena places a hand on
the girl's thick hair and guides her out. 'Oo-er, sweetheart,
what will I get?' Fay ponders on the pavement, chewing on
her jaffa cake. 'Nobbut lines. You en't smashed their gypsy
faces in, or whatever.'

Sheena takes her shoes off and walks on the warm sand. She
sees what Paul meant. You adjust. The surface sifts, you can feel
the millions of grains. It is sexy, kind of, the sensation thrilling
up from the bottom of her feet through her body to her mind.
You still have to watch out for broken glass and nasty odds and
sods, though, floated in from the ocean. She swims out to a
rock in her sunglasses, scarcely able to believe the glittering
loveliness. She lies on the rock, shivering a bit in the whiffs
of seaweed, and vows to take charge of her life. Paul is a part of
that life. It is just a question of being bold. She isn't sure about
the name, though. Paul. He is more a Jody. Leo. Rafe.
     That evening in the hotel bar she gets through a bottle of
Listán Negro. A youngish off-the-rack-gorgeous local in a
white suit and aviator's shades buys her a drink and tells her
she is the most beautiful woman he has ever seen.
     'The light is low,' she jokes, 'and you've got your shades on.'
     'I am agree.'
     She laughs, which is a bit cruel. She only knows about twenty
words in Spanish. He is smoking a thin cigar she likes the smell
of. They go up together to her room at two in the morning
and make love with an unswerving dedication to the surface
of each other's bodies, strangers to the end. She is sure she
hears him whisper 'Mama' at one point, nuzzling her tits.
He goes back to his own place and Sheena lies on the scattered

146

pillows and cries as she watches CNN unroll the world's miseries and injustices, though her tears are never for those.

He didn't even stay to tidy up the bed. His mouth tasted of dung behind the toothpaste. That was the cigar. Imagine suddenly waking up, she reflects, with someone else's mouth instead of your own.

Fay doesn't come back at all until the week after Christmas. Her mum was bad, and Ken got cuffed by the police, a night in the station, released with a caution 'for possession of a controlled substance'. He then got 'very paralytic' because he was upset, and pulled Rochelle (the mum) by the hair until Rochelle screamed and he nearly got done for domestic assault. On Christmas Eve. A single breathless sentence with the broad accent. Google translation where are you?

'You *have* had an exciting time,' says Sheena, helpless to know what to suggest. The odd thing is that the girl seems to love and even admire her stepdad, who has 'a big heart'. He never lays a finger on the girl. Only the mother. Back in Hemel Sheena's dad would occasionally lose his cool after a hard day supervising the buses with a biro behind his ear and slap his wife across the face. But Sheena's mum would take her revenge ten times over by going almost mute for days. It infuriated him and he did suffer, oh how he suffered, coming back from the Green Line depot in his purple tie to that silence. Until the next explosion, fuelled like Ken's by drink or worse (Whitbread Trophy with his mates in Dad's case). Again, he never laid a finger on his little girl.

'What did you do for Christmas, Sheena?'

'Slept. Slept right through it.' Giving out soup to the derelicts down Monks Road, like every year. Distraction. Taking her life in her hands.

Fay is very keen to go over to Chapter Seven with some of her savings in a purse. To see if they've got any dog books. Sheena gives her fifteen minutes off, despite her safeguarding suspicions about Mike (totally unfounded, she admits to herself). The girl returns after twenty minutes with *Dog Training*, showing a retriever on the cover with a fat bird in its mouth. Not what she wanted, she says. It's for hunting. One quid fifty. She seems disgruntled.

'How was our Mike?' asks Sheena.

Fay glares at her. 'In a mard. I hate him. He's a cruel *twat*.'

A mumsy looks askance, all but shielding her three-year-old's ears, except that they already have a pair of furry white muffs on them. Sheena brings Fay away to the scullery with an encouraging arm on her back.

'What did he do?'

'Nothing. He's just a fucking old cruel— Mmmf . . .'

'He can be ever so grumpy,' Sheena says, removing her hand from Fay's moist little mouth. 'He's famous for that. But Fay, can you not swear in my shop, please?'

'Why don't you shut your hole and do one?' shouts Fay, having wiped her lips with the back of her hand. And then she's gone. Sheena is actually trembling. The girl's feral. You can never tame a wild animal. How very disappointing. That bloody Mike.

She goes across to see him as he's closing up, usually an hour later than her (he claims a lot of people come along after work, but she's never exactly noticed the queues). He looks surprised. Well, it's her first time in. It's dark and dingy, chaotic ain't the word, old books stacked not just on the shelves but on the floor. The golden rule: never show too much stock. That's not the only rule he's broken. Not enough light to read, which seems self-defeating for a bookshop. And he doesn't greet his latest customer, or not properly. A grunt and a scowl is worse than nothing.

'I hope I'm not intruding,' she says.

'If you're here to purchase, not at all.'

Is that supposed to be funny? There's a smell, hard to define. Dead mouse somewhere. Ancient papers. Dust. Gone-off wax floor-polish. The floorboards were last painted black in the nineteenth century, it looks like, and are now scuffed back to bare wood by footfall, but not evenly. Hers are hidden by a high-quality Heckmondwike Supacord carpet, a calming aquamarine. Even resists infant vomit. You can't arse about in a retail environment, to quote Tony.

'My work-experience trainee popped in here today. To purchase, in fact. A slim fourteen-year-old with red hair called Fay. A sweet girl, difficult background. Popped out again rather smartly, however. Shame.'

She thought that would be enough. Mike Watkins looks down at her from a battered wooden footstool on which he is standing with a column of books hooked in his right arm. The bookcase is hopelessly full. As he is simply staring and not replying, looking over his small oval spectacles like something out of *Harry Potter* (the beard, the beard), she adds, 'The thing is, I'm just checking if everything, well, that nothing . . . She's not used to bookshops.'

'So we saw,' he says.

We? As in 'We are a grandmother'?

'Oh dear. What happened?'

Mike returns to his shelf-stacking like an unhelpful employee in Asda. He somehow finds room, even if it means squeezing them on top of the others. 'What happened,' he says, eventually, 'is that she stole a book.'

'Did she? She said she'd paid one fifty. What was it called? *The Hunting Dog*, or something.'

'She paid for that one, yeah. But she didn't pay for the one I saw turning her right-hand coat pocket into a kind of brick. *Listening to Your Dog* is the title. First edition, signed by the author. Worth twelve pounds fifty. When I pointed this out, she called me an unrepeatable epithet connected to self-pleasuring. And then some more.'

'Apologies,' says Sheena, suppressing a smile. What a pretentious shrivelled-up wanker. Literally. It probably gets caught in his beard, like cobwebs. Ugh. To think she waves to him almost every day, despite getting a bare nod back. She's much too nice. Solidarity my foot. 'I'll buy it right now,' she adds, taking out her purse. She can't possibly fall out with him. It would make life on Totter Hill a daily ordeal. She's known retailers get nervous breakdowns with the strain of avoiding the glance of the enemy opposite.

'You can't,' he says. 'You'll just hand the said book over to her.'

'Exactly what I intend to do.'

'Appalling lesson for a juvenile.' He alights from the stool with another grunt, slapping his hands free of dust. Presumably never exercises. She's dependent on her weekly workout at the gym club for her sanity. 'Reward for thieving, insulting an adult? The stolen goods.'

Sheena sighs away her desire to thump him. 'Oh, come on. She's a street kid. Dysfunctional and impoverished family. Fiery temper. A redhead!'

'That's a myth,' says Mike, going over to the door and turning the tatty OPEN sign to CLOSED. 'Like the myth of impoverishment. Free school, free healthcare, free transport to school, free council house, free school trips, just about everything. And what do I get? Higher and higher rates, charges for this and that, and bloody Oxfam selling used books. Even book tokens for Christmas have gone out of fashion. Ergo, the final retailing day of 2011 is a complete washout. I could be at home in front of the fire.'

150

'I can see,' says Sheena, who unfortunately could not disagree with his basic thrust, 'that Fay will remain disappointed.'

'And don't try to get anyone else to buy it for her, as *Listening to Your Dog* is not on the shelves any more. It reminds me of what was a very unpleasant and even shocking experience.'

Sheena feels for him, suddenly. Fay could pack a punch. She has a tongue on her, as Mum would say. Nothing like that has ever happened in this shop, she realises. It is an earthquake in an earthquake-free zone. She can see the books tumbling off the shelves.

'I think it'll teach her the appropriate lesson,' she concedes. She is very good at conceding. And they are both on the same side, as retailers. Sticky fingers, large pockets. Mike says nothing, only nods. With a touch of impatience. He is a sort of Paul Cannon type, but the bad version. Paul is the good version. The grumpy but good angel. And hot too.

A week later, and no Fay. Of course she isn't feral, she's a suffering creature. A victim. God, we all hope Mike didn't *do* something when she was alone in there; he's a bit of a dark horse. One little public hint of that and the local vigilantes would burn down his shop, or at least heap his books up in front of the cathedral and torch them. With a sign on it, misspelt: PEEDO. And him on top, his beard catching first. Whoosh. Full of dust and dry gravy and dried spunk.

Sheena considers contacting Fay, but by now she isn't sorry that the girl is temporarily (she presumes) absent from her life, as the latter has taken an unexpected turn. *Previously on Sheena's Diaries* . . .

The young dark-haired customer in Paul's shop that time was seated at the bar in the Short Straw during the lunch break, when frankly the world might have suffered an apocalypse, it was so quiet. Despite the sales, she had had the second worst day of the year, as she joked to Hannah, whose creative ideas (for example a blackboard bearing a stick of chalk below YOUR NEW YEAR RESOLUTION?) draw the masses. Crap!

So what's good about January? A young man raising his glass at her. She went over, ordered hers (Pinot Grigio spritzer with a hunk of lime), sat on a stool and remarked on his steel-capped black-leather boots. 'Glad you found a pair.'

'Vegan,' he said, keeping straight-faced, looking down at hers rested on the brass bar rail. His eyes lifted, burying themselves in her ample cleavage. The boil on his nose (for such it appeared to be) was subdued by the low light – a gloomy lunchtime, and Clive refused to recognise the need for artificial light until nightfall, like a Victorian lamplighter. As, no doubt, her forty-something wrinkles and sags were softened. He was positively pretty, with fine features, bony cheekbones, his jet-black hair transformed thankfully into a sort of 1920s cut, sleek and neat. And Sheena liked men with eyes so dark the pupils vanished into the iris, giving the gaze a hypnotic quality, if a little like those black gobstoppers you used to get. He was twenty years younger but clearly fancied her. Sheena needed this. No woman teetering a couple of years off from fifty did not need this. It was Sheena's mother who had said, a generation earlier, 'No man ever looks at a woman over fifty.'

His name was Gavin. She didn't think he was drugged up. He was also in the retail sector, an assistant manager in a convenience store, day off today, but had other ambitions. 'Like?' He smiled modestly but winningly. Pleasant, lilting voice. Hidden depths. 'To make the world a better place.' An idealist. Sweet. She smiled back, raising her Pinot Grigio. 'It's 2012. Go for it.' They touched glasses. 'And how would you go about it, Gavin? Improve your face-to-face transaction skills?' She was on her third spritzer by now. Their fingers touched when they simultaneously went for the peanuts in the little bowl that Clive always had to be asked to provide. His skin felt cold only because hers was overheated. She felt twenty-something because that's what her heart still was. Her face too, when she forgot.

'It's a long story,' he said, sticking to her with his gobstopper eyes.

'No time to tell it now, then. I'm opening in fifteen minutes. A wee bit pissed too.'

'I could tell you, like, this evening?'

'We can resume our acquaintance at five thirty. Come to the shop. Ring the bell on the rather flaky green door to the right. That's my private entry, as it were. You know where it is, I've seen you loitering in front of Chapter Seven.'

He frowned. 'I never loiter. You know what I do? I stand in a state of high expectancy, very alert.'

'For what? Shoplifters?'

He was taken aback for a moment, then understood and found it funny. The thread became (yet again in her case) the curse of shoplifting, which was of mutual interest, he being an assistant store manager, and they shared stories. Wealthy kleptomaniacs were her area. Disturbed. Pocketing cardies for their nieces or nephews, possibly imaginary. His were the offshoot of poverty or generational tradition (not just grimy travellers) or bloody students. 'And *I'm* a bloody student! Part time, though. Currently pausing to earn my bread so as I don't starve.'

He didn't pay her tab, but then men were forbidden to be gentlemen, these days, and he was saving up. As she left, pausing at the door to glance back, he gave her a thumbs-up and a meaningful look, like the handsome stranger in a film to an innocent young woman stranded in a one-horse town. Except that this was Lincoln, and he was (judging from the very slight twang of an accent) a county native, so he didn't quite pull it off. Not everything can be perfect, but it made him even more munchable.

Completely ridiculous, but she returned up the hill with a spring in her step. God, you're only young once, and that felt longer ago than it actually was, pushed back into the past by a daily intake of youthful mumsies. Even those who'd put their careers first and waited to their mid-thirties, and now looked drawn and worn. Even they seemed young these days.

Gavin turned up after closing time only ten minutes late, pressing his face against the plate glass to see inside. She had just switched off the lights after tidying, the interior a dim and sickly yellow in the overspill from the lane's sodium street lamps. Otherwise the shop was a stage or a TV screen. No privacy for a retailer; it's all public. He was a thin shadowy form, and she thought she saw Mike bloody Watkins beyond, on the other side of the lane but as close as ever, fiddling with his bargain box. Unlucky.

She ushered Gavin into the narrow hallway. 'I'm upstairs,' she said. 'Cup of tea?' She cast this back over her shoulder on the way up the crooked little stairs – brightly, despite a sudden qualm that was part embarrassment, now the spritzers had settled to a sticky pool in her head. What was she up to? She felt about as sexy as a bed-and-breakfast landlady.

He was just behind her on the tiny landing. 'What's your name again?'

She wanted to laugh. 'Sheena. Old enough to be your grandmother,' she added, testing. Actually, only old enough to be his (young) mother.

Gavin liked the flat. He liked the wood-and-brass ship wheel on the wall and the big landscape and the bright metal

154

butterfly (souvenir of Sandro). She made him tea. 'I've got wine in the fridge,' she said. No, he'd have tea. She pulled a face. 'Have you got a headache too?' 'Look, Sheena, I think you're mega-sexy and I only want tea first because I'm thirsty. Have you got a biscuit? I like digestives but anything'll do.'

He was so sweet. So young. 'Sit down,' she said. 'Take your coat off. Let's give this a moment to settle.' Her heart was alight. 'I'm very glad you find me sexy,' she called from the kitchen. 'I find you extremely sexy.'

That wasn't quite true. She found him cold and enticing. Above all she felt like teaching him something, because she knew that underneath his cool exterior he was jelly. Or maybe it just boiled down to the fact that he was in his twenties, that he was a young man, that this had to be one of her last chances to seize youth in her arms on an equal basis, and that the bloody Paul issue was going nowhere. This would make her more attractive, she knew it. Her skin would glow; her pheromones would cluster; she'd feel less like a bloody mini-roundabout in Hemel. Paul would smell it on the wind.

Happy Almost Unused Year.

She turned the fake-log fire up full, and it blazed merrily with that subtle giveaway hiss. She didn't think music would be a good idea, as her taste would expose their age difference in an unattractive way. He looked faintly goth, or probably had been once. All that black. Mungo didn't head for the stranger's lap, oddly. He was usually very sociable. He stared at him with those hawkish eyes, flanks twitching and tail flicking as they did when he spotted a bird or a bee in the tiny back garden, then disappeared upstairs into the spare attic room – a sacrifice, because it's only heated when used, although warmed feebly by the rising air from the rest of the flat.

Gavin sipped his tea on the sofa next to her with great concentration. 'I'm chill as a cucumber. On ice.'

Of course he was the opposite. 'Look, if you want to leave it, Gavin.'

'Leave what? My lovely tea? By the way, are you his woman?'

'Whose?'

'That gay guy in the shoe shop,' he said, smirking.

Sheena pulled a face. 'I don't believe he's gay.' This was such a bad idea.

'So you *are* his woman.'

'No, I'm not. Maybe I'd like to be, though.'

'I could see that. I'm pretty perceptive.' He drained his mug, his Adam's apple bobbing in his elegant young throat. 'In fact, I am a *sensitive*. You know what that means?'

'Gavin, would you like a whisky? I have a Chivas Regal. Twelve years. Or ordinary Tesco's, but you don't notice if you have enough.'

His face lit up. Poor soul. 'The former. Neat. No ice, yeah. A wee dram.'

He watched her as she glugged the stuff into her best tumblers. They clinked and he took a considerable gulp. She felt the Scotch course through her fierily, so fierily. The bottle had dust on its shoulders. Why had she deprived herself? His hand was now on her knee, on the hem of her skirt, gripping rather powerfully. He did not come across as someone strong, or heedless of his own strength like other men she'd known. 'You are beautiful,' he said, having drained his Chivas. 'I can't believe my luck. I knew something really special was going to happen to me today. It's like I've imagined this kind of encounter so many times? Like I said, I'm a sensitive. I can kind of literally *see* the supernatural, like it's just behind what other people see?'

She placed her finger on his lips. His inane chat, snagging more and more on a local accent, was sounding childish. That's not what she wanted. The whiff of an armpit, overlaid with some awful male deodorant smelling like rotten pine-apple, both excited and demoralised her.

'Does the idea of a joint shower grab you, sweetheart?'

'Oh my God. I'm looking at myself and thinking, Hey, is this Gavin?'

Sod it, she thought. Live for the day.

Gavin comes round after supper. That's how he likes it: in the evening, well after dark, in secret, like his own shadow. The lane, being steep but not famous, is virtually empty after seven o'clock. He's been three times this week, and this is the end of the first week of the affair. It makes her feel good about herself, if a little more tired. She thought he would be tentative and shy in his lovemaking, but instead he arrives knowing exactly what he wants. 'Motivation is my middle name, doll.' She's happy to oblige because she finds his lean, young and pale body extremely attractive, especially in the bedroom with the dimmer switch low or with only the odd candle to gild his limbs. He finds her opulent and mature flesh (never fat, darling) high on the 'kissability curve', especially the chest region. 'These two are still holding their own,' she agrees, looking in the wardrobe mirror. 'Gavin, get in me.'

He starts to get a little rough in the second week, slapping her buttocks or pinching her neck. This again seems to be programmed. Then it occurs to her as she is dropping off to sleep after a particularly complicated and sweaty session: he watches porn. All his knowledge comes from watching porn. He watches, then he wants it reproduced. It's sex-by-numbers. It's a carnal pleasure kit, rubber band included. So why does she find it so exciting? Why does her body feel replenished, transfused with new blood? Because she is depressed, probably. She has to seek out these perverse remedies. And because Paul is so bloody hopeless. Perhaps he *is* a closet gay. With his miserable pseudo-Buddhist talk of having to suffer, having to be deprived.

She will end the affair in a few weeks. Two months at most. When it's the spring sales, the daffodils out in the park. It's a temporary reprieve. It makes her feel empowered and sinful in front of all those goody-goody two-shoes of perfect mumsies. It's a passage, not a cul-de-sac. Her brief stint with a shrink last year yielded one excellent piece of advice: Don't try to manage the unmanageable.

January is a dull and gloomy month, we all hate January, but this one's buffed up by the affair. Sheena has no precise idea where Gavin lives, only that he shares a small house with other young people near Sincil Dyke. She did sit down in front of her Mac one day and tap *Gavin Henderson* into the Whitepages directory, adding *Lincoln* in the address box, but it only came up with a Gavin Henderson in Swinderby, a good few miles south of Lincoln. *Other possible current occupants: Maureen Henderson.* His mother, from the sound of it. *Sourced from the Electoral Roll 2010–11*, it says. This doesn't mean that Gavin has lied, just that he hasn't bothered to update his details since last year. Or maybe he doesn't vote.

The Dyke is a dead-straight concrete channel of brown water going on as far as the eye can see, so his shared house could be in any number of streets. 'Roman, originally,' he informs her. 'In the time of the Romans, that is. Now it's ex-Roman. Full of ghosts.' Sheena's memory of it dates from twenty years ago, when she lived in the same insalubrious area. He reassures her that it's no longer as full of dumped vacuum cleaners, shopping trolleys, bloated corpses or wind-blown plastic bags, because the area's being tarted up. 'Don't recall any corpses,' she says. He runs a chill hand smoothly over her stomach, then kisses her navel. Even his lips are cool. 'Have

158

you got poor blood circulation, Gavin?' He pauses, pulls back the sheet, points at his cock, straight as a lighthouse, and says in an American drawl, 'Not where it matters, bitch.'

He asks her to shave her pubic hair, and she draws the line. He asks her to screw in his car, which she has never seen, and she refuses. 'It's January,' she says, curled in front of the fire in her silk negligée, the one that he likes because its delicate French lace shows her dark nipples. He presses up against her from behind, close as a spoon in a drawer, and says, 'I can put the heating on, if the engine's running.'

'Mine's only a Mini Cooper,' she tells him. 'And yours?'

His fingers stroke her neck but she winces: the knuckles are freezing. 'Have you just washed your hands or something?' 'You're just on heat,' he sighs. 'You're really hot-blooded.' His hard-on at least is warm, pressed up against the small of her back. She reaches behind her and lazily, casually, starts to fiddle. He groans, scrabbling around her muff with his cold hand. My toyboy, she thinks. Dressed all in black.

Mungo comes in and hurriedly slips out again as if shocked.

Afterwards Gavin says, 'Your cat doesn't like me. Jealous. Cats are cruel. They have cruel hearts.'

She sits cross-legged away from him, letting the flames dance in her eyes. She's forty-eight and feels nineteen. She is firmly in control of her life. In years to come, when Gavin's married with screaming kids to a dull woman with a double chin and stringy hair, this brief period will be his golden age. She suddenly feels desperate for a fag. She gave up six months ago.

'Gavin, lay off my cat.'

'I prefer fish,' he says. 'I can talk to fish.'

'Whatever floats your boat,' laughs Sheena, trying to remember where she hid her fags.

*   *   *

Ghastly time of year. These spots of light and warmth in the week: Gavinised! The sales season has been disappointing so far. Tony is on to her, wondering *why* on the phone.

'Tony, have you noticed the recession? Austerity? Lincoln is not Chelsea.'

'But the well-off are weller-off than ever, Sheena!'

'Online shopping, hun. A gradual recognition that all your stock is massively overpriced maybe.' Bedraggled, half-starved Asian kiddies sewing on pearl buttons, blue denim dye swirling into the drinking supply of ultra-poor countries. She's seen the documentaries, Mungo on her lap. She likes documentaries.

Tony sighs and says, 'Only the fittest survive. Develop your loyal client base, pronto. Think about the customer journey, yeah? From way before they've come in to way after they've gone out. Empathise. Hey, bloody Hell, we're not talking about hitting targets but *smashing* 'em.'

'Have you been on one of those silly courses, Tony?'

'I hope you're not past it, love. The tits still buoyant, are they? And don't forget Australia Day, 26 January!'

'This one's for Tony!' she cries that evening, riding Gavin backwards at his request, facing his toes in front of the faux fire while he slaps her buttocks, pinches them, prises them apart so she has to say whoa. This girl is so athletic, so strong. East German Olympic gymnast, 1980s. And she doesn't even do much yoga. Each of his toenails is painted black, like Samantha Cameron's (according to the *Mail*). Isn't that a bit . . . ? Or just goth?

Afterwards, Mungo pads in from down below, the cat flap just audible – always a welcome sound. Sheena *thinks* Mungo's got the idea that cars are lethal, while not understanding that a Dolce & Gabbana daisy-embroidered dress (£435) is not a convenient litter. They are toasting each other with an Argentinian red on special offer at Majestic. The cat stops, stares at them with huge yellow eyes, gives a plaintive mew and scuttles off up into the attic room. 'That's not funny, Mungo,' Sheena calls after him.

Gavin snorts. 'Animals don't have a sense of humour,' he says flatly, staring into the fire. 'That is a uniquely human trait. Neither do vampires. To spot a vampire, apart from them having red hair, right, is what you do is, you tell a good joke and the one what doesn't laugh . . . '

Sheena replenishes her glass. You only live once. Gav's favourite TV series, he told her once, is *True Blood*.

'Or you can scatter a packet of rice,' he goes on. 'All vampires suffer from OCD. They'll spend hours counting them, or rearranging them in neat columns.'

She sees herself folding clothes neatly, lining up the sleeves exactly. It wastes so much time. She reveals her upper teeth. 'So check me for fangs, darlin.'

He laughs his sweet little laugh. 'Pure dreaming, Sheena. I'd be so frickin lucky.' He flexes his fingers around an imaginary neck. 'Wait till the Romanians come. Then we'll be kept busy.'

Watching a late-night documentary about junior doctors, charged up and unable to sleep, she recognises something in the gaze of the male ones as their tutor dissects the cadaver, which is called Tom. It is Gavin's gaze as he kneels next to her equally naked body, his long slender fingers at work. You have to show a cadaver respect, it is explained. The gaze is a mixture of wonder, fear and outright bloody sadism. A surgeon's gaze. She's known one or two in her time.

She stirs her Horlicks and reads the poster in the kitchen for the first time – properly, that is. She can't recall where she got it from. It's gathered grease spots and acquired a ripple from the steam. Funny how your belongings come to mirror you, like your pets. *The happiest people do not have the best of everything, they make the best use of everything they have.* She does get lonely, of an evening. Her young beau breaks that. Never weekends, though. They now get through a couple of bottles of decent wine afterwards. He brings nuts from his foodstore, where he has an office, shared with only two other people. She opens her packet of fudge from the monastery out near Kirmond le Mire (present from Tony, the smarmy bugger), and the lad finishes it off methodically. 'I'd like to be a monk,' he says. 'Fudge and not being disturbed by stupid prats. Ever been to it?'

'Not on your nelly.'

'I'll drive you out there one day. Nice walks. A decent lake with swans.'

Sheena nods. What a terrible idea. Is Gavin the type to go on nice walks? Well I never.

'You know what,' he says one time. 'I didn't ever want promotion. I have six people under me, loads of responsibility. Less time for making the world a better place.'

'That's what my Tenerife hotel said. Please to reuse your towels. Make the world a better place.'

They are sprawled on the bed, his head like a concrete bollard in her lap. His hard-on is history, thanks to her attentions. The supply seems inexhaustible. Now the soldier is the size of a thumb. 'Tom Thumb,' she murmurs, flipping it up and down. 'It's all a question of blood,' he says, staring up at the ceiling. 'It's not muscle. How are your tofu boots?'

She laughs. 'My boots are very tasty,' she jokes, not wanting to think about Paul, who is frowning at her from above. Appalled Paul.

162

He throws his head back, pressing her belly down with the heaviness of his skull, and laughs most peculiarly, a sort of soft high-up howl.

Sometimes she wonders if he is on some type of drug. *Todo es posible*, as it also says in her kitchen. No, it's a drug called youth. The golden elixir. Sometimes irritatingly immature. 'You'd better be going,' she says. 'I am truly knackered.'

'Scented candles,' he calls up, descending the stairs in creaks to the front door. 'That would be useful. Frankincense or rose. There's a good place on Sincil Street.'

'What a kind thought,' she says. He's not brought a single thing so far, except a sprig of holly and some free nuts. He looks surprised. She folds her arms and squints down at him. 'And a bottle of red, why not? Go for it, Gavin.'

It's bloody cold out. There's a wind. Flat, desolate country. Bracing, some say. That's one way of putting it. The blasts of freezing air on the coast. The locals. Ah, the locals! Missing Lincs, as the joke goes. At least two decades behind the rest. But you can find your nest and keep cosy. Anywhere, really. She supposes her shop would find better soil in Chelsea or Notting Hill, but she'd be serving the wives of Russian oligarchs, the oppressed nannies of Qataris. The occasional real quality, Sloanies and dressed-down aristos. The toddlers would be just as sweet, presumably: impeccable Montessori spawn. Spoiling as they get older. Ruined by the age of eight. Dwarf masters and mistresses of the world.

She phoned Paul last night and he's invited her for an early herbal tea. She would rather a strong coffee, but she'll pull with the tide on this one. He sounded as if he was thinking about something else on the phone, and her heart sank. The fact is, she wants to find closure with Gavin (the whole thing

163

is mad and potentially quite dangerous vis-à-vis the clientele), but not without Paul in the wings. She's decided that he is chronically depressed and thus without initiative. She needs to provide the initiative.

As she passes On the Hob – pricey toasters with a mirror finish, retro 60s kettles, trad enamel bakeware – Hannah is hoovering and shouts something through the open door. Sheena pops her head in; they've not talked for days. The Hoover dies with a whine.

'Sheena! What's happened to you? You look fab!'

'In what way, precisely? My red nose? My blue ears?'

Hannah puts her free hand on her hips and appears to be assessing. 'I dunno, you just look really, really fab. Younger. You know, about twenty-five?'

'Exaggeration. Try harder.'

'OK, thirty-five. I'm thirty-six. You've got a really good colour? I mean, it's bloody January; most people look like walking corpses!'

That's what having an affair does to you, baby. Ask Shirley the hairdresser. She can spot it a mile off.

'What's all the green and gold for?'

'Australia Day! The 26th. This Thursday coming. I thought I'd give it another whirl. See these amusing porcelain ornaments? For the kitchen? What do you reckon, babe, honestly? A sly touch of humour?'

I'd rather be playing rugby.

'Knock me over with a feather.'

Paul has a cold. He's feeling sorry for himself. He's not got a good colour, not at all. He snuffles in the pantry at the back and says, 'I'm vulnerable to flu and stuff. My buggered spleen.'

'That's rotten,' says Sheena. What she really wants to say is, Notice me.

'I don't think it's flu, though. It feels like it, but I haven't got a temperature.'

'It's called man flu,' Sheena says. 'Women just have a simple cold and carry on. Woman flu. Ignored.'

'You're probably right. Rebecca used to say that.'

'Can I cheer you up with a Chinese? This weekend? I imagine Indian isn't your thing, outside India. Or there's good old-fashioned British at Peelers, in the High Street. A lemon sole to kill for. Warm bread rolls. Tomorrow evening?'

Paul blows his nose carefully, an operation Sheena does not concentrate on, pouting at her tea instead and scorching her lip.

'Can we make it next week? I'm feeling pretty poorly.'

Bloodless, that's what he is. But then he does have man flu. It's emphasised his eyebags, as colds do. Deep breath, Sheena doll. 'What happened to Rebecca, then?'

'Rebecca? Oh, she left. Ten years ago? Walked off with the plumber. An Israeli. Installing the new boiler. They run a surfboard rental business near wheresyerface. Tel Aviv. Interesting architecture.'

His eyes are on hers.

'Oh, I'll bet you mean Igal,' she says. 'Very good-looking but short. Like it's all in miniature. Except the necessaries, I suppose. Fantastic with leaks.'

He starts crying, can't help himself. He covers his eyes. No, he's not crying, he's chuckling. A bit like a growl because he's breathing in, not expelling – she might as well be tickling him on the tummy. 'Oh dear,' he says, wiping his eyes, 'I think that's done me good. Thanks. Sorry about that.'

She sips at her chamomile and feels a bit of a prat. 'At least he wasn't from Leigh-on-Sea.'

He looks up, puzzled. She goes for it.

'A randy young plumber from Leigh
Was plumbing a maid by the sea.
She said, "Stop your plumbing,
I hear someone coming . . ."
Said the plumber, still plumbing, "It's me!"'

He nods slowly, as if she's recited from the Book of Common Prayer. Probably a mistake. Bugger-it-all-up Sheena.

Blue Monday followed by Blue Tuesday. Already the third week of 2012 and it still sounds futuristic. February round the bloody corner, as if it can't wait. And then Fay appears in school uniform, albeit with her shirt hanging out. Apologises for being 'lippy'. Her fleeced coat looks even bulkier on her; she seems thinner, or Sheena has just forgotten. She is such a serious kid. 'Forgotten all about it,' Sheena says in the middle of checking a size. She thinks of what Mike said, but it all goes out of the window in front of the actual child. Because that's all Fay is: a child.

It's two thirty on Wednesday. 'School pack up early, did it, Fay? Another conflagration?' The girl looks shifty in her uniform, multicoloured backpack frayed at the corners. She's already taken off her coat, hanging it carefully on the hook in the pantry, and is folding the Kenzo rompers that some wild three-year-old strewed over the bench, 'helping' his proud mother. 'You know what, sweetheart? It's good to see you again. I have been wondering.'

'Wondering what, like?'

'Whether you'd ever pay me the privilege. Why don't you make us a cuppa?'

'I can stay for supper, if you want, after work.' Her emerald eyes are gleaming with hope.

Oh no. Not with Gavin coming, scented candles and all. Unless Gavin is cancelled. For 'security reasons' he's refused to give her his mobile number. If she's not in, he said, too bad; I'll go down to the pub. He's a little paranoid maybe, but she feels more secure that way. No texts to be discovered. No voice messages. Not that she's afraid of being found out. She's not breaking any regs, but the newspapers can make a scandal out of anything. 'A string of sex partners . . . running a toddlers' clothes shop . . . reputation in tatters . . . middle-aged curvaceous blonde . . . predatory baby-snatcher . . . school questioning its work-experience policy in the light of . . . an application of more robust safeguarding arrangements . . .'

'Sorry, hun, I prefer you to get the school bus,' she tells Fay, 'as it's a school day. I don't want trouble.' Fay nods, used to disappointment. She is picking golden hairs off a cloche hat of dark-green felt, the kind of task she enjoys: the whole shop, Sheena tells her, is a magnet for hairs and dustballs. Fay spends the afternoon religiously dealing with it.

When the girl goes off to the loo upstairs just after five, Sheena finds herself discreetly checking that the light fingers haven't been at work again. An old book is one thing, a Sonia Rykiel pink tulle dress with diamanté is something else. She does a quick visual sweep of the empty boutique, then attacks. The backpack – a well-worn Adidas sports bag, the zip awkward – is happily loaded with school textbooks and a pencil case, but no stolen items. It smells a little of cigarettes, but that might just be the ambient fug in the Ermine abode. Or maybe in the school, which (Sheena checked this too, when first contacted) has only just emerged from Ofsted Special Measures. She feels awful.

After ten minutes she wonders why Fay hasn't come down. Maybe she's checking in turn. Sheena feels a flush of panic, but why should she care if there's a trace of Gavin? She changed the sheets this morning. He only ever brings himself, wrapped in a long charcoal-black coat and dark grey scarf. You can't leave those behind by accident, not in her cream-orientated flat.

She hurries upstairs, her feet sore from the day's work, and finds Fay lying on the bed with a purring Mungo, a curtain of hair blending into the cat's head.

Sheena smiles. 'You two don't really get on very well, do you?' They both give her the same long look: green eyes, yellow eyes. Straight-faced. No sense of humour.

Two peas in a pod.

She's already tiddly on Scotch by the time Gavin turns up. Less than two hours before she had put on her big fur coat and walked Fay to the bus stop through the dusk's icy swirl. A few flakes whitening in the street lamps, the cobbled pavement a glistening limb-breaker, no salt in sight (council cuts). She felt guilty: hard and merciless. Love follows you, she said in her head. 'Come round whenever you want on Saturdays,' she told her, 'and weekdays if you're not bunking off school.' She pecked her on the crown and smelt Mungo in the red hair. 'Put your hood up, angel, you'll get earache.'

'I'm not a kid,' complained Fay.

Sheena felt a shudder rise through her – no, more a ripple, a spasm of maternal loss. It just never worked out, the whole kids angle. Time whipping past like the wind. Never the right man. And Paul just down the lane, sort of waiting. Lazy Sheena. Lazy, stupidly shy Sheena.

Then Fay, as if reading her mind, turned round and asked if she was seeing her 'bloke'. 'Eh?' 'That bloke who has the shoe shop. With the ponytail.'

'Could be,' Sheena replied, tightening her fur over her chest. 'But keep it secret.'

The girl, instead of grinning, glowered at her, her eyes aglow. A flake landed in her hair and instantly melted. The bus, by some miracle, was only ten minutes late. It growled towards them, all brightly lit like an aquarium, and carried her away into the night. In Sheena's hand was the crumpled fiver that she'd intended to stuff into Fay's mitt at the last minute. Bugger it. Next time.

And tomorrow's Australia Day. For which she has prepared nothing. Not a koala, hun.

7
MIKE

The month of the black ashbud is beginning as it means to go on: in misery mode. It's keeping dry, however, so he's lugging out the vintage trestle table, opening it with three practised jerks. Blowsy Sheena (local and typically uninventive nickname Lego-ver) is watching him from behind a cigarette in front of her overpriced kiddies' boutique bang opposite, with its bubblegum colours and bug-eyed cartoon cut-outs. The familiar dilemma: should he turn and greet her properly or just nod? What do you say when you cross someone's line of sight every day for years and years? The lane is narrow; you can smell her perfume under the nasty smoke: a proper street would have been easier. A cheery wave rather than a word.

Trouble is, they've fallen out. An unfortunate incident for which he's been unjustly blamed. It's *Gesellschaft* rather than *Gemeinschaft*. Her latest boyfriend is the ageing hippy who runs the shoe shop down the lane. Mike's spotted her struggling up the hill with him, pushing his wheelchair. Laughing. They do electric ones these days, but maybe the poor bloke likes the exercise. He presumes he's her boyfriend, or maybe she's just being kind. He doesn't probe.

171

He settles the trestle's metal legs to the right of the door, chocks of wood under the appropriate feet to counter the slope, and the board receives the usual: a battered pinewood box full of 50p bargains. The lure to get the attention, entice the unwary inside.

He notices the addition around midday. Slipped between *This Was My World* by Viscountess Rhondda (cracked spine repaired with gaffer tape) and *Making Floristry Your Business* (1947, badly bumped corners), the intruder is a familiar book. It provokes a racing of his heart. Only he knows why. And Sheena, annoyingly.

This has happened before: tyro poets product-placing their first pamphlet; spiral-bound notebooks of obscene and racist apophthegms, whatever. Always posted immediately into the pseudo-Edwardian street bin two doors up, like the apple cores, Magnum wrappers, dirty tissues or half-sucked boiled sweets with the sticking power of superglue. A used nappy once.

This one is different. It was originally – until yesterday – in the basement stock room, his overspill area. It was, in fact, concealed within the seventeen volumes of the complete and unsellable Works of Thomas Carlyle, like a stick in a forest. Between *Sartor Resartus* and *French Revolution 1*, to be precise. He didn't notice anyone descending to the basement, defying the NO ENTRY sign above the stairs.

Sheena has gone back inside. Mike is not into remonstration. He slips back into his lair. At closing time, in the sodium-shafted darkness of the lane, he humps the box and the trestle inside. He removes the intruder from the box, but instead of returning it to the basement, where the books are double-shelved, he slots it into the Animals, Pets section.

Hardback, good jacket, first edition, signed by the author, who stares out like a complete jerk, cuddling an enormous flop-eared dog.

£9.50.

After a few days he has almost forgotten about the book, until its bulk yawns open and grows enormous, a vicious black-and-white hound springing out from its pages. The bloodthirsty snarls wake him up. He makes a cup of Horlicks with a dusting of cinnamon and pads about his semi-detached labourer's cottage. As it's situated on a lonely road between Lincoln and Saxilby, he keeps the lights on. A house for two. Mum chose it in the wake of Dad's untimely death. Mike was fifteen. There was room for her loom, and she felt her teenage son needed the comfort of nature. Now that she's in the care home, it's all his except in name. Including the dusty loom. Plus her elderly cat, Mary-Shelley, with a slight drag to the hind legs.

And then, in the middle of a quiet Tuesday afternoon exactly a week later, his eyes slide carelessly towards the Animals, Pets shelf. A slight lean to the serried verticals because one of them is missing. An immoderate flash of shock in his chest, which is infuriating. He goes straight out to the bargain box and finds the stray placed on top of the others, flat and twitching, but the twitching is not of its own volition. A frost-charged easterly, straight from the North Sea's whitecaps, is also messing with his beard.

His best friend Alex, when told, goes back to Theory 1. Theory 2, which he's dismissed, is that Sheena Fleming is a practical joker. Theory 1 is that it's a customer. It's what customers do: finger and soil and leave. They do it to his electricals. He's forever tidying them up, reboxing, recoiling, rehanging. Alex, originally from Manchester, now in his forties, runs the legendary second-hand electrical store up a dank snicket halfway down the hill. Jug-eared, so thin he almost disappears from the side, he is permanently dressed in a white lab coat smeared with grease and oil. A man of solid sense.

They stand outside Chapter Seven, studying the box like real customers. Mike has the errant volume in his hand: on the slim side, octavo, 160 pages. The author's signature in emerald-green ink: pretentious. A minor TV celebrity, now forgotten, with long sideburns like hirsute caterpillars. It is open at 'First things first'. Socialise your puppy. You have until five months, after which it risks becoming a yob, barking like a maniac at everything that moves, crapping in front of shops – particularly bookshops. 'It's happened twice and it's all too carefully done,' Mike explains. 'Too deliberate. No one except me knew it was down in the hold.' He looks up suddenly: Sheena Fleming opposite, staring. Smug expression. Pathetic. He turns his back.

Alex wonders aloud if Mike isn't getting into a mither about nothing. 'You're sure you didn't put it there yourself? Sub-consciously. It's your kind of humour.'

'Alex, are you suggesting I've not got both oars in the water?'

His friend pulls a face. 'You just asked me that. Don't you remember?'

It's possible. The first signs of senescence, slight rubbing of the boards, mildew spots. Mike is fifty-five, the book is forty. Books last longer than people, though, or he'd be out of stock. Even the crummiest paperback.

Alex pulls out a mud-brown specimen with bowed covers and a tape-shadowed spine: *Plywoods: their development, manufacture and application* by Andrew Dick Wood. He bets Mike a trip to Fantasy Island that Wood's *Plywoods* will be sold within a year.

'I don't want to go to Skeggy and slip on vomit.'

'Fantasy Island's in Ingoldmells, not Skegness. It has extreme rides, Mike. It'll take you out of yourself. You need to find your inner child.'

'Haven't got one.'

Alex smiles. 'Worried someone'll actually buy this, then?'

'Part of the first job lot from Hemswell. When plywood was the latest thing. How about this instead?'

It's the *Blue Peter* annual for 1968. Jason and Petra in front of the ship. More dogs! Plus the cat, he can't remember the name. The puzzles have all been done in blue biro. Yellowed square of tape on the spine head, back strip part-detached, bottom spine-end missing. Nobody will ever want it. Alex nods. 'Done. See you on the Twister.' They shake on it.

Instead of returning the wanderer to the Animals, Pets section inside, Mike leaves it in the box, slotting it between a bilingual German-English number of *Welder's World* magazine (there are about twenty more in the basement, 50p for the lot) and the book about plywoods. Someone's about to make a nine-pound profit, but he no longer cares. He glances up: Sheena is a shadow in her window, watching him. He gives her a minimal wave. She doesn't wave back but turns away into that alien interior flocked by dwarf humans with super-size larynxes.

People do not flock to Mike's shop. There is a certain seepage from the outside world. He smells that outside world on the eddies of air that seep in with them: a faint whiff of fry-ups, with the occasional overspill from the rendering plant at Skellingthorpe. Mostly the same faces, over and over, accumulating the marks of age. Their medical histories, catheter and all. Their polite verbal pogroms of Poles, of chavs, of people saying 'duck' to each other. And their jokes. Rib-ticklers about bookworms, illiterates, low-flying combat aircraft, Poles, chavs, people saying 'duck' to each other. They don't buy anything and they expect you to laugh.

So the next alteration is less surprising. On Monday morning, after driving into town through a fresh and glittering world emerged from a Sunday of heavy showers – catkins on the hazels, crocuses and daffodils glowing on the verges, a peacock butterfly just missing the windscreen – he carries the box out and notices it has been rearranged, except that there never was any arrangement. Alphabetically, with Wood last, straight after *Welder's World* (no author, so by title). There, of course, is *Listening to Your Dog* by Cecil Bigstaff. It follows the opener, *A Laboratory Manual of Semi-Micro Inorganic Qualitative Analysis.* An error because Edward Arnold is the publisher and you shouldn't count the article, definite or indefinite. Reassuringly amateur. Smiling, he places it second to last, its author being one E.T. Thompson. The *Blue Peter* annual is in third position, being similarly authorless.

He can't remember how the box looked when he took it inside on Saturday. Not like this, though. This has a touch of reproof about it. Not quite the Dewey system, but a suggestion that he's a lazy sod compared, say, to bloody Oxfam.

He now begins to keep a proper eye out, but he is no surveillance camera. Alex offers an antique black-and-white model from 1984 for a fiver: 'Makes everyone look like a phantom.'

'Then what does it make real phantoms look like?'

'Oh, you'd just come out invisible, Mike.'

Maybe the culprit is a child. All children are half feral, but even most local urchins know their alphabet. He hasn't been one himself for about four decades. Or maybe he never was – despite the fading photos, despite what his mum would tell him when she still had her marbles. He's always suspected brats of nicking the odd book from the box, in the mistaken belief that they're making 50p.

A thin little ginger-haired rat scuttling about. The thought frightens him for some reason. It couldn't really be *her*, could it?

Or else it's someone with obsessive-compulsive disorder. Mike thought at one point many years ago that he was an OCD sufferer, but it was just the result of what he dubbed the categorisation complex. There are books that don't quite fit any shelving category, and he learnt not to care after days of agonising over a loopy personal memoir about the Avebury circle – Archaeology? Body, Mind, Spirit? Mathematics? Memoir? Mysteries? Nature? New Age? Parapsychology? Religion? He left it in Oxfam eventually, losing a potential £4.50 (bumping on the corners, tears, some foxing). He then vowed NOT TO CARE, and the shop began to take on its charming air of disorder, its reputation spreading to London via the snaking rails of the commuter line. 'All you need,' said Alex, 'is an integrated online presence. Then your London fans don't even need to trek out here.'

'Fix it,' said Mike to his astonished friend.

It took two years. It has made no difference: city folk like to breathe deep of the shop's scented mustiness, creak its planks, nod confidentially at the Beard, chuckle at the framed Lear poem, stand bowed over deckle-edged antiquarian tomes or some near-worthless Penguin paperback with a coffee ring on its green cover and feel they have been time-lapsed into a yesteryear when everything was solid, sensuous and real. They finger, gently and lovingly, the full set of the 1973 *Encyclopaedia Britannica*, the shelves groaning under its gravitas, while holding numberless if less sanctified *Britannicas* in that little casket in their pocket called a mobile phone.

Chapter Seven's distressed frontage is not affectation; it has stayed still while the rest of Totter Hill has moved on, the street's scrubbed period architecture frequently used for film shoots. The building's owner, from whom Mike has rented for over twenty years and who keeps the flat above (separate entrance) as his pied-à-terre, is too rich to bother with minor matters like upkeep. He resides in the British Virgin Islands, wherever they are, and comes back about once every three years to have his skin cancer dealt with. Mike likes it that way; the facial bush, which educated locals call Tennysonian, developed out of sheer neglect. 'You could always shave it off, go for a new, snappy young image on the website,' Alex advised. 'Do I see bird shit on your collar, by the by?'

> There was an old man with a beard,
> Who said, 'It is just as I feared! –
> Two owls and a hen, four larks and a wren,
> Have all built their nests in my beard!

Mid-week, the glorious spring sunshine enduring through occasional blustery attempts to extinguish it, he steps into the big outdoors and finds the box's contents rearranged in reverse order – beginning with Wood, ending with Bigstaff. He checks the latter for clues: inserted matter, scribbles, a sketch of a dog pissing on a book. A wry Post-it. Nothing. His hands tremble as he puts it back. He is seized with a desire to act. He has to take the wretched thing somewhere he isn't known. The charity shops all have CCTV cameras and go on red alert at his Ben Gunn look. Here's Mike the treasure hunter! These days, they are too canny. Oxfam's website dismays him. What's the point in going on?

'The point,' Alex reassured him in the pub, 'is the shop. Your shop. It has soul. It is human. Like mine. We are the last of a line.'

Meanwhile, someone is playing around with his head. By Friday the box has been rearranged by title. *Listening to Your Dog* is sandwiched between *Legacy of Kings* and *Meteorology for Glider Pilots*. He pretends to descend into the basement only to scamper up again abruptly, startling the customer whose guilt he wrongly suspected. This darkens his reputation for eccentricity even further.

Like a boy detective, Mike scatters flour on the spine and cover.

'What are you looking at my privates for, Mike?'

'I'm looking at your hands. Show me your hands.'

'From off your stock, friend.' Alex spreads his fingers wide. It is dust. Very unprofessional. 'You need an assistant.'

Having an assistant worked quite well for a few years. Students, gap-year types, unmoored graduates. Qualification: an affection for books. Motivation: preferring to wield a feather duster in the warm and dry to a broccoli-cutting knife in the cold and wet. He paid them a pittance on the understanding that their CVs would be boosted by 'trimming the sails on the *Marie Celeste*', as one Oxford-bound wag put it. These days he'd pay them nothing, for the same reason, and call it an internship instead of slavery. Anyway, Mike was able to nip out on errands without closing the shop, and the opening hours began to coincide with the type-written paradigm on the door. The dust diminished. The pan in the kitchenette below would be properly decrusted of porridge. Heavy boxes were shared and his back improved, even if it got no straighter. One of them even suggested using Coca-Cola to destain the loo bowl, which he thought was cheeky.

Another pair of eyes would definitely be useful, given the present circumstances. Sharper, younger, fleeter. He pictures a pair of wine-dark eyes, a sylph-like form behind the counter, and the dust banished. His own Eurydice. Could there be another one like her? She was recruited some four years back, for the summer. Her smile, her saffron cardie, her fresh loveliness threw back a curtain on the gloom and increased the number of male customers.

The light golden hair on her forearms. The wink of wet on her lips. The astonishing smoothness of her young skin. Mike almost started to believe in God, as he would on country walks or when reading his favourite passages from Shakespeare. For who else could create something so lovely? *And I'll go to bed at noon.* Chloe was drifting through a fine arts degree at the university proper and this merely added to her attractions, put Mike in mind of Botticelli (absurdly, since she knew very little about the great masters). He considered inviting her along on one of his fenland hikes, sharing his binos and conversing, pointing out the circling buzzards waiting to zoom in on a field mouse. Mike knew nothing of modern youth; she knew nothing of literature. Or birds. *If I could write the beauty of your eyes . . .* Then she graduated and was swallowed by Manchester.

He can't possibly stretch to an assistant these days, although it would be a welcome luxury. Internet orders mean an increase in wrapping and posting, activities which he loathes. Can young people wrap precious things in brown paper, impeccably, these days? One wonders. Work experience and unpaid interns are more trouble than they're worth. There'll never be another Chloe. Never. Missed the train on that one.

Monday, just before lunchtime. *Listening to Your Dog* is propped up against the window, the author grinning gormlessly out. It's ghostly pale from the flour, but he searches

180

in vain for fingerprints. It could have been any of the passers-by shadowing the many panes of the bay window. And there was him popping down to the basement too, several times.

Sheena is currently having a fag. It can't really be Shagger Sheena, can it? It can't be Lego-ver, surely? She looks at him as if concerned for his health. He decides to address her. They haven't spoken in months. Not since the incident in January. He scarcely has to raise his voice to be heard across the cobbles.

'Sheena, was someone here just now?'

Pause. The bastard has addressed me. 'What, you mean waiting?'

'Fiddling with my box. It's been going on all week.'

'I thought it was *meant* to be fiddled with.' She laughs, sending across a puff of magnolia scent mixed with tobacco. She's jollier these days. More irritating. Daft not to have spoken before. 'Just a bloke walking past. Something nicked again?'

'They didn't stop?'

'I've only been here a couple of minutes.' The cigarette pauses at her mouth. 'Mind you, 50p is 50p, I suppose. It all adds up.'

She can't have asked someone to do it, can she? One of her myriad lovers.

He slips back inside, flustered. Again he's made a fool of himself. The jingle of cap and bells. His mind is decided.

The cathedral's shop is in the crypt, its halogen spots glittering on all-glass cabinets and gleaming off pale pinewood display cases. He fails to locate the books at first among the glass and china ornaments, the pin cushions and key rings, the baskets full of fudge and the rolled-up fascimiles of Magna Carta: he is looking for spine-crammed shelves. Beyond, in the far corner, a few glossy volumes are facing out in a display case, as if online – no more than ten or so.

He places his volume casually on top of *The Legend of the Lincoln Imp*, hiding his action from the security cameras with his body. The new arrival could be misread as *Listening to Your God*, although the faded photo on the cover is a giveaway: that grinning oaf with the large sideburns in an awful sweater, hugging a hound. Well, he might be God, who knows? Why should God keep up with the times? Only mortals bother with such trivia.

No one approaches him. He is not seized by a uniform.

He ascends to the main concourse and parks himself in a pew. It is lunchtime, the service over, but he isn't hungry. He is ageing and useless and full of the wrong assumptions inside this shadowy majesty of limestone. William the Conqueror again, making sure we all feel cowed. My castle isn't quite enough, *mes chers*; they need divine reckoning too, those Anglo wimps. The nave looms high above him. He has not been here for at least two years. His fleshly life crouches as his spirit soars up to the gilded roof-bosses, the height shrinking them to fancy buttons, their patterns imperceptible without binoculars.

He keeps those for the birds. God's true miracles. On his way out through the minster garden he notices a robin on top of Tennyson's head.

He does feel a little smug the next day, with a curious confidence that God's house is the best sort of security. Even though he knows God is a figment of the universal imagination to keep the howling black emptiness of the universe at bay.

He humps out the trestle table and then the 50p box with a spring in his step. The early morning sun that glittered on dewy webs in the grass around the cottage is now, by lunchtime, actually warm. No one has seen anything like it. It's been a

182

week of blissful blue skies, perfect for the Red Arrows to scribble their smoke trails over, and it's only the end of March. 'Welcome to Florida!' cries a passing wag, face vaguely familiar as so many are. Totter Hill is not a suntrap, the buildings either side see to that, but at midday his patch is bathing in liquid gold. Hannah further down is showing her midriff again, scrubbing the cobbles in front of her shop, something he ought to do much more often.

He waves at Hannah, who looks surprised. He must make an effort to be more sociable. Sheena actually waved to him today. *I thought it was meant to be fiddled with.* Jezebel! Tits heaving, absurdly short skirt! He raised a hand coolly back. The sunshine's waking obscure corners in his obdurate soul. He should have opened a shop in Provence or Greece. There is a nurse at his mother's care home, a young Romanian woman with lampblack hair. It makes him think of Tennyson's *black ashbuds in the front of March.* Her name is Cosmina. He is quite sociable with her, it has to be said. At least he makes an effort. They only coincide when she's on the afternoon shift. He is old enough to be her father, but in her presence he feels more like her brother, or (better) cousin. She doesn't seem interested in books, however. Or maybe not in used books. Hateful term, like used tissues.

It is almost afternoon opening time, but Hannah is approaching, her neck swaddled in a bright-blue scarf purely for the look. She bears a takeaway coffee in a paper cup from Quickies, the unfortunately named sandwich place a few doors down. She does this every so often, but he's never grateful, not only because the coffee is foul (cheap and watery, tasting of its paper container), but because it puts him in her debt. 'For me? Hannah, thank you. Take a book from the box in return.'

He glances down, runs a quick, nervous eye over the battered spines. *Herself Surprised*; *Farmer's Glory*; *This Was My*

World; *Meet Me at Midnight* . . . Gone, gone! Safely down in the cathedral crypt like an entombed corpse! A graven martyr! Hannah is as over-grateful as she is overnice, flicking through the poor rejected souls as if it's Christmas: 'Oh, I so love second-hand bookshops, but I daren't enter or I'd have to be surgically removed!' She pulls out *Approach to the Ballet*, a seriously edgeworn hardback from the 1950s. 'Perfect. Thank you *so* much!' He wonders why it was ever in there: it's probably a collectable. He is trying to prise off the coffee's plastic lid without burning his fingers. 'You do ballet, then?'

'Cripes no, I was whizzy at it when I was six or something, but I'm far too fat these days.' Hannah only says this because she is slim and lovely, and knows it, apart from an attractive fleshiness to her belly. But Mike can't stand her teeth-grating presence for more than a few minutes. 'Hey,' Hannah goes on (as she always does), 'this is *perfect* for decor. The shop's. Casually leaning on the pepper-pot shelf. Awesome. Thank you *so* much.' He is still struggling with the lid, but the paper walls of the cup are too flexible. 'No,' says Hannah, touching his hand. 'It's got a sip lid – you sip it through that little hole.'

She meets his bewilderment with a shiny-eyed gaze over a pitying smile. If her chatter didn't test him beyond endurance, he would have fallen madly in love with her at first sight. She is as pleasant and smiley as his mum was, before her affliction, but the latter only talked sense.

How did his mum's affliction begin? 'I'll make us tea,' she'd say as he came in from work, only to find the tea cosy already harbouring a now tepid and over-brewed pot. 'Oh, silly me.'

'Never mind, Mum, join me in the ministry of the terminally vague, along with most of my customers.'

He sips through the hole in the lid, which is half off and therefore unstable, spilling a little of the contents. What he really wants is his favourite Samuel Johnson mug and the usual teaspoon of coffee granules boiled up in milk on the dented pan in the basement, stirred to a sepia creaminess and dusted with cinnamon, a little umber island in the middle like a spinning galaxy. That's how his day starts. If it doesn't start like that, the day is always hopeless.

She is looking up at the multi-paned, proto-Dickensian bay window, in which reside (at present) two of his favourite wares, displayed on wire easels: a signed morocco-bound slightly foxed Kipling and a rare edition of Wilkie Collins's *Basil: a Story of Modern Life*, one page of which is badly browned by a now skeletal pressed flower, the vegetal fragrance still detectable whenever Mike brings his nose to the cleft between the pages.

'Oh,' she cries, suddenly pointing, 'look at that simply *divine* doggy book. His wonderfully awful haircut and totally cheesy sweater!'

Mike follows the line of her slim finger, extended by a dark-purple and very sharp false nail. With a familiar electric flash from toes to scalp, he spots the addition at the back, like a ghoul in a group photo: that idiot with his sideburns, bouffant hairdo and Zappa moustache in a thick polo-neck sweater with diagonal stripes, crouched with an arm around the vast dog and gazing out, stupid and intense, with a hazy English field beyond. The book is leaning against the horizontal metal rod that Mike installed himself two decades back, a subtle separation of window display from the shop's bowels.

'Christ in Heaven,' he growls, to Hannah's surprise. He has spilt more coffee because his hand is trembling.

He leaves her clutching her ballet book on the pavement, the door jangling to a close. He stares at *Listening to Your Dog* as if it's a rucksack left on its own in a train station. Hannah is watching him through the grubby panes. He smiles dimly at her, raises his paper cup, then retreats to his cubbyhole where customers pay at an ancient mahogany desk. He has sticky liquid on his hand – he has to wipe it before touching any book, even that book. The box of tissues in the cubbyhole is empty. He groans, descends to the sink in the basement.

The trickle of water must have hidden the tinkle of the bell because the floorboards above are creaking. Unless the door hasn't been opened at all. He gazes up at the beams. Last night, in the deepest middle of it, he woke with two original lines of verse in his head. Idly, as if to dictation, he completed the fragment, from two lines to four over a Horlicks down in the kitchen, scribbled it all in his notepad and then went straight back to bed. This occasionally happens because Mike at one time wanted to be a poet more than anything else – encouraged by his mother, for whom, along with weaving, poetry was everything, especially the works of A. E. Housman. Of course he failed, failed himself and totally failed his poor mum. This morning he found the scribble and assigned the lines to memory, partly as a way to exercise the latter's battered powers.

> Will I leave my dreams and go,
> Or should I gather them to me now?
> Might you be there to greet me, so
> I know just where, and why, and how?

He finds himself repeating the lines down in the hold. He's in a mess. It will either be Hannah, wondering how he is, or a customer, the first of the afternoon, infuriatingly bang on opening time. Give me a break! He retrieves his coffee and mounts to the upper world. No sign of Hannah. Deborah Phipps, a loud-voiced retiree on the arts festival committee who likes her drink, looks up. 'Good gracious,

Michael, you never struck me as the takeaway type. Did I disturb you down there, in your secret takeaway hideaway? Spot the rhyme!'

The ribbed paper cup sits shamefacedly in his hand. It's a relief, for once, to see the dreadful woman.

'Sorry to disappoint, Deborah.'

'Do you still have the Solti biography? I've had breakfast with him on two occasions, both memorable.'

'You were only in here the day before yesterday. It's not greatly in demand.'

'Oh,' says Deborah through her signature snort, like a trumpet with a sock in it, 'do you keep tabs on us all? You should do OAP discounts, by the way.'

'You know my policy on discounts. Same with deposits.'

'I do indeed. '

The tall elderly lush disappears into the Music section at the back, huddled along with Fashion, Textiles, Psychology and so on in its own narrow niche, the L of the ancient floor plan. He is glad of her company, for the first time ever. Someone must have known exactly where to find the offending tome and brought it back from the cathedral shop. On the other hand, every one of his books sports a Chapter Seven slip, with the address and a tiny woodcut of his distressed frontage. He must have left it in by mistake: what a useless criminal he would be! Maybe it was left when he was on the loo before opening time: a helpful verger, popping in and not knowing what to do with it. He switches on the radio in the cubbyhole and drops the paper cup into the waste-paper basket; it seems to explode. He is slopping up the mess with loo roll, swearing under his breath, when Deborah emerges from the back.

'If you're doing so badly, Michael—'

187

'Who says I'm doing badly?'

'You should have filter coffee, wicker chairs, that sort of thing. Like that marvellous place in Much Wenlock. Philosophical and literary debates. I'll chair them.'

He straightens stiffly. 'I could just have customers who actually buy books,' he says, staring her down. She has the icy blue eyes of a death-camp guard. Deborah has a problem with money. With spending it.

'Oh, listen. I thought it was. Panufnik. I adore Panufnik. *Sinfonia Sacra.* "Hymn to the Virgin". The poor man's reputation just disappeared when he fled to England, having been numero uno in Soviet Poland. Can't you turn it up? It's hardly background music.'

He swivels the tranny's volume knob on a crackling blaze of static. Not just a bus shelter with books now, but a concert hall.

She unrolls a poster. 'Now, I'd be grateful if you'd do your bit for integration and put this up somewhere prominent.' BALTIC POETRY AND PANCAKES DAY. Last year's had been an unexpected and rip-roaring success: heaps of grilled sausages from Estonia, Latvian almond cakes shaped like pretzels and some equally delicious Lithuanian doughnuts. He sold a few books too.

'You ought to do one for Romania,' he says.

'One step at a time. Poland's in the wings, for next year.'

'Deborah, do you have a dog?'

'A lovely little cat called Robert. The poor thing has weak kidneys.'

'It's all the same,' Mike says. He removes *Listening to Your Dog* from the window and thrusts it at the woman, to her astonishment. 'It's an amazing work, a collectable, and I want you to have it. With my apologies.'

'Apologies for what?'

'For never having precisely the right book in stock. The book that you would actually buy. So I'm giving you one. I'd be incredibly happy if you'd accept.'

'I do believe,' said Deborah, glaring at him, 'you are taking the mick. And given that I am a regular customer . . .'

Mike is alone again with the last moments of the *Sinfonia Sacra*. He sits behind his desk in what Alex calls the Imperial Throne (carved baronial chair in honey-coloured oak, Victorian, picked up for a fiver long ago) and closes his eyes, drowning in the trumpets' final summons, their call to prayer and battle. Someone is playing a game. He hopes they are a stranger to him. He turns the radio down. *Listening to Your Dog* is still in his left hand. He expects it to twitch or turn rotten and send gangrene creeping up through his forearm as in an M.R. James story or some idiotic horror film.

He leaves the book on his desk in the cubbyhole. It's better visible, out in the open. He pictures himself driving down to Mablethorpe and hurling it into the sea. That's the answer! Add to the litter on the Lincolnshire coast! Or let it be taken by the currents to Siberia!

It'll come back. Like driftwood. Salt-swollen and cracked. Leaving a puddle on the old coir mat by the desk, with its barely legible WELCOME ABOARD, or on the new coir mat by the door (a gift from Alex: *It's NICE to be NICE*). Or it'll wait in a corner, crouched and growling, ready to give him a heart attack.

Tonight is care-home night. He tries to go two or three times a week and once at the weekend. He managed to jot down the personnel's shift rota for the months of March and April: the Romanian nurse called Cosmina will be there until ten this evening. If he coincides with her no more than twice in a week, it won't look too suspicious – too much

189

like courting. She also does night shifts and morning shifts, but they are hopeless for him.

He spots Sheena taking another cigarette break. She's started smoking again. Of course it's that pestilential woman from across the way. Who else could it be? She's three paces across the cobbles, the sloping lane is that narrow; she has a motive, vengeance. That half-feral girl did a bunk, possibly in distress, back in January. But he had nothing to do with it! Nip in, nip out. Coast clear. It's been going on exactly a week; it feels like months.

The girl's face taunts him from almost every shop in Lincoln, but the posters already seem overfamiliar. Some have been taken down, presumably as more details have emerged of the girl's home life, her truancy, her being caught shoplifting in a community supermarket on the day of her disappearance and 'a string' of similar offences, including petty drug-dealing on behalf of her renegade stepfather, initially arrested on suspicion of murder (another cock-up by the brainless boys in blue). No way was Chapter Seven about to display a MISSING poster. Pointless, anyway, given the light footfall. Sheena must have noticed that he wasn't displaying Fern, or Faith, or whatever her name was. Is. Teaching him a lesson.

He ought to have a word with the woman. No, better: he can give her the book. Fly the white flag and hand it over. Quits. It's so obvious it shrieks.

The next time she's having a fag, he steps over, the book tucked out of sight in a hessian bag. Her latest catch, Paul of the shoe shop, can't approve of the smoking. He's always been pretty uptight about clean living, would buy the odd cut-price tome about yoga or vegetarianism over the years. Now he's crippled, as you're banned from saying. That must be truly terrible, but Mike never knew him very well. He wasn't the chatty type. Maybe it was because Mike never bought the man's shoes. Overpriced and made out of fungus or something.

'Sheena, hi, how's things?'

Her eyes narrow abruptly under their blue-shaded lids. Her ample cleavage is braving the chill, for it is, as usual, uncovered. The woman's a tart!

She picks a shred of tobacco off her painted lip and tucks the hand under her other arm.

'I see you had that dragon to keep you busy first thing.'

'Deborah Phipps? Never buys a thing. She's all bluster. Comes in for the company. One of my best customers, as we say in the trade.'

'Bluster. That's a nice word,' she says reflectively. Not sardonically. Mike feels an unexpected twinge of affection for the harpy. Unbelievable!

'Here.' He produces the book from the bag. 'I want you to have this. It's been weighing on my conscience.'

She looks down at it but doesn't move a limb. Not a tremor of guilt. 'I don't have a dog.'

'It's not that. It's the book Fern tried to, um, remove. Faith, sorry.'

Sheena stares at him. 'It's the thought that counts. But you can give the book to Fay yourself.'

'Fay. That's it. She's not here,' he pointed out, discomfited by her stare. Of course it isn't Sheena. She's an adult. She's beyond such things.

'Oh, she'll be back. A bit wiser.' Sheena taps her forehead. 'I sense it. That she'll be back. No worries. I told her I was an ever-open door.'

Swing-door Sheena, Mike muses. Lincoln's very own Circe. No, Lady Audley. Jezebel, anyway. He can see Fay looking at him from the shop's interior. Maybe he should relent and put a poster up. Might make a difference.

191

What on earth was he becoming? Someone who believes in ghosts? But Fay isn't a ghost. As Sheena says, she'll be back, breathing and fully fleshed and ready to call him nasty names again.

'Let's hope so,' says Mike, giving up.

Sheena's large eyes are gleaming in the soft afternoon light. A watery sniff now. Oh, God.

Turning on his heel brusquely, as if fearful of contagion, he crosses the divide back into his own domain and slips *Listening to Your Dog* into its former place in the Animals, Pets section. With a furtive air, like a reverse shoplifter.

At the care home that evening, while Mum's having a nap, something unexpected occurs. Cosmina has a chat with him about Romania.

His heart does stuff that it's not used to: swelling and contracting, for instance. She is alone and lost, far from her family. He is alone and lost too, but in the land that he was born into. With a charming old cottage crying out for scenes of domestic bliss. Books, an open fire, a Rayburn (although he mostly uses the microwave). He has so much to offer her, and she has even more to offer him that can't be quantified. She likes going to rock concerts, there are big music festivals in her country which she never missed when she was living there, taking along her father. Nine Inch Nails, Above and Beyond. You escape yourself! He nods as if going to rock concerts is his favourite pastime.

From now on it will be. As it once was. After all, why are his ears so lousy? He was at university in Sheffield! Descending every week into the sticky-floored, acoustic jacuzzi of the Limit nightclub, squeezed between a chippie and a sweet shop, scouring his lugholes with the likes of Siouxsie and the Banshees or the Cramps. Mike Watkins, long black hair, jumping up and down like a madman. Over thirty years back. There's a lot people don't know. Cosmina has never heard of the Cramps. Or Siouxsie, for that matter.

He comes back home and makes his Horlicks and sits until two in the morning staring into the fire, Mary-Shelley purring on his lap. He can hear wedding bells. They ring for you. Chloe never fired his heart, only his imagination. Somehow, half of his bottle of Jameson slips down his throat, merely adding to the blue flames of unrequited love, his heart a Christmas pudding and applause all round. He could hire Cosmina's eyes to keep watch, but she has a full-time job and he can't afford to pay her anyway. Unless they were to marry and she became his business partner. We're all as one in Europe: he's looked it up, and in January 2014 – in less than two years – Romanians won't even have to have a work permit. They'll be a proper part of the family.

He chuckles inwardly, as if he's divided into two people. One romantic, one a total cynic. Then he harrumphs. Like a character out of Trollope. Your number's up, mate, once you start to harrumph. One obstacle to love is that he can't imagine a woman kissing him without a shiver of disgust. His own disgust. Imagine kissing himself! Ugh. What a thought. So how could anyone else do it? He's always thought this, ever since his first bout of acne at fifteen. Or maybe since his father died. Around the same period. Cosmina's exquisite face moving slowly towards his own, the bearded gargoyle. Maybe he has to begin loving the gargoyle. Start with the mirror. He holds his crystal glass up and looks into its bevelled flank. Ugh. Thank God for the beard.

The shop opens late, at eleven. No one seems to notice. The city isn't in crisis, full of wailing sirens, although some minor roadworks a few doors down get him wincing as the jackhammer starts. He could begin at eleven as a rule, stay up after the bewitching hour and sleep in. Or do an early spot of gardening to stop himself becoming a Lincolnshire lout. Prune the roses. The garden has not been at its best since Mum moved to the home.

His only buying customer is a gaunt young bloke in a charcoal-black coat who seems familiar, but Mike has no desire to chat. Spot on his nose, needs dealing with. Maybe a boil. The youth hangs about in front of the Animal, Pets shelf, so Mike keeps a wary eye. Eventually he's handed *Kitty Love*, to his surprise. Hardback. Stock photos of cute kittens, a pink bow adorning the fluffy feline on the cover. Present for a younger relative, presumably. Spine in good condition, pages clean.

'Call it two fifty.'

'Wow. Cut-price. Reverse inflation. Celebration time. Funny to think that raptors kill small cats. Like, we're all prey to something, even if we're predators ourselves. Mother Nature takes no hostages?'

Overcome with a flash flood of nausea, Mike tells him he has to make an urgent phone call. Give them an inch of rope, they'll hang you with boredom. 'Have the book on me.'

He picks up the phone and dials the home. It can always guarantee a few long minutes of medical detail. The young man turns to leave, trailing a strangely supercilious smile below a pair of eyes that look like the twin entrances of a railway tunnel. He opens the door and the jackhammer's urgent stutter grows a lot louder. 'Fuck off, roadworks!' He's grinning into the room.

Mum is very 'settled' today. Increased dosage, probably. *Listening to Your Dog* hasn't moved an inch.

He picks up a MISSING poster at the police station ('It all helps, sir') and pins it on his corkboard, next to Baltic Poetry and Pancakes Day.

Fay Sheenan looks directly at him. Now that's a coincidence: Sheena, Sheenan. Life can be stranger than fiction, mate. In fact, Fay's emerald-green eyes follow him *wherever he goes*. Even when he's at a sharp angle. Sliding round to the side. The toothy smile. The dapple of freckles on the nose. Disconcerting.

A temporary measure until things calm down.

He checks the Animals, Pets shelf regularly. No change! However, he has this strange sense now that the book is just a material object. Not all books are. Over the years, from time to time the bound and glued wodges of paper, board, card, leather and ink, nothing in themselves without a visiting intelligence, lifeless as stone, have all started shouting, bursting into a combined bedlam. Thank God it's only ever been a split-second awareness. All those impacted words, like the energy of the sun in coal. Mike's harem, Alex calls it. (He won't tell Cosmina that.) Mike suspects that Alex himself, however, has never had anyone, male or female. Not part of Lincoln's gay scene, nor any other scene. Sexless. Man-child. In love only with his gadgets, his machines, his screwdrivers. Mike doesn't probe.

Cosmina's afternoon shifts for March and April are on Sundays, Mondays and Tuesdays. A cluster. Otherwise he has to visit in the morning or over lunchtime, or impossibly late on Friday to catch her night shift. She has Saturdays off. Unless he changes his opening times or simply closes the shop on Thursdays (an unimaginable revolution), he won't see her before Sunday. He has to endure the desert sands between now and then.

Listening to Your Dog is grounded, it seems. So it *was* bloody Sheena, the tarty toerag. She's only come in here once, late last year, a few weeks before the brat did a bunk, and that was to shout at him from out of her fresh tan. The incident!

Admittedly he has never stepped over her threshold. Chalk and cheese. Paper and rain. Sometimes there's overspill from her fancy boutique in the form of upmarket mums looking for an 'original' Beatrix Potter, Dr Seuss, Tove Janssen, their offspring intent on hand-printing pages with slime and chocolate. 'They begin at £350,' he enjoys telling them. But then the mums have come straight from Mother Hubbard – whose name is pure irony.

A client in a grey blazer over a white T-shirt is browsing the Travel shelves today: probably a Londoner, judging by his red sneakers with zips up the side, his snazzy jeans, his handsome urban cool. He emerges from the Asia section with a big glossy hardback of photographs from Nepal, *The Land of Mystery*. What he really wants to look at is the Patrick Leigh Fermor in the window: a crisp first edition of *A Time to Keep Silence*. Mike reaches over the iron rod and plucks out the book. 'I quite like Fermor,' the customer says in a shy voice that no doubt serves to get people jumping about in some hip agency. 'Have you actually read this one?'

'An account of his stays in various monasteries. Spell-binding language, even if you dislike Catholicism as much as I do, which is a lot.' He snaps his mouth shut. Mike's five years among sadistic tonsured pederasts who liked to feel their frocks flap around their ankles is judiciously reburied.

The man starts to flick through the book. He pauses on a page and brings it closer to his face. '*It was a wonderful room to wake up in,*' he reads out loud. '*Dreamless nights came to an end with no harder shock than that of a boat's keel grounding on a lake shore.*'

'To be honest, most of it's as good,' says Mike.

The man looks up. His striking hazel eyes are shining. 'I'd like to live like that. I keep plugging away in bloody

Hammersmith and sleep very badly and wake up feeling shit. This book is talking to me. The first sentence I saw.'

'Bibliomancy,' says Mike. 'A type of divination. Opening a book at random to see what comes up. *Sortes Sanctorum*, if you use the Bible. The Romans used Virgil or Homer.'

The man slowly shakes his head. He is slightly stubbled.

'Bang the bongos, that's amazing.'

'Lovely first edition,' Mike continues. 'Still with its dust wrapper, almost no shelf wear. A spot of rubbing on the spine tips and corners, otherwise very clean. Demand is rising for Fermor.'

The bell tinkles. It's Alex. Mike would like to shoo him away. The sales pitch can't be interrupted, you have to keep the pressure lightly applied.

'How much again?'

'Two hundred. I'll let it go for a hundred and eighty but no lower.'

Snazzy jeans thinks about it, turning the pages less imperiously because it might be his at any moment. Mike finds his honeyish scent intrusive but pleasant, like an expensive cigar. The man's mobile is bound to go off, smashing the sale's delicate construction. *Sorry, I'll come back another time. Hello? Hello? Yes, it's me . . .*

Ingvar Lidholm's *Kontakion* on the radio. The right atmosphere. Alex is hovering in his lab coat and sticking-out ears looking as geeky as ever, holding two sherbert dips. Please, not now. Mike scowls at him, mouthing *Go away.*

'Yup, it's a deal. Oh, and I'll take this as well,' the man says, tapping a book that he has left on the table. Mike hadn't noticed. From the 50p box.

It's the 1968 *Blue Peter* annual with the yellowed tape on the spine head, half-detached back strip and all the puzzles done. Incredible. Mike, feeling generous, says he'll throw that one in.

He adds that if the local Lincolnshire poet, Lord Alfred Tennyson, is of any interest . . .? Or speaking of dogs, he's got a classic, signed by the author, Cliff Bigstaff. Sorry, Cecil. Cecil Bigstaff. Cecil Bigstaff himself. Do you have a dog, by any chance . . .?

Alex has gone, doubtless in a huff.

'Er, I'll take those three vols on Lincoln Cathedral too. How much?'

'They're scarce. We'll say a hundred.'

'Done. And the Nepal book. That's for my son. Gap year.'

'It'll take up most of his rucksack,' Mike quips, gratification bubbling in his chest.

The man is turning over its smooth pages: impossibly lofty mountains and impossibly ethnic locals in smudgy clouds of incense, stimulating reader inadequacy as much as inspiration, at least in Mike's case. Anxiety in the man's. 'Joey's going for six months,' he says. 'I am frankly shit scared. Earthquakes and avalanches.'

'Tell him it's a present from me.'

What's four pounds fifty? And it's one of those stupid super-wide formats that stick out of any shelf, however deep.

The man murmurs his thanks, sounding embarrassed. 'Hey, I'd love you to write in it. Just put *For Joey* and then your name. If that's OK? I've told him about this place,' he adds, glancing at the cuttings.

Happy Journeying, Mike scribbles after the lad's name. 'And I'm sure he'll be fine.'

Known as far as Hammersmith. That's a galaxy away.

Alone again, Mike turns to Fay and gives her a wink. Everything from now on is going to go very right. Sunday is only three days off. He scratches his voluminous facial growth, months thick. His lips are no longer visible. He seldom washes it, let alone grooms it. It is probably seething with its own indigenous life. He might as well own a poodle. He needs to move on.

On the way home he stops off at the new Romanian shop on the edge of town and buys a packet of spicy sausages, a six-pack of Kalnapilis beer and a jar of green walnut jam. The place smells exotically foreign.

That evening, after his delicious supper, he clips away at his beard until it is no longer eccentric. Neither is it hipsterish. His face seems to emerge, blinking, into the light. His mouth is liberated, lips fatter than he remembers. He uses it to sing along to a couple of tracks on *A Kiss in the Dreamhouse*. Incredible: he remembers most of the words. *Handcuffed in lace, blood and sperm / Swimming in poison . . .* The needle sticks and he thumps the bare floorboards outside the bathroom with his foot: it works. He feels twenty years old.

Apart from their pallid prisoner-in-a-dungeon tint, his overall looks are revealed as being acceptable. Why the Hell did he stick so long with that absurd accessory? That ridiculous backwoods mask? There is a pile of brindled curls on the bathroom floor sufficient to stuff a pillow.

'Michael,' he remembers his mum saying in her soft voice, when he came back with it from his first year doing English at Sheffield, 'don't you think you should shave more regularly? Or are you growing a fashionable beard? I'm not sure I like men with beards.' They were sitting having tea in the cottage garden. Fitful sunlight. He asked her what was wrong with bearded men. 'Oh,' she laughed, looking up at the hazy cirrus, her long weaver's fingers rippling in the air. 'That's a long story! You do whatever you want. Far be it from me to dictate.'

Later that summer, among the photo albums, he found a loose snapshot featuring his mother on a horse with a dark-bearded, thickset young man holding the bridle, in long boots and braces. *Me with Dan* was written on the back. A long story, no doubt.

She looked about nineteen, her hair black as night. She has no photos of herself as a child: she was taken in by Dr Barnardo's at the age of four. She believed her unknown mum was from Poplar. On leaving the orphanage, Janie Watkins remade herself. Mike has always marvelled at her indomitable courage, her capacity to look forward. Now he wonders if death wouldn't be kinder.

He's nervous of what Cosmina might say about his new look. But she isn't there on Sunday. His heart nosedives. She has emigrated back to Romania, claims Bronwen, one of the other nurses, whose fat smugness Mike finds as repellent as her body odour. 'Ooh, you've gone all pale.' She laughs. 'April fool! No, our Cosmina's got one of them so-called migraines,' she adds with an attempt at withering scorn. 'Did your beard fall off or what?'

The person who has taken up residence in his mother's head is more abusive than usual and calls him Magnus. It's because Cosmina isn't there.

'What's my own bloody name then, Magnus?'

'Janie. Janie Watkins. I can read you some Shelley?' She adored Shelley, once.

'Not on your nelly. Go fuck yourself, Magnus.'

It's as if Mum's early, mysterious years before the orphanage have erupted into the daylight, smelling of coal and gas and outdoor lavatories.

'Oh,' says Sheena, addressing him across the lane on Monday. 'Hello stranger. You look quite good,' she adds, with a note of surprise.

He mumbles some inanity and scurries back inside. You look quite good. They probably said the same to the Elephant Man when they put him in a suit.

The *Blue Peter* bet lost, and it being Good Friday, as suitable a day as any other for a painful and protracted death, Mike spends his windfall on the trip to Fantasy Island at Ingoldmells, with Alex driving calmly between the leafless hedges. The sun's out, but there is a thick frost clinging to the winter cabbages, the churned mud frozen in shock. 'It's getting warmer,' Alex reassures him. 'Spring is champing on the bit.'

He gets drenched on Log Flume, all but vomits on the Twister and thinks he is going to die on the Odyssey, hurtling and looping and corkscrewing through the sky at the equivalent of sixteen storeys up, an icy sea wind adding to the drama. He screams primally, to his dismay, when spun round very fast and upside down on Amazing Confusion. Alex's face, when he glances across to look, is an alien's, quivering like a blancmange. But Mike does get in touch with his inner child, just as promised – reliving the terror (thrashings from the holy brothers at St Bartholomew's, his Catholic grammar, their concomitant threats of Hellfire – Mum and Dad entirely ignorant). The humiliation, too. The ghastly fumblings. *I have been one acquainted with the night.*

'Robert Frost, Alex. A very suitable name. Can I go home now? Please?'

On the drive back, his gastric juices settling after the whirl-pool, he tells his friend the latest news (the book in the window, the poster, the hip poseur in snazzy jeans and zip-up sneakers), like someone recounting long-past battles from the comfort of his sitting room. He has not yet spoken of the original clash with Sheena, let alone of his brief encounter with the flame-haired runaway; Alex is always telling him to lighten up, tick the generosity box. He should have let the girl keep the bloody thing in the first place.

'I saw the poseur,' remarked Alex. 'You never noticed me. But then he was a handsome sod. By the way,' he went on quickly before Mike could expostulate, 'I'm not sure they'd have allowed you on the Odyssey with your old-style beard. Could've got caught in the machinery.'

Mike anticipates recounting it all to Cosmina, making her limpid blue eyes widen with wonder, but one of the inmates up the corridor chooses to die noisily surrounded by a gaggle of even noisier relatives and he hardly sees her. Mum scowls at the chocolate egg and six-pack of ginger ale (her favourite drink) that he's brought along; she doesn't open her mouth either to eat or talk. 'She won't touch anything fizzy,' Bronwen tells him with an air of intense satisfaction. The telly's showing some poor young milkman being offered a wad of cash if he'll do his round in a pink top hat and flowery apron, among other humiliations. *A Year in the Life* used to be one of Mum's favourite programmes, uncharacteristically, even when it deteriorated into total trash. Now she couldn't care less, ignoring the audience's shrieks and screams. He watches it vicariously: it reminds him of when Mum was hale. It belongs in an ancient tradition. Degradation and irreverence. Did Shakespeare watch the bear-baiting next door? Bound to have done, now and again.

He goes back home with the six-pack and makes himself a Gordon's gin buck. It's so oilily pleasant: the juniper mingling with the ginger, the lid of lemon knocking his upper lip, the overall alcohol level levelling his mind to a satisfying mush. He's survived. You need diversions from existence. An induced coma, for instance.

On Easter Sunday Mike with a headache instead of a rucksack walks twelve miles in the Wolds through a landscape of tender greys and ends up in an isolated pub he's never tried before, sipping timorously at a pint of Yella Belly Gold. If the advertised roaring open fire were more than a damp log smoking on embers, he'd feel sufficiently Lawrentian to find a meaning in life. But at least his head is full of nettled paths and lone churches, sweeps of early corn, knolls and dips of rough pasture against nothing but the sky swept by cirrus, as if the entire county is lying on a high Himalayan plateau. A pair of circling buzzards, a sparrowhawk, loads of crows, spirals of noisy rooks, the usual. His calves brushing early cow parsley beside the thickening woods. Fitful sunlight for an hour at midday, a bit of mizzle, then both again at three, the weather with no idea what it's up to. Nepal would be a good idea. Tibet even better.

The book – *the* book – stays put on the shelf. A synonym for the state of play with Cosmina. She is always busy, with a mere glance into Janie's room just to check. Short of staff. Maximum profit for the owners of Snowdrops Care Homes (who apparently live in Ibiza). Inmates ill or expiring just at the wrong moment. Cosmina has not noticed the loss of half his facial hair. He is not the centre of her universe. Not even a twinkle on the night's starr'd face. And then, two weeks later, the sun shafting dramatically through Turneresque skies charged with imminent storm, she has to take his mum's blood for some test or other, and she asks him to hold the brittle wrist as the needle probes the faint vein in the crook of his mother's arm amid the blotched and sagging folds.

'How is it called, what you feel with this?'

Mike feels slightly faint, watching the needle pierce the storm-coloured skin. 'A prick?'

'Yes, thank you. Just a little prick, Janie my sweetie.' The two of them are so close he is all but resting his lips in the cormorant plumage of her hair. His bare forearm – he's rolled up his shirtsleeves in the care home's hot fug – brushes her soft pale cheek. Mike's heart swells like an old leathery balloon become smooth and beautiful.

'You're a qualified nurse then?' he comments in what he considers an admiring tone.

'HCAs are allowed to do such simple things,' she says defensively, the syringe now almost full of his mother's crimson juice.

'HCA?'

'Healthcare assistant. Please, don't you worry for your mum. There we are, Janie. You didn't hurt one bit, did you?'

His mother glowers, mute for once, her toothless mouth a crumple of grievance. The dentures were hurled at the wall yesterday: he has to sort out the insurance.

'I wasn't worried at all,' he mutters, dismayed. 'Only admiring.'

Anyway, what use is he to her, to this sensual, passionate, slender young woman? Who could have been a film star or whatever, with those looks? And then, at the door, she turns and says, 'You are so lucky, Janie my darling, with having such a helpful son.' And gives him a brief but dazzling smile that he is too taken aback by to acknowledge, but which pitches him into the torment of adoration all over again.

He can't sleep. The announced storm is over the sea and closing in, the air full of electricity. His neat grey beard itches, more than before the crop. Why does she sound so mature? Is it a nurse's thing? She's young enough to be his daughter. Come on warmer, a voice murmurs in his ear as he's slipping into sleep, come on warmer. It brings him up short. It could be the first line of a poem: *Come on warmer, come on warmer, like a full brush upon the snowy paper.* Something like that. A brush full of burnt sienna. A loaded brush. A loaded brush upon the snowy page. He used to take watercolour lessons out in the Wolds, half the age of anyone else. She is his Muse. He smiles to himself. These things happen. Poetry curled in the dungeon of his soul, wakening to the light.

Sleep is instantaneous, and the keel slides up the shore of day with scarce a bump until a clap of thunder hauls him fully awake. The rain is released as from a series of Olympian buckets and after breakfast he has to run the few yards to the car. Alex, who enjoys such calculations, has measured thirty-three inches of precipitation by the evening. A cruelly wet and chilly April so far, and we're well over halfway through.

Every book in Chapter Seven is microscopically damper than at the beginning of the month. Sheena's *Daily Mail* hangs like a wet tongue out of her letter box. With luck it'll be unreadable, tear to soggy strips in her fingers.

The next visit, and there's no sign that he has occupied so much as a cupboard in the mysterious palace of Cosmina's mind.

'Sorry, Mr Watkins, do you know how you're fixing a puncture?'

He doesn't, not without a puncture kit. She knows a bike shop but that's back in Lincoln. At 10 p.m. he loads her bike in the back of the van and drives her home. They talk mainly about his mother. His heart is a tom-tom in a tangled jungle. Try to be polished, he tells himself. No, try to be cool. 'Do call me Mike, by the way.' Home is a shared house in Shakespeare Street, near the football club on what he tells her is the wrong side of the tracks. Shared with a female friend, thank God. At least she's well south of the Monks Road area, one of the poorest in Europe and with a population to match. He doesn't tell her that, of course. Too close to the immigrant bone. Although he might advise her to avoid the road at night. Scary-looking types. Alcoholic derelicts, addicts, the lot. Muggings galore. Welcome to England!

There's a late-opening pub two doors up. 'I'm parched. How about a drink, Cosmina? You deserve it.' It's all perfectly natural. Unless the tom-tom lets him down with the excitement and he has a coronary.

He strains to hear her, although they are seated opposite each other at a small table. The music, his lousy ears and the yowling clientele – mostly in their twenties – combine to render human intercourse almost impossible. What he does find out is that her father was brought up in the Jewish district of Bucharest, in a street where there were three synagogues and which is now a wasteland for cars to park on since Ceaușescu flattened the entire area in the late 1980s, wrought-iron balconies and all. 'Oh, sounds like any British city in the 1960s and 70s,' he comments. Her parents were rehoused in a new North Korean-style apartment block off what was then called the Boulevard of the Victory of Socialism. She is having to shout and he doesn't catch every word but is completely entranced. Mike feels by his second or maybe third pint that this is probably the best evening of his life, that he has spent too much of the latter scowling out at the world from behind a wall of decrepit reading matter. She drinks a couple of spritzers. The young male yowlers keep glancing at her. He's never felt so strong, so male, so young, so interesting. When she asks him about his childhood, he avoids telling her about the wicked monks or his father's protracted demise from a burst of shrapnel decades before. 'Basically, the most exciting thing you could hope for was a trip with your parents to the big shops in Sheffield. Redgates toyshop, Pauldens for everything, Saxone for shoes. Later, it was Violet Mays for records and Sexy Rexy for poly-ester shirts. What a name! The shirts stank when your sweat hit the synthetic cloth as you grooved about to your Hawkwind vinyl. La Favorita for coffee. The arcade, what was its name – Barney Goodman, that's it – for throwing your paper-round earnings away, then a matinee in the Classic Cinema. Oh, and the Old Blue Bell to get truly pissed in for the first time.' He goes on maybe too long. It's way past midnight. He scratches his chin and chuckles. 'Sorry, I get carried away. Nostalgia.' But it's one of his tape loops and he couldn't have stopped it, and she's nodding and smiling in a totally un-English way: no sourness, no contempt.

He drives very steadily and measuredly back to the cottage but still gets home in record time.

Well, I know the road blindfold, officer!

Mary-Shelley, waiting for him on the sofa, is not impressed. Her chin stays firmly on her paws, eyeing Mike with one large hawk-golden eye, the pupil retracted to a minimal and very wary vertical slit.

He did not lunge, in the end. She thanked him politely on the doorstep and vanished into the little terraced house like Eurydice into the Underworld, leaving him staring at the front door, its red paint chapped and peeled like the sunburnt skin of an adventurer.

You look quite good. He gives himself an inner thumbs-up.

He fishes out his own ancient bike from the basement – he uses it for local deliveries, part of the service – and pedals over to Shakespeare Street at lunchtime on Saturday between hesitant showers. He has a crisp Keats *Poems* (Everyman, of course) in a plastic lunch box in the pannier and a jar of Mum's last batch of home-made marmalade from 2008. His van would have given the wrong image, reminded Cosmina of the care home, that scrunch of gravel disturbing the eerie calm. He waits ten minutes at the level crossing for two goods trains of inordinate length, thus doubling his journey time. His plastic cape crackles around him and appears to have a leak.

She's not in. Why should she be? She has Saturdays off. She gets out and about. He should have phoned.

The rest of the weekend is a literal washout. An East Midlands monsoon. Even the primroses on his lawn look grey. On Sunday afternoon he stubbornly walks several miles through it, his face soggy again with wet. Some of this wet may, for all he knows, be self-supplied and salty. Sunday supper is a packet lasagne for one, scalding from the microwave. He sits in the shop on Monday and frowns at people. Both of them, to be precise. He's behind with his website orders. People who order by Internet are lazy sods. By the end of the morning he feels he's sitting on a thistle.

Fay looks on with that smile twisting into a smirk. She approves. There are knotty oak beams behind her head. Of course, the snap would have been taken in Sheena's place. The brat really bothers him; she seems to be eyeing his every move. Yet she's on his side now. In collusion! His unpaid assistant! Work experience! The book has ceased its peripatetic life, staying put for weeks, happy in the menagerie of the Animals, Pets section. This makes it worse, because he's actually grateful. He could take the poster down. But he doesn't dare. Not because he's afraid of Sheena, but of the possibility that she might not have been the culprit, after all. Too earthbound. Never a trace of her sickly perfume, for instance. If he were to tell anyone else other than Alex, they'd put him into a clinic or keep him in the community on medication.

At the height of it, having read an article online about adolescent girls being unwitting poltergeists, he searched on the web for exorcists and found someone in Grantham calling herself a spirit rescuer, coaxing earthbound spirits 'back into the light'. Out of the gloom into the great outdoors. Ursula would be bringing along her grandmother, dead for ten years, and Archangel Raphael, guider of lost souls. The only spirit needing rescue, he decided, was his own.

Next to the poster, his clippings grace the corkboard like old blooms on a grave, illuminated by a shaft of sunlight for about twenty minutes on clear days. NEW BOOKSHOP FULL OF OLD CURIOSITIES. MIKE'S TAKING ON THE GIANTS. THE MUSTY SMELL OF SUCCESS. Their nasty paper is urinously tanned, crisp and curled at the edges; the colour photo in the Sunday magazine article of 2001 has not so much faded as fogged up: ECLECTIC AND CRAMMED WITH KNOWLEDGE: AND THAT'S JUST THE OWNER! He looks amazingly younger in his ungreyed and pre-crop brown beard, though wearing the same open plaid flannel shirt that still does duty, albeit now minus one button and frayed at the collar. He loathes being photographed or filmed: it shatters the vague illusion (as he once put it after a few pints with Alex and Alex's many friends) that he is not a freak of nature. '*You're* not a freak of nature, Mike,' they all chorused faux-sympathetically like nurses.

Nurses!

He gets up, unpins the clippings and carefully secretes them in a drawer. They feel as brittle as thin toast. That's a quiet revolution. The corkboard shows their absence as vague ghostly shapes, where dirt hasn't settled. He looks down and sees traces of egg on his cardigan. Rest-home egg. Mum likes being spoonfed, sometimes.

Spasms of showers after the weekend deluge, the street still gurgling with run-off, the box safely indoors. His second customer in the last hour, a silver-haired woman in slacks, unknown to him, leaves after half an hour's browse with only a cheery wave. A relief, as she kept pulling out the hardbacks with the tug of an arthritic finger on the top of the spine. Mike felt the damage in his nape. He's given up actually snapping at people these days. He's mellowed in his middle age. He feels a lot clearer without the cuttings.

Cosmina. The first Romanian he's ever met. Incredibly attractive name. Like Bathsheba. Bathsheba Everdene. Yes, there is always reading. He finds *Far from the Madding Crowd* on the Classic Fiction shelf. Murder and attempted suicide! Unwanted pregnancies! Miscarriage! Runaways! Thomas Hardy did not flinch. Fay is staring at him knowingly. Fanny Everdene, of course. God, kid, supposing you ran away because you were *with child*? Who knows what your ilk get up to? The stepfather, the drugs! (Heroin, apparently. Local swanky businessmen involved. Big-time farmers, even.) For Mike the local estates are far-off planets. He is deeply ignorant. He is poor old Boldwood, never Gabriel Oak.

He closes the cheap Penguin paperback and returns it to its place. Incredible that it should contain so much within its flimsy cover (light wear, creases like white hairs down the spine). Hidden now. Silent. Ready to erupt in the mind for three quid. Sometimes the thought of all those characters crouched between covers scares him. Thousands of them, when you think of it. Good and evil and in between. Unfathomably evil in certain cases. He's got five editions of *Macbeth*. He takes out the most precious, although it's unsellable: a single volume of a Shakespeare Collected: London, 1785.

There was a fire over Christmas in a manor house in Norfolk known to have a fine library, and he swooped, but other predators had got there first – the type that scour the obituaries then offer grieving relatives derisory sums for vast and marvellous collections, boxing-up included. He was left with the detritus. He cradles the ravaged *Macbeth* in his hand. Nothing left but the guts: namely, the undamaged text block, its spine like charred bark, the glue split by the heat, small patches of the sewn endbands exposed, while the leather covers and boards have gone completely, revealing undamaged marbled endpapers. Yet the words become more charged, somehow, looming out of this wreckage. *Come to my woman's breafts, And take my milk for gall, you murd'ring minifters, Wherever in your fightlefs fubftances You wait on nature's mifchief!* He buries his nose in it and breathes deeply: an incense of soot and rag paper, the trapped port-and-tobacco fug of a Georgian study with horsehair wigs and languid hounds. Or was the sweet port smell emanating from the ink? Ink made from gall nut, not breast milk!

210

Cosmina sometimes emits a whiff of perfume, when it's not overwhelmed by the care home's tang of bleach and other olfactory horrors.

Surfacing, Mike feels the present like an abdominal pain. Almost everything good has been thrown aside – horse-drawn waggons, dew ponds, hay stooks, folk remedies, small book-shops, flowering meadows, letterpress printing, looms. The list is endless. The villages of England used to be sleepy, grassy little places. Now they're metalled and scrubbed, sub-picturesque drive-thrus. They'll do the same to countries like Romania; they are already doing it to Poland. Intensify! Advance! Grow up, you ignorant peasants! Or starve!

Sightless substances. That's exactly what all these characters are. Just that. They exist, they outlive their authors, number-less and teeming, but they are invisible. He finds himself staring back at Fay. She goes on staring at him in turn, green-eyed and mocking. What if she's a sightless substance now? God forbid. But she's too garish for that, somehow. She's completely of our benighted present. So out of place in here, he can't bear it. Never read a book in her life. No. She wanted to, but he stopped her. Stopped her outright. Teaching her a moral lesson! Now he can almost hear her voice, shrill as a whistle. *Wanker!* It's a jingle hanging in his mind, a plucked stem of cleavers, a blackberry thorn, a kind of intimacy. A cheek, anyway.

And then, turning at the door and glaring at him as he went on remonstrating, 'Shut the fuck up, you piece of shit!'

A tongue on her. A tongue blistered by the poison of her upbringing. By the violence of gutter-level England. All out there, crouching, its thighs trembling, tattooed and drooling, only just held at bay on a straining leash.

Shut the fuck up, you piece of shit!

211

Now why should Sheena dictate to him what he displays in his shop? Deborah Phipps's poster for Baltic Poetry and Pancakes Day was about his limit. Where's his authority? Where's his pride? His sanity, even – believing the red-haired foul-mouthed little scrag had anything to do with that hip guy and the Fermor deal, like an ancestral hearth goddess . . . *O, that way madness lies! Let me shun that!*

Anyway, the big-chested harridan barely notices him these days, his clipped beard notwithstanding – buried as she is in her new mobile phone, sending texts to her boyfriend or googling or whatever. Hardly ever using his own bottom-of-the-range Nokia mobile, purchased merely to be available to the care home in emergencies, he finds all this messaging lark a mystery. But it makes life easier in the narrow street. Not wondering what to say, when or when not to greet.

Wa-anker!

Shut the fuck up, you piece of shit!

Whispered now, not screamed. Whispered is worse. Right in his ear. He springs from the chair, seizes the MISSING poster by the side and yanks it away, ripping it from its drawing pins, which hold fast. Scrunching it up in both hands. A new decisiveness. He will not be in thrall to some blowsy bloody slag of a shopkeeper, exhibiting her giant mammaries! Four corner shreds are all that's left. He removes the drawing pins with some difficulty and the shreds fall like confetti.

The scrunched paper ball sits in the waste-paper basket, a green eye still visible, watching him as if through a keyhole.

Wanker!

Oh, sod it.

He takes the basket out to the tiny yard at the back and tips its contents into the wheelie. He comes back feeling even clearer and bolder and glances at the Animals, Pets shelf. He glances again for confirmation.

A leaning aft of the neighbouring tomes. A crevice. A fissure. A crack that seems to enter his head, the kind of crack that the rain gets into and worsens, putting the whole structure into danger.

What's he to do? Search the whole shop? Didn't he check this morning? Or was that yesterday? Something is nibbling his neck like an over-affectionate Mary-Shelley. It's called fear.

The book is not in the 50p box, which is still inside, its contents arranged as they were before, by title. He feels an icy draught through the flush of panic. No sign of Sheena. Anyone could have come in while he was out in the yard. He trusts people. That's why the redhead brat so annoyed him, why he reacted as he did. She broke that trust. She didn't understand the rules. Steal from Tesco's or WH Smith's, fine, but not from struggling Mike's. Not from Chapter Seven, for Chrissake. It's all he's got. He reaches into the drawer for his emergency hip flask, rarely resorted to. His grandfather's originally, to screw courage to the sticking post in the mud of the trenches. A quick swig to calm the nerves. Noiseless, on tiptoes, the brandy circulates through him, quelling the cold, stoking the embers.

He slips the flask back as the bell jangles. Oh no, it's Derek Bintwell. Retired architect, desecrator of (among many others) Grimsby, Nottingham and King's Lynn, owner of the oldest cottage in Lincolnshire (a thatched jewel in the Wolds). The old man hobbles sweetly in with a dangerously wet umbrella. Mike usually cries, 'Ah, the Visigoths have arrived . . .' and Derek takes it on his stubbly chin with a smile. This time Mike cries, flushed with courage, 'Ah, Nicolae Ceauşescu has arrived!' and the joke doesn't work.

'I was intending to have a peep in your treasure chest,' Derek says in his quavery voice. 'The Tennyson. The wife's at the hairdresser's,' he adds conspiratorially, like someone conducting an affair. His wife is younger than him: a red-cheeked beaming bundle of knitwear called Claire. 'No rain damage? I was quite concerned. They're still pumping down by the Witham.'

This is a familiar ritual. A locked glass-fronted cupboard holds the first editions – Dickens, Thackeray, Hardy, Woolf et al., and Derek likes to finger them. Mike finds the key in his desk drawer and gives the cabinet's ancient door a little tug, shivering the spotted glass. He pulls out the precious volume by its slender spine: *Poems, Chiefly Lyrical*, with Tennyson's modest rather childlike signature crouched on the title page. The sumptuous deep-blue leather binding (Riviere, c.1950), each corner blossoming with embossed gilt, is cradled in Derek's arthritic fingers as he turns the pages. At £1,150 it is beyond the means of even a retired architect, but the man's eyes are as wide as ever, and one day he will crack.

'I can't see the print very well,' he moans. 'I do wish you'd get some proper lighting, Mike.'

Not quite this time, thinks Mike. The book is slipped back between the crisp *Bleak House* (damp staining to the board, significant spotting and handling marks) and *The Mill on the Floss* in three volumes (some wear to the spines and extremities, hinges tender, sunning on the cover). Both first editions, both a snip at £750. Mike leaves Derek to it and returns to his desk. The old man now has his withered head all but inside the cabinet; he's studying at close range the three rows of delicious spines, mostly in tooled and ribbed leather of every hue, from amber through copper to burnished ochre. He is audibly inhaling the complex fragrance of sweet tobacco and vanilla with its zest of coal smoke, when he says, 'Now what in Heaven is so special about this one, Mike? A crummy-looking tome.'

He is holding up a familiar book. 'A pauper among kings, I'd say.'

The cabinet has not been unlocked for weeks.

'Oh, that,' says Mike. The heart is sending messages through the jungle again. Curiously, he wants to laugh. A hysterical giggle, more like. A high-pitched howl. 'It's a unique copy. Haven't found any others.'

'Curious.' Derek is flicking through. 'Looks like cheap rubbish to me.'

'Signed by the author.'

'So? Not exactly Henry James, is he?'

Mike blinks slowly, leaning back on the desk, heart curiously shifted to the top of his head. 'Cecil Bigstaff was a top member of the Illuminati. The clue is that striped polo-neck sweater. Those in the know would leap at that book. It's got messages in code. About the future, about the plans of the secret organisation that runs the world.'

'Mike, you're pulling my blasted leg. This utter crap's for the 50p box!'

In literary fiction of a certain sort and period, characters are given to sudden galvanised movements that wake up the soporific reader by the glowing fire as if an eight-pounder has been let off in the room. Mike does a perfect real-life imitation. Derek all but totters backwards as the book is snatched away.

'Who runs this shop? Who decides?'

'But, of course, I wasn't implying . . .'

Derek appears frightened, which does something strange to Mike. It stirs something furry inside his mind, like the abdomen of a hornet. He's smelling the helot's blood; he's breathing in short, sharp pants; he's spotting the twitches of terror on the flanks of an old and weakening zebra. He leaps, he sinks his teeth into that rusk of a neck. 'Ah, the 50p box, Derek. Yes. Everything for the 50p box. Utter crap like Gothic churches, Georgian squares, Victorian warehouses, ancient ginnels or bay-windowed shops like mine.'

'Pardon?'

'All flattened on the orders of the Emperor Nicolae Bintwell. Swing low, sweet demolition ball. Pulverised for pieces of shit shut-the-fuck-up concrete. For boulevards the size of motorways. For ring roads and their attendant pedestrian underpasses. Or should that be underpisses?'

As Derek backs away to the door and opens it, Mike raises his voice. 'For dickhead shopping plazas, office blocks, multi-boring car parks. Derby, Leicester, Grimsby, Nottingham, ye-es, all for the 50p box! Not forgetting poor old Wolvo!' He stands on his threshold with his hand cupped around his mouth, shouting down the lane at the old man's retreating back. 'Remember the Black Boy Hotel? You were there, Derek, yelling, *Utter crap, all for the 50p box!* . . . Thank you, Derek! Thank you for your regular custom! *Wa-anker!*'

He's dancing on his toes like Basil Fawlty, entranced by the manic fiddle of his rage.

The man in question has vanished round the corner on his arthritic legs, moving faster than he's done for years – downhill, of course, which is more dangerous. The odd passer-by stops and backs away, thinking perhaps it's a terrorist attack, but the others plough on, a few so deep into their mobiles they haven't even noticed: he might just as well have been wielding an axe. Oh, it feels so *good.*

It feels so good to have courage! To go over the top!

Sheena is watching from her shop door. Kids behind her, anxious mothers clasping them by the shoulders. Mike swivels and gives them all a vigorous double thumbs-up. A kid waves back. The slag frowns and goes back in, saying something to the mums. Call the cops! Mad Mike on the loose!

He pulls his own door to, turning OPEN to CLOSED. His legs are jelly. He has to sit down. A real lion wouldn't shiver after an attack; he'd just tear off another fleshy chunk from the still-living animal, brain hard-wired to survive and not to feel pity. Otherwise there'd be no lions left. No felines at all. No canines, for that matter. No dogs, no wolves, no jackals. Listen to your dog, listen to it properly, listen to its profound heart, its deepest thoughts, and you'd end up a serial killer.

He laughs, a brief yelp. The book has vanished again. He looks around without stirring from his chair. It was in his hand, definitely in this very hand; he must have dumped it somewhere. He'd like to tear it into shreds, into confetti, page by page. He'd like to marry Cosmina. Cosmina, Cosmina, Cosmina. The lion's mate. The lioness. She does all the hunting, isn't that right? In the real wild world? While the lion slumbers or eats his rival's cubs? Yum yum. The beautiful and noble king of the jungle, cracking the cubs' bones like Twiglets.

The phone rings. It's the home. The Spanish nurse, Esperanto or something. Mum's taken a turn. His chest lurches before the voice says, 'No in any immediate danger, Mr Watkins, but better we let you know. Your mum, he's a bit more confused. A'right?'

'I'm coming. Right away.'

Not quite right away. He rescues Fay's poster from the wheelie bin, slipping on the wet flags. And there, a layer deeper in the pungency, nestling on a banana skin, is *Listening to Your Dog*. He smooths the poster out but it stays badly creased and stained by a rotten tomato.

He stocks up with another quick swig and takes the stupid book with him. Mum would like the illustrations. By the time he arrives, she's recovered, swearing and glowering as of old. No one except Cosmina gives her the time of day, he's noticed.

217

And it's Cosmina's day off, which varies depending on needs (the home's, not hers).

The husband of the old dear next door is seated in the lounge with its rubber plants and washable easy chairs when Mike comes in with a coffee. The husband says, 'You'd think they'd give her somethink, wouldn't you? Your mum. Somethink like a sedative. To calm her down. It's not easy for Diane. My missus. All that swearing.'

'Mum'll be dead soon, don't you fret.'

'Oh, I didn't mean . . .'

Mike feels the power of being a nasty man. Insatiate. There are whole fields of wryness between grumpy and nasty. His brandy breath is a flame-thrower. But the man is so cockney-nice that the poor thing evidently feels guilt, continues to be pally after a brief pause. East End Jewish from his swarthy face and prominent nose. Mike's always had a soft spot for Jewishness. And for cockneys.

'That pleasant nurse, the Romany one, says you sell old books.'

'Did she?' She's been talking about him. 'Romanian, not Romany, by the way. Yes, I do.'

'Do you have back numbers of *Motor Sport*? The thing is, I used to be nuts about cars, threw all mine away. My magazines.'

'I don't, no.'

'A bit of an inventor, I was. Anything engineering-wise. That so-called collapsible steering column, first found on the Triumph Herald in 1959? It's in my file marked AUTO IDEAS at least five years earlier. What was I, fifteen? A flash of inspiration when fiddling with me old toy telescope, then working it all out by crouching in the footwell of my maths teacher's Standard Eight. Which was replaced by the Herald, if you recall. I don't mean to be rude, but you could be old enough. A tube sheathing a solid bar, fixed by an adjustable Allen screw passing through to a nut on the other side. Genius! Name's Howard, by the way. Howie to me mates.'

Mike nods. His mind is being washed, laved by another's loneliness. It is relaxing. It makes him feel more normal. The voice continues.

'I can still smell them seats. Thermo-plastic fabric. Especially when she was parked in the sun for a bit: Tygan, wasn't it? Or Vinolene? Washable, resistant to all stains. The future is here! Yet the dash was still all hardwood veneer you'd polish up to show the grain. Get the chrome bezels on the dials shining. Craftsmanship, eh?'

'Pure craft.' Mike nods. 'All gone.'

'Well, that's the thing. And I was right up with the modern times. Worked for British Steel. Special Steels Division. Up the road. Jets. Big Rolls-Royce engines. Vulcan bombers. Thermonuclear capabilities, that's what kept us open when that handbag horror was laying waste. Do you know how many times she – the Vulcan, not Thatcher – had to refuel on the way to the Falklands? Have a guess, go on.'

'Fifty-one.'

Howard's face falls. 'Oh, come off it. Thirty-two.'

An uneasy silence. Then: 'I never understood why, with all that water to the east, they couldn't use that to fly over, like them Typhoons do now from Coningsby. Know what I mean?'

Ten minutes later Mike is back in his mum's room. He picks *Listening to Your Dog* off the blanket and offers it to her again. She takes the book and throws it at the wall. There it lies, splayed like a tent on the stained nylon carpet by the old Georgian tea table he insisted on bringing from home as a comforting reminder. Nurse Bronwen comes in with the trolley on its horribly squeaky wheels and picks up *Listening to Your*

Dog. 'Ooh, this looks fa-ascinating,' she says. 'Could I have a peep over my tea?'

'It's all yours,' Mike says. 'Keep it.'

'Not at all,' she replies. 'Wouldn't dream of it. You brought this along for Janie. I don't have dogs, anyway.'

'You could put some WD40 on your wheels. Unless it's part of the torture.'

'Eh?'

It sits on his passenger seat on the way back, demure and silent. Enjoying the drive, probably. In the way dogs do, muzzles catching the wind. He has to brake suddenly when a farm lorry takes the lane a touch bullishly and he wonders whether his own steering column is collapsible. Bye bye, Mike. A click of the fingers. Gone.

What will he do when Mum goes? Can't be long now. He's got to be present at the expiration, the final breath. He can't let her wander off into the shadows alone.

That's why he succumbed to a mobile phone. Day or night, he's told them. Day or night. The first sign of deterioration. OK? The first spot of mould. Contact me. I *have* to be there.

I have to be. I want her to go holding my hand. That's very important.

It might as well be the Arctic again. The blustery May Day sky throws down spiteful shards of rain between harsh sunlight that reveals every facial flaw in Lincoln's streets. We all look old, Mike thinks, in our thick scarves, while the young are mostly nowhere to be seen. Then he spots Cosmina bicycling past. She looks unbelievably foreign and glamorous: a grey-black fur jacket down to her midriff, leather sleeves and trousers with visible zips. This is probably normal in Romania, but here in Lincolnshire she still looks weird, especially on a bicycle. There goes the woman who changes the nappies of the woman who changed his own over a half-century ago. He stares after her like someone on drugs. He'll invite her for another drink. Meanwhile, he'll have a little warming top-up, solo, in the Adam and Eve.

The next morning he wakes up wondering where he is. Prison yard. Factory precinct. Snow blowing in. A goods entrance. The back of Littlewoods, now Primark. No, it's his own kitchen. His brain is smoked by 70cl of Talisker 10 (the empty bottle on its side) and preceding vodka shots in the pub, never mind the ales. He's worthless. Library remainder, heavy soiling and shelf wear, frayed and browned, beginning to separate at the spine. Pen underlining to pages throughout. Give myself away; 50p would be a rip-off.

How did he get back? The van is there, crookedly, one wheel on the front lawn. Automatic pilot. He's still emanating high-octane vapours at lunchtime.

The following day is beautifully, suddenly warm. *'Wel-come be thou, fair fresshe May,'* he cries, driving in briskly, no longer feeling on the edge of death. A new MISSING poster is in place; the old one was crumpled, tomato-stained and torn, impossible to restore. A little tiff, he's calling it. A little tiff with Fay. No hard feelings. All is forgiven, kiddo. He's opening up the shop each morning with only a minor ripple of anxiety. The book no longer moves, but for the last few days it has done so in his dreams. On his desk. In the window. Secreted on the shelves at the back. Philosophy. Or Gardening. Or Modern Fiction, buried in the phalanx of dog-eared Rushdies. Yesterday he woke up with the book in his hand, its slab of pages fading away as his real hand swung into view, empty. In reality, it is back on the Animals, Pets shelf. Home again among its own. Business is still quite brisk on the virtual realm. Computer orders keep him out of mischief. He is becoming screen-bleary, like an office clerk. Above all, he never wanted to work in an office.

The warmth lasts a day, before plunging back into unseasonable temperatures, although the sunlight lingers. Due to untrustworthy showers, the trestle table stays folded. He sits in the corner of the Short Straw with Alex after three full days of abstention, having imagined it continuing a year or the rest of his life.

'I'm thinking of moving to, I dunno, Tibet.'

Alex nods. 'About the only place you could upsize to from Lincolnshire.'

The next day Mike is humping flimsy cardboard boxes overladen with surprisingly crisp Victorian volumes mostly bound in gilt-stamped half calf, job lots from an auction, when the sky cracks open. As he struggles across the road, a gust drives the rain horizontal and into the back of the van, where two boxes remain. Sheena watches him from her threshold, impassively. They haven't exchanged a word since he lost it with Derek Bintwell. Maybe she's scared. Who cares? Hannah is still civil and Alan and Des merrily twiddle their fingers at him. He buys a quiche there now and again.

It helps to finger his rosary of Shakespeare quotes in repeated murmurings, with one in particular thumbed to smoothness: 'Love goes by haps; Some Cupid kills with arrows, some with traps.' Perhaps people think he is talking on a mobile through earphones. No crazier than anyone else in the streets, these days.

He scans the shelves from his cubbyhole through the perpetual twilight of the shop: all these little histories, pleading to be turned into tarmac binder or snow pellets; to be transmogrified into something useful. 'The greatest university of all is a collection of books,' as Carlyle put it. What a pity he turned neo-fascist before fascism was even invented.

*   *   *

Mum has reached a plateau of near catalepsy, which the staff are relieved by and have probably encouraged with some chemical input. Only Cosmina seems to bother to talk to her as if to a person. The May timetable includes a 2 p.m. to 10 p.m. twice-weekly shift, so they coincide several times without effort. He sits by the bed and watches out of the corner of his eye those full lips move as she talks. It is enough to watch them move, that miracle of muscular effort, upper lip dancing with the lower, touching and not touching. He registers again how slender she is, maybe on the thin side. Clavicles clear under the smooth skin, like hard ripples of sand on the beach. He hopes she isn't anorexic. He is happy simply to worship silently, unnoticed. The drink and chat in the pub has made no difference: if anything, she is a little shyer with him. There is something deliciously agonising about all this. He'll wait a few more days, then suggest another outing. She's a gazelle, easily sent leaping away.

He does declare, clearing his throat, that if she wants to improve her English skills, he has some excellent language books in the shop. Cheap, second hand. Then he worries that he's insulted her, twice over. 'Your English is very good, of course.' Which makes things worse. And implying she is poor. But of course she is poor. Her country is very poor. Until Mum passes away, so is he. She says she hardly ever goes into the centre of Lincoln (he doesn't tell her of his sighting on Saltergate). He tells her about the website, although he hasn't updated the catalogue for weeks. 'We're in the twenty-first century,' he jokes. She shakes her head: her iPhone is smashed and the computer at home belongs to Anca, her flatmate, who protects it with a password.

'That's a bit selfish,' he remarks. 'Did you get cross with your iPhone?'

She's on the chemicals round, unflipping the lids on the plastic transparent pill-box. His mum meekly sticks her tongue out, waiting. The tongue is furred and white. One of those pills might be a heavy tranquilliser. When he remarked on Mum's calm the last time, fatso Bronwen said, with an unattractive raspberry noise, 'You should see her first thing in the morning. A right old rascal she is.' Which he considered unprofessional.

'No, it was broken by a car,' Cosmina says, placing a white pill on Mum's huge tongue. Who decided on the pills? Mike hovers with the follow-up glass of water. The tongue stays out, a slab of discoloured meat. Will the pill stay on?

'Broken by a car?'

'In it goes, Janie sweetie.'

The tongue vanishes. There is a struggle to swallow the ensuing water, which Mike is holding to the crumple of dry lips and tipping in, much of it dribbling from the corners of the mouth. One operation, and he's goofed. Cosmina is ready with the tissue and the kind words. Is she having him on about the iPhone? Or is it just her English? *Broken by a car.*

'Run over, you mean?'

'Exactly.'

She tells him calmly how she was knocked off her bike. He can't bear it: she might have been killed. The pills operation is over. He tells her she should wear a helmet. She doesn't respond. No Romanian wears a helmet, cycling. But European rules? His thoughts feel boring, as asexual as a flotilla of shiny desks in Brussels. He mentions the shop again but it sounds too insistent. Unthinkingly, perhaps, she parts her black velvet curtain of hair and shows him her ear for a few seconds, seconds that stretch forth into a nirvana of timelessness, as if he's floating far above the moment, looking down on the crusty, unbandaged wound and saying, in an echoey voice like

God's, how it will heal quickly. Despite the mess, he thinks the undamaged part is one of the most beautiful things he has ever seen. Pale and opalescent as the whorls of a seashell, like the dog whelks and periwinkles he would collect in Mablethorpe as a kid. Vaguely honeyish scent from her curls, her skin.

There was something so intimate about the gesture. Did Bathsheba ever do such a thing?

'I will definitely come for books on the nature, Mr Watkins,' she's saying, as she smooths out the coverlet and switches on the telly with an overwhelmingly attractive twist at the waist. He can't bear the telly blaring out, and now it's killed the moment, but his mother is half deaf. She ogles it uncomprehendingly, yet they think it does her good. The telly itself is hers, a small but bulky cathode-ray model from home. He reckons the object comforts her as much as the crap it shows. She has the electric bed-height control in her hand and is pointing it at the screen, jabbing the buttons. The staff took the batteries out long ago: they use a foot pump and manual lever to adjust the height and position. He was shown how.

The screen is now full of snow.

'Call me Mike,' he says, fiddling with the rabbit-ears aerial. He knows this telly well. 'Mike the TV repairer. We call this phenomenon *snow*, for obvious reasons. I like it. It's a relic of the Big Bang. The founding of the universe. What you're actually seeing here is fossil radiation, Cosmina, thirteen billion years old. The telly's struggling to turn it into an image. So I used to think that I could see the Big Bang itself. As a kid. Although we've changed the telly since then. It's not *that* old.' He turns round. She's dabbing his mother's brow with a wet wipe, but is she listening to him?

She looks up. 'In our country we say, Oh, look, the TV has fleas! Again!'

225

Mike finds this genuinely funny, mainly because she became, in a brilliant flash, a comic elderly Romanian frustrated by her country's endless hassles. She is clearly gifted, highly intelligent, with a wonderful sense of humour. An actress! Maybe a dancer, with that lithe waist! He feels he has broken through to new territory, as golden with possibilities as his heart is right now. Then, as if swept forward by the impetus of this breakthrough, he says he knows someone who can mend anything, anything at all. 'Let me try him with your broken phone,' he says. 'He's a good friend. Name's Alex. He has a workshop on Totter Hill. Name of my hill. Nothing to do with tottering.'

A few minutes later he has the gadget in his hand, its screen a starburst, unlit and (apparently) unlightable, the case behind cracked. She has left it with him. She has held this white object many times in her moist palm, held it up to the beautiful shell of her ear, brushed it with the soft pulp of her lips. The TV's game-show inanities are pin-sharp now but swirling about his ankles like waste matter: everything belonging to his old life. This is the first moment of the new universe. 'What a load of rubbish,' says Mum in an apparent moment of clear judgement. It's *A Year in the Life* again, once her favourite programme. A repeat. But her head's on one side, pressed into the pillow, and she's looking out of the window at the garden, the dusk revealing her own reflection floating in between like a moon in water.

As his favourite philosopher wrote, 'You always kill yourself too late.'

Children are the number-one enemy, damp is number two, customers in general come in at three, especially when their mobiles go off. Mike shows the iPhone to Alex in his workshop. Sitting in his shirtsleeves crouched over flexible tubes, electrical bits and two halves of an old-fashioned red-and-cream vacuum cleaner of the sausage-dog type, Alex has an eyepiece screwed into one eye, like a watchmaker, and a tiny screwdriver in his hand. He doesn't look up but says in a cod-American voice, 'Nothing sucks like an Electrolux. Forty years old and still sucking strong.'

'How did you know it was me?'

'The tread. A waft of old books and tired shirt. Very tired shirt.'

'Clothes bore me.'

'Snap. But I do buy new ones now and again. And iron them. It's great when you get the hang.'

There are two reactions to the iPhone: the first, what the heck is the man who still thinks offset printing is newfangled doing with the future at his fingertips, and the second; youch, this particular future is now the past.

'Seriously?'

'Unless one of the art students at the uni can recycle it as a degree-winning piece of found sculpture. Title: *Child Miner, Congo.*'

'What to do?'

'I presume you, or the rightful owner, got in a right strop with Apple and stamped on it repeatedly.'

'Run over.'

'Nice one. HGV in this case. Whose is it?'

'Can the contents be saved?'

Alex laughs. 'Mike, we call it data. All depends on whether she did a back-up. If she didn't, start from zero and get a replacement phone. A bottom-range smartphone won't cost you much.'

'How do you know the owner's a she?'

'Dearie me, the blush has still not died. And I don't think it's your mum's, somehow.'

Mum pulling and pushing the exact same model of vacuum cleaner and saying, *It's never done.* His childhood. Jesus wept.

'Still going strong,' Mike comments drily, patting the handle, 'but, um, kaput.'

'A minor hiccup on the circuit board. No built-in obsolescence in the 1960s. The engineers were in charge, not the accountants. Professional pride. I can make even modern bobbins, made to last a couple of years in obedience to the profit motive, last thirty. I'm a danger to the entire liberal-capitalist enterprise, cock.'

Mike nods. 'As someone who believes the greatest catastrophe in human history was the Industrial Revolution, I can but wish you good fortune, friend.'

'Is that Shakespeare, then?'

After a lot of incomprehensible patter in the downtown phone shop, Mike walks out over £500 poorer, which is a shock but he'll ride it. This is the golden ring. He walks down the street feeling twenty years younger, virile and in love, Pierre to Cosmina's Natasha. A swift screeches overhead, having spent the winter above the Congo. Now there's a subject he could enthral her with: the miracle of swifts. Perhaps they nest in Romania as well as here. The lazier ones.

All she has to do is activate the new phone. He'll write a little note to explain, slip it in.

He wraps up the clean white box in his special Shakespeare wrapping paper and feels solemn, almost holy. His chest expands with pride. These are unknown sensations. He's never been very good with gifts, let alone technology.

He takes the iPhone to the home on the following Sunday, when he knows she's on night shift and they'll not coincide. She'll find it, press it to her heart, and the next time he'll invite her for a coffee near the cathedral . . . He places the jiffy marked *FOR COSMINA*, double underlined, carefully on the claw-footed table. His mother can't remember who Cosmina is.

The book has stayed put, meanwhile. The new MISSING poster! The only incident during the last week was a gust of wind barrelling down the lane that sucked open and then slammed shut the front door, cracking a pane and sending his yellowed typewritten notices tumbling onto the mat: DO PARK RIGHT IN FRONT OF THE WINDOW AS WE LOVE THE DARK . . . COMPLETE SET OF DICKENS NEEDS TO FIND LOVING OWNER WITH DECENT LIFE EXPECTANCY . . . The wind came out of nowhere. Nothing between him and the North Sea but fields the size of Lichtenstein, the steep and narrow lane like a chute, a funnel. It all but gave him a coronary.

The fact is, as he explained to a long-suffering Alex one day, he's relieved the book is not moving, but the anticipation of the contrary is killing. First thing each morning he unlocks and shoves open the door and glances straight away at the precise spot on the Animals, Pets shelf. Complacent, he's getting. It's building up and up. The suspense. *Listening to Your Dog* looks completely innocent, the one character you never suspect.

The drag is, he imagines that the slightly bumped condition of its front board has suddenly become a serious buckle, the inner spine cracked, the corners gnawed. As if someone – or something – has been handling the book clumsily. Or he discovers a serious, slightly discoloured water stain in the middle. Or, somehow the worst, he pulls it out and sees the cover photo faded by sun and the pages within dark and brittle. 'This was when?' asks Alex, frowning. 'No no, I imagine it. Because then I'll know that years and years have gone by, maybe as much as my lifespan, and I'll turn round and outside will be a dry wasteland.' Dust barrelling over the same old cobbles and flagstones but the houses deserted, their windows shattered, their roofs collapsed, and the only sign of life those wild, famished, big-toothed dogs, as large and as clever as wolves.

'Mike, you've been at that poetry again. Who's the one?'

'T. S. Eliot. Coming back late from the hyacinth garden, arms full and hair wet . . . And so on.'

How is he supposed to respond when she thanks him profusely for the phone, which she's bound to? *My pleasure entirely. What are you doing tonight?* As in the telly soaps? Sounds like verbal rape, almost. It's a dilemma.

Fay surveys the shop, meanwhile. Helping him out. It's a combined ops.

On Monday he expects a phone call. Nothing. All day nothing. He knows she's off tomorrow, when he's due to visit Mum in the evening, and that she's back on Wednesday from 6 a.m. to 2 p.m. Never before in the fuzz of his life has he bothered much about timetables, agendas. He'll close the shop and drive down to see Mum again for Wednesday lunchtime, whether Cosmina's called or not. Why should she call? She has yet to activate the iPhone, no doubt. But he's secretly disappointed. A crack. A fissure in his happiness.

Tuesday comes and Alex pops by in a daft *Ho Lee Chit* T-shirt. The weather has abruptly, without warning, over a matter of twenty-four hours, gone from bloody cold to summer hot. It is fairly bewildering. 'Fancy a pint, chuck? It's almost beer o'clock and I am beyond parched.' Mike tells him he is knackered, sleeping badly, has to visit Mum. 'Squeeze one in,' Alex suggests. 'Happy hour starts at six.' Then as Mike is locking up, feeling a quiet contentment at the thought of idling in the pub with his friend for an hour, the phone rings. He leaps on it with a pounding heart.

Alex has to pull out. Forgot a dentist's appointment. Suspected abscess. Already had to wait weeks. Squeezed me in at the end. Sorry!

Mike says not to worry. He's surprised at his own disappointment. He'll go anyway. He can already taste the ale . . . A quickie before hitting the road for Purgatory. Or Hell. Or Heaven, if Cosmina is there by some freak occurrence: you never know. He will hold his mum's chilly hand and read her some Housman. Of course, she won't remember what happened to the envelope. A microwaved tikka masala after. Everything in abeyance.

Strange, being trapped in one body, one mind. Who chose him to inhabit Mike Watkins? Pub thoughts. Lone-wolf musings. The Royal Society of Loners. What are days for? Ah, solving that question . . . He's sitting in a corner of the Short Straw, a pint of Black Sheep, a bowl of peanuts. The three tables in the yard are already taken. He dreads one of his customers snaring him in talk: how Kindle's great to take on holiday, how useful Amazon is and so much more efficient these days and the starred reviews really help and (naming some best-selling international feculence) how it's really gripping if you don't mind the writing. And so on and on. He refreshes his glass with half a Yella Belly Gold (he's driving, after all) and restocks on smoked almonds. He used to come here much more regularly. Brian Ashton's still propping up the corner of the bar as he would every night but Sunday, hardly talking, anything to get away from the wife. Ageing gracefully. Mike puts on his universal bonhomie accent, chipping the edges off his intellect. *Hello, Brian, a'right? A'right mate, yourself?* Forty going on sixty. There's always been one in every pub he's known. Stalwart. Hollow-legged. Silent.

Companionship.

He feels pleasantly floaty. He could always skip the home, nest down in this corner seat on a quiet Tuesday evening until closing time. Not even many students, thank God. Just sit here and anticipate tomorrow. Hoping Cosmina isn't rushed off her feet by the mean bastards who own the place. One of a chain. Snowdrops Care Homes. Snowdrops being winter flowers. Or very early spring. Better suited to a maternity home.

The beer's going down too fast. Some ales are like that. Hoppy and quite dry, quite light, this Yella Belly Gold. Not a lot to shout about, but slips down harmlessly enough. An edge of bitterness which he likes. He might manage another, drive very carefully. It only gets dark now around nine o'clock. He could do the road blindfold. An hour with Mum and he'll still be at home by dusk, have supper on the lawn. He feels a mild ripple of warm anticipation. Put on a Siouxsie vinyl just for the Hell of it. See if he can remember the lyrics. Usually Mendelssohn or Mozart when he comes in, but . . . He must have been the same person. Kohl around the eyes once or twice. Look at him now. The original old codger.

Everyone else seems to be studying their mobiles, thumbs whirring. iPhones probably. He went to a jazz concert at the arts centre recently and it was the same there. Coltrane ignored. He's never really taken to gadgets, but now he checks the Nokia, just in case. Turn for the worse, or worse. The latter would mean no more trips to the home. No Cosmina.

Nothing. At least he's remembered to charge the thing up.

The car's tucked into the tiny yard at the back of the shop. It's stopped raining and he should drain his glass and go. He sees her anorexic wrists above the blanket. He sees Cosmina's wrists too. Slender but pulsing with life. Tomorrow!

Things have a habit of turning out for the best, in the end. He's never seen this before but now he does, he really does. He's abruptly suffused with optimism, a wild love for his fellow creatures. The pub's filling. All these happy folk. In T-shirts and short sleeves, at last. Some in shorts. Heedless. Yap yap. Guffaw after guffaw. Too loud. Doesn't make you dread loneliness the less. Ending up like Brian there, a permanent fixture. The bar girl changes the music to non-music. Thrash and boom. Savage screaming. That's what his mum thought of Siouxsie, mind you. Even The Cure. It all comes round.

He has to keep suffused. Don't let that feeling go.

He took a walk on the beach near Mablethorpe day before yesterday, after leaving the iPhone in Mum's room. Strong wind. Such a strong wind, flicking the waves back so they whipped up into a froth. *O wild West Wind, thou breath of Autumn's being.* That was such a strong wind, Sunday. But it never goes anywhere. That's the point. You don't have to go anywhere. You can be taken by the moment. The wind clean on your face. The swirl and crash of the sea. Herring gulls. The odd dipper. Beyond windswept.

'Great book,' comes a voice.

Jarred out of his reverie, Mike squints up at the face, in silhouette against the window's blaze of westerly light.

'Cute kitties,' comes out of the silhouette. 'Every one a bundle of fun.'

Mike then remembers with a kind of inner seizure of dismay.

'Glad to be of service,' he says. Wasn't it for a younger relative? 'Mind if I . . . ?'

'No no, go ahead,' he says quickly. 'I have to be off somewhere.'

'Where?'

'Somewhere I'm late for.'

'I'm chill. As a cucumber on ice. Cheers.'

The youth sits down and raises his pint, and Mike has to respond by raising his and taking a generous mouthful to finish it quicker.

'Shit, they're playing The Prodigy. Can't get better. How's tricks and trade, Mike?'

'Brisk as ever.' He doesn't like that *Mike*. Intrusive.

'Name's Gavin, by the way. Blame me mum. You can't blame me dad because he's moved on to the real world. I was six. Coronary. Wham bang thank you, Sam.'

The eyes are still as black as Marmite, with the same glassy shine. 'Sorry to hear that. I was fifteen when mine . . . Very slow-moving war wound.' He gestures emptily. Stop the tape machine, pull the plug out of the socket.

'Have you altered your beard, Mike?'

'Oh, a little shaping.'

The lad doesn't smile, he frowns. 'Gotta look smart for your customers. Know how I started? Stock replenishment assistant at Asda. Now I'm a store manager up in the Ermine. Why do they call it the Ermine to rhyme with fine? Because it ain't. Scores high on the Multiple Deprivation Index. Like multiple injuries. Multiple sclerosis.'

'Right,' says Mike. 'I assumed you were in higher education.' *Or possibly the sixth form.*

'I am. Computer science at the college. Part time. Taking a break at present. Too much pressure.'

'Good to take a break now and again.' He looks at his watch.

'Crikey, is that the time?' laughs the youngster in a sort of falsetto.

Knowing, playful, everything a lark. One step ahead. He still has that big pimple on his nose. Otherwise what Mum would call a pretty boy. Now in a white shirt and collar, though, sleeves rolled up. Work outfit. He's placed his shiny black smartphone on the table between them. It reminds Mike of the white iPhone, and his chest flutters. 'You don't have to pretend,' the boy goes on. 'There's too much pretending. I always knew I was different. Well, I knew at fourteen. I've known for twelve years, like.'

Fourteen plus twelve . . . Twenty-four, twenty-six . . . Twenty-six! Mike reckoned the youth was barely out of his teens. There you go. You can't tell. He tries not to look at the pimple, or maybe boil, on the thin nose, pulling his gaze away to the middle distance, where the guffaws and gabble are thickening, competing with the heartbeat-infiltrating music. The intruder is leaning forward and goes on talking. 'I have six people under me, lots of responsibility. By the way, you're a sensitive, right?'

Mike nods mindlessly as he works at the last quarter of his pint, then registers the interrogative lilt of the last few words. 'A what, sorry?'

'A sensitive. That's why people like Sheena Fleming reckon you're an unknown factor, behind that beard. The old major beard, anyway. It's minor, now. Suits you better, to be honest.'

'Sheena Fleming? I don't care a toss what she thinks.' He regrets his defensive tone. Secretly, he feels he knows what she meant. Jesus, Sheena fancies him rotten.

'Mind you, the term *unknown factor* is a euphemism. I will not sink to her level and repeat the words she actually used. This was a few months back. January? A lot happened in January.'

Mike blinks. His chest is bubbling with stress. 'What did she say, then?'

'The Romanians are coming, however. Then stuff's really gonna happen. Ouch. Double ouch. And it's gonna happen for us sensitives especially. Dark and perilous. Really perilous.' He's off on a different register, now: probably *on* stuff, like half the county. Rotted out by heroin, if you listen to Alex. Certain big farmers, even. Posh retirees. All in on the game.

Mike, still seated, is gathering his coat prior to standing and scarpering when a hand is suddenly placed on his wrist. A chilly hand. Yet it's warm out. The hand leaves and its forefinger indicates a tattoo on the back of its owner's pale neck, where the nape emerges from the raven-black collar. A cross. A jagged cross. Lightning bolts. The skin looks scuffed in some way, this close up. A goth thing, no doubt. Or maybe something Nazi. The nastier edge of the disgruntled right. *I was sort of a goth once, long ago,* Mike wants to say. *It all goes past too fast.*

'They'll know what this means, yeah? The Romanians. I'll really have to be on my guard. But they'll be nervous too. Shadow kisser,' the boy adds, his eyes straying here and there as if already seeing an immigrant in every happy group, before they settle again on Mike like two shiny horseflies.

'I know a Romanian, a very nice and very bright Romanian, actually,' Mike protests quietly. He's blinking into the shadows of his own mind, bewildered by the brief touch of the hand on his, the way its cold instantly triggered heat, the heat rippling through his body and making his ears buzz. No, he thinks. No no no.

'Oh? Tell me more, man.'

The text comes through as he's unlocking the van squeezed into his stone-flagged yard. He's over an hour late. The lad got on to poltergeists, that was the trouble. Books thrown from shelves, plates flying about. He wouldn't reveal what Sheena had said. Perv, paedo, prat, you name it. A dangerous woman, Mike. Avoid her from now on. Don't even wave.

Poltergeists, green-eyed vampires with red hair, the undead.

Another pint to hear the boy out. It was like being confronted with your very worst fears. Macbeth and the witches. *And his eyes have all the seeming of a demon's that is dreaming.* A pint's worth of idiocy. He probably shouldn't have mentioned Cosmina by name, or where she worked. It was somehow wheedled out of him.

He fishes the buzzing mobile out of his jacket pocket with some difficulty. It's still new to him, after a couple of years. He got it in case of emergencies. 'You love your mum, don't you?' said Cosmina in that pub in Shakespeare Street. Why didn't he reply, 'I love you more. And even more than Shakespeare.'

The text is from the Spanish-or-whatever nurse again, the short one called Esmerelda, though here she signs it *Miss D'Cruz*. He stops to reread it. Take a grip. He's leaning on his van's dented wing. The English doesn't seem quite right. *I am very sad about informing you . . .*

A lurch.

He reads it again, just in case he's got it all wrong.

8
FAY

27 January 2012

Fay loves Pooch and Pooch loves her. Six years they've loved each other! Six years as last month! Someone had to run off his energy or the council would charge them for dog damage to the maisonette. Ken goes round to the butcher's looking for big bones and Pooch splinters them like they were sticks.

'Too bloody wild,' says Rochelle, wheezing. 'Look at that snarl. Them horrible yellow teeth. Fur all manky. Someone run him over I'd give 'em petrol money.'

'Born to be wi-ild!' Ken sings, rocking it over the toast, but he doesn't practise the guitar enough to be a star, like he said he was going to be. He hasn't been asked to play a session for months. After the White Heather damage he went back to working the street spot outside Smith's in Cornhill with more of his ancient Led Zep and Wishbone Ash numbers and stuff, and he was ace but then he goes and spends it all on a new set of strings or summat and what he calls 'essential refreshments' from the beer-off. Now and again he plays for Ermine East's Youth Dance Club, but for free.

Fay used to go along to the club sometimes, but she wasn't good enough. They are all well up themselves that side of the Ermine. Someone told her to stop being shy and she clobbered them, or tried to. Nowt to do with being shy! Would've helped to've had proper dance clobber. She even goes along one day to Caraway in Waterside just to look but them girls who are snoots and never skint, well, they all gid her a glare on account of her manky old coat and the shoes were costing twenty quid cheapest even though she did have that fifteen from Nan (God rest her) 'for your golden future' and so what if her top friend Evie goes to weekend dance cos you're spied on while you prance about in your leotards. 'I'd rather be doin nefin then. I'd rather be doin nefin,' she said to Evie during art class this morning and Evie laughed and said nefin's what you are. It was just bants, though.

And anyroad she has to look after Rochelle.

'Fay? Where are you? Come back to earth, duck. She does this, y'know,' Rochelle moans on, turning to Ken. 'A million miles away.'

'Are you reading me?' says Ken, pinching his nose.

'Him's never snarling, Mum. It's a smile.'

'What is? What're you rattling on about? Go and get on with whatever you're to be getting on with, Fay, only not under me frickin feet. Bless,' she adds, as she always does. She is superstitious. If she doesn't say it . . . Sometimes she grips Fay's head and gives it a slobbery kiss, with tears shining in her eyes.

Fay takes Pooch up for his training, bunking off afternoon school. It's Friday, who cares? She doesn't even care if she's excluded again. She's hardly slept, though. Last night her walls were flashed by blues and she thought it was the bizzies coming for Ken and she was ready to warn him, but then Rochelle met her on the landing and said it was over yon side, bab, summat up again with that mental family from Hull. A massive domestic, shrieks and shouts, lippy Gary from three doors up yelling and swearing out of his window at the lady coppers down below like they did on TV, just a big show-off, what a tosser, just gagging to get cuffed up or even tasered, which Ken said was like the most painful ache you can imagine. 'How do you know that, Ken?' 'Cos I know.'

They all went back to bed and she heard the bin men come round, then headbanger Heidi next door set off for her paper round on her squeaky bike, and then Heidi's dad heading off to his work at the scaffolding depot, and Pooch snoring. Morning school was so boring she felt ill and had a nap in maths and little Mr Davis had a go at her. Fuck off, Diglett! 'Yesterday was Australia Day. If the surface area of Australia is . . .' Frickin Australia. Who cares?

Today is Day 1.

The big field feels different because it is a weekday, Friday'n all. It's wet and slippery. The solicitors' car park is full of smart cars: at least three Audis. She throws sticks over and over but he just chews them up with his big teeth. He'll only get scraps for dinner. After an hour her voice is hoarse from shouting and she is angry with the dog. She tries to make him play dead by pressing him down but he twists round yelping and catches her on the ear with a fang. There is blood.

'Yer grufty Staffie mongrel!' she shouts.

She checks her ear. Just a messy bump on the top. A scratch. The cold wind makes it prickle, like nettle stings but worse.

The field is misty and too huge and there are people in a group watching her from the back of the solicitors'. It's too far away to see their faces so maybe they're just smoking. If she goes even further into the middle of the field she'll still be in sight, all alone and tiny. Not at school. They'll phone the filth because the bizzies are in league with solicitors, one came and gid a talk when she was in Year 6 at primary. He makes jokes that no one laughs at, then pats her on the head afterwards like Gary Glitter.

Nonce.

She leaves the field and goes to the playground instead, running some of the way so as she gets there in ten minutes flat. She throws sticks again but then some boys come in and she recognises them, they're from the year above. Bunking, like her, but she has a reason. She pulls her furry hood over her face and crouches down, stroking Pooch's stiff hairs at the neck, feeling the muscle. His fur smells manky from the wet, like Ken's socks mixed up with Rochelle's spit when she'd wipe stuff off your cheeks. The lads yell rubbish, but they are pathetic. They head off towards a smashed-up old warehouse in the distance, throwing metal stuff inside so it echoes. It is going to be a massive Asda or something.

She needs them frankfurters. That's what Uggie learnt on. Hot dogs. Sausages. Lincolnshire sausages, best in the world. Reward-focused training, the trainer called it. All animals need rewards, because passion's never enough on its own.

The foodstore has just had the discounts in, but she's only got 30p on her. The frankfurters are too much. The fancy Lincolnshire sausages are even more. There is loads of cheap Polish stuff, but Pooch'd throw up or a load worse. Pass away, even. She stares at the beef mince under its plastic film, like trapped blood-stained maggots. Lean beef mince. EXTRA 20% FREE. ONLY £5. VALID TILL 27 JAN 2012. That's today! Her heart is going quicker, out of excitement. Pooch needs a reward, that's all there is to it. Her ear hurts.

Nobbut does nowt for free. She sees herself in a shimmy sequin bodysuit, lights flashing, Pooch holding his paw up in a glittering gold collar, and Rochelle stuffed into a size 30 silver outfit down to her swollen ankles and never moaning. Even Ken wouldn't grumble at the telly, watching it.

Cashier service only, machines out of order. She turns her back on the surveillance camera. She's not done frankfurters before, the shelf is higher than normal. Pooch is watching her through the glass, jerking at the lead. She pays for some Wrigley's banana chuddy and is nearly at the door when the security hunk who looks like Seal puts an arm across.

'Hey, you should be in your school.'

He's a foreigner of course. PIOTR on his name badge. Polack or Latvi. Go back home.

'Me mum's disabled. I'm her carer.'

'That's make me cry. Look, my tears. Empty pockets, please.'

Reward-focused training, that's all you need. She tries to brush past him to get to Pooch, but the arm is solid steel, he's an eastern European android. His other hand clamps her shoulder. The second guard is behind her now, producing the frankfurters like a magic trick. Pooch is staring through the glass at the packet, not at her, with his tongue dripping. It would have worked, she knows it.

They are emptying out her coat, turning it inside out. Its fur is the same manky brown-grey as Pooch's.

'Your dog, is he? What's the name, my duck?'

He is a foreigner too.

'Uggie.'

'Ugly, more like,' chuckles a new bloke in a posho suit, smelling of aftershave. He has a girly voice and a zit on his nose and is phoning on his silver Samsung, like. Davos Man. But he isn't a foreigner. 'Deputy manager,' he says. 'Step this way, please.'

And we don't lift a finger, thinks Fay as her hands and then her legs begin to tremble and shake.

9
SHEENA

When the bell rasps a little early, she is on the loo and curses. She passes Mungo, still on the bed where Fay left him – head raised, ears cocked. She opens the front door to an absence: expecting him to be standing there in his usual huddle of black, it's as if she can see his phantom presence, blurring Mike's shop beyond. A movement to her right: he steps out of the gap between the boutique and the place to let next door.

'I found myself a crevice,' he says. 'Lincoln has a lot of crevices.'

'Don't need to know the gory details.' Once he is inside, along with a gust of refrigerated air, she looks him up and down. He's shivering, nose blue, the spot on it red. Schoolboy look. What is he, behind all the bluster? 'I was on the loo, Gav. And you are quite early. I'm concerned Mike opposite might spot you. He goes home late on occasion. He's what I call an unknown factor.'

'Like me.'

'Oh no, you've not got a beard.'

He raises the bag in his hand when they get upstairs, Mungo shooting off somewhere as usual. 'Got the scented candles.'

'And the wine?' 'Who said anything about wine? I mean, I pay the petrol to come here. You never shift your beautiful arse a single inch, like.'

She faces him. 'How old do you think I look?'

'Old enough,' he says, smirking. 'I don't like them too young.'

'Gavin, I don't think you've had anyone at all before me. Not properly.'

His face twitches. He looks about the room. 'Summat to stick 'em in? I should've bought block candles.' 'What's a block candle?' 'Thick ones that stand on their own.' 'You've a broad vocabulary, for your age.' He chortles. 'I'm a deputy store manager, remember?'

Sheena produces a couple of her Lanzarote volcanic rock candleholders. A bit of thrusting and turning, but they fit. He produces a lighter and the sitting room fills with what Sheena is told is frankincense, sweet as honey and sickly. It makes her boring Argentinian Malbec taste mulled. It makes her feel promiscuous. He looks at the stairs and asks what's up them.

'Spare room. Converted attic.'

'I want to do it up there,' he says. 'A change of scene.'

She climbs the winding stairs and turns on the radiator and the blanket. The room smells faintly of damp. She switches on the red-shaded lamp and kills the main light. Clever boy. Yes, she is excited, her breath coming short. The radiator is wheezing and tapping. What she didn't tell him is that her mum passed away up here. Nursed to the end. No way was Mum ever going to a home. Or a hospice. She could admire the roofs of lower Lincoln, the towers of the cathedral. Mum even sat in the shop now and again, quietly in a corner, before things got too bad. 'Why do folk keep stopping and taking pictures of the shop, dear? Are they planning a break-in?' 'It's because they are tourists, Mum. They love everything that's old, pretty and typically English.' 'Then why don't they take a picture of me?' A hoarse laugh. Heads turning, the tots looking scared and curious. 'Mum, keep your voice down, will you?' The happiest period of their relationship, weirdly. Four months in all.

He is peculiarly pressing that evening in bed, under the eaves, a chill draught finding the gaps in the sash windows. Hasty, almost violent. So much energy and force! So much appreciation! Were they too loud? She imagines squares of light popping into life up and down the hill, curious faces peering out as the howls increase beneath the clustered stars, swept bright by the easterly wind. Like a film, really.

He wanted to take a film of them in action, on his swanky Samsung. She downright refused. 'Oh yeah, and then download it for the world to see?'

'Who do you think I am?' he said, looking really cheesed. That's the point, Gavin. I don't really know who you are. But that's how I like it.

She is so exhausted that she dozes off next to him, both naked under the duvet, deliciously giving way to the urges of sleep.

She wakes up needing to do a pee, thinking it's near morning. Dare she look at her clock? 12.43 in luminous green. Frick me, as Fay would say. Strong moonlight, thin curtains. The hour you begin to question your life choices. The space beside her is empty. She likes this nest under the eaves, though there are watermarks on the plasterboard between the roof beams. The pantiles probably need checking, tidying up, a few cracked. Heritage area, so they'll be sending their drones over to check you've got it right. Only the most expensive materials, please, for all those millions studying the city from a helicopter. Hush, child.

He's presumably gone home, thoughtfully leaving her to recuperate. No wine needed. Who needs wine after that vintage crate of sex? What an adventure! A pity about Paul, though. Even when he has a cold, she likes being with him. Inexplicable. It must be love. Love, and not much lust. Paul Cannon.

She feels a touch lonely without the toyboy here.

Oh. His clothes are folded neatly on the chair, clear in the silver-blue moonlight. Now that's a funny thing about Gavin: a young feller who folds his clothes along the creases. His wallet and mobile on the little table under the dormer window. He must be downstairs, brooding or snacking or whatever. She grabs her knickers and sweater from the floor, pads over to the wallet, shivering. She cracks it open and there is a driving licence among other odds and sods. Gavin's photo makes him look like a schoolkid, which he was then: German tin-helmet cut, in fashion in the noughties. Every lad in Lincolnshire had one. He appears to be down in the dumps and is acne-riddled. The address is the Swinderby one. His mum's. His mum called Maureen. Hasn't bothered to change it. Or he fibbed and this is his present home address. Still living with Mummy. The licence confirms his age, at least. She doesn't probe further: receipts, a few fivers, credit and loyalty cards . . . she's not a snoop, nor a bloody detective.

His mobile. The swanky Samsung. She picks it up. It's like a drawer that you can't resist opening. She doesn't resist. She presses Camera. No pictures of her, no films. The photos slip by under her thumb. Selfies, as off-putting as selfies always are. His navel. His dick, unaroused. Oh my. An arty one of trees at night, lit by headlights. Oh. Sweet. Kittens! Sweet little big-eyed bundles of fur. Who'd have thought it? Roadkill, Christ. Some poor little beast run over. Now that's horrible. Arty Gavin. Bloody Hell, from several angles. An unhealthy interest. Her thumb is trembling. More selfies, showing his teeth in a snarl. She hears a sound from down below. She freezes at the table. That's not a Mungo sound.

248

She snaps the mobile shut, replaces it next to the wallet, creeps down the twisty stairs in bare feet. Only the penultimate step creaks and she avoids it, using the beamed walls either side for balance, alighting on her toes like a ballet dancer. The bedroom door is open a crack. The light spills from the frame into the dark sitting room, catching the sequins on the sofa cushions. No sign of Mungo. She hears a click, which could be a gun but is in fact the latch on her wardrobe door. She approaches the light, heart thumping even more vigorously, right out to her ears.

Peeping round the door jamb, all she can see is the reflection in the full-length mirror: Gavin is stood in her big fur coat, the dark-grey one. His reflected face is a bit wonky, which is normal. Just staring at himself, lips slightly pouting, arms dangling either side, the coat shrugged a little off the shoulders, one white thigh sexily protruding. He is starkers under the coat, that's clear, although the fur is covering what is likely to be an aroused dick. Below the hem of the coat, which comes to just above the knees, are a pair of stocky legs covered in swirls of black hair.

She'd have preferred a bit of a flounce, a prissiness, like the little overweight double-chinned girls in front of the shop mirror flouncing and preening in their striped party dresses. It's always tragic and pathetic – it makes Sheena want to cry – and then they march out scoffing their way through a mega-size packet of Monster Munch or whatever. Gavin's stare isn't tragic or pathetic; it's concentrated. He's not even fiddling with himself. It's as if the coat itself is normal. That even with the fur covering him, he's still naked. He's a narcissistic prat.

He turns, gives her a suggestive smile. No surprise, no shock.

'We can do it in this,' he says, unabashed. 'Have it away in this.' Bloody cheek.

249

'Where do you live, Gavin?'

'Eh?'

She repeats the question.

'I told you. Near the Dyke.'

'Swinderby, that's where you live.'

'That's where me mum lives, not me. Right?'

She will have to take the coat to the dry cleaner's. His armpits. Stale sex. Then she sees it: her dress crumpled on the bed. Her favourite dress: the deep-V silk wrap, marine blue, with the long sleeves. Diane von Furstenberg, for Pete's sake. In a sale but even so. Cost a fortune. She looks gorgeous in it. He folds his own carefully, couldn't care a toss about anyone else's. It's been tried on. Oh no.

His glance is furtive now. 'Snooping on me, then, were you?'

'Are you really a store manager?'

'No, I'm an alien. Believed me, didn't you?'

'Of course. I watch too many weird documentaries.' She sighs, worn out suddenly. 'An alien who lives with his mum in Swinderby.'

'Anything wrong with saving on rent and keeping a lonely old woman company?' He chuckles. 'Sounds familiar, does it?'

Her entire body is trembling. Men are shits. 'It was nice while it lasted. Hang that fucking dress properly, please, before you depart out of my life.'

She goes off to fiddle in the kitchen, rinsing the wine glasses, hands trembling dangerously. This is how things break. Still no sign of Mungo. Stuck outside or in some interior hiding place because the poor puss hates Gavin. A few creaks upstairs: he's back in the attic room.

She feels molested, as if he's put on her own skin. She can't help it. It's the way she is. She dons her dressing gown and waits.

He appears in the living room in his usual black outfit. She hands him his long coat and scarf, like a dresser. She feels so bloody tired. But she's glad: tomorrow is another dawn, clearer and simpler, albeit a Thursday. Paul will get over his man flu. Gavin will get over this. Back to his shelves, his responsibilities, his mum.

'Sheena—'

'Thank you. Please go.'

He stares at her with eyes that look hollow. Shit, they're kohl-smudged.

'It's for the best, Gavin. More for your sake than mine, mate.'

His face hardens, goes all knotty. Hit the spot, evidently. He nods slowly, adjusting his scarf, then makes for the stairs. On the top step he turns.

'Before I go away out of your life for ever and ever, can I just say a little word, kind of?'

'Not really.'

'It's my democratic right.'

'Go ahead, then. The very last word, please.'

He stands at the top of the stairs. He is being reasonable and mature, thank Christ. Two responsible adults. It'll be a clean break. 'The thing is, like, this has been a really interesting learning experience. I have got such a lot out of it. For instance, there was this bloke with white hair in the pub a few months ago, right, who was holding his pork pie prior to consuming it, and he remarked to me that shagging old women was like eating this . . . comestible. That was the word he used. Comestible. I didn't know what he meant, so he explained.'

His teeth have got larger, he's doing a kind of snarly thing as he talks. Her heart is banging hard against her chest. Let me out! Let me out!

'So you bite through the crust, right, then you chew on the jelly to get at the meat. I didn't quite understand it at the time, see, Sheena, but now I do. He was right, was this white-haired geezer. I now know that shagging an old woman is *exactly* like eating a pork pie. So thank you very much for that.'

He has to fling himself down the stairs, feet scrabbling on the sisal runner, because Sheena is throwing stuff at him. Anything she can grab hold of in the immediate vicinity. She is screaming and throwing – useless cushions, a table lamp, Mungo's scratching post, the leather poof from Fez, the Thai Buddha decorative wall plaque, a file of shop stuff that explodes mid-air, until her fingers close around the heavy paperweight from the Algarve as Gavin is scrabbling with the double lock in the little hallway. He gets the door yanked open just as the paperweight speeds past his head and into the night, cracking off the cobbles with a splintering bounce and then (as she scrabbles down herself and reaches the cold air and peers) rolling noisily and jerkily down the hill at Gavin's heels.

It must have woken the whole neighbourhood, but no lights come on. Maybe there's no one left alive, she thinks, tightening her dressing gown and breathing in far too much night frost as she pants. The empty lane glistens, his dark shadow flickering in and out of the curly wrought-iron street lamps all the way to the bend. Maybe everyone's as dead as herself, and just getting on with life as if we aren't dead, not at all. Shivering so hard her teeth are, yes, actually chattering like in the books.

When she goes back upstairs and shakes the cat bowl, Mungo does not appear. He has found a hiding place that works. Survival technique. It's not the first time. When the Chinese take over, cats will be used for handbags. She clears the hall and stairs of the debris, hoovers the sisal and then the bedroom and the attic and the sitting room. It's well past two by the time the overheated machine whines to a stop, her ears ringing. Mungo hates the Hoover. She'll give her darling until lunchtime tomorrow, then she'll put up a MISSING notice. Several.

Roadkill. Jesus Christ.

It's Thursday. Today is Australia Day, and she's the first person in the United Kingdom to think it. Sorry, Tony.

She struggles through until Friday and then goes on a long weekend with man flu, pulling a sickie on the sofa under a duvet, downing chocolates with Chivas Regal and the occasional Lemsip, watching box sets and stuff like *About a Boy* for the tenth or so time, her baby purring on top of her, in cat Heaven. He was there on the sofa in the morning, fur chilled by a night outdoors. Sensible Mungo.

Not-Britt takes over down below and the place doesn't burn down. Trade is reportedly brisk, especially for the Icelandic-Chinese sweaters. She has a lot of brooding time. She expects eggs to come out of her ears. She even watches, without changing channels, all them grey suits gathered in the snowy mountains for the bloody World Economic Forum meeting in Davos. The 'Great Transformation', they call it. That's what we all need. A great effing transformation, on the personal level. But it won't happen, neither on the global nor the personal. It's all wishful thinking, dearie. As her mum would say. When you realise your parents were right all along, it's way too late. Them Swiss mountains do look heavenly, though.

There is a notice on Itchy Feet's door, run off a computer in fancy lettering. The wintry air feels very out-of-doorsy to Sheena but it's full of damp and it's Tuesday morning; nothing good about the last day in January after three duvet days except that she's still alive.

Due to unforeseen circumstances, we are closed until further notice. Apologies for any inconvenience caused.

*   *   *

She swears under her breath, heart pounding in her throat. The blinds are down. The place is dead and Paul Cannon is dead. Perfect spelling, so not his. He's got himself killed. WE ARE CLOSED. Who's WE? Him and the shop? He can't be dead if it's WE.

Although it is just a formula, a way of putting it. She knows that. UNFORESEEN. It doesn't mean anything.

She never got his bloody mobile number. She trots back up the curve to On the Hob, defying gravity. Hannah always knows everything. The ex-primary school mistress. Miss Fox. Please, miss. Jason's cheating. Samir's nicked my fags, miss.

She's hoovering again. The Hoover dies. Sheena catches her breath, although she's slowed down for the last bit. She doesn't want Hannah to suspect.

'Hi there, Hannah,' she pants.

'Training for the marathon? So should I be. Are you better? You look white.'

Every year a mass of locals run the streets laughing in aid of Cancer Research, and there is always someone who drops dead, still in his funny hat.

'It's the bloody slope. Need to be on my feet more.'

'Brittany said you were in bed with a raging fever.' Hannah has this lovely deep posh voice. Padded hearts hang on threads between them because it is Valentine's coming up. The kind of thing that annoys customers, but Hannah will learn.

'A stitch in time. How's tricks, Hannah?'

'Really quiet, after a good start. Mind you, it's winter, it's the recession, it's bloody cold. And it's Tuesday. Did you know the first day of February has the highest number of suicides in the UK?'

'That's tomorrow.'

'Better to be warned.' Hannah always puts things a bit strangely. *What is Your New Year Resolution?*

Sheena acts away. 'I can't even push the carnal love guff, not on toddlers. I'd be arrested. Missing that classroom already?'

'Like, er, no.'

Hannah is young, not even thirty-five, with hair streaked in lollipop pink and a very slim figure that Sheena envies. She feels rounded in front of the woman, who is always showing off her midriff. Sheena could have done that, once, if the style had demanded it, but now her stomach is starting to roll up against her belt. It isn't diet, it is muscular deterioration, like old rubber bands. She'll never eat a pork pie again in her whole life.

'Don't let me stop you vacuuming so industrially, but I've a query.'

Hannah laughs, Sheena isn't sure why. People do laugh louder these days. 'Fire away, Sheena, once you've got your breath back.'

'What's happened down the road? I mean, Paul – that – that quiet sort of hippy bloke's place. The shoe shop. Itchy Feet.'

'Oh, crikey,' Hannah gasps. 'Of course, it was on Friday. Awful. Did no one tell you? I only knew yesterday evening, mind you. I left you a message, actually. That was right to the fore of my mental diary, and so why did I forget just now? Weird.'

The awful hearts. Keep bumping against your forehead. Spangled, like migraine. 'Awful what?'

The phone goes. Some customer, bound to be, yacking on and on about whether Hannah has got in some pointless decorative crap or not and he or she has tried everywhere else and Christ these people ought to be strangled at birth and yet Hannah is listening and nodding and talking back like sugar, like syrup, because the client is always right and meanwhile a real heart is pounding so hard it is ready to explode.

The second the phone goes down, Sheena says – too angrily, too urgently – 'What awful *what*, Hannah?'

'What what?' The girl is still coming out of client mode. Or she's on drugs. 'Oh, that. Poor thing. Yes, you wouldn't believe it. Awful. The silly billy went and broke his back. Paragliding. Weird name, sounds like gliding for the disabled, doesn't it? Sorry, that was tactless. I mean, it's—'

'Broke his back?'

'Uh-huh.'

'When?'

'I said, Friday. Awesome.' She glances at the calendar. 'The 27th? Only heard last night, as I was leaving. I did try phoning you. Should have texted, but my boyfriend was waiting, battery flat, well done team!'

'Not rock climbing?'

Hannah is propping a red velvet heart behind a set of Danish cutlery. There are too many hearts. Maybe there's a big heart between Hannah and Paul. No, no, no. No way. Sheena feels some kind of energy filling her out to the tips of her fingers.

There'll be no one else to push him.

She has to sit down, her legs jellifying. A few hearts spill onto the floor. Hannah goes out to fetch her a nasty tea in a nasty paper cup because she has nothing to make it in, not in On the Hob. The cathedral bells start pealing. Sheena thinks, sitting there alone and hoping no one comes in expecting to be served, now it'll be all over town, like the ringing bells. Sheena 'n' Paul. Paul 'n' Sheena.

Silly billy. Silly sod. Taking the day off. Friday. Today's Tuesday. She didn't know for three days. He didn't phone her. Not family, is she?

Better than Gavin 'n' Sheena, though. That was a close call.

*　　*　　*

She recovers her legs quickly – psychosomatic, Hannah reckons – and tells Brittany to hold the fort for the morning and heads straight off to where they've taken him: Nottingham. The university hospital's spinal unit. World renowned. It takes almost an hour and a half with the horrible traffic. There are other people visiting him, loud friends from the paragliding club. She feels a bit silly and shy, bursting in on all this, and hangs about in the hospital corridors until they've gone, studying the shiny floor.

'Hello, Paul. I was just passing.'

'Yeah, very likely.'

He blinks at her as if through a pale mask. This is such a mistake. She is about to give him the Ferrero Rocher and go when he says, 'Hey, I like the boots.'

'Picked them up for a song somewhere. Can't think where.'

She is surprised to see him looking intact, without a single bruise on his face. Now she knows what the tan was: he went paragliding every weekend, in the wind and rain and sun. 'My personal two fingers to the flatlands,' he explains. Over in Derbyshire or, if he couldn't face the drive, up near Louth or skimming the waves at Mablethorpe or across the Wolds with the help of a tow winch. The quiet type. This last time it was a Friday because it was so dead in the shop he thought he'd die too. Headed for the Derbyshire Peaks, off Mam Tor. A wind shadow near a line of very tall pines had snared him as he was descending in the afternoon, had collapsed his wing and shoved him down on his arse instead of his feet when he was about twelve feet off the ground. He knew the worst straight off, he says. He just lay there in the field near Bakewell, arms akimbo like Jesus, crying his eyes out. He'd heard his vertebra blow. It had seemed to travel up to his head and crack there like a twig in his brain and his big flying boots wouldn't shift in the grass and he couldn't breathe at first, his

257

lungs had collapsed like his wing, he saw them full of blood, like his big blood-red wing. In fact, his whole head was filled with warm red blood and it was crazy – for a moment it was like a high during meditation, this kind of amazing glow. Then that drained away and he just lay there with tears streaming over his face, staring up at the blurred sky, feeling bloody freezing. Someone came running over. It was Chas, his paragliding friend. Big worried face.

'Oh God, Chas, oh God, oh *shit*.'

Chas knew straight away that this was the extreme that they all feared but never anticipated. He didn't even take Paul's helmet off.

It was just a freak accident, wind shadow, a whirl in the water of wind. But he'd miscalculated.

They don't know, not yet. He tells her he's blown his L1 vertebra, which is just above the small of the back. They have already put in titanium rods and screws to stabilise the crushed bone and manage the pain. A cage, they call it. Six hours under gas, yesterday. Or was it the day before? At the moment he can't feel his legs or lower back, but the X-ray and MRI scans show the nerve hasn't been completely severed. There is this tiny glimmer of hope.

'Your luck ran out,' says Sheena, holding his hand when the words stop. He had to explain the technical terms like wind shadow, thermal, cloud suck. It was like he had to get it all out. 'Whatever happened to Hugh of Amersham?'

He screws his face up. Trying to stop himself laughing? 'Hugh of Avalon. Went off to Amersham, maybe. Or the wild swan got shot.'

Nothing to do with luck, he explains. Luck isn't what paragliding is about. It's about skill and being organised and not making a bad landing. It's about being aware of your body and aware of nature, becoming a bird, a gliding hawk. He probably made a bad decision, flying that day, because the air felt jumpy. It was his last flight of the afternoon. He'd thought he was far enough away from that line of trees. Or maybe it wasn't the trees at all. It was like something shoved him out of the way. From underneath. Shooting up from underneath, honestly. Collision. Like another hang-glider almost, spiralling up, but there was no one else in sight, only Chas's tiny white face looking up from way below, firmly grounded. Anyway, it went all mushy and he found himself in a stall. He was going over it, over and over what happened, but it wouldn't undo its knot. Do you know what Nirvana means? The place of no wind. Maybe he hit Nirvana, like a black hole. Some weird wind current, some vortex smacking up into him. Sheena nods, thinking of Gavin in her flat, on the stairs, turning to her and opening his poison mouth.

'What time was it?'

Why should that matter? But it's what you ask. You want to lock it down.

'Around four o'clock? Four thirty? I'm scared,' Paul adds as if amazed. 'So they tap my feet and I can't feel them. I'm blindfolded. I won't be able to read the ground.'

You won't be able to walk at all, Sheena thinks, but all she says aloud is some drivel about it being early days and so on. She has never known him talk for so long. He's probably used up more words with her in twenty minutes than over the last ten years. Half of it mumbled, as if he's on medication. Morphine, maybe: there's a drip feeding into the veined back of his hand, which makes her feel whoozy. Or some kind of uppers that have brought him out of himself. Even after her boob op (silliest decision ever), she felt high from the anaesthetic for hours, made amazing plans for her life, told the doc he was an angel in disguise. Just chemicals. Better than booze.

She goes on holding his hand. It feels like it has been in the fridge. Warm it up, warm it up. As bad as Gavin's, God forbid. She wonders why he doesn't paraglide barefoot. Presumably the landing is too tough on the feet, even for a barefooter. She can't really ask, not now.

His face peeps above the sheet and blanket like a little boy's, very pale under the tan.

'You never told me you went paragliding,' she says.

'I knew you'd make a fuss.'

'Did you?' She gulps. 'I mean, you knew that I'd make a fuss?'

(Which meant, You actually care what I think?)

He lies there, as if thinking about it, not looking at her but staring up at the ceiling as if it is the sky. It is hot in the hospital, the sun pouring in. There is a lot of noise coming through the door, like some continuous wild party, with the medical staff shouting and laughing, ever so jolly it sounds. And crashes of metal things, squeaks and bangs. Ever so jolly. His face makes little spasms. Flashes of pain. Everything is delicate. Almost religious.

'How's your man flu, at least?'

He smiles briefly. A lovely smile, affects his whole face. 'Great thermalling but then the wind got jumpy,' he murmurs, so she has to lean closer. 'My thinking was haphazard. Chas had copped out. He was out of his harness. His mind is very honest.'

There is a pause because Sheena feels love for him flood her insides right up to her throat. She wishes she hadn't gone with Gavin. That was her swansong. With Gavin it was a total miscalculation, got sucked in. Now it is all Paul Cannon.

He is in a special room three floors up, with high-tech equipment everywhere and two drips, a monitor and, of course, a catheter. At least it's warm. His X-rays are in a big brown envelope on a trolley, and she looks at them, heart pounding with happiness. He'll be all right. The nerve isn't completely severed; it'll grow back again, like a stalk. If he is careful. And he is encased in a spinal brace, so he can't not be careful. It itches, he says. But not my feet. I can't feel my feet, itchy or not. His morale goes up and down, maybe the morphine or whatever kicking in and out.

His ex-wife doesn't know about the accident, not yet. Maybe she'll never know. Israel's a long way away. He mumbles on; she listens, also relieved his ex-wife wasn't contacted. The friends were, though. What the heck. The hang-gliding fraternity. She says she's never done anything scary in her life. The scariest moment in her life was seeing Gavin naked in her fur coat, but she doesn't tell him that.

He says you've no idea how free you feel up there.

She can see the spine snaking up on the X-ray, its vertebrae like stacked tea cups ready to fall. He shows her where the crushed vertebra called L1 is: a bit flatter than the others, that's all. She expected worse: splinters and cracks and stuff. She screws up her face in imaginary pain. It might have been higher up, affecting his arms, his neck. She has no idea whether it affects the willy, whether it paralyses the willy, blocks all those feelings of pleasure. She doesn't care, not for herself. Only for him.

'I'm trying to send these kundalini energies down,' he says.

She nods. She likes the idea, though she's never been into alternative medicine. Better safe than sorry.

'From your India days?'

'Oh, don't talk about India.'

Stupid of her. His face purses up in pain. She squeezes his hand then bends towards him and kisses his forehead and lays her cheek against his for several moments. She feels his hand on the back of her neck, stroking it.

'You made me chuckle,' he says. 'Igal the plumber, fantastic with leaks.'

'Did I?'

'That's when I fell for you. Hadn't occurred to me before, to be honest.'

'I didn't mean to make you chuckle.'

'That's exactly it.'

There is salt on her tongue, suddenly. Either his or hers. Doesn't matter. Mingling.

'Lonely hearts both,' he murmurs as if mind-reading.

Then a nurse comes in.

'Oh,' says the young nurse. 'Hiya. All right then? Don't let me stop you lovers. How's it going today, Paul?'

Sheena sits up and smiles at her lover. The floodwaters are breathable. They are leaping fish in the floodwaters, leaping up and out and into the wind. Wild swans. Great white wings of swans. Her lover is telling the pretty young dark-eyed Asian nurse how he is.

'To be honest, I'm annoyed. I'm kicking myself.' He suddenly looks stricken. 'You know, I was always quite cautious. I wish it was Friday morning and I'd decided not to go. I wish a lot of things.'

The lovely smooth-skinned nurse is taking his pulse. Bound to be from Sri Lanka or somewhere else paradisal, originally. The nurse says, 'Cautious men don't jump off cliffs. They keep their feet on the ground. They're boring.'

He smiles, looking at the nurse. She smiles back, gently placing his wrist back on the sheet.

A more senior nurse – she is older, anyway, about Sheena's vintage – comes waddling in to see how things are, and her plain age-swollen face makes Sheena unpleasantly aware of her own seniority. 'Oh,' says this nurse, whose belly is prominent under her blue top, 'I know they're a bit naff, but I love Ferrero Rocher.' The pretty nurse has left.

'Have one,' says Sheena sharply, 'if that's what you're angling for.'

'*You're spoiling uz, Mr Ambassador,*' the nurse quotes in a fake French accent. Stupid cow.

Sheena thought the chocs were posh. Not too pricey, but posh. The overweight nurse takes three, of course. Fat and getting fatter. Should know better. 'I brought the paper,' she says, dropping the *Daily Mail* on his blanket. 'Its owner has just left us.'

Released? Or dead? Sheena frowns at the paper, wondering about hygiene. It looks creased and soiled. She didn't have time this morning to look at hers.

The nurse folds her arms. 'Lincoln's in it today. You *are* from Lincoln, aren't you?' Paul nods. 'Well, you're in it today, in the paper. Lincoln. Young teenager gone missing, along with her dog. Can you imagine the parents? A few days ago now. Blink and you miss it, but you're on the map. Even Lincoln!' Paul thanks her but she doesn't go. 'Lunch,' she adds, 'is classic lentil roast or pork pie.'

'Classic lentil roast,' says Sheena too quickly.

The nurse looks surprised. 'I can see you know what's good for him. Cauliflower or chips?' 'He doesn't eat meat,' Sheena explains. 'Cauliflower *and* chips,' says Paul. The nurse nods and says, smiling, 'How does rhubarb crumble *and* custard grab you for dessert?'

'Oh,' Sheena says, 'I think I'm going to, what's the word, *admit* myself. Just for that.'

The nurse doesn't find this funny and leaves them in peace. She and the pretty one probably wash his nether regions. Shut up! Thoughts! Of course someone has to!

263

'Who's naff, then?' says Sheena, smiling at him through a mash of silly interior voices. It is a little comic episode they have both shared.

He stares at her. 'Who says I don't eat meat?'

I'm kicking myself. Christ, he's probably *paralysed.* It takes time to absorb. It is from another world. Like watching the nine o'clock news and then the news appearing all around you for real.

'I assumed it.'

'You're kind of right,' he says. 'I like chicken, though. They usually bring round this form with boxes to tick. Probably run out, like they run out of nurses. Staff shortages.' Then he says, a bit like a teenager, 'I'm thirsty, like really suddenly?'

She hands him the glass. If he doesn't get better, he'll need shoes even less. Will his feet feel the cold even less? Of course he'll get better. Pick up thy bed and walk. Just take bloody care in the meanwhile.

He dribbles from the corner of his mouth as he drinks and she isn't sure whether she ought to pull out a tissue from the box and give him a wipe. Instead she takes another look at the X-ray. She turns it upside down. The spine has exactly the same slow curve as Totter Hill like that: the L1 vertebra is roughly where her shop is.

'I always wanted to go to Queenstown,' he murmurs.

'Where's that? South Africa?'

'Otago in New Zealand. Probably the best paragliding spot anywhere. To jump off a mountain in Otago. Snowy mountains around a blue lake on the edge of the world. You can't hang around for things until it's too late,' he adds. Was he looking at her meaningfully? He's so pale that it's like a stocking over his face.

'I thought Lincolnshire was the edge of the world,' she says, which isn't helpful. She picks up the paper. 'But now we're in the *Mail.* Do you want me to find it?'

She rustles it as you do but he shakes his head. She stands up, drops the paper on the chair and goes over to the window. Little Portakabins down below, like a shanty town, gleaming in the sun. Trees that look lost, sandwiched between the hospital grounds and what looks like a retail park. The usual mess. Swallowing everything up. The big names eating away at their efforts. She's never liked Nottingham anyway. Robin Hood my foot. A helicopter passes in the far distance like a bee.

She turns round. He is looking at her again, his chin shiny. She knew it. She knew he'd be looking at her.

'Perfect day,' he says. 'Look at it. Perfect blue perfection of bloody sky. Not a cloud. You'd see the curvature of the horizon if you were up there. Infinity of blue. How many times is it ever that?'

She turns back to the window. He was looking at the sky beyond her head, in fact. That's where he belongs.

'Hardly ever,' she says out loud. 'To be honest.'

10

CHRIS

17 August 2012

The bells ring after lunch for the office of None. *I love you, Lord, thou art my strength.* He raises his head skywards as they leave the chapel. A few fleecy clouds; mostly sunny. Normal service resumed for August, at last. The morning was cool and clammy from a sea fret that hid the surrounding fields then lifted in a few minutes around midday. They are twenty miles from the sea.

An afternoon of humble labour awaits him. Picking blackberries, on Brother Barnabas's orders. Yesterday it was up the ladder in the apple orchard. He has thick gloves, a large basket with a chequered cloth folded inside, a beech-handle sickle and an ancient chunky pair of steel secateurs stamped 'England', the tools carried in a patched canvas shoulder bag retrieved from one of the clapboard sheds by the kitchen. His postulant's smock has been swapped for a pair of worker's overalls, circa 1950.

He sharpens the sickle on a whetstone, a task he relishes, by the rain barrel at the entrance to the vegetable garden. You have to sweep the stone away from the body. Away and away and away. He feels a lot more male in overalls, it has to be said: they're tight at the crotch.

Chris loves foraging. One of his first jobs here was to cut nettles for soup: Brother Barnabas throws in potatoes, carrots and leeks, and scatters nettle flowers over the dark-green surface. Beyond delish. Chris's taste buds have changed over the last months, since the Great Transformation (as he secretly calls it). They have become more sensitive, more appreciative. He likes to help with the cooking, savouring the colours, the textures, sinking spiritually into the cellular depths of God's bounty. Other people would call it the result of permanent peckishness. The starvation diet.

Blackberry picking is hard work, he knows, especially in heat. Sharpening a sickle is even hotter work. He dips the whetstone in the rain barrel and sweeps down the blade again and again. Mid-August, and the first time this summer that the temperature has remembered where it is, seasonally. Just in time for the weekend: according to the forecast it'll start to drop on Monday. They're all glad of the cavernous cool of the abbey church. Personally, he finds it easier to tune in to God's ultra-high frequencies there. The voluminous cowls with their endless folds of white cloth have been discarded, but even the sleeveless black scapulars, hanging down over the shoulders to the ankles, look sweaty. He's glad of his postulant's grey smock. Few of the monks use deodorant; washing is purely hygienic, and a bodily honesty now wafts through the communal spaces, medieval and spicy.

Visitor numbers have shot up with the thermometer. He doesn't mind the retreatants, but the tourists are a distraction. Yesterday there was a whole German biker gang all in leather: 'Angels, but we are coming from Hell,' as their leader joked to Brother Vincent, manfully grinning behind the shop's counter. This morning he stepped into the pigsty and shouted his usual 'Hi, guys' only to hear a giggle from the wooden fence: a girl in her teens had her hand over her nose, in convulsions with her friend, their naked bellies upfront like laughing mouths. One had a bead in her protruding navel. Doubly distracting. Pass me the hair shirt, guys!

He tests the blade with his thumb. Pretty good. His collar is sodden with sweat.

At forty-five, he is the third-youngest of the fifteen. The youngest is in his early thirties: Brother John from Liverpool. Brother Lawrence is next, unless he's an undead and centuries old. He's the only member of the community that Chris can't quite get through to. A kind of sinister piety. Most of the others are in their sixties or above. White-stubbled scalps, deep-lined faces, some hobbling, with Brother Felix in a mobility scooter. Working the cross-cut handsaw through endless logs, Chris feels useful. He feels young.

A brief letter came yesterday from Emily. Joey is probably anorexic, says the doctor. Never goes out. Hardly speaks. He's on pills. She didn't say which ones, but – hey, that's just so important! *Look what you're doing to him, Chris. He didn't even watch the Olympics. Should have been trekking in Nepal by now!* Unfair, that. Joey's not a kid any more.

Early this morning he prayed for his son, eyes tightly squeezed, until his knees hurt. Years of jogging on the pavements of Balham. Jesus resisted all distractions. All temptations. However urgent.

I can only follow suit, Chris has concluded.

A cascade of fruiting brambles runs all along one of the lower woods, around a bumpy meadow where a lost village once stood. It's good to go out through the side gate into the wilder grounds. He takes a shortcut across the visitors' car park, striding healthily. Last week he started his Canadian exercises and tweaked a muscle in his left shoulder. Otherwise he feels better for them, as he used to feel better when he was a gym regular. His hands have calluses from the axe, the hoe, the broom, the heavy kitchen pans, you name it. His body is, on the whole, slimmer and tighter; it's finding its younger self, when he was contemplating a sports career after uni. A skiing nut. Or slamming to victory in professional squash. He went into TV instead, thinking it was more creative. Illusion after illusion.

His mind is clearer too. But the bits that aren't yet there seem to be knobblier, denser, ganglion-like. *Loving Jesus and loving one another* seems simple enough as an aim, because if you love Jesus then you love his Father, and if you love God then you love the cosmos, but he's just not sure where the Devil fits in, if by 'the Devil' we mean the heartless narcissists, the bullies with giant fists. The demons, minor or major, smashing and poisoning and draining the good energy. He knows it's in his own veins too. Look at these shiny cars in the car park. Look no further.

As he skirts the rear of a beguilingly battered old camper van, he sees, sellotaped in its dusty rear window, a face staring out at him from a poster. MISSING. A young girl's face. A young girl, missing. He stops, clutching his basket and his bag of tools.

A bucket of ice-cold water has been dashed over his mind, dripping down into his heart.

It's her.

What the fuck is she doing here?

He comes closer, mouth open. She has long copper-red hair and a toothy smile. *Did you see Fay?* He has to read the details twice before they go in. Hasn't been heard from since the end of January. Vanished along with her dog. Fay Sheenan. *Any information, no matter how insignificant . . .* She lives – or lived – in Lincoln. Last seen *at 16.22* – CCTV, obviously – *wearing a reddish-brown coat with a furry hood.*

He stares at her staring back at him. She's got a name, then. Fay Sheenan. Now that's all wrong, all wrong. A car reverses before turning with a scrunch to drive away; watching it in a daze, he's aware of the faces inside looking out at him in turn, an elderly couple under muffs of grey hair.

He touches the sand-dusted metal of the van, warm as a television, and meets the poster's eyes again. Sea-green, rather large. Exactly the same. And the freckles. Beyond, in the real world, inside the vehicle itself, there's a clutter of mattresses, blankets, toys. Beach buckets and spades. A draped, deflated dolphin-float with a toothy grin, flat as roadkill. Take the Pacific Coast Highway. Be a hippy. Make love in the dune grass.

He steps back. Below the rear window is a large oval sticker and another dolphin, leaping from Planet Earth and encircled by *EcoForce: may the Green be with you.* There's a smaller sticker on the bumper: the blue silhouette of a kiwi with the New Zealand flag inside; but the vehicle has a British registration. These people are far from home.

There are no two faces exactly alike. He knows this is the same face. A toothy coppernob angel with freckles spattered over her nose like flicked ink.

His angel.

The whole world goes suddenly quiet.

It's already mostly quiet here: WE LIVE IN SILENCE shouts from the gate. That very first time, threading out for their Sunday stroll – the one time in the week they're allowed to natter – it sounded as if everyone was bellowing. There was a familiar roar and they all looked skywards: the Red Arrows were practising rollbacks. Unfortunately, the presence of a silent monastic house far below has never been enough to make the Arrows change their route.

271

'Bless them,' a brother murmured, still wincing at the noise. That was very impressive. In the outer world it would have been *Fu-uck off!*

It was Easter Sunday, the monastery closed to visitors. They had kept the vigil from well before dawn, and celebrated the Eucharist. He had, he supposed, been plunged into the holy deep end. The stone was rolled away from the tomb. He was reborn with a bloom of Pinot Noir from Surrey in his mouth. He had only arrived on Thursday, just in time for the Mass of the Lord's Supper.

Everything felt different. Two suitcases like starting boarding school. Plus a rucksack, which felt adventurous. Yet only ten days earlier he had been scouting locations in Lincoln prior to doing Morocco with Emily. Joey and Flo not coming, for the first time ever. Eighteen, post-A levels, Oundle finished with at last, doing their own thing before uni. Then it all changed.

He bought a book in that nicely messy second-hand place.

Oh, and that huge domestic with Emily in the car a week or so earlier – on the fast lane of the M4. 'I want happiness,' she said. 'You have just one life in which to achieve happiness. Right now I'm sad. I've been sad for years. Look at this shit. This is me, heading down the congested, totally depressing motorway of life. So I want a new start. I want to come off. I want a divorce.' He protested; she began to shout. To weep. To have hysterics. So they came off at Membury for a Starbucks cappuccino. Welcome Break. 'Last time I was here,' he said, trying to keep it light, 'it was for a shoot back in 2003. A year in the life of a motorway services cleaner. Remember? It hasn't improved.' She went hysterical again. Everyone looking. His mobile pinging away.

Bad timing, the whole thing. No way could he have taken so much as a day off work: panic emails flooding his phone all Sunday. So it was straight back early on Monday to their stupid new open-plan office in Hammersmith. Nigel Hunter red-flagging everything, talking about meltdown on the upcoming shoot in Romford. *A Year in the Life* of a toilet service driver. 'Never call him a portable-toilet cleaner, OK? He's uber-sensitive.' No time to sort out the catastrophic domestic problems, oh no. The two-year contract terminating soon, as it had terminated so many times before. Always voluntarily renewed. Stupid system, the TV world. This time he'd only be renewing himself. Cultivating silence.

Emily thought it a great idea. Or pretended to. Her reaction was a shock at first. She wanted him out of the way.

No more Nigel at least, sitting up very straight in his swivel chair, fussing at this and that. Camp twiddles of his fingers, the nails clipped with millimetric precision, like his jawline beard, not a curl of his horribly home-bleached hair out of place. All the time plotting, plotting, plotting! Tight-arsed: the man could hold an ice cube between his buttock cheeks without it melting.

'So long, Nigel. It's been a pleasure.' Get thee behind me, Satan.

A parley with the twins about his planned 'retreat'. They scoffed, secretly found it cool. 'You'll be back in about three months, Dad.' Joey working in Pizza Hut towards his Himalayan journey, planned for April. Flo to do a newspaper internship in Madrid. A very big hug.

It was the beginning of a process that will only end in the golden light of the Godhead: total absorption, as Father Jeremy puts it, in the centre of immensities. So much better than the term *death*. He can imagine no better end for his body than to be tucked up in the little cemetery, facing the woods and the distant fields where the original pre-Dissolution brothers were also laid to rest, apparently, before the smash-up.

However. Right now he is looking at an angel called Fay Sheenan. He feels he's been whisked back to Go. Base camp. Pre-shoot panic. Massive bump onto solid concrete. Way, way off-piste. He has to lean on the van for support.

One day, a week into his postulancy, returning to his cell at dawn after Vigils, the sky was full of rooks like flecks of soot, cawing, chuntering and squeaking – there are rookeries in the belt of ash trees fringing the monastery lake. It was reassuring. Praying for all those fearful of the coming day, you forget you might be fearful too. He'd had an awful dream that night and woken up sweating despite the cold; the stove had gone out, but the bells had not yet rung. Two o'clock? Two thirty? The short-wave static was his stomach. All those lentils.

Sleep was out of the question. He slipped out of bed, fumbled with the Danish stove and prayed. The indivisible One, awake at all hours. No answer came before the bells.

He read Psalm 42 again at his little desk: *Deep calls to deep at the roar of your waterfalls; all your breakers and your waves have gone over me.*

He went back to bed. He was flying over the fields for an aerial shot. The helicopter was a Sikorsky, piloted by Nigel Hunter, naked in a hooded cowl. The blades wouldn't fit between the trees. Nigel howled triumphantly.

Chris woke up with a yelp and a full-on erection. The nightmare had left greasy black deposits on the walls of his mind. He was scrubbing them dutifully with an oven pad when the bells of Vigils gained on his reverie at the border of sleep and scattered it, his alarm tinging in sympathy. Maybe he'd slept when he'd thought he was awake. Maybe you can actually dream that you're awake, fooling your own mind.

He remembered what Father Jeremy had advised him during his first counselling session: *You are God's idea, not your own idea.* Like a character in a TV series. God the screenwriter.

He swept out the boiler room after the office of None with mindful concentration. Even a cuppa had become meaningful. The glazed brown mugs from the pottery studio are two-handled, medieval-style – or like an infant's mug, reminding them to retain the faith and humility of a child. A friend once said to him, years ago, that faith and religion are two quite different things.

That evening he decided to adapt the well-known *Sortes Vergilianae* method of divination and opened his Bible at random. His finger fell upon a verse in Ecclesiastes: 'Better is one handful with quietness, than both the hands full with travail and vexation of spirit.'

He slept very well that night. He considered he was over the glitch.

There have been several other glitches before today. The first happened at the end of his observorship: writing an email to the monastery, replying to the vocation director's positive decision, he ended it with a chatty *Wonderful!* His finger missed by millimetres on the last letter, but he only realised once he'd sent it off. The vocation director? Brother Lawrence.

Wonderfuk!

Hunger was a major issue, especially for the first month or so. He'd crave the granola lumped in the chunky stoneware bowl, but there was never enough. When, every other day, a fresh loaf appeared on the platter before him, still warm, he could barely resist grabbing the bread knife. He even yearned for the tinned tuna with overboiled gnocchi. Cooking fudge, however, put him off fudge. Cold was another preoccupation, in the spring months. The wood-burning stoves in the cells, despite being the latest thing from Denmark, struggle to make their mark: the ration of fuel is too small. The rest of the place has no heating at all. And he still shifts on his jogger's damaged knees as he prays with the others. Some too old even to bend at the knees, though their heads are permanently lowered by their corkscrewed spines.

These are all physical problems. The two latest glitches are not. They are deeper.

Joey, and Fay Sheenan. Let's work it out. Clarity and chronology.

A trio of visitors crunch over the gravel, returning to their vehicle. Not this vehicle, though. Bleep-bleep of car doors, remote unlocked. Nasty sound. A posh young voice saying, 'It's fairly niche, isn't it, as an excursion?'

He glances again at the face on the poster and then walks away abruptly, off towards the brambles. Salvation comes through labour.

Fay Sheenan. Her eyes are following him. It's all so incredibly *wrong*.

To reach the blackberries, he has to cut a path with the sickle through a swash of six-foot flowering nettles that sting his exposed wrists now and again, sweating in the sun's blaze. He'd always thought nettles to be a painful nuisance, but they are wonderful, full of nutritional benefit, essential for other friendlier plants and for insects such as the butterfly. As good as broad beans! But not in late summer. Now it is mushrooms, nuts and hedgerow fruit. The sloes, for instance, have never been better. So he was told by Brother Odilo.

The tussocky field is full of frantic clouds of midges. The wood's hem casts the patch into shade, tricking his eyes that it's actually black until his pupils widen and the rhodopsin levels return. The air is heavy with the satiated vegetal perfume that the word *Amen* gives off. He ought to be feeling very, very good. He takes off his gloves and begins to pick the inky berries, sneezing and coughing in clouds of pollen dust off the nettles, dropping the fruit gently in the deep wicker basket. When he tries to pick more than two or three at once, they end up squashed. The key is patience. Right now he's rushing it. The thorns are vicious. They snag on his sleeves, inject his fingers with their needles. Imagine a crown of them slammed down onto your head, ripping into your veined temples.

Fay Sheenan!

And things were going so well too. Better and better. The peckish angle, for instance: his wooden spoon no longer scours the bowl for the gold of a last bran. Now, when a lay brother brings a fresh jug of water, Chris ignores his thirst and denies himself a second cup until the others have helped themselves. He even refrains, after washing in the chill stone basin along the refectory corridor, from drying his fingers on the roller towel, leaving it less soiled for the others. He's retained the generic postulant expression, which is somewhere between mild curiosity and gentle wonder. The new-guy gene, as it was known in his former life.

The absence of sex is an issue of course: sublimation, wet dreams. Dreams involving Emily's smooth, bared shoulders, his hands slipping over their coolness and down, down. Burying his face in her hair. But she's never his actual wife in the dreams; it's always an affair. The fiendish subconscious. This will improve! He's praying it out of him, as it were.

Even the day's exhausting schedule has turned out to be manageable, in the end. He thinks of the seven communal prayers in the huge abbey church as ripple marks on the broad beach of the day: firm against the bare soles of your feet. The rhythm keeps you going. Nothing comes and tears it all up, as work used to do, or family cohabitation. You just follow the bells. And the summer has been lousy: not much sun, unseasonally wet and registering extremes of temperature either way. 'You know it's bad when the weather forecast says "partly cloudy" and your heart lifts,' remarked one of the jollier monks as they set off for their communal walk one grey Sunday. To be honest, his heart has been lifting almost every day. Until now.

Accumulation. You have to watch out for accumulation. The fragile eggs piling in the bowl.

There have been other shocks as opposed to simple glitches; it's not quite true to say that it's all been plain sailing apart from hunger, cold and exhaustion. Let's not talk it up into a dreamworld, guys.

During Terce one morning at the end of April (he'd been here barely a month) the great chapel shivered to a clap of thunder like an explosion. They stopped singing. The sky turned so black it might actually have been night again. An obviously faked curtain of rain stretched on and on over the fields. A colossal amount fell – a month's worth in twenty-four hours – and the accompanying gale left a hole in the roof of the chapter house, part of which dates to the fourteenth century (nothing much else does, thanks to Thomas Cromwell). The lake overflowed into the adjoining meadow and drowned the cabbages in the field beyond.

Following the monastery's mud-splattered Mitsubishi jeep carrying ninety-five-year-old Brother Felix, they picked their way up the main track through its ruts and puddles to have a look. The monastery lake had brimmed several yards over its banks, the trees now paddling in their pinafores; a dirty brown gush was obliterating the little waterfall at the outflow end. The stream was so swollen and full of leafy, broken branches that it was more a cove. The whole place smelt like an intertidal mudflat: he expected to see starfish or crabs.

The press called the gale a tornado, with clips on YouTube showing it twisting over the fields as if Lincolnshire was Kansas.

A number of significant trees had succumbed, showing their uprisen root balls, tearing down others on the way. At least the rookeries were more or less intact. The whine of a chainsaw began. When the water level had lowered itself sufficiently, the fitter monks helped clear the stream, white habits or even black scapulars swapped for dungarees and wellies. Chris enjoyed this teamwork, for all its discomfort. A sharp shout from near the outflow: the others made the mistake of hurrying over. Lying in the shallows was the most horrific sight Chris had ever seen in his entire life: a white-fleshed, bloated form with patches of fur and the grinning expression of a disfigured pig showing large pointy teeth, empty eye sockets writhing with worms.

'Dog,' said one of the brothers. 'And I don't think it drowned yesterday.'

'This is why we are advised not to swim in the lake,' commented Brother Lawrence sternly, turning to Chris as if he'd been doing nothing but splashing about since he'd arrived.

He had to back away, apologising because the stench seemed to be pulling his features down to a deep pool of nausea, saliva rising in his throat. A brief debate about what to do with it. They decided to bury the poor creature on the edge of the beech clump to the south of the monastery, where the earth was soft and loamy, and say a little prayer. A lay brother fetched a sheet of plastic and rolled the corpse in with the help of a spade. Chris left them to it. He now knew what a demon would look like, and how it would smell. The teeth were yellow, with huge curving canines. Pump in smoke and screams and a red flickering, have it up on hairy goat legs and cloned ad infinitum, and you'd beat Hieronymus Bosch hollow.

A mongrel dog.

Months later Chris's stomach still gives a sympathetic lurch. Blood on his hands from tiny stingy punctures and scratches, clusters of blackberries tempting him to overreach himself. Why did God make thorns? Evolutionary protection device, blah blah. The better question: why did He make blackberries? The pads of his fingers are stained a dark grey. As when he'd churn out agitprop on the Roneo machine at uni, type his mediocre essays on his portable Olympia. All wiped out by computers the moment he joined Granada: first rung on the greasy ladder.

Cause and effect, that's the thing.

No, clarity and chronology, the two key words in his former life. PowerPoint simple. That's why his presentations were sought after, even in the seen-it-all TV entertainment world. Clarity and chronology, guys.

That rainy spell subsided and it was suddenly hot for a few days, as if the divine caretaker had returned from an extended break and thrown the switch. The ooze and slop of plastery mud in the huge fields grew snakeskin scaly, while the lake was still high but scintillant and much clearer. The brothers had to admit that their main water feature looked rather grand and lovely. A few ducks and moorhens patrolled and dippers perched on broken branches, curtseying in their stark white bibs. Someone suggested installing a giant fountain, another felt a stone pagoda would be suitable, as at Stowe. They were not being serious, and everyone laughed. Laughter is very much part of the monastery's soundtrack.

A meeting in the library: the accounts were laid bare by Brother John, the community's official bean counter. He had done the calcs. Not good. An astonishing estimate for repairs to the chapter-house roof earned a general gasp; the competent carpenters among them offered their services.

Chris cleared his throat. 'Look, speaking from my former swim lane, if I may,' he said, 'I suggest a video clip for the website. Better than photographs. A talking head with a brother or two, some chanting in the chapel, a glimpse of a cell, a few exterior wide shots? Finishing in the gift shop, close-ups on products?'

He seemed to have talked for ages, but it couldn't have been more than a minute or so. An apologetic tone full of humility. The white hoods – it was cold in the library – didn't seem to have budged. He felt suddenly illish.

'A *take*,' echoed Father Jeremy, scratching his close-cropped snowy beard.

'Oh, several,' Chris said without irony. Emily would have to bubble-wrap the camera and send it, he realised. Would she do that for him? 'I've seen it on some other monastic websites. Especially the American ones. Those weeny embedded fifty-second clips too.'

The hood containing Brother Lawrence stirred. 'Adverts. I can see the faithful instantly hammering at the door.'

There was a chuckle from the others. The word *adverts* might as well have been a well-sharpened hatchet. He was back in nursery school, being patiently told the difference between his shorts and the loo.

'Now what did that new feller say?' shouted Brother Felix, less gaga than he looks.

Whether encouraged or not by this humiliating episode, the deepest shadows descended around the middle of May. The first stinger was a letter from Gillian, his nicer sister-in-law, the previous week. Joey had stopped all his sporting activities and cancelled his gap-year plans and was stuck in his room most of the time, smoking skunk and playing video games in his undies. Emily had made no mention of this. Gillian implied

Joey was in depression because his dad had become a monk. Too 'freaky' for him. Chris felt the tentacles of the outer world rippling towards him. Joey may well have got depressed anyway as a result of the upcoming divorce. Or because he was in transition. Between stations. No mention at that stage of the anorexia.

Seated in a leather-spined niche of the library, he wrote Joey a long letter, each penned word pulsing with love, the whole thing blotted carefully. But it was difficult, and not just because he hadn't used a quill pen in years. He'd never really had time to feel fatherly, and the kids were only at home in the holidays. There was no reply.

Then came a spell of simple interference, of snow on the screen, of hiss.

Up to then he would scrub pots or unload the antique dishwasher in the scullery – his least favourite jobs – with a song in his heart, transposed from the key of grudge into celebration. Even working in the fudge room with plump Brother Barnabas – no ventilation, sickly-sweet sludge – was converted to gladness. The observorship finished and his mind made up, he was barely a fortnight into his postulancy when a brown envelope full of treeware arrived: forms. Emily was filing for a divorce on the grounds, not of incompatibility, but of his decision to become a monk. Unreasonable behaviour and desertion. But his decision to become a monk was spurred by the unhappiness of their marriage, by Emily wanting a divorce: she's distorting it all! She can't bear ever to be in the wrong! If the forms weren't filled in and returned, it would be assumed that he agreed with the proceedings, and the divorce would go ahead smoothly through the decree nisi and on to liberation.

A burr in his chest, a deep rankling that she had made out that the slow-motion car crash of their marriage was all him at the wheel. But that was old thinking. That was Chris Barker 1. Chris Barker 2 was free of retribution or remonstration. Chris Barker 1 knew full well that Emily would never acknowledge the mote in her own eye, that it was always everyone else's fault, that her world view did not include personal humility, that she'd been brought up that way by his dreadful Tory in-laws, both of them surgeons who had never approved of him. But Chris Barker 2 knew something else: that he couldn't do anything about it, and that letting go was the sensible option, combined with prayer and meditation.

That way lay internal peace. He had no more need of material wealth, of status, of gross things: the double-fronted house in Balham with the plum tree and pond, the nippy Honda Accord coupé, the Quad speakers in his study, his K2 Apache Crossfire skis with only a couple of seasons' use, his Tecnifibre Carboflex 130 squash racket with its purple wrap grip barely stained by sweat. The kids would inherit his vast collection of videos, half of them only playable on antique machines. They would curse him for it, probably. Books too. His precious Hornby Dublo 1930s electric train set that had belonged to his father. Yes, a slight twinge of pain, but no true sacrifice is painless. Everything to be sold or given away the moment he became a full monk. In six years' time. By then he wouldn't care.

Joey and Flo: adults, now. On their own paths. Quarrelling finished. They would visit him from time to time, their weirdo dad, from their respective unis. Quality moments. Skyping was out of the question, though.

He filled in the divorce forms at his cell's wooden desk. There were days when he was all but back in his T-shirt, his hand-stitched jeans, his Zanotti red leather Hi-Tops, his splash of Serge Lutens Fumerie Turque, saying things like, 'I'm all over it, guys.' Today was one of those days. What was he doing dressed in this party robe? Who was he, a drag queen? He'd eagerly entered into the treasure house within him, he had seen the things that were in Heaven, as Isaac the Syrian had put it long ago, and now there was a dark screen yanked in front.

Back in the fudge room, he reflected on his name, Chris: its genial banality, the longer form hopelessly posh. The day he became a novice, in under two years' time, he would change it. Brother Barnabas had been Des once. Des from Nuneaton. Chris fancied Gideon. Or something exotic like Theophylaktos. Or French, like Matthieu. Brother Matthieu. He'd probably adopt a slight French accent too. All long-game stuff, obviously.

Then a sudden flash of panic in the stifling air, worse than the crisis in his cell: who am I? What am I doing here? The molten fudge, bubbling as it boiled, was the laval pits of Hell. What a terrible death that would be. He deserved it. *Chris, you're a selfish git.* That was Emily. Neat rows of fudge squares cooling on greaseproof paper. Ready to be packaged. Ready to be gobbled up, rotting out strangers' teeth. He was hungry, but he was sickened at the thought of all this edible pleasure. A great surge of sexual longing out of the blue. Sweet, edible Emily. He had to sit down on the bench. Brother Barnabas glancing over from the packaging department. They couldn't talk to each other! At least, it wasn't recommended. The Rules of St Benedict. Lots and lots of them. Fifteen hundred years old!

Monotheistic religion, he muttered to himself, is one of the stupidest inventions of the human race. Christianity, Islam, Judaism. Almost as stupid as TV. Or cars. But even more murderous. And here I am in the thick of it. Obedient as ever.

The thought of Joey in his undies, staring at the screen, manically thumbing the game controller; it was overwhelming.

A hand on his shoulder. Brother Barnabas, that broad and friendly seen-it-all face, terrible teeth but never mind, softly saying, 'The end sanctifies the means.' As if he'd understood. Trappist telepathy. Happens all the time. Chris nodded, apologised in a whisper and girded his rebellious loins to carry on making fudge for the good of the community. Waitrose were stocking it in all their East Midlands branches, and they could barely keep up the supply.

Brother Barnabas opened the window and birdsong scattered its joy. One of the community's cockerels was crowing over and over as if it was dawn . . . along with the tarp clapping loose on the chapter-house roof.

In the solitude of his postulant's cell, in his sacred desert, Chris prayed so hard that his knuckles showed teeth marks. He had to pull on a skin-tight mask of merriment. Keeping awake to God's mystery meant he would nod off during Vespers, finding the usual nap at midday impossible. Since posting the forms in May there had been the sense of some transcendent curve having been casually broken. 'Let nothing be put before the work of God': Rule of St Benedict, Chapter 3. After all, God sacrificed his only begotten son to save us from eternal death. From our sins. The greatest sacrifice of all, as a recent sermon from Father Jeremy reminded them. That's the real work of God. And he was putting his own domestic concerns before it.

Smoking heaps of resentment, lit by spite.

Emily had mentioned that her husband was undersexed on her desertion statement, as if becoming a monk was the result of a dysfunctional libido! How far from God's purpose can you get? She knew this assertion would hurt him, which is why she included it. It was all lies, again. She would push him away, turn her back on him, regularly banish him to the spare bedroom. Not a word about his idiotic fling years back with that pretty intern of the delicate neck, because her own occasional flings would have been exorcised. Him in TV, her in fashion. They were always grown-up about it. Back in January, during an overnight stay in Lincoln for that Babylonian orgy on televisual ways of saving the whales, or whatever it was, he got very, very high on uppers and alcohol and was found passed out by the cops down an alleyway. She laughed. Now she's mentioning it in evidence. That was his final binge too, after a year or two of chemical exploration. There were some very pleasant moments. Tapping into the planet's life force just the other side of the smoked glass we call the daily grind. But it was stupid and pathetic, really.

Please, Lord, help me work through my acrimony and out the other side.

Soon after this crisis came the vision-dream. According to Father Jeremy, dreams are closer to the spiritual realm: they momentarily constitute reality and that mental reality is far more 'elastic'. This dream started realistically enough, though: no Dali component, no melting watches. The brothers were walking in the fields on their weekly outing, when nattering is permitted, but in the dream they were in complete silence. They were returning to the abbey by way of the lake. It was black with silt in the dream, as if the scouring storm had never happened. Brother Felix was on his feet, spry as a gazelle.

It was a sodden, miserable June in the real world, but the dream's weather was bright and cloudless. As a postulant you are only permitted a grey hooded smock and white trousers, but in the dream he was a proper monk in voluminous white habit, hood right up like the others. The whole dream was non-diegetic, anyway: he kept getting shots of stuff he couldn't have seen himself, like a wide-angle of the whole group, tiny in front of the water. Then all of a sudden their habits began rippling and shaking and lifting, until they were billowing out like laundry on a line, each brother struggling to press the cloth to his thighs.

Where were the fierce gusts coming from? The soaring ash trees were breathlessly still; the corn in the adjoining field likewise. They looked up at the sky together, as if at a signal.

The black dot of a lark.

Then something bigger, probably a buzzard. Then, impossibly, a swan with huge sun-gilded wings. But it wasn't a swan; the neck wasn't long enough. And where the swan's head should be was a girl's face, maybe even a young woman's – at any rate of an unearthly gentleness and beauty but at the same time completely individual. This shot was really close in, and he remembers worrying about nose shadow, that they had forgotten the eye light. Green eyes too. Glowing? It was all wrong! The wind machine kept coming into shot. He could feel the stress mounting. This was the take of a lifetime and had cost an arm and a leg to set up.

The faery wings slowed (she was, in fact, somewhere between angel and faery) and she started her descent towards the water, like a hang-glider pilot ready to land. She had a small freckled nose and dark red hair that rippled upwards. She tucked her wings right behind her, then spread them out again wide and made a graceful landing feet first on the very surface of the lake, barely puncturing its blackness, the reeds unmoved. She was squinting. The lights were too close, Chris wanted to yell at someone, but the entire crew were off on tea break and there was something about the gaffer having broken his wrist.

There was a loud click, a shiver and a shake, then she gave them all (a clumsy hand-held zoom onto the face) a toothy and totally endearing grin, turned her head to the left and soared away with – to his huge surprise – a massive cross that surged out of the water vertically with a great whoosh. It swung beneath her feet like some outsize prey dangling from an eagle's claws. And then she vanished, breaking up through the sudden lid of cloud.

The monks' cries turned into a post-wrap discussion about the technical aspects of the visitation, about speed and velocity, about the very powerful grip of an angel's toes and so on, during which he shouted, 'We need silks!' The effort woke him up.

An early morning dark. His night light wavered. He was hungry of course. Remembered every detail of the dream. When he was in it, it was real. Wrote it all down in his diary, as they are encouraged to do. The Faith diary. Ups and downs. Little things. Observations of flowers, birds, light.

If it actually was a dream. It was more like a message. A vision. A visitation. The cross was identical to the one that stands in the rough grass beyond the main gate, erected in the 1950s: a massive upright of oak beam, with an equally thick crosspiece attached by a shiplap joint. But why should the angel carry away their holy cross?

And why pull it out of the lake?

Monastic history is strewn with visions. They are, in some ways, what keeps the whole show on the road. Chronic hunger helps, although Merton himself warns against starving yourself in return for glimpses of Heaven.

He did not go back to sleep.

A mere postulant granted a vision. Or even a visitation! He told no one. It would not have gone down well. Monks are human beings, not saints. After twenty years of office politics, he's learnt a thing or two about envy.

The angel had done away with the interference, however. His screen was needle-sharp. Full colour. The clouds of depression and doubt were scattered. Blue sky only.

In the days following he allowed himself to drift into the seamless ocean of chants and prayers in the duskiness of the church, every brother looking somehow nobler in the soft candlelight. *Ad te clamamus exsules filii Hevæ, Ad te suspiramus, gementes et flentes* . . . On chillier days the others would come in white, in full hooded cowls instead of the black scapulars, looking as if they were carrying laundry over their arms. A gathering of Druids. Comedy, almost. As though pushing the boat out for laughs. 'Our loving prayers penetrate to the depths of Hell,' Father Jeremy told them in a sermon, 'and to the furthest reaches of the cosmos.' That puts broadband into the shade, thought Chris, apologising with a prayer. He was cocky, almost. Dangerously near the smug zone.

Once, during the blissful smoky murk of Compline, his gaze caught on Our Lady's face in painted wood, full of compassion in the lone candle's glare. The dream-angel's face was real, like flesh. Why would an angel be so endearingly toothy? Don't they have orthodontists in Heaven? He was chanting without listening, his mind adrift. Jesus was said to have been a redhead. There are red-haired angels in paintings. With freckles, maybe, like Flo. Ssssh.

The silence.

Every time, after the moments of the Eucharist, there is a silence such as he has never known silence in all his life. The silence begins after the last prayer and holds firm until Lauds almost seven hours later. Silence and stillness that, as they all fan out from the sweet-fumed cavern of a church to their separate cells on a whisper of leather soles, moves towards him with the open arms of complete freedom.

289

That was how it remained for weeks after his dream. He was happy being a silent conduit, a kind of satellite dish. His dream was not a conventional visitation: the Virgin did not appear on the cloister lawn or in the vegetable garden – as had happened to more than one brother, according to the monastic diary – her sandals glittering between the lettuce, her slender finger raised. No, it was an angel, a seraph. Gifted with love. Filled with ardour. Pure light.

He had recommended his spirit unto God. And he had been rewarded. Was there just the teeniest crumb of pride?

Now, in the troubling season of late summer, never his favourite time – a time when you realise that everything you had been anticipating for months is as illusory as the sunlit England of the adverts – he sees that the salvatory angel with the gift of love is only a face mentally recorded off a poster, stored and forgotten.

Recorded when? She's a local, a Lincolnshire girl. Background of old house-beams, suggesting a middle-class upbringing. He made two trips to Lincoln early in the year, a few uppers swirling in his head. The first visit was at the end of January, for the conference. Around the time she went missing. There may well have been posters up already. The second visit was in March, scouting locations. The town would have been full of posters by then. His vision was a trick of the mind, card-flicking memories. The cross was the mind recalling . . . no, not her death. She's only missing. He sneezes in the pollen-rich air, blows his nose. Missing, presumed dead. Or not. Groomed by some evil bastard, then abducted. Or not.

He so needs some foot-on-the-ball time!

He attacks a swathe of nettles obstructing a waterfall of blackberries glistening with ripeness. O, the joys of the sickle, the need to regularly whet the blade. Who needs a lawnmower, a strimmer? Death's sickle must need plenty of whetting, hitting all that bone and muscle over and over. Death with huge, strangler's hands would be more likely. The last, fought-for breath. The rattle.

A sudden claustrophobic panic seizes him. He might never leave here for years. He'd always wanted to see New Zealand. The Galapagos Islands. Sleep in a bamboo stilt house. Go trekking to Angkor Wat.

The angel dream suddenly feels confused, distant, a jigsaw you can't pick up without it buckling into fragments. He's not even sure that the dream happened, that he's not inventing it. It's as if his memory cells are breaking up as well, turning opaque like the surface of the lake brushed by a breeze. But this is ridiculous because he wrote it all down in black and white in his Faith diary. Time is no longer a chronological line, emerging from nothing and travelling on into nothing, but space itself. He can stretch out his arms and touch time with the tips of his fingers: it's like a roomy, clear plasticity all around him. Behind him, before him. The dream itself is both in front and behind, as is Emily and the job and his childhood and the kids and everything.

He sends up a little plea for help, but God is busy on the other line. There are problems in Syria and Egypt that need urgent attention. Neil Armstrong has just died, floating up to the moon like a tuft of old man's beard before the welcome in Heaven. Chris mutters a prayer for the missing girl. Dear Lord, please let Fay be found alive. Watch over her, wherever she is. Huddled in the mouth of the Tube with her mongrel dog. Hell's mouth, which he would enter every weekday in his old life, ignoring the homeless.

Wipe that. Fade up a small mound of earth, a rough, home-made, matter-of-fact cross.

A cross. Each buried monk has his own identical cross. Take up your cross daily until it stands on your grave. He turns his head away from the blackberry cascade and towards the monastery. The top of the great wooden cross is just visible. He doesn't like it. It's too broadbrush, too heavy. We don't need it. It shouts. There's not even a suffering Son of God nailed up there. Passing under it on the return from their Sunday walk recently, he asked Brother Simeon – former secondary teacher in Woolwich, expert on the abbey's history – how old the cross was. 'Nineteen fifty-seven. It was erected at a difficult time for the brothers, I'm afraid.' Chris didn't probe too deeply, but the difficulty involved a nearby school for young Catholic delinquents set up by the abbey in the 1890s, which provoked all sorts of 'problems'. The school was finally closed down in the 1960s, the brothers on the staff taken on by St Bartholomew's RC Grammar, an excellent school which was expanding at the time 'and which still goes on rising in the league tables', added Brother Simeon.

'What kind of problems?'

'Just don't go there,' the monk advised with a kind of simper.

The cross was a statement of confidence, or maybe defiance, funded by 'sympathisers' in Ireland and America. Chris didn't go there, no. Instead, he commented on the golden froth of gorse blossom spreading beyond the upright. Nature is always a safe bet.

He's been here nearly five months. It's nothing, and it's everything. It's not a sabbatical. It's a rendering up.

So many peak moments. For instance, hoeing between the broad beans in the vegetable garden a few weeks ago with Brother John. The usual peaceful silence. No need to make conversation, to juggle with status, to oil the wheels with chit-chat. The ferocious complexity of beetles and ants. He watched a worm wriggle in his hand, its little body surprisingly chill. I am a monk, he repeated to himself. This fact has a clapperboard crispness. Astonishing and ordinary. Clack. He took a deep breath, sucking God's eternal breath out of the early summer air and into his soul. He'd never thought of it like that in the old days – before Easter, in other words. He'd never even thought about breath, or breathing.

If you like broad beans, his mother would say, you've achieved adulthood. He adores broad beans: their flat, earthy ordinariness.

Hoeing was good. Three afternoons of it. He'd stay in his smock while Brother John kept to his tunic and scapular. It was a medieval scene. The uprooted weeds quickly went limp and dry. Of course he thought of the Parable of the Sower (Matthew 13), where Jesus suggests that he'll be personally sending his troops of angels to deal with the human weeds sown by the Devil, casting them all into the furnace of fire. Nice. Ah, but even weeds are merely wild flowers excluded by our agricultural arrogance. His hoe churned away, heartsease and speedwell and goosegrass biting the sod. Farming is mostly a branch of the chemical industry, so the Lord must be in goggles and white suit, spraying Roundup over those deemed sinful. He glanced at Brother John, who would never have thoughts like these. Bland and smooth as a choirboy.

The ordinances. Not to nurse a grudge. Not to hate anyone (even Nigel Hunter). To have no jealousy or envy. It occurred to him that his dream angel may have been demonic, tempting him into arrogance. She planted a thorn of pride that is now infected; either it was a divine test or he'd let his defences down. As Nigel would have said, looking disdainful, you've bigged the whole thing up.

293

He's sweating as he picks and plucks now, wondering why the basket isn't filling quicker. Go with it! The berries are warm, come away easily. There are rustlings under the brambles: voles or field mice or birds. No one treads lightly on this earth. Heaven will be weightlessness. Could be a bit dull.

The thing is, there was such intent in her face. In the dream. Staring at him. Such intent.

Ouch.

There is a small musty room in the oldest wing called the Conversation Room. It has a couple of frayed floral easy chairs with toothpick legs and an electric kettle. The decoration consists of a faded poster showing a cathedral's portico: possibly Santiago de Compostela. The previous abbot introduced the idea in the 1970s: when two monks have a relational problem, and the weather is too unpleasant for a walk outside, they can ask the abbot for permission to go to the room and vocalise rather than bottle it up.

Few do these days, but Chris sat in it one day last week and pictured surly, sardonic Brother Lawrence in the other chair, down to the round medieval-style specs, the cadaverous cheeks, the lupus (or whatever serious skin condition) that has pocked and rutted the man's face. The room smelt of mice and stale coffee. Brother Lawrence has taken to hiding inside his scapular whenever they pass in the corridor: pulling the black hood forward, the face disappearing into shadow, he is like a medieval Death figure. A sightless spectre sometimes, because the round glasses catch the light. God's aide! He would be permanently on his mobile if they were allowed them.

He imagined sitting down with Brother Lawrence and getting things sorted. But he was afraid to. So the conversation was held with his kids instead. It went quite well. He even pretended to make them coffee.

Now he imagines sitting down there with Fay Sheenan. Why did you fool me with your great wings, Fay? To lead me by your small hand into illusion and pride? The lake element. Yes, why the lake? Jungian perhaps. He can't remember his Jung, it's been so long. Whatever, she says. Duh. It's easier to land on water, yeah? He studies his inky fingers.

Along with the cemetery and its open view, the lake is one of his favourite spots. There was that Sunday stroll around it just the week before last, in the solid waking world. They gathered on the cloister lawn, less sharply mown these days for ecological reasons and thickly sprinkled with daisies and buttercups, soft with clover, popular with butterflies – mostly orange tips and small whites. Chris wouldn't have had a clue what their names were in his former life; at least that's a gain.

The weather was glorious, for a change. Everyone except Chris the postulant was in tunic and scapular, a black-and-white procession with a grey note. They had a look at the vegetable garden first, the cucumbers ready to be mashed for Our Lady of Grace's best-selling body cream (which provoked a few jokes). Brother Odilo, ex-biology teacher in Middles-brough, pointed to various spots and moulds due to the wet weather. Then outside the walls for the orchards, the hives, the greenhouses, the near-lightless mushroom sheds and the cabbage field. They contemplated the huge wheat field beyond the hedge. A problem: the farmer uses foliar feed, herbicide and fungicide and there is overspill. This year was terrible for fungus so the farmers didn't hold back on the chemicals. 'Nathan Dobson is his name,' said Brother Odilo, pulling a face. 'And the Dobsons are not to be meddled with. They're very proud of their high yields.'

'Working against nature,' sighed the abbot mournfully, shaking his head. Chris, who had never given it a moment's thought while in London, nodded in sympathy. The ripe wheat was ready to be harvested: it swayed like liquid in the summer breeze, looking pure and innocent. It was, he now knew, thoroughly toxic. How on earth do you tell the good from the bad? But he was learning so much!

They headed down to the lake. Out of the trees' shadow the water was a glittering aquamarine and there were oohs and aahs of admiration. Dragonflies and mayflies darted and swooped: he could now tell the difference. Great lace doilies of elderflower. Brother Odilo spoilt it somewhat yet again by saying that there were several invasive species of waterweed flourishing in there, helped by the chemical run-off from the fields. They would have to be yanked out at some point.

Sometimes we know too much. But it makes no difference. We do not do evil in ignorance.

Straggled out into smaller groups, they circled the lake on the narrow towpath. To his alarm, Chris found himself next to Brother Lawrence, all hooded halitosis, with Brother Eustace – Italian expert, fine baritone singer, built like an ox – making up the rear. The conversation, circling around the frescoes of the Brancacci Chapel and then expanding into a general overview of the Quattrocento, was way over his head. He began to feel thick. Their even voices, in which Italian names bobbed like lost holidays, lulled him into a rancorous sleepiness.

He contributed absolutely nothing, not a word. A degree in history, and then he'd languished in the crap telly world for over two decades. Well, it was hip at the time, back in the Blairite 90s. Popular was in, it was classless. Saying you were a producer on *Have You Got My Size?* went down better at dinner parties than if you said you were with *Panorama* or *Arena*. Shifting to Viper's Bugloss Productions, *A Year in the Life* revealed fans even among his own circle, perhaps because it was not yet trash, but falling ratings at the end of the 90s meant they had to drag it down into silliness, daft stuff, cash prizes, audience votes and shamelessly giggling presenters. The show's founder, Ricky Thornby, was horrified, but he'd been sacked years ago in a crafty buyout and restructuring. And Chris had learnt everything he knew from Ricky, before the guy moved to Texas. Audience skew got older and older: sometimes he reckoned it was mostly rest-home residents, staring at it vacantly over a milky cuppa and stale digestives.

Twenty years of his life! The last five or so were dreadful. Checking the TARPs (variable target, withering audiences, declining ratings), working at weekends, hire-and-fire, the old two-hour lunch breaks in a pub whittled down to a deskbound pasta salad out of a foam clamshell. *A Year in the Life* hanging on to its teatime slot by its fingernails, the chasm of the 9.30 morning death slot ever yawning. Tight-arse bastards like Nigel Hunter keeping you on your toes while executive mothers doing ten-hour days, their young kids fraying them to a pair of dark circles around the eyes, spat at you in emails. He didn't even go out on shoots very much when he became a full producer. Any personal opportunities opening up and you still had to be in there like swimwear or you'd lose out, be cast adrift, die of mortgage strangulation. When *A Year* got the Daytime Television Award in 2008, Nigel – the man who'd plagiarised every single one of his ideas – got a full page in the *Sunday Times*. No mention of Chris Barker. Not a squeak.

Now Chris Barker is picking blackberries in Lincolnshire. No one's telling him how he can do it better.

So what did Nigel reply to one bright lad eager as a puppy for an unpaid internship, the CV over-gilded with achievement, the photo bursting with enthusiasm? *You look pretty shit. Have a nice life eating out of bins.*

Chris knows now how the lad must have felt.

At least he knew what the Quattrocento was; it was just the detail that had gone. Two decades-worth of obliterating trash! The lake's water was so clear, shafted into by spot beams of intense sunlight, that he could see the waterweed (there was certainly a lot, good or bad) and drowned boulders, lazy flickers of fish, countless water boatmen. He reckoned he'd have to make regular visits to this very spot, drinking from its beauty. His sort of place. No wonder he'd dreamt about it, or rather no wonder God had tendered him such a dream.

He allowed the two monks to get ahead a little, and he was the last in the line. The front lot were already on the opposite bank, chatting and gesticulating against the belt of ash. A guffaw, stirring the ducks.

The sun on his face, kicking up off the water in sparkles and flares. He let the art-history symposium move out of earshot.

There was a shiver over the water, and another, shadows canoodling with sunlight in the summer breeze. Puffs of old man's beard sailed past, the feathery tufts still dry. A brother had told him that old man's beard was once used to weigh souls. He could imagine that. He remembered taking Joey and Flo to sail their toy boats on that huge pond on Clapham Common, where the sleek vessels would sway and lean and be attacked by pirates. Pure fun.

Then the breeze dropped and the lake was absolutely still. Only an impression of stillness: picked out by an intense beam, a dense ripple of waterweed streamed out a few feet off from the bank, more dark red than green, and fixed under a rounded boulder as pale as bone; then the air brushed across it again, and the surface took over, dimpled like glass in a bathroom window.

This was the precise view he'd had in his dream, he realised. The angel had touched down on the lake somewhere between where he was standing and the far bank.

He took a deep breath and stepped back on to the path, walking faster so as not to give the idea that he wanted to keep his distance. Brother Eustace, unhooded like the other normal brothers, swivelled his head as Chris approached, the thick fifty-year-old neck bulging with muscle.

'Ah, the prodigal son returns,' said the monk in his velvet baritone. 'Did we bore you stiff?'

'Not at all.'

Brother Lawrence didn't even deign to look, the pointed hood firmly pulled forward. Chris felt he was scuffling along in their wake, a kind of spiritual and intellectual dwarf. This will improve.

He pops one or two blackberries into his mouth. Pure succulence. You cast your own shadow. The great cross of suffering casts a shadow. It is not about ridding yourself of the shadow, it is about asking questions of the light. Big questions. Remember, as his dad used to say to him: it's not all about yourself.

Ask the right questions, the right answers come.

His hand jerks all by itself: reaction to a sudden thought. The flash of a thought. An answer! Snared in the complex curves of the brambles, pulled out too fast, the skin is lacerated just where the veins bulge by the kuckles. Not really lacerated, but a handsome and painful rip that he sucks on. The basket is almost full, after a slow start: a decent poundage.

He covers the fruit with the cloth and walks briskly back, crossing the car park again. Sweat is trickling down his spine. The camper van has gone, leaving only ruts in the gravel. He returns the gloves, sickle and secateurs to the greenhouse tool room and deposits the basket on the table in the empty kitchen, the vaulted space poised in its own shadowy calm and smelling of damp sponges, Ajax, interminable simmerings of lentil soup. His heart is thumping; he needs to take a deep breath and slow down. He might be having some sort of breakdown. The dog. That bloated vision from Hell. How could he have forgotten?

As he gingerly washes his hands (rip superficial), he counts the big pans and skillets hanging in a row against the lime-washed wall. They are so sensible, so real, so weighty, so gratifyingly enduring and reliable. So ancient. Whenever he helps with the cooking, he can barely lift the largest of them onto the Rayburn.

He has dedicated his life to the ephemeral.

He slips out of his work gear and into his postulant smock and sandals, the overalls joining the others on a row of pre-industrial iron hooks, the boots shelved at knee level. Everything shared, and it works.

It works. Just take your time. A proper breath. Reach in carefully, don't grab. All his life he's grabbed. He'll miss the kids as they accelerate (or maybe drift) out of adolescence. Will they miss him? He tries not to worry about Joey. Trust that everything will turn out fine. Don't grab.

A monk passes him on the way out through the cloisters. Chris catches the flash of a single circular lens as the face swivels to glance at him from deep inside the scapular's black hood. He shouldn't have been hurrying. Of course the monks do rush about sometimes, especially the lay brothers, but hurrying is not the done thing here, it's as alien as adverts. Stupid to have hurried.

He glances back once again from where the little path to the lake begins: the curving track is empty, the monastic buildings patchily visible to the left, the great black cross now out of sight beyond spreading branches massed with leaves. He slips down the path like a felon.

The lake looks different. The sky is veiled with thin cloud, one massive soft box, diffusing the light to an evenness that flattens everything, including personal mood. The water is no longer a sapphire blue but a molten pewter, reflecting the sky with no Rembrandt lighting to probe the depths. And it's the morning, not the afternoon: the angles are all different. The air is heavy and full of midges that fancy his sweaty neck above the smock's collar.

His sandals scuff the path's complex surface of shed leaves, berries, twigs, repeating last week's circuit through the tussocky grass. He thinks he's near the spot where he paused, but it's hard to be sure: it looks the same all the way along. The green sward, the patches of wild growth, the waterside bushes and trees still with Tibetan prayer flags of plastic and cloth caught on their branches from the flood . . .

He stops and looks out over the lake, trying to recall the view opposite. It's as if the actual place is obliterating the memory of it. It could have been anywhere along a hundred-yard stretch. He squints: the haze of cloud has thinned. He moves his head to get out of the glare zone, but everywhere's a glare zone. The white sky angles off the water with a tungsten intensity.

This is ridiculous. He needs to get himself sorted. There's not enough distance between his inner mind and the outer stuff. Get a grip on the giant skillet. Then he notices, after advancing a few yards, a cluster of reeds up against the bank, an alder trailing its lower branches in the water and a spray of white parsley-like flowers he doesn't know the name of. He checks the grouping of the tall ash trees opposite with a trio of raggedy Scots pines to the right: the memory plays tricks, the trees seem less tall for all their bulk, although without the little human figures in front there's no scale to play with.

This is it. This is where he saw it, just ten days ago. That long ripple of redness, the pale lump.

He approaches the grassy edge and peers in, sitting on his heels to get closer. The alder shields the sky's obliterating whiteness, which helps, and he begins to see below the pewter surface, beyond the mirrored alder leaves. Or perhaps the light has changed, the great titan arc in the sky stronger. He makes out nothing at first but a muddle of pebbles, drowned branches and twigs, a suspended something coated in silt, dark green waterweed – long stems but a different type of leaf, curly, not even reddish. Tiny creatures darting, feeding, all feelers and minute busying legs. A trout investigating, a relaxed and superior giant. Minnows nibbling at the algae on a large drowned rock, but it's not got the same roundness as the one before. The world down there is miraculous, alien. Why does Brother Lawrence despise him? Or is that just a projection? What is Emily doing right now? Why is Joey hunkering down in his room, not eating, wasting away? Has anyone tried talking to the lad?

He sighs. He has so far to go. He can smell incense off his sleeves. The sweetness seems opulent and strange among the background odours of vegetal life and the faint whiffs of silt and decay off the metallic water. The incense gets in everywhere, especially the ancient floorboards, where it sticks, apparently, in the wax. The cloths, the tassels, the curtains. Soaked in it. Orange peel, cloves, pine sap.

Something long and wavering, not much more than the suggestion of a shadow, a few feet out into the lake.

He shifts along the bank a yard or two closer and kneels, leaning out as far as he can, but the current over the decades has worn away the bank around the alder roots and he can't get close enough. Anyway, wasn't the reddish waterweed nearer to the edge? Or was that just an illusion stemming from the underwater clarity, lit up by the sun last week? Or his faulty memory? He traces the shadow along its length but there's no sign of the pale boulder with its hollows and cranial smoothness, unless it's that lighter blur there. Could be, yes.

He tries different positions along the bank, either side of the alder, but can't pierce the surface sufficiently. There's always a challenge to delusion: it's called reality. He looks about him, thinking he heard a twig crack above the lapping of the lake, desperately hoping he hasn't been followed. The bushes look innocent but could easily hide a man. So what? He'll say he's discovering nature, the multiple rivarian delights of a summer's day. Please go back to your Pharisaic card index of mortal sins and multiple transgressions. Something's whispering in his ear. It does this sometimes. Your own voice telling you what to do. High and insistent.

Nowt but your scanties.

He pulls off the postulant smock via his head, the rough cotton scraping his gums accidentally, unbuckles the sandals, stands naked to his underpants. He wades into the water with the determination of a Channel swimmer. After a moment's reflection, the water shifts from cold to liquid steel blade. The only ground is slime of uncertain depth, as in the origins of the universe; he finds it hard to keep steady. He has no idea where he is: from a yard or two out, the grassy bank from where he started appears different. His ankles are being nibbled at. The slime envelops his feet, the soles heavy against sharp- nesses and hidden knobs, as if someone's discarded a console, given it a lake burial.

His lower legs up to his middle thighs have ceased to exist. He stares down at the water, ferociously unhelpful now it has the white sky clamped to it. He's there, grinning back up, mouth agape, while underneath, in the unseen depths, a slippery mass of dark red tendrils clings to his right foot, pulling on it, pulling him down.

Flounder towards the bank, trip on a rock, crash forward full length, shattering the surface; pain hurts happily now it has something to do. Is gainfully employed. Scramble to feet, wipe face with silt hands, smell the sulphurous foulness of rotting matter, taste the said rottenness in mouth, clutch self where a sharp rock poked the rungs of the ribs as the horizontal was lost.

Tussocks, grabbable for lift and leverage. Out onto the dry tickly wickerwork of grass, where a pair of sandals is occupied by human flesh, rising to the white hem of a tunic.

For once the creature has thrown back the black hood; the expression is stern but not nasty. A human hand is offered. Tang of sharp breath. The man known as Chris, seldom as Christopher, clambers to his feet unaided, clutching himself and shivering.

Brother Lawrence, strict about listening rather than talking, makes no exception for the emergency. He gestures, *I'll fetch your clothes if you tell me where they are.* Or, *What the fuck are you up to?* Or, *Look about us at the Almighty's wonderful creation.*

Chris can't speak, anyway. Teeth are chattering instead. Brother Lawrence is staring at something on his body, below the right breast. True, watery blood is fleeing a small gash on the side of his torso. His nipples are white and hard and uncomfortable. The hands hurt, just to make life more difficult: he checks the palms like a Muslim praying. Maybe there was broken glass, or sharp pebbles, or the spikes of shattered branches when the hands selflessly broke his fall. Brother Lawrence takes his hands and holds them by the fingers, palms still up.

Chris wishes he wouldn't, frankly. He half-heartedly attempts to pull away, but the grip tightens. His hands shake as they are held, wired up to some sort of generator. He wants to get dressed and run away. He wants to be normal again, a normal person, but he can't remember how. Look at those goosebumps on his arms! The miracle of flesh!

What were you doing?

Need to get dressed, Chris manages to mouth through bodily shudders he can't control.

'Did you find what you were looking for?'

The voice seems horribly blatant, couched in its smoke and flames of hidden decay. The little round spectacles have dropped like a butterfly nut further down the bridge of the nose. The eyes look over the rims, their black gleams resting on the postulant, on his near-nakedness.

'I think I know something,' Chris stammers.

Tell me.

Chris looks down at the stigmata, the worthless scratches, one of them bruised blue with a little manhole cover of bloodied skin. They hurt. Nobody has touched him for months. He can't possibly tell this man anything. Open his box of secrets. *I am hetero, I am hetero*, he hears himself silently hissing.

What do you know, exactly? says Brother Lawrence's expression.

'Just let me get dressed; I'm seriously cold,' comes the whisper. Or shout. Hoarse, anyway.

His hands are freed and he lopes over to the alder, where his clothes cower against the grey trunk. The other watches him as he dresses. The smock clings loyally to the wet flesh.

The monk is approaching him over the grass at an even pace. He clears his throat, crosses his hands behind his back as if handcuffed. The lupus is bad again, worse in the outdoors

light. Get it seen to, lad. 'When we'd go for a dip here, and
we did do so occasionally, we'd either be naked or in our
swimming trunks. Now we are advised not to. Health and
safety. You should have asked. Or did something impel you?'
Voice more up in the nose than usual.

'I just felt like it,' Chris replies. Why is the gorgeous silence
being broken so casually?

'You said you knew something. It can remain between us,
Chris.'

Chris. Who looks out over the water. Not Brother Chris.
Nigel would wheedle his way in like this, soft-snouted. As if
he had every right. The fellow producer but younger, still in
the first form, Chris in the sixth. Made no difference. Young
Nigel always had to know what you knew. Everything.
Clambering into your skull. Looking out from its bunker eyes.
So maybe Nigel did fancy him, deep down: Emily thought so.
'But then everyone fancies you, Chris, male or female. Don't
know how you do it.'

The other waits patiently. The lake is an even sheet of
peroxide white, the odd water bird in silhouette. The ash trees
and the black Scots pines are a gathering of shadows under
the false ceiling of translucent cloud. His core thermostat is
fucked. God is supposed to touch everything here. Only on
monastery land? Supposing it's rented out? How far does the
sacred stretch? How far down, for that matter?

One thing God is not supposed to be: aloof.

'Mayflies,' says Chris, pointing at the flickering forms, eager
to shift subject, draw him away. 'A day or two of life. Brother
Odilo says their sole aim—'

'I know. Procreation.' There is a silence. Which is now the
norm. Chatterbox, the rest of the world. Never stops. Nature
weaves in softly. Eventually: 'You saw something that frightened
you? In the water.'

'My own face.'

'You're feeling overwhelmed? Very common among postu-
lants. Most leave after a few months.'

Chris knows he doesn't have to say anything, but he ought
to take the initiative. There is no monstrous thing in the
lake. It is all projection. Above his work desk there was one
of those goofy signs: BETTER OUT THAN IN. His damp bum
reminds him of skiing, snow collecting in his ski pants. The
kids in their Ray-Bans squealing on their sledges, or curving
down the nursery slopes with their arms out wide, then in
a matter of no time snowboarding with acne. Shit. What
right has the man to decide? He says, looking out over the
water to the raggedy pines, 'You ought to get medical
attention. Possible case of lupus. I'm only saying. My late
dad was a GP.'

The monk frowns slightly, blinks as if his eyelids are being
blown on by a child. He straightens a little and says, 'There
is Dettol in the sickroom. You need to wash those cuts
thoroughly. Apart from anything else, the pesticide and
fertiliser residues and so on, the water has fecal run-off from
cattle in the pasture further up – it's full of bacteria.'

'Lupus can eat out your innards, if left untreated.'

Brother Lawrence's frown is a reef knot. He has taken off
his specs. He meets Chris's gaze head on. His knot slips into
smoothness. 'I do not have lupus,' he says. 'I have HIV.'

The sting of the Dettol is all he deserves. Brother Lawrence
insists on administering it properly, cleaning the cuts with
a sterile wipe. He was a medical orderly once. Chris has
apologised and the subject hasn't come up again, mainly
because they haven't talked since the lake. *Better is one handful
with quietness.* The man is hypersensitive to UV of course,
but now the hood is down. The puncture wound in Chris's

side is properly dressed, and in silence. The one-room infirmary has a single picture, a faded Victorian effort with tiny flies in the glass: Archangel Raphael lifting great kingfisher wings. The healer. *St Raphael, pray for us!* There's an empty drip stand and a hospital trolley. The spider plant needs watering.

Brother Lawrence clears his throat and says, 'Would you like to use the Conversation Room?'

Chris stands and pulls his smock gingerly back on, being careful with the cuffs. 'Yes.'

The room hasn't seen anyone since he was last there, you can tell. It needs a vacuum and a dust. Santiago de Compostela. Now that would be a good idea, taking the road to Santiago, rucksack and boots, don't forget the water flask. He has no idea how to unscrew things with Brother Lawrence, who is boiling the kettle. 'Tea? Nescaff?' Trying to prise open the tin's lid. Rusted, probably. 'There's no milk up here.'

Start with an apology. Brother Lawrence waves a dismissive hand. 'You followed me,' Chris goes on. The tea is chamomile, dried leaves from the herb garden, tasting of straw and old socks. Yes, it's vital to air this whole thing out.

'You seemed in a flap. I was concerned. We once had a suicide among the retreatants.'

Eventually but softly, Chris confesses: 'I had this dream. It got muddled up with reality. Or *vérité*, as we'd say in my former life.'

He summarises, from his dream of the angel to the MISSING poster and all the way to what he imagined he'd seen in the lake. The whole thing wouldn't pass a sense check, but it is such a relief. A short silence. 'Dipping deeper, though, I think I know what really lies underneath.'

Brother Lawrence raises a quizzical eyebrow. 'In the lake? We can always dredge it. Get a police frogman.'

'No, no. Metaphorically. Psychologically. Concealed monsters.' Perhaps the monk is slightly Asperger's, incapable of metaphor. Of getting jokes. That fits.

'Did you know the poor child, then?'

'Not at all. It's auto-suggestion. She's probably still alive. I hope so.'

'The dead are never far from us in our daily life. Those we were close to.'

He doesn't appear to have got the point. 'My son,' Chris says in a firmer voice. 'Eighteen. And a half. My son is having difficulties. He might be having a breakdown.'

'Because of your decision to obey the call?'

'And the divorce proceedings. My wife. I'm getting divorced. OK. Which I don't want to go into.'

'What's his name?'

'Joey. As in Joseph. His twin is called Flo, as in Flora. Joey and Flo. Like a double act on kids' TV. Rosie and Jim. Bill and Ben. Bad idea, possibly. Not one you can hug.'

'Do you feel you should be at home with Joey?'

He shrugs. The chunky mug is warm. He's glad he has something firm to hold, and he grasps it by both handles. He never used to when he first came, just found the extra handle irritating, craved his old tomato-red mug at home. *King of Awesomeness.* Birthday present from Flo. Brother Lawrence watches him for a moment, then takes off his round specs and idly cleans them on his scapular. 'When family are in trouble and need us, we can go. Temporarily or permanently. Follow them, if you know what I mean. You just need to let the abbot know.'

'After breakfast tomorrow,' Chris says eventually, staring down into his chamomile, where the withered leaves have plumped out again, pretending to be fresh, poised in the amber liquid. All his life he's been on the wrong latitude. His wounds are telling him this. Landsman at sea. 'Actually, I'd like to stay at least for None. I mean, I have to be around for Brother Barnabas's apple and blackberry crumble.'

The monk stretches a smile as far as it can go. His eyes without the specs are bleary, short-sighted, soft.

'You bet,' he says.

11
FAY

27 January 2012

After the shop she goes back up to the playground, not caring about the boys: only two on 'em, she says to Pooch. She has something called a caution. One more time, my beauty, and it's an ASBO. Davos Man twitching his trousers up to bend at the knees and give her a talk about the retail sector suffering because of thieves like her, people losing their jobs, if she didn't go to school she'd end up on benefits and stay stupid. His face was too close. They were in his weeny office with a desk and computer. He said, 'What's your name? Apart from Ginger?' 'Fay.' 'How are you feeling today, Fay?' 'I'm great ta, how's you?' 'I'm feeling cool today, Fay. My shift's nearly over. I'm getting married this weekend to the girl I love.' What a tosser. Zit on his ugly nose. Gay perfume like.

He took out a form and she had to fill it in. Name, address, school, parents. Phone number. She wrote rubbish for the phone number. She put 'England, the World, the Univerce' after 'Lincoln'.

He looked at it and then he said, 'Actually, I'm pulling your leg. I haven't yet met the girl I'm going to marry. Unless you want to volunteer, like.'

She couldn't help saying it, but she said, 'That's pervie talk.' Instead of calling the bizzies and arresting her, he chuckled, showing his white teeth.

Then he reached in his jacket pocket and gid her a packet of best Lincolnshire sausages. She tried not to think of Janice's older brother's story about them, about how he'd used a Lincolnshire sausage in his girlfriend's ma's fridge as a condom in an emergency. After emptying out the meat, *of course*!

She thanked Davos Man and he'd not touched her. Otherwise she'd have done him for abuse. They'd been told that at school: don't be afraid to report abuse. Even a close family member. Just stroking your leg. Whatever. Grooming with best Lincolnshire sausages. Nobody has called her 'my beauty' before, not ever. Nor 'kitten', even. Not with them freckles, her bony body. Her tooth. Retard.

'Take care then, eh? On your journey. My name's Truth, by the way.'

'Yeah. Thanks. Bye. Have a good weddin.'

There is a whole gang of lads outside the old warehouse now, about ten on 'em, sounding like wolves, looking for trouble. She wishes she could go to West Common, like they do with the school to see wildlife, but Ken said two dogs from round here dropped dead of poison off the golf and probably more were done, the owners were gutted. Rochelle said who were the owners but Ken looked shifty and said it don't matter who they are, they're gutted. Next to the common with all them horses is Whitton Park. It is outside the estate and she's only been there once with Janice and her friends, but she could trot it now. Never mind it is mizzling. This is when she wishes she had her own mobile, but Mum said not likely, they can't afford it, not before she's sixteen.

It takes her twenty minutes, hurrying past Suicide Towers without looking up in case she meets one of Ken's mates, who scare her, especially the one Rochelle calls the Nazi. And the other one with the red Land Rover who pretends to be an old gent. 'Never get in it,' says Ken. 'Just scarper.' Then that long dead-straight stretch down Burton Road that'll probably never end. She looks back at the beginning but the overpass is not even a dot. Pooch doesn't like the lorries.

The park is bigger than she remembers. It's on a slope and has a load of trees and bushes and a duck pond and swans and the main part is really quiet: the play area for kids is busy, but it's in the middle and fenced off. Even the goalposts are hardly ever used. The houses around are new and only for the quality. She opens up the packet on one of the big grassy areas away from the playground. It has stopped mizzling and the grey has been pushed away, like that advert for milk. But it'll be getting dark soon, before you know it. She wouldn't mind swarming up a few trees, but there en't time.

Pooch runs helter-skelter over the grass, not minding the cold and the wet. She waves the Lincolnshire sausage about in front of her, but he only stops to sniff at it once and then takes no notice, even though his tongue is hanging out as he hurtles about – so fast he sends bits of mud and grass shooting up behind him. When he comes close she can hear his panting and the thumps of his paws, but he isn't hungry. Dogs are always hungry, that's not normal for a dog. She's not often hungry, but that's because a lot of food makes her feel manky. What the heck. He only stops once for a piddle and then is off again, chasing birds and squirrels then chasing invisible birds and invisible squirrels in and out of the trees. He reaches the big pond and has a good jabber at the swans, who spread their wings and hiss, coming closer so he actually gets frit and runs off back to the squirrels. The swans' heads keep moving left and right like there's a person's arm up their neck.

Necks like socks with a hand stuck up in the head. Kids' telly. Jabber jabber like.

After half an hour of this she is shouting at him, aware of her teeny little voice disappearing into the sky. It is the cold air that does it, there is too much of it, her breath is showing in a mist and her neck is cold and wet. It's different in a room: she pictures a gym, like the one they use near her school for sports lessons. Echoing shouts. Mr Jackson, the new sports teacher, with his whistle that goes straight into your brain like a needle. He is dead fit but knows it: even Janice drools over him, never answers him back. 'Wish I were his missus,' she'd say. 'I bet he keeps her busy, like *proper* busy every night.'

It is probably Mr Jackson's lesson today that she's missed.

Pooch has not returned this time; vanished into the trees. She runs, calling, towards the dark area on a slope under the trees where you get these old rusty swings without the swings.

'Pooch!'

A streak of dog. She runs after it, laughing. She is buzzing. She's looking at a snarly face. Suddenly. Not a dog's. A man's snarly face. An old gent bent down a few feet away, hands on his knees; he's making an ugly horrible face at her, a werewolf face. Snarling, showing his yellow teeth.

Pooch has gone again, off to the left. Her legs feel icy, almost paralysed. Fuck knows how she gets them working again, but she does.

Frickin heck.

The face hovers in her thoughts all the way back home, a dirty old man's horrible distorted face, snarling at her, full of hate. Werewolf, could've been. The park is ugly to her now. It has evil in it. A perv with yellow teeth. Not the one with the red Land Rover, though.

She pulls the hood up to hide herself in, it makes her feel safer. She'll have to go back to the massive field, up towards the dual carriageway where it is more private. Burton Road seems less long this time. She scampers on it like Pooch is doing, keeping up so his lead is loose. She wants to be back in the Ermine, in what she knows. It's Rochelle's programme in a bit, they'll watch it together on the sofa if she's not too manky. With a big cuppa, some biccies. *A Year in the Life.* Mum's favourite, the only thing that makes her happy. Today it's that prat with a spanner from last week, the bet gone up to six thousand. A plumber from Inverness, wherever that is, in nowt but his scanties.

'I got some Lincolnshires,' she says, dropping the packet on the kitchen table, where Ken is sitting and having his morning mug of coffee, hair all over the shop, except it's the afternoon. There's a packet of Mr Kipling Viennese Whirls on the table, Special Offer, two pounds. Unopened. She remembers Sheena likes them fancy cakes. She wants to see Sheena right now like; she's owed a tenner for the work she did day before yesterday. About to tell Ken about the werewolf but then remembers she should've been in school. It's boiling in the maisonette. The heating is on but the window's wide open: Ken has hot blood, likes fresh air, but hardly ever goes outdoors to appreciate it. He is always saying the flat is too hot because there's a problem with the valve, whatever that is, the frickin council can't be arsed to come round and fix the valve.

She unclips Pooch's lead and puts it in her pocket while the lazy doggone star drops into his basket – a manky cardboard box really, with QUALITY PRODUCE on it because that's what Pooch is. She takes off her coat and smells wet on it like the mould in her room where the sill leaks. Her legs buzz like they are electrical. Her face shines: she imagines herself as a light bulb. She's going to explode. No sign of Rochelle. She's fed up of her mum being upstairs and poorly.

She'll have to go fetch her down right now for the telly show. Fuck sake. Then after the show there'll be time to scarper to Sheena's for the tenner. Nobbut works for nowt.

'Best tell Mum her show's on in five minutes,' she says.

Ken doesn't listen; he's checking the packet because the plastic film on top is torn. She put the training sausage back after brushing it free of dirt.

He tells her to be sure to cook them proper. 'Full of inbred country shit,' he jokes. Then he leans forward, reading the label carefully. 'Meat free! What the fuck's all this about, Fay?'

'It can't be,' she says, although she feels a pulse of relief. Dogs aren't vegetarian, are they? There you go!

'The thing is,' he's saying, tapping his head, 'when you go shopping, you have to concentrate, right? That's three quid gone. Christ. Three quid. And it's torn, so you can't even get a refund!'

His face has gone ugly, like that dirty old werewolf's. He's scowling at her with his hair all over the shop and bloodshot eyes and stubble on his cheeks and chin, and he is still in his stinking manky *Life's a Gas* T-shirt that he kips in. She's never seen him as ugly before, not like this. Old and ugly.

'Then go shoppin' yersen, Ken,' her voice shouts suddenly, as if not part of her. She is trembling all over. She can hardly breathe in here, it is so hot. 'Why don't you? Why don't you get off yer fat lazy bum and go do it yersen?'

And she grabs her mouldy coat and the unopened packet of Viennese Whirls in one flash and runs off out the maisonette and down the concrete stairs, burning with satisfaction, Pooch scampering after her without a whimper as Ken yells after them, and she looks back just once and he is in his bare feet at the door, yelling at her to come back, for Chrissake. Just come back.

ACKNOWLEDGEMENTS

I am very grateful to the following for giving so generously of their time, thoughts and support; without them, this book may not have seen the light of day: Edward Way, Sacha Thorpe, John Fuller, David Steward, Zoe Swenson-Wright and Sigrid Rausing. Also to Duncan Minshull at the BBC for initial guidance, and to John Owen for an insider view of bookshops.

Thank you to Tom Williams, Clare Bullock, Victoria Murray-Browne for their critical suggestions at an early stage.

Many thanks to the Nyika family of Lunca de Jos in the Pagan Snow Cap Region of north-eastern Romania for their warm-hearted hospitality on the farm: especially to Istvan for translating and to Erica for recounting her experience of working in England.

With thanks to my editor Robin Robertson for his exacting judgement through later drafts, to Ana Fletcher at Cape, and to my agent Lucy Luck.

As ever Jo, you made it all possible and stuck by me. This is your book as much as mine.